ABUNDANCE LEGACY

THE ABUNDANCE SERIES- BOOK 5

SHANNA SWENSON

For my fellow sonographers,

We do it better in the dark ;-)

(And for my fellow Crohnies, fighting a daily battle no one else understands)

~

To our military, your sacrifice does not go unnoticed or unappreciated. God bless the USA!

Abundance Legacy
Shanna Swenson

Abundance Legacy is an original work of fiction. Names, characters, places, organizations and incidents either are the product of the author's imagination or are used fictitiously. Any resemblance to actual persons, living or dead, events, businesses, companies, or locales is entirely coincidental.

Paperback ISBN: 978-1-7329626-4-4

www.shannaswenson.com

For permission requests, write to the author at shannaswen@gmail.com

Cover Design
OliviaProDesign

Works Cited
Shakespeare, William. *Romeo and Juliet.* 1591-1595. Act 2 Scene 2. Lines 2, 3, 43, &44 (noted with superscripts 1 and 2 in Chapter 6)

❀ Created with Vellum

ALSO BY SHANNA SWENSON

THE ABUNDANCE SERIES

Abundance: An endearing romance novel

Return to Abundance: The Abundance series- Book 2

Escape from Abundance: The Abundance series- Book 3

Stars over Abundance: The Abundance series- Book 4

Abundance Legacy: The Abundance series- Book 5

Starlight Valley: The prequel to Abundance (FREE ebook)

OTHER WORKS

PERSONAL FOUL: The Prequel to the Gods of the Gridiron series (A book in The Fire Within: Conquered by Love anthology)

LEARN MORE AT WWW.SHANNASWENSON.COM

FOREWORD

To my readers:

I hope you've enjoyed heading to Abundance, Texas the last two years with me and the gang at Kinsen Ranch and Starlight Valley. It's been a true pleasure sharing my characters with you!

This finale was fun, exciting, and bittersweet to write, but I'm eager to share Savannah and Austin's story with you all—I think you *might* just have a new favorite Abundance cowboy after you read this one ;-)

I want to thank you from the *bottom of my heart* for reading my work, sharing your thoughts with me, and coming back to Abundance for more.

Without further ado, welcome back to Abundance, one final time.

—Shanna

PROLOGUE

"*D*addy, grab his head for me, will ya?" Dallas Kinsen-Callahan moved her big pregnant belly aside as her father grabbed the head of the stubborn stallion. The big lug wouldn't cooperate with the de-worming pill she was trying to give him and it was beginning to frustrate her further. "It's like they're extra unsettled today, I swear."

"Maybe they sense that you shouldn't be out here in the snow and ice to trip and fall," her father scolded. "Or better yet, that you're on the verge of giving birth at any minute now…Imagine that!" Jack smarted with a grumble.

She just pursed her lips and narrowed her eyes at him. She had work to do and wasn't going to let a baby who wasn't due for another couple weeks stop her from it. She was hard-headed like her old man in that aspect.

A lot had happened, since Cole had proposed to her, over the last ten years. Dallie and Cole had gotten married in her second year of vet school then they'd moved into the home they'd built on her father's land. Upon graduation, she'd tried her hand at a trauma clinic not far from the town she'd been named after. Horses had always been her passion though, and Kinsen ranch was where she belonged—right alongside her father as she'd always been—so after the chaos of helping run a busy clinic for three years, she'd decided to come back to her roots and start a practice of her own. Her father had, very willingly, agreed to the idea of her opening her own large animal clinic right on their property, not far from his barn and training facility. She'd delivered many a foal, and in turn, had trained them as well. It had been her dream job come true and she couldn't have been happier. That had been two years ago.

Now, she had a delivery of her own to make here soon; her and Cole's first bundle of joy. A baby girl who would be named Lilian—a combination of Lily and Anne—Rose, after all three of the baby's great-grandmothers; one of whom Dallie had never met but had heard of for years now.

Lily Kinsen had been Jack's beloved mother, who'd died while he was in college. If she'd been even half as wonderful as her son was then Dallie knew her child should have the name too. After all, Jack Kinsen had always been one of Dallie's favorite people in the entire world—even if he was giving her the death glare at this moment as his big arms crossed over his broad chest.

Her father hadn't changed too much over the last decade, in fact, he was even more handsome as the generous spattering of grey hair only served to make him more distinguished looking, like a younger Sam Elliot or Tommy Lee Jones; he had few wrinkles on his face and his athletic build was as big as ever. Time had been good to Jack Kinsen, Dallie saw as her eyes evaluated him.

Her mother was thriving too and dabbling in the world of fiction writing, now with her children all grown—well for the most part. After all, Jackson was almost sixteen now and just like his father, he was compassionate, hard-working, and loved his family and the horses he helped tend to and train. Despite being the baby and a teenager, he had a good head on his shoulders, respected his elders, and didn't cause too much trouble.

Savannah was the Kinsen clan's prodigy, with a B.S. in engineering *and* a master's degree in astrophysics. She was currently living in Houston, about to achieve her doctorate, and had, unsurprisingly, gone to work for NASA two years prior—at the age of twenty-three. They had all been completely blown away by her. Despite her genius level IQ, Savannah was down-to-earth and kind, like the rest of them, even if she did walk around with her nose constantly in a book and her head in the clouds.

Dallie was excited for their baby girl to arrive and so was Cole, one of the best mechanics in town. He and her Uncle Nate worked together a good bit and enjoyed it. Her Aunt Jordan was doing well too and had gotten into wedding photography shortly after she'd shot Dallie and Cole's wedding.

Morgan, Dallas's cousin, much to her uncle Nate's silent dismay, had gone into the construction business instead of horse training. He had an architectural engineering degree and owned his own company, Butler Homes. He had done very well for himself and had actually drawn the blueprints and built the home that she and Cole lived in as well as his own, both of which were on the Kinsen/Butler property.

Dallie's grandparents were doing alright. Her Paw-Paw had had a mini stroke just last year and her Grandma was starting to have issues with her heart. Dallie went to see them as often as possible at their little cabin not far from her aunt and uncle's, and they'd reminisce about old times when Dallie was just a little girl. Her Nana wasn't doing well at all, and Dallie feared she wouldn't live to see her great-granddaughter be born. What had started with pneumonia this past October had become multiple hospital visits over the last few months, and Dallie knew it wasn't good; her lungs continued to have fluid on them that had to be repetitively drained. Just two days ago, they'd found fluid on her heart and her kidneys were starting to fail. Dallie prayed daily for her health, but knew it was only a matter of time. Life was unpredictable that way and being a doctor, Dallie knew how short it could be.

"Y'all almost done down here?" Jax asked as he ambled over, and

Dallie smiled at her handsome little brother. His curly light brown hair peeked out beneath his tan Stetson and his blue-green eyes held a seriousness far beyond his age.

"Yeah, Doc, are we done yet?" her father asked.

"Yes, yes. He'll be fine, I reckon." She patted the stallion's neck and turned to throw the packet of medicine back into her kit.

She heard a splash hit the floor of the barn and felt a sudden dampness between her legs. She gasped and looked up at her father and brother in shock.

"Uh…what was that?" Jackson asked.

Her father gave a heavy sigh as he frowned into Dallie's gaping face. "*That* was your sister's water breaking."

$\sim$

"*O*f all the days this child had to pick…a blizzard in December just *had* to be one of them, huh?" Jack stated and gripped the steering wheel a bit tighter as he felt the wheels slide on the ice-covered road. "Well, baby doll, she gets that stubborn streak from *your* side of the family, you know? The Butlers for sure," he said to his wife with a laugh to ease some of the tension he felt emanating from her. After twenty-six years of marriage, he could easily sense her emotions and read her like a book; it was a gift he'd cherished over the years.

"Dad, it's not like it ever snows here. What are the odds? I mean we live in Texas!" Dallas said from the back seat and breathed in through her nose, clutching her big belly.

Jack gritted his teeth. He hoped like hell he could make it to the hospital before his grandchild decided to grace the world with her presence.

After Dallie's water broke, Jack went into action, picking her up, and carrying her up to the house. They'd gathered a few belongings and hit the road, despite the inclement weather. At least this wasn't his first rodeo with childbirth; he was better prepared this time since he'd gone through this twice now.

"Never a dull moment in this family," Jax added, smiling at Jack from the backseat.

"Ain't that the truth?" Natalie grumbled next to him as she gripped the handle above the car window and squeezed her eyes shut in the drifting downpour of giant snowflakes. Jack's hand reached over to grasp her free one and she clasped it tightly.

Her eyes came open then and she looked over at him. Jack knew his grin must be silly. He was still so in love with her after all this time. If one were to ask Natalie Kinsen, she'd say that her dark hair was going gray and wasn't quite as full as it'd once been and that her complexion wasn't quite as flawless as it was the day that they were married, but none of that mattered to Jack; she'd always taken his breath away, and he loved losing himself to her touch, her body, her eyes. She'd had him under her spell for so long now, he knew he'd never stop being love-drunk on her.

"Oh jeez…" Dallie gasped then huffed. "Mom, how in the world did you do this *three* times?" Dallie groaned in pain, and Jackson leaned in to take her hand.

"Dallie? You're already having contractions that bad?" his wife responded, looking at her watch then gazed up at him, apprehension in her eyes.

Jack focused back on the road and tried his best to see through the wall of white in front of him; good thing he knew the road like the back of his hand. Hopewell, what a great name for this road! It had been the beginning of all the wonderful things that had happened in his life.

"Where's Cole?" Dallie asked and blew out again, her breathing becoming rapid.

"He's on his way, sweetie," Jack responded.

"Oh God," Dallie cried and gave a scream. "This doesn't feel right."

"Uh, Dad?" Jackson exclaimed, alarmed.

"Yes, son?"

"There's a lot of fluid back here and it's got some blood in it."

"It's ok, honey," Nat answered. "It's going to continue until the baby's born. That's normal."

Dallas grimaced and leaned forward, and Jack watched her eyes as her hands moved.

"No, it's not normal, Mom," Dallie's voice sounded panicky.

"What do you mean?" Nat turned in the seat.

"I feel a foot...she's breech!"

~

*W*aiting was the hardest part. Jack got to the hospital just as Dallie's screams began to tear through his heart and riddle him with fear. She'd been rushed in, and he'd parked and prayed with all his might that his eldest daughter and her child would safely make it through labor and delivery. He'd walked in and headed to a small, dimly lit waiting area where he and Jackson paced and waited.

And waited.

And waited.

Just when Jack's hope was starting to shatter, Natalie came in, crying and smiling, and Jack huffed out the breath he'd been holding. He grabbed his wife to him and hugged her tightly, taking comfort from the mere presence of her, her touch, her scent.

"How is she?" Jack asked as he pulled back.

"She's good; resting now. Lily's perfect, Jack. She's beautiful. You boys wanna meet her?"

He and Jackson just nodded and smiled nervously.

They followed Natalie down the hallway and into a room with a heavy oak door. Jack heard the mewling of his grandchild as they entered. His relief was palpable as he looked over at Dallas, whose rosy-cheeked face greeted him with a big smile. Cole caught his gaze then and Jack saw the love glowing in his eyes at the birth of the daughter he held, Lilian Rose Callahan. Jack knew that feeling. Becoming a father had been the most wonderful thing that had ever happened to him, aside from marrying the woman of his dreams. It had all started when he'd adopted Dallas when she was five years old, and his blessings had just multiplied from there—another beautiful daughter, a son, a son-in-law, and now a granddaughter.

Cole walked over with a bundle of pink, and Jack laid eyes on his tiny granddaughter for the first time. She was an absolute angel, and Jack felt tears come to his eyes as Cole placed the little infant into his arms. Jack held her close and moved the blanket down from her chin, so that he could take a good look at his first grandbaby. She'd been cleaned up and her little almond-shaped eyes opened to look up at him. Right then and there, his heart simply melted.

"Well, howdy, my lil' darlin. Look at you! You're so beautiful, Lily Rose. Just like your Mommy and your Nee Nee." The tears fell, unbidden, down his cheeks. His heart swelled to bursting as he took in the sparkling blue eyes that gazed back into his, those fat chubby cheeks, and white-blonde hair. Lily yawned and cooed at him, and he sighed, falling immediately in love.

Cole patted him on the back then. "We did pretty good, huh, Dad?"

"Y'all did, indeed!" Jack gave a hearty laugh. "Isn't it amazing?" he asked. "Just when you think your heart can't possibly love any more than it already does..." He glanced over at his wife, who grinned at him as she sat in a chair next to Dallie's hospital bed and grabbed Dallie's hand. He mouthed an, "I love you," and pursed his lips at her in a kiss. She returned it, her eyes doing incredible things to his insides. Jack then moved over to his oldest daughter's other side and placed her baby into her arms. He kissed Dallie's forehead and cupped her cheek. "I love you, pumpkin doodle."

"I love you too, Daddy." She covered the hand that held her cheek and looked up at him, tears glistening in her sapphire blue eyes.

"You frightened me there for a few minutes," Jack admonished, recalling the panic that had overcome him when Dallie discovered the baby was breech.

"I was pretty frightened, myself. I didn't know how that was going to end there for a little while." Dallie gave a nervous laugh.

He sighed. "Me and you both, baby. I'm so glad you and our little Lily Rose are alright." He glanced down at Lilian and stroked her small cheek with his finger.

"Me too." Dallie glanced down then suddenly back up to him. "Thank you."

"For what?"

"For everything! I wouldn't be here if it weren't for you, Daddy." Jack drew his brows, confused at her statement. "I'm serious! You weren't just Momma's knight in shining armor the day you rescued us on the side of the road. You were mine too."

Jack just gave her a knowing grin and patted her cheek, looking back down to his granddaughter. Little did Dallie and her mother know, Jack was the one who'd been rescued that fated September day some twenty-seven odd years ago. His heart had been filled with so much love over the years between his wife and children that it oozed out of every pore in his body. And now he had yet *another* beautiful soul to love; for Jack Kinsen—tough guy that he was—was already a sucker for the tiny infant before him. Her name was Lilian Rose and she was going to be quite a sight, he could tell, as she cried at the top of her lungs.

There would be yet another little finger he would be tightly wound around...

Jack stepped back and propped himself against the wall, arms crossed as he took in the scene before him. His amazing family. The family who'd always completed him and continued to grow stronger with each new member. He sighed in contentment.

Jack couldn't believe it! He was a *grandfather*. Life was good.

CHAPTER 1

FOUR YEARS LATER

Savannah Grace Kinsen huffed, wiping the unwanted tears that streamed down her face as she pulled her luggage—two oversized duffle bags, really—down the sidewalk. She hated that she was crying, hated that she'd given Siddharth Bhushan three years of her life that she could never get back. For him to end it all for some dumb blonde super model skank was mortifying.

As if Savannah hadn't absolutely worked her ass off the past two weeks, only to come home to the apartment they shared together and be literally kicked out, all her stuff forcibly packed and probably a mess of tangled and crushed items, into the two big suitcases she was now lugging down Texas Avenue towards the bus stop. It had been utterly humiliating to say the least.

When she'd opened the door—wishing only for an Alka-Seltzer and her bed—she'd been taken aback to see Sidd standing there, arms defiantly crossed over his chest, with a stunning blonde she recognized from commercials behind him giving her a Cheshire cat grin. Savannah had literally balked as her eyes lowered to see her two red suitcases stuffed to the max.

"Sidd, what the—?" Savannah started, only to be cut off by him.

"We're through, Savannah."

Since when? Savannah wanted to ask but before she could, Ms. Bimbo spoke. "Siddharth, doesn't want you anymore. You're mousy...and boring," she'd harrumphed and added for good measure. Savannah had just gulped, unable to hide her shock. If he'd been unhappy at all, he'd not let on to it.

"O...kay...well, let me just—"

"All your stuff's in there," Sidd interrupted again. "Just give me the ring and the key."

As if that's all there was to the breakup of a three-year relationship; simply giving him the ring he'd proposed to her with back and the key to the apartment they'd rented together. Where did her heart fit in? Would she get all the pieces of it back that he'd taken in the course of thirty point seven seconds?

Savannah had only nodded—*for what else could she do?*—and began pulling the sparkling one-karat diamond from her finger and handed it over. She hadn't been able to keep her hands from shaking as she fumbled with her keyring, trying to pull the key off of it. When she finally removed it, she handed it over as well then began pulling her bags over the lip of the door saddle, struggling with the one that probably had all her books in it—she did have a *lot* of those. Sidd shoved and finally the bag came over the sill. Before she could say anything else, the door was slammed in her face, and she was alone in the hallway of her apartment complex, looking around to see if anyone had heard the embarrassing encounter.

All had been silent, for it was still early on a Friday morning. Begrudgingly, Savannah had rolled her bags down the corridor, hopped back on the elevator, and thought about where she was going to go and what she was going to do. Sleep had been all she'd wanted and heartbreak had been what she'd been given.

Now, she meandered towards the bus station with only bags to show for seven years of living in Houston. She guessed she should probably go home, to Abundance. After all, it'd been a while since she'd been home to see her folks and siblings. She would go to

Dallie's first. She couldn't call her mom and dad, for if she did, her dad was going to show up in Houston and beat the absolute tar out of Sidd Bhushan, she knew.

Jack Kinsen had never cared for the cocky Indian cardiologist that Savannah had brought home a few Christmases ago—not that he'd ever cared for either of the two men she'd brought home—for her dad had the demeanor of a drill sergeant when it came to his daughters. He and her mother had always been super protective of their girls and super suspicious of outsiders. Savannah knew why now, and thank goodness hadn't dated much in the span of her thirty-one years to have to deal with the intolerance of her father, but she knew beyond the shadow of a doubt, he was gonna kill Sidd when he found out how she'd been treated today.

So, Dallie's it was, until Vanna was ready to face her father and enlighten him on what had happened. She needed a break from work anyway. The last two weeks had been ridiculous, and she'd spent the better part of her days engrossed in her project for a new satellite NASA was testing out. Many nights she'd not even gone home or she'd slept on her office couch a few hours before once again hitting the computer and test facilities and going back to the literal drawing board. Her work was demanding and highly stressful, but as much as she loved it, a break was completely overdue; she couldn't even remember the last time she'd taken a vacation.

Savannah pulled her bags to a stop at the crosswalk, pulled out her phone, and called up her boss, Royce Slayton. She told him she was going on leave, and he could email her the paperwork later because she had a family emergency. She didn't feel like it was much of a lie; her nerves were shot and she felt sick to her stomach.

He didn't protest her impromptu sabbatical, knowing she'd been the forerunner, overseer, and head developer of their latest project and had seen it through to the end without much sleep and an over-abundance of caffeine.

She replaced her phone, grabbed her luggage, and was strolling down the sidewalk, her eyes burning as she was passing the window of a darling antique toy store. A gorgeous white wooden rocking horse stared back at her from inside, and she couldn't help but smile, for she knew that her niece, Lilian, would absolutely love it.

But where the hell am I gonna put it? she thought, even as she proceeded through the automatic doors.

As she approached the vintage horse, she was thinking that she might have it shipped and moved her bags in, setting them to the side. She reached out to touch the handle on the weathered wooden toy, seeking the price tag tied to it when a hand dropped down on top of hers. Savannah gasped, immediately looking up into a ruggedly handsome face shaded by a tan cowboy hat.

"Pardon me, ma'am, but I believe I saw it first," said a deep voice with a thick southern accent.

"Like hell," Savannah countered. She'd been had by enough men for one day; she wouldn't be overthrown by this one too—no matter how buff he was in his fitted white t-shirt and equally as skin tight Wrangler jeans.

The man laughed heartily and gave her a big smile. Of course he had to be drop dead gorgeous with straight white teeth and dimples that his scruffy, blonde beard didn't cover. The hair beneath his hat was sandy blonde as well, thick and wavy, and his skin was golden tan; he looked like he could've been a surfer from California. What the hell did he want with an antique rocking horse?

"Sorry, sweetheart. It's mine." Eyes the color of rich amber burned into hers.

"First off, don't *call* me sweetheart," Savannah scoffed. "And second, have you bought it?"

"Well no, not yet, but—"

"But nothing! If you haven't bought it yet then it's not yours...technically."

"*Technically* not. But I intend to buy it." He crooked his head at her and gave her the once over, that damn smug-ass grin of his tugging at the corner of his sexy as Hell mouth. "Unless, of course, you can convince me why I should let you have it."

Let me have it? Boy, this guy was unbelievable.

"I don't have to convince you to do *anything*. I saw it first and I'm buying it. It's that simple."

"Well, I could say the very same thing, darlin'. As it were, *I* saw it first."

Savannah wasn't going to sit there and argue property rights with this ignorant cowpoke. He didn't own the rocking horse and therefore had no stand where it was concerned.

She tilted her chin up higher, not caring that her mascara was probably streaking her red, tear-stained cheeks, that her makeup had been applied almost twenty-four hours prior or that her clothes were disheveled and her thick, wavy hair was unruly. He wasn't going to get the best of her. Not today!

"Ladies first," she retorted.

"I'm a hard supporter of women's rights, so since y'all want equality and all, I'm gonna contend that you're being sexist with that statement- *I* saw it first."

Savannah's mouth just dropped. She saw red and the next thing that came out of her mouth shocked even her. "You're *fucking* kidding me, right?"

His brows shot up to the brim of his hat; he was taken aback.

"Listen buddy, I don't know who the hell you are, but this rocking horse is mine. You got me? *Mine!* I'm buying it, right here and right now, and I *dare* you to try and stop me." With that, she jerked the rocking horse up, despite that it was far heavier than it had originally looked. "I've *had* it with men like you today." She struggled as she tried to move the rocking horse away from the cowboy's grasp, looking up at him to drive her point home. His hands were up then, palms out and he was shaking his head, as if he didn't intend to physically fight with her over the horse. "Now, are we going to have a problem? Or do you yield?" She huffed as she set the heavy-ass rocking horse down and planted her hands on her hips.

"Why, yes ma'am. You've done gone and degraded my manhood,

so what other choice do I have *but* to yield?" he smarted back, crossed his arms over his broad chest, and glowered at her. "You should be glad you're not a man."

"If you were a woman, I would pull your lovely golden locks out one by one," she countered.

Whoa, Savannah, she scolded herself. Where had this angry, haughty side of her come from? *Getting humiliatingly dumped by my piece of shit ex-fiancé and running on little to no sleep for weeks now,* she reminded herself. She held her ground...waiting for him to lunge at her, fight her, protest in some way. If he got physical, although he didn't seem inclined to do so, she was ready. She knew karate and tai chi; she'd been trained from childhood and could beat his ass if it came right down to it, despite that he looked to be as big as her father—six feet two inches tall and over two hundred fifty pounds— all broad and big-shouldered like he was. On second thought, fighting him was the last thing she wanted to do...*Dammit!* Why did she have to meet him today of all days? He simply oozed sex appeal.

He just stared her down for a few more minutes, his unique eyes moving over her once again before he scoffed and gave her that dimple-shining grin. "Damn, lady, you drive a hard bargain. How's about I offer you double what it's worth?"

Did this guy ever give up?

"I believe I've made my intentions clear, sir. I won't be making a deal with you. Not now or ever." Savannah picked up the rocking horse and started lugging it forward, toward the front of the store.

"Yeah, well, go figure you ballbuster," the man mumbled.

Savannah stopped, dropped the horse, and turned to face him, cutting her eyes at him.

"Oh? Well, you're nothing but a hotheaded male chauvinist."

"And you're a sassy little minx who needs a good bare-assed spankin' in the worst way," he retorted.

Savannah gasped, completely taken aback, but before she could reply, he was winking seductively, turning, and walking out of the store.

$\mathcal{K}$elsey Boyd couldn't hide her excitement at seeing her best friend, Savannah, for the first time in far too long. She grabbed her and pulled her in for a much-needed hug as Savannah held back tears.

"Oh, girl. Sidd was a total dick and he didn't deserve you. Better you see that now than to have married the bastard and found out the hard way."

Dallie had called her as soon as Savannah came into town that morning, and Kelsey left work early to come console her dearest and oldest girlfriend.

Now they were sitting out on Dallie's back porch enjoying the mid-spring afternoon, mojitos in hand, all except for Dallie, who was five months pregnant and wasn't partaking in the libations.

"He did have some killer green eyes though, I'll give him that," Savannah said dreamily as she stared off into the rolling hills of the back pasture.

"I bet his dick was small," Kels countered thoughtfully and laughed back at Vanna, who smirked at her and shrugged. Not like the poor girl would know either way, she'd only ever had two of them.

"Well, it doesn't matter what his dick or his eyes looked like. He was a complete jerk and I'm glad you're rid of him," Dallie said, putting her two cents in.

Kelsey just nodded her head. They'd all known Sidd wasn't the one for Vanna. He was handsome, successful, and a great doctor, but he was cold and unfeeling when it had come to his bride to be. Everyone had seen it, especially Savannah's dad; he had a way of reading people unlike anyone else Kels had ever known.

Kelsey hadn't been so successful in love herself, any more so than Savannah had. She was thirty now and had yet to settle down. She'd fallen in love, years ago, with Morgan Dean Butler, but he'd broken her heart into a million pieces and she'd never quite been able to put those pieces back together. She'd tried; even just recently with a local cop she'd gone to school with named Brantley Burgess. But he'd been too possessive, and Kelsey couldn't see a future with a man who couldn't even trust her to go out with her girlfriends. She'd literally just broken it off barely two weeks ago.

Aside from her love life, Kels was happy as an elementary school teacher. She loved kids, always had, and looked forward to seeing those seven-year-olds every day and educating the future generations. She had a nice, quaint little home and enjoyed her fairly uncomplicated life.

"I just can't believe he treated me that way…after three years. To just kick me out like I meant nothing. And that stupid blonde—"

"Yeah, well, give it a month. I'm sure she'll be tired of him soon enough. He works as much as you do, Vanna. I'm sure he won't be able to devote as much time to her as she feels like she deserves." Kels rolled her eyes.

"His patients just love him," Savannah murmured and took another sip of her drink.

"When do you plan on telling your Daddy is what I wanna know?"

Kelsey knew that if it was her own father, she would hold off as long as possible. Luther Boyd had been close to killing Morgan after he broke up with Kels twelve years ago. She'd been just eighteen years old then and was head over heels for the rugged, dark-headed, blue-eyed entrepreneur, but she hadn't been what he wanted, especially after—

"He's just gonna say I told you so," Vanna moped.

"Now, sister, you know that isn't true. Daddy would never!"

"Well, maybe he *should*. I didn't listen to him and look where it got me," Vanna sniffled again.

Kels sighed. It was hard to see Savannah, their resident genius, so upset. Savannah had always been so ambitious, organized to a fault, and enthralled with the way the world worked- literally. She wasn't one for sulking and always grounded Dallie and Kels, not the other way around. She'd never had time for boys in high school, didn't even have her first boyfriend until college, but then she was always younger than the men she was around in school and at work due to her early graduation. Sidd was ten years older than Savannah after all, and they'd met during a project at Savannah's work. Vanna wasn't one for meeting men the traditional way- bars or clubs. She'd always had her head in the clouds or a book or was too busy painting or writing music.

"That's it! I know what we're doing. We're gonna get this girl up, we're gonna wipe her tears, and we're gonna take her out for a night on the town," Kelsey offered. "After all, when have the three amigas been back together and able to enjoy each other's company?" It had been years.

"Kelsey, that's a great idea! I know Cole won't mind to stay with Lily."

"That's the spirit, Dallie. Savannah?" She wasn't gonna let Vanna tell her no.

"I'm not in the mood to go out. I look terrible and I don't feel like it." Vanna pouted.

Kelsey rolled her eyes. "Wrong answer!" With that, Kelsey stood and dumped the contents of her glass on top of Savannah's head.

Savannah gasped and sputtered. "Kelsey! What the hell?"

"You're getting your whiny ass up and gettin' in the shower. We're curling that sexy head of hair, we're stuffin' your skinny ass into the tightest dress I own, and we're takin' you out to the bar tonight to get laid!"

Dallie laughed at that and shrugged over at a stunned Savannah. "I mean, rebound sex doesn't sound so bad for you, Vanna. Maybe it's exactly what you need."

"Ok, who *are* you and what have you done with my sister? Do you even hear how ridiculous you two sound?" she asked incredulously, swiping at the mint leaf stuck in her hair.

"Lighten up, Vanna. You're as uptight as a nun in a brothel."

Vanna scoffed, "Seriously? Am I the only sane person left in an insane world? Kels, I expected as much from you, but Dallie, you're my sister. Why would you *ever* encourage me to have meaningless sex with random strangers?"

"Oh, Savannah, relax. I just think you need to let your hair down some. You've been overworked and overstressed for a long time now. And Sidd has only added to that. I'm not encouraging you to be a floozy, but if you happen to encounter a handsome guy at the bar and end up in bed with him then so be it." Dallie shrugged.

"Dallie, Daddy would actually *die* if he heard you say that!"

"Vanna, you're a grown woman. You're the most responsible person I know. Besides, they make condoms for this very thing."

Kelsey busted out laughing when Savannah just gaped at her sister again as if Dallie had grown horns or something. Finally, Savannah seemed to find her voice.

"Dallie, you've been around Kelsey *way* too much." She sat her drink down on the patio table then and stood, planting her hands on her hips. "I'm taking control of this conversation right now and telling you that I will *not* be going home with some jerk who won't bother to give me a call come tomorrow. You can bet on that!"

Kelsey just giggled, thinking about how drunk she intended to get her best friend before the night was through. "Alright, Ms. Goody Two Shoes, take it easy. Just be ready to go when I get here at eight. We're gonna have some much-needed fun for a change."

"And just where are you going?"

"Duh! I'm going home to get you a dress," Kels confessed as if the answer was super obvious.

"I should have a dress," Dallie recommended.

"I'm sure you do, but not the dress I have in mind." Kels winked then grinned at Savannah before standing to leave.

~

*S*avannah laughed at Kelsey as they curled her hair into sexy long ringlets.

"God, you're such a horn dog, Kels."

"I can't help it that your dad is a walking sex god."

Kelsey'd had a crush on Savannah's dad since they were kids. Savannah was suddenly wondering now if all those nights she'd come to stay the night were more motivated by her infatuation for Jack Kinsen than for hanging out and enjoying her childhood with his daughter.

"I mean, he's a total stud. If I didn't love your mom as much as I do, I would absolutely fuck his brains out."

"Eww, that's my dad you're talking about. Gosh, get ahold of yourself!" Savannah swatted at Kels plump bottom with the paddle brush she was holding while Kelsey operated the curling iron.

"Sorry. But he's got just the right type of build to give a girl a good pounding." She bit her lip probably more from trying to squeeze her legs shut than concentrating on Vanna's hair.

Savannah's mouth dropped as she looked dubiously up at Kelsey's image in the mirror. "I'm goin' to pretend like I didn't hear that." She closed her eyes at the mental image that was drawn in her subconscious, shuddering before hearing Kelsey cackle at her discomfort.

"Oh, Savannah, you're as prudish as a dang born-again virgin. That's exactly what you need... A good pounding."

"What am I? A piece of meat that needs to be tenderized?" Vanna shook her head and rolled her eyes.

Despite her scolding of Kelsey Boyd, the wild child she was, Vanna could appreciate her enthusiasm and lively personality. Kelsey had been her best friend for as long as she could remember. She and Kels were just 9 months apart and had been raised like cousins, seeing each other every weekend they were allowed and spending almost every summer attached at the hip. Despite their obvious differences, both in looks—Savannah was olive-complexed, green-eyed and dark-headed and Kels was tanned, blonde and hazel-eyed—and in personalities, they complimented each other well and always had. They enjoyed the same type of movies, music and could carry on a conversation about practically anything and everything without one offending the other. They could spend hours talking or in the same room doing separate things, usually Vanna playing or painting while Kels read magazines or talked in chat rooms online. Kels was the extrovert and Vanna the introvert. Kels was the hothead while Vanna was the voice of reason. They were more like sisters and had been known to call each other that from time to time.

If anyone could ever be honest with Savannah, it was Kelsey. She could give Savannah advice, or feed her the harsh truth, without pushing the wrong buttons.

"No, but your vagina does? It needs to feel the love. I bet Sidd didn't even believe in foreplay, did he? He seemed like a straight-to-the-point kinda dude. Am I wrong?"

No, she wasn't...of course. Sidd had always been in too big of a hurry when they made love or was completely exhausted by the time they'd gotten around to doing it. They lived busy lives with little time to appreciate one another, which had ultimately led to their break-up.

Savannah just grimaced in response, not wanting to talk about Sidd. Kels must have sensed her hesitation for she offered her another sip of rum and coke.

"Drink up, I want you good and buzzed before we ever even get there."

"Jeez, you lush. You want to party or put me to sleep?"

"Oh, shut up. You've had one drink, Vanna. You're such a light-weight." Kels giggled and fluffed Vanna's hair up from the bottom, giving it some volume. She then stepped back to admire her work. Savannah was an artist with a brush, but what Savannah could do with paint, Kels could do with a brush and a curling iron. "Damn, you look like a little sex kitten." Kels meowed and giggled again.

Savannah looked at her long, ribbon-curled, maple-brown locks that perfectly framed her heart-shaped face, the sea green eyes that stared back at her and the tight, black halter dress that fit her like a second skin and she gulped. Her eyelids were covered in an array of smoky hues, her lips red and her eyelashes coated with the best mascara money could buy.

"Wow," Dallie said as she came in. "Smokin' hot, sis."

"You're pretty sizzlin' yourself, hot mama," Kels whistled at Dallie, who'd donned a mint green, short-sleeved wrap dress that complemented her fair skin tone.

Dallie and Savannah didn't share the same father, but they both had their mother's lips, cheekbones, and thick hair. Dallie had inherited their mother's eyes and skin tone but had gotten her hair from her biological father's side of the family. Savannah's nose and skin tone were from the Kinsen genes but her eyes and hair were color combinations of both her parents. Jackson, on the other hand, was the spitting image of his father, save for the lips and curls he'd, too, inherited from their mother.

Savannah smiled up at Dallie and Kels as they looked at her in the mirror. She admired Kels's silky red dress; it fit her personality—flamboyant and friendly.

"Well, ladies, let's go paint this town red," Kels stated, as if reading Savannah's mind.

Savannah nodded and pushed her feet into the ropy silver stilettos of Kelsey's, noting that she would probably break one of her ankles before the night was through. She wasn't used to wearing anything other than a wedge, even in her business dress attire.

She was thankful she'd taken a good long four-hour nap at Dallie's before going out for a night at the Rusty Spur. She'd laid down once Kels left to go plunder her closet, at her sister's insistence —and after showering the club soda and rum out of her hair—and surprisingly, she'd fallen asleep quickly and soundly. She'd awaken to the squeal of her darling little niece, Lilian, from the living room and had ran out to greet her. Lily had been thrilled to see her Aunt Vanna, as Savannah knew she would be. She was four years old, with curly locks like her momma, and had the most adorable personality...and she absolutely adored Savannah. Savannah had squeezed her tightly and oohed and aahed over her latest art project from pre-school. They'd watched a movie about penguins while Dallie and Cole cooked dinner then they'd all eaten. Dallie had made a delicious southern supper of fried chicken, collard greens, slaw, black-eyed peas, fried potatoes, and cornbread. Dallie had taken after their grandmother on the cooking end, for Savannah rarely cooked—and never cooked like that. It was a feast fit for a king and as good as it was, Savannah feared her stomach wouldn't be happy with all the butter, grease and animal fat of it, but damn, it was good.

Once they'd gotten Lily into bed, they'd snuck off to the guest room and started primping. Kels had joined a short time later to doll Savannah up. And now they were heading out.

"Be safe, my angel," Cole called to Dallie and rubbed her growing belly before taking her hand in his and bringing it to his lips. God, the two of them were as bad as her mom and dad, and Savannah envied the way Cole looked at his wife. That look that said more than words ever could. A look of love, lust, pride, submission and dominance all wrapped up into one. Sidd had never looked at her like that...had he?

Cole and Dallie had been married for going on eleven years now and looked to be as in love as they'd been that beautiful fall day on their family's land under a gorgeous arch at sunset. Savannah hadn't been able to hold back her tears that day, especially when Cole then her dad had started crying. Dallie had been absolutely stunning that day—not that she hadn't always been—but she'd been a bride completely in love with her groom, and Savannah—growing up with parents that couldn't keep their hands off of one another—had been glad to know that Dallie would have that too.

And she wanted to feel it herself. Perhaps that's why she'd even paid any mind to Sidd's advances in the first place...well, that and the fact that he was incredibly handsome. But she should have known. He hadn't been as polite to her once they'd moved in together; he'd never held the door for her, walked her out to her car, or chosen the outside edge of the street when they'd walked together. In fact, he was mostly self-absorbed, even when they'd made love. She cringed at that thought and turned to leave, waving at Cole and thanking him for letting her and Kels kidnap his wife for the night.

"Just bring her back in one piece," Cole chuckled. "And still pregnant preferably."

He was referring to one of the last times the "three amigas" had gone out on the town with Dallie so pregnant. Kels'd had drama with some dude getting touchy feely with her, and Dallie had ended up in labor and delivery later that night with Braxton-Hicks contractions. Lilian hadn't come then—no, she'd chosen a winter blizzard instead—but needless to say, it had given Cole ample fuel for the fire. He'd been a worried husband and father-to-be and told them after it happened, "No more Rusty Spur."

And now here they were headed back to that no-good bar...

Cole hadn't been off base; the Rusty Spur was a death trap for fights, drama and break-ups. Her mother and her aunt Jordan had enlightened them over the years with various stories. Even her uncle Nate had been arrested one night after a fight at the Rusty Spur. It probably wasn't the best place for them to go, but it was the only place in Abundance open after eight PM on a Friday night, and it wasn't fair for them to ask five-month-pregnant Dallie, their designated driver, to drive them all the way to Denton.

The drive was quicker than she'd remembered from prior drives —or it could simply be the two rum and cokes she'd downed in the last hour—and her heart leapt into her throat at the expanse of cars in the gravel lot as they pulled in and Dallie parked the car.

Savannah stepped out of the back seat and shut the door, looking up at the dilapidated old neon sign humming back at her from a towering height and gulped. She had a feeling she should just get back into the car, go back to Dallie's, watch *Sweet Home Alabama* and binge eat Ben N Jerry's, but Kels grabbed her hand and pulled her toward the front door as Dallie headed up the rear, giving her a sweet smile. Oh, her angel of a sister, bless her, she'd just wanted a night free from pull-ups and cartoons; she didn't see how disastrous this night could be just lying in wait.

As if the thoughts of meaningless sex and barroom brawls weren't swirling around her head at the sight of the place, the smell of the musky, once smoke-filled bar assaulted Savannah's nostrils immediately upon entry.

It was as loud and boisterous as she could remember from prior visits. The same old wood bar, poker and billiard tables, dance floor and mechanical bull were located in the same spots. She noted a few more neon beer signs and a new disco ball, but aside from that, the place hadn't changed a bit in the last four plus decades...or, well, it sure didn't look like it had.

Kels pulled them to a high-top table not far from the bar and ran over to grab some shots. Savannah smiled hesitantly over at Dallie, rubbing her bare arms from the inner nervousness that suddenly crept over her. She scanned the place, looking for both familiar faces and new ones too, her introversion rearing its shy head. The bar was pretty full, much to her dismay, and she saw lots of cowboy hats in the crowd of people sitting, playing billiards, dancing and just hanging out. She didn't immediately recognize anyone, so she was able to relax some. As if it wasn't bad enough to get dumped, she sure as shit didn't want to have to talk to people about it.

Strangers. They were good.

"Here ya go, shots of Patrón," Kels yelled over the sound of the raucous country-western music playing over the speakers.

"*Patrón*! Are you out of your mind?" Savannah shook her head and pushed the shot glass away. "Are you just trying to get me sick?"

"No, I'm tryin' to get your panties off!" Kels laughed and pushed the shot back over to her, insisting with her eyebrows. "Live a little. It's gonna be a fun night!"

Fine. Savannah thought and shot her glass back at the same time Kels did.

The smooth tequila didn't burn her throat but did her belly, and she hissed as it hit even as Kels pushed yet another one to her. They both shot another one back, and Savannah looked over at Dallie, who grinned behind a glass of milk.

"What's so funny?" Savannah asked.

"Nothing! It's just been a while since I've seen you drunk. I'm gonna enjoy this."

How the hell could she say that? Savannah wasn't a fun drunk. Not that she got drunk often. She got a little brave and somewhat wild...or she had the last time.

Kels looked around the bar and sang along with the music as Savannah felt her veins hum with the alcohol she'd just consumed in the span of twenty seconds. Dallie looked over at the bar and smiled big.

"I'll be back," she said and walked over to an elderly man who sat on one of the many barstools there, nursing a large stein of beer. He had white hair and a beard with a brown cowboy hat and jeans, from what Vanna could see in the dim lighting.

Savannah shrugged when Kels asked who he was, for she didn't know. She couldn't identify him like her sister had, but smiled when she saw the recognition hit his eyes, and he hugged Dallie.

"Must be someone she knows," Kels stated the obvious. "Let's go dance!"

Before Savannah could respond, Kelsey was pulling her onto the slick old wooden dance floor, and they fell into a line-dance, Savannah stumbling around for a minute before getting used to the rhythm and steps. It didn't take long before her heart was pounding, her feet were moving and her head was reeling from the booze. She laughed along with Kels when the song came to a stop and a rap song started. Their backs hit as they began to bump and grind like when they were teenagers again; gyrating, hips swaying and twerking. It wasn't too many songs in before her legs and abs began to feel the strain of those old movements, and Kels was pulling her back to the table they'd claimed, out of breath and cackling like a hyena.

Thankfully, Dallie had prepared and had two waters sitting on white napkins, sweating and ready for them when they came back. They both chugged greedily.

"Damn, I didn't realize how old I'd gotten until I start dancing like that again."

"Right?" Dallie laughed. "But y'all looked good out there. I was afraid for a minute you'd have a swarm of men all over you. You caught a few eyes…just sayin'." Dallie looked at Savannah almost apologetically as Vanna frowned at her.

Why was she wanting Vanna to get drunk and go home with someone before the night was out? Who was this woman who sat across from her? When had her moral code become so lax?

"Uh oh, milk is kickin' in. I'm gonna go pee. Y'all good?"

Any other time, the three of them would take a group trip to the bathroom, but Vanna wanted another shot and Kels must have sensed it, for she just nodded and looped her arm through Vanna's, pulling her to the bar and towards a tall, middle-aged bald man whom she called Barney.

"Four more shots of Patrón, Barney." They took the two empty spots at the bar top, getting looks from the men on either side, and Kels' eyebrows went up. Savannah just rolled her eyes.

"You got it, doll," he stated and grinned at her. It was immediately evident to Vanna that she had him under her spell.

Kels turned her legs into Savannah's and leaned in suddenly, frowning. "Morgan's here."

Savannah stilled, knowing what that meant, and took in the sudden alarm in her best friend's eyes. "Where?"

Kels just tilted her head, indicating for Vanna to look behind Kelsey. She did.

Her cousin, Morgan Dean Butler, sat there, looking up at the TV. He looked good; healthy, happy, well-groomed in his dark polo shirt. His raven-black hair cut short, shorter than she'd remembered seeing on him last, and his beard trim. She couldn't help but grin, trying to get his attention; he was her cousin after all. But Kelsey's pull on her arm immediately shelved it.

"I don't want him to see me."

"Oh, Kels, c'mon. It's been twelve years since y'all broke up. Either talk it out or move on." Savannah could say things like that. It was Kelsey...and she was buzzing.

"I know, but I just...I can't, Savannah. I'm still not ready."

Kelsey and Morgan. They'd been sweethearts since they'd first met, immediate sparks flying in all directions. *Everyone* had seen them that day at the summer barbeque all those years ago, as if they'd been live wires, and knew Kels and Morgan were meant to be. They'd been hot and steamy all through Kel's high school career, not able to keep their hands or eyes off of one another then one day right before Kelsey started college, they'd up and split. Kels had told Savannah years later why and she'd understood, for the light had been extinguished from Kels's eyes as if he'd taken her very soul with him when he'd up and walked away. To this day, neither of them had ever spoken to each other about the tragedy that had befallen them. But Vanna could see, even now, the pain was still so raw in Kelsey's eyes.

When Barney handed the drinks over, they quickly retreated back to their table, and Kels visibly relaxed. As much as Vanna wanted to press the issue, now wasn't the time or place, she knew, and shot both her glasses back, one after the other, as Kelsey did. Kels sat with her back to the bar and looked Vanna over.

"Thanks," she murmured.

"Of course," Vanna answered with a nod. She just wished things were different, and they could've worked it out. They were such a great couple.

Suddenly, Savannah's eyes settled on the man sitting next to Morgan, zoning in on a face she recognized, not because it was familiar to her, but because it was one who'd pissed her off earlier that morning.

"I'll be damned," she stated, not believing her eyes.

"What?" Kels subtly turned her head and looked where Savannah's head nodded.

"That guy! I know him!" Well, she didn't *know* him know him.

"Oooh, he's hot, Vanna," Kels purred. "You should go talk to him."

"No. He's a jerk!"

"Well, he's one *sexy-looking* jerk," Kels surmised, looking thoughtfully back to Savannah.

Come to think of it, it was Vanna who'd been the jerk, not necessarily the handsome cowboy who now sat at the bar. Now that she looked back on the incident with liquor-tainted eyes, she'd practically taken the rocking horse right out from under him...and with no remorse whatsoever. He honestly hadn't deserved how she'd treated him about it. She'd been unreasonable and completely unfair. And he just happened to be an innocent target on her woman-scorned warpath. She suddenly remembered his cool demeanor, his big stature and his sexy deep southern accent. He was absolute sex on a stick, sitting there looking comfortable in his skin with his tan cowboy hat atop his head, leaned over the bar nursing a beer. She remembered suddenly that he'd suggested performing some kinky foreplay on her before leaving the store...perhaps she *should* go talk to him. He deserved an apology after all.

When Morgan suddenly got up from the bar, presumably to go to the bathroom, she took her opportunity.

"Vanna?" Kels asked as Savannah stood. Vanna gave Kels a knowing grin, and with a bravado she hadn't believed she could possibly muster, she moved towards the bar.

CHAPTER 2

*a*s Savannah closed in on the California dreamboat—if he wasn't a Cali man he could have been their poster boy—her mind fired off doubtingly at her insecurities. Her heart hammered in her chest and her ears rang with the blood that accelerated to them. She was just squeezing into the stool next to him, his eyes focused on the TV above the bar as she cleared her throat and let the vulnerable, sex-starved inner vixen take over her thoughts. She noted the jukebox playing "Hot-Blooded" by Foreigner and smiled. *How fitting!*

"Did Houston run out of rocking horses?" she began.

His head turned quickly and his beautiful amber-colored eyes sought hers. She'd never seen eyes quite that color before, a seeming mix of equal parts brown, yellow, and copper. A big smile lit his face as he recognized her from the store. He gave an incredulous laugh even as his eyes descended down her torso, making her skin hot where they touched her.

"Well, I'll be a son of a bitch! The horse thief." *Horse thief indeed.* Taking that rocking horse away from him had, in retrospect, been the highlight of her day. "So," his deep voice grew even deeper as he leaned in to her slightly. "Stealing my horse wasn't enough, huh?

You've come to steal my heart too?" That sexy dimple popped into his cheek as his eyes appraised her tight dress once more before returning to her face.

She grinned. "I see you're not completely devastated over your loss."

"All is fair in love and war, they say. Besides, beer and gorgeous women make *everything* better. I gotta ask though...are you stalking me?" His eyes moved back to her breasts, trying unsuccessfully to see through the thin silk of the keyhole halter top. "Because I must tell you, if you *are*, feel free to extract your pound of flesh, my dear."

Savannah wasn't sure if it was his confidence, her breakup, his gorgeous self, or the alcohol that gave her the heady feeling his words elicited. She assessed him with her eyes. He was still clad in the same jeans, but must have changed his shirt, for this one was a black button down, the first two buttons undone to expose the V of his impressive chest, the sleeves were rolled up, hugging his bulging, dark-inked biceps tightly. He had a blonde-bearded square jaw, a straight nose, and lips that simply begged to be kissed. His blonde hair stopped midway down his neck and was unruly with wavy curls that haphazardly stuck out from under his tan Stetson. He was cocky and all male, and she suddenly wondered what an unscrupulous night with him would be like.

He fingered the neck of his beer bottle before tipping his hat to her casually and extending his hand. "My name's Austin, ma'am. I didn't catch yours."

"Savannah." She easily slid her hand into his and felt a shiver run through her.

"Sa-*van*-nah," he enunciated, his deep voice as smooth as honey. "What a beautiful name for such a *sassy* little minx." He winked, and she felt her sex tingle. "Savannah," he said again, only deeper as he leaned in a little closer, "Savvy. Yeah, that's about right." If she was turned on simply by him saying her name, she couldn't even comprehend what his hands and mouth on her would do. She gulped. "Why are you here, Savvy?"

Her hand was still clasped in his. In fact, she hadn't even been sure she'd properly shook it, but his thumb was now stroking her knuckles ever so lightly, so she wasn't tempted to break the contact.

"It's girls' night out," she said breathlessly, his touch pulling prickly ribbons of silky heat from her center. She motioned over to Kelsey, who suddenly forced her eyes in another direction as they looked over to her. He briefly took in Kels before averting his eyes back to Savannah's. "What about you?"

"It's Friday night...not much else to do in this lil' town." Savannah just nodded and tried to calm her pounding heart. "So, girls' night, huh? Y'all celebrating somethin'?"

"You could say that."

"What are we celebrating?" He half-grinned again, and she felt her panties melt right off.

"New beginnings."

He cocked his eyebrow. "Yours?"

"You could say that."

"What do you do for a living?"

She wasn't expecting all this small talk. Couldn't they just go out to a vehicle or to the bathroom and make out? If he kept asking questions, her brain would take over and convince her this was a bad idea. She needed to drown it out. She looked to the bartender and debated her choices.

"Damn. I'm sorry. Forgive me for my rudeness. Can I buy you a drink?" Austin motioned Barney over with the hand he wasn't stroking hers with. "Barney, I'll take another Bud. Savvy, pick your poison, darlin'."

Savannah debated once again; she'd had two rum and cokes and four shots of Patron. She should probably stick with rum and coke, but her stomach wasn't digging all the carbonation.

"Cosmo, please."

"Comin' right up." Barney nodded, and the sly look on Austin's face stilled her.

"What?"

"You look like a cosmopolitan type girl."

He had no idea; her head was constantly in the cosmos.

Before she could respond, he gave her an expectant look, and she realized he was still awaiting an answer from her in regards to her work. This was the last thing she wanted to talk about, for it brought her thoughts back to Sidd, so she decided to consult her inner sex goddess who responded with, "You'll never guess in a million years what I do. What do *you* do?"

And just like that, Venus nodded at her, for he smiled big and took the bait. Being the arrogant male he was, he brought the attention back to himself. "I'm a horse trainer."

*Go **fucking** figure!* Vanna shook her head in defeat. What were the freakin' odds? Of course he was a damn horse trainer!

Not that Savannah had ever looked down upon her upbringing, small town, or family. She adored her namesake *and* life on the ranch. She'd simply surmised that she'd fit in best with people like herself. Due to her superior IQ, she'd sought all her life to find individuals who could understand her complex intellect, who spoke her language, who got her. Upon meeting and befriending many a scientist, doctor and fellow physicist and engineer, she'd just assumed those types would be the only people on the same level playing field...but then the only brilliant doctor she'd gone and given her heart to had neither understood nor even paralleled her. Maybe she'd been wrong all along and had looked for love in all the wrong places...or maybe this was fate's cruel joke. *Well played, karma! Well played!*

"But it seems as if I need to switch over to taming tigresses." The eagerness in his voice was unmistakable, and Savannah grinned at Barney as he sat her drink down in front of her. "Cheers." Austin clinked his new beer bottle against her martini glass before she brought it to her lips to savor it. He tilted his head and studied her. "Not in a million years, huh?" He pursed his lips and rubbed his bearded chin with his thumb and index finger. Finally, his amber eyes narrowed and his finger went up. "I got it! Deducing from the fact that you were wearing business attire this morning, you looked as if you hadn't slept much, you were ready to murder me over an eighty-year-old rocking horse and the fact that we *were* in Houston, I'm gonna go with rocket scientist."

Damn, but he was close. "Well, you're not far off."

He gave a big chuckle before he realized she wasn't laughing too. "Wait, you're serious?"

Savannah nodded. "I work for NASA."

"No shit! How cool is *that*? I seriously just pulled that straight outta my ass." He looked her over again, this time with renewed appreciation; she immediately felt sexy as hell. "I'll be damned. I've never met anyone that worked at NASA. So, are you like an astronaut?"

Savannah laughed. "No, but I'm an astrophysicist and engineer."

"You're the hottest engineer I ever saw."

She wouldn't mention that she had a PhD in astrophysics, a bachelors in engineering, *or* that she'd gone to Harvard, for that might emasculate him even more so than she had this morning. Plus, he was awe-struck enough for the time being; no need to brag.

"It's actually pretty difficult to be an astronaut, you know?" She wouldn't get into the rigors of astronomy with him or discuss the competitiveness of the space programs, for that hadn't been her focus when she'd started her internship at NASA. Research and development had always been her dream. The stars simply fascinated her.

"I would've loved to have been an astronaut. Talk about a super cool job. I'm downright jealous," Austin confessed. Savannah just gave him a knowing grin. Despite all the glamour that came with working at NASA, it was grueling, unfair and at times redundant, as with any job, a soul was practically married to it. "So, since you don't get to walk in space. What is it that you do?"

"Well, I study and develop equipment and instrumentation, analyze data, research thermodynamics. I've helped integrate many of the current space programs. I've worked with a good bit of astronauts over the years, helped build and test satellites and crafts, assisted in onboard Avionics improvement, done a lot of research on the effects of space travel on the human body and implemented programs and systems to help assuage that impact. I've even analyzed samples of extraterrestrial materials." She could go on and on, but decided to stop there so she didn't overwhelm him.

"Man," Austin whistled after several moments of reverence. "Extraterrestrial? I would ask, but I'm sure you'd give me that B.S. answer, 'It's classified'." Vanna nodded in response with a smile. "But, dang, that's *so* interesting. So that must mean you're like a super genius then?"

"Oh, believe me, there are many who are *much* smarter than I am."

"I doubt a single one of 'em is as gorgeous as you are though." Gorgeous? Wow! He'd said it twice now. He was at least helping mend her broken ego. As if sensing her demeanor change, he asked, "Now, was it an extraterrestrial that had you all riled up this morning? Or are you planning on sending an antique rocking horse up in space next?" For his accent to be so strong, he had a cunning sense of reading between the lines. Who was this guy?

Vanna suddenly realized she'd forgotten to tell him she was sorry. "Oh, my. I do owe you an apology for my behavior this morning."

Austin held his hand up and just shook his head, indicating her apology wasn't necessary. "Nah, I owe *you* the apology. My momma would've worn me out if she'd 'a heard me talkin' to you like that."

"Well, you had reasonable justification for it, I suppose."

"It made my day more interesting is all." He winked again and sipped his beer. "But I sure would *love* to know why you were so mad." His insistence, at any other time would have been off-putting, but the way he looked at her made her want to tell him everything... with all her clothes off. His beautiful eyes pulled so much from her.

"I, uh...I came home from working eighty plus straight hours to my fiancé shacked up with another woman," she blurted out before her brain had time to register what she'd just said. "My suitcases were already packed and waiting for me at the door." She couldn't hide her cynicism as her lips and brows drew.

"You gotta be shittin' me! No wonder you were fit to be tied." Savannah said nothing as her cheeks continued to flame red. "Well, I dunno who your *ex*-fiancé is, but he's a total dumb-ass." *Houston Memorial would say he's a genius interventional cardiologist.* "A woman like you would be damn hard to leave. Those lips were *made* to be kissed...over and over again." Austin's statement made her sex clench, and she pulled on her bottom lip with her teeth, something she was known to do when she was nervous. He licked his own lips as he gazed down at the mouth he'd just mentioned then his eyes shot back up to hers. Savannah gulped; his intentions were unmistakable. Looks like she'd found the man for the one-night stand Kels and Dallie had been pushing her towards.

She tried to come up with a smart response, but none was forthcoming; yup, the booze was starting to take hold and kill some of her billions of brain cells.

"He obviously didn't agree," she finally spit out, sarcastically.

"Yeah, well, he's truly missing out. What's his name?"

Ugh. Did she really have to say it out loud? "Sidd," she murmured and tilted her glass to her lips, hating that she'd cried that name in orgasm as recently as a couple weeks ago. She swallowed down two big gulps of cranberry, triple sec, lime juice and vodka before looking back at Austin.

"Sidd? Not a very solid name, I have to say." He shrugged. "I'm gonna let you in on a little secret, Savvy." He had her full attention—not that he hadn't from the beginning—as his hand fell to her arm and he rubbed her skin gently with his thumb. She gulped. "If Sidd could see all the things I wanna do to you, he would be remiss to have given you up." His boldness should appall her; any other man who'd said such a sexist comment would have angered her, but she just sucked a ragged breath in as her attention-starved body reacted wantonly to his sentence. "Don't think for one second that I forgot about the bare-assed spankin' either because I haven't." He winked.

Savannah shivered as sparking heat engulfed her body. She knew she should protest; tell this man he had the wrong impression of her, scold him—albeit playfully—for not being a gentleman. But she didn't want a gentleman; she wanted a cowboy. *This* sexy cowboy. For she'd never been with one, and he looked to be every bit as untamed as the horses she knew he trained. She wanted rough. She wanted wild. She wanted rugged, unfiltered sexual renegade, Austin. "You ever rode a mechanical bull?" The answer was rhetorical, so after three seconds, he continued, "Why don't you show me how you move those curvy hips of yours on ol' Sherman over there? Show me all that passion I know you got hiding behind that sexy dress of yours, and tonight I'll make you regret every lover you ever had before me. Ride Sherman, like you're on top of me, and if you give me a good show, I'll ride Sidd right out of your system."

Motherfucker, if she wasn't wet as a rainstorm in that moment. He was a girl's wild west fantasy come to life. His words, his voice, his overwhelming sex appeal.

She wanted to hurl herself at him and beg him to take her right then and there—against the wall, on the floor, it didn't matter—for she just wanted his infectious aura to invade every cell of her body and erupt in a mountain of glorious mind-blowing release.

But her sensible brain intervened then, one last attempt at rationality, "What makes you so different than the lovers I've had before and why would I be so quick to hop right into bed with you, cowboy?"

His grin was so damn cocky, but it was his words that stilled her. "You and I both know you're simply dyin' to see what I got hidden in my pants, darlin'." When she gulped, he laughed confidently. "Most men don't have the proper equipment and furthermore don't know what to do with it." He winked. "I, sweetheart, ain't *most* men."

He knew then that he'd hooked her, for he was pulling her to the opposite side of the bar, and she was going willfully, his arm wrapping around her waist as they approached the old pitiful metal replica of a small steer. She hesitated only a moment before Austin lifted her and she straddled the imposter bull, the cold metal touching her smoldering womanhood, making the flame of it seem even hotter. She regarded Austin, who looked at her like she was his next meal— which wasn't far from the truth. He stood inside the railing and propped his confident self there, crossing his arms over his broad chest and grinning like a shit-eating possum. He gave her a thumbs up before saying, "Give her a good ride, Lane."

With that, the bull began to move slowly beneath her and in her startled daze, she gripped the bull rope with both hands, feeling a wave of both panic and excitation in that instant.

"Now darlin', I didn't take you for a cheater. Just one hand."

Savannah looked over at her soon-to-be fall from grace and raised her left arm above her head and gripped the rope with her right hand, letting her thighs squeeze around the strikingly cold metal. She grinned as she pulled her posture up and felt her confidence kick in as her body grew familiar with the position. She came from a long line of riders, it was in their blood—on both sides. She knew what game Austin was playing, and in her drunken state, decided she would play right along as she let her hips move slow like the bull. Back and forth, back and forth, she swayed and rolled her body, locking eyes with the man who would soon be her lover as she arched and bucked with the bull between her legs. If his grin and gaze were any indication, he was enjoying the show she was putting on for him and her bravery increased as the blood surged through her.

"C'mon, Lane. Is this all Sherman's got? I could ride all night with this pace." Savannah faked a yawn. She saw Lane look over to Austin, who nodded at his unspoken question. The speed increased, and Vanna's grip tightened as the metal moved somewhat faster and bucked a little harder. It only served to increase her adrenaline and arousal and to her utter horror, she found herself asking again, "You gonna give me a challenge tonight or what?"

With that, the bull's pace increased, and she was being flung side to side, her grip ever tighter around the strap. She kept pace though and although her brain was buzzing and flipping around wildly, she continued to match the rhythm of the bull with her hips. Austin's admiration seemed whetted and he smiled over at her seductively. She should be happy with that, but she had to press her luck, after all, Savannah was and had always been an overachiever. She asked Lane, "You call this a bull ride? I could do this in my sleep." Lane looked to Austin, shrugging. Austin gave her a surprised look, but again nodded, and that's when Vanna knew she had asked for too much, her teeth chattered with the force of the jerking and gyrating bull, her female parts slammed hard down onto the unforgiving metal as the machine went berserk. She tried but failed to keep her grip as the bull went one way and Savannah went another. Suddenly, she was airborne and felt her body crash into another, then felt the weight of that body on her as she hit the cushions with an expulsion of breath.

She laid there for a moment, trying to catch her breath and let her mind center itself before she looked up into Austin's gorgeous face, his eyes burning into hers. His big palm cupped her cheek and his hot breath fell over her face.

"Are you alright?"

The adrenaline coursed through her veins and made her buzz even sweeter. She couldn't contain the laugh that emerged from her throat then. She laughed and laughed and even got a short one out of Austin as he looked her over for signs of damage. His slow, stroking thumb stymied her outburst, and she gazed back up at him.

"That wasn't meant to be a *real* bull ride, ya know?"

"I know. I just didn't want you to be the only one having fun."

He smirked. "You're quite a woman, you know that, Savvy?"

She started to nod but felt her head reel, from the alcohol or him she wasn't sure. "I think everyone must have seen my panties," she whined.

"Well, don't worry. I didn't," he remedied.

"You will soon."

With that, she arched up and planted her lips on his; a soft, sensual kiss that left them both surprised and wanting to explore as his mouth opened to her searching one. He didn't rush the kiss, but when she thrust her tongue in, he groaned and let his tongue tangle with hers in a fight for control. His tongue was strong and eager as it plunged into her mouth relentlessly until he pulled back.

"Save it, cowgirl. Or I'm gonna take you right here in front of God and everybody," Austin practically growled. Vanna stilled and let herself be taken away in that moment just staring up at him, his body solid against hers. His hand fell to her ribcage and he lightly fingered the bones there, she visibly shivered and could see he'd ticked off an invisible mark in his head as he gave her a devilish grin. "Wanna get out of here?" he asked. She only nodded, for to say anything aloud would be an admission of guilt, and she didn't want to admit that this overconfident cowboy had stolen not just her breath but her moral fiber as well.

~

Kels looked over at Vanna and the sexy blond cowboy that led her to the mechanical bull and smiled. Good for her! He was definitely gonna make for a fun night. Kels grabbed Dallie on her way out of the bathroom and pulled her to the dance floor where they danced the "Macarena" and then began slow-dancing to Garth Brooks song "The Dance". Dallie asked where Savannah was and just as Kels was about to answer her, Kelsey felt her elbow being roughly jerked and her face planted into a hard chest. Her temper flared and as she looked up at the scruffy jaw of Brantley Burgess, her stomach plummeted. She gasped and sputtered.

"Damn it, Brantley. What are you doing?" Kelsey tried to pull away from the big hands that suddenly clasped her wrists, but he was too strong.

"Dance with me, Kels. I'm sorry. Damn, I'm sorry," he mumbled, his breath reeking of Jack Daniels. Son of a bitch! He was sloshed, which meant he was so much worse than usual.

Kelsey thought of a way to handle this as she resisted the urge to push him away. He would only get more physical if she fought back. No, she was going to wait until he relaxed his grip then slip right out of his grasp. When she stopped resisting, he relented and dropped his hands to her hips. She visibly cringed.

"Brantley, you and I are done. It's not gonna work. I don't know how many times I have to say this," she yelled over the next song that came over the speakers.

"No." He shook his head vigorously.

Dammit. Why was he here? And why couldn't he just leave her alone?

"Brantley, you don't fuckin' own me and that's what you don't understand!" Kels felt her anger surface. She looked over at Dallie then who'd inched her way closer to them, frowning as she sensed Kels's apprehension.

Dallie was like her big sister, so intervention was coming whether Kelsey wanted it or not.

"Brantley," Dallie cooed to him. "Why don't you go get her a drink?"

"She don't need another damn drink!" he bellowed and growled at Kelsey.

"See! This is the shit I'm talking about. You don't get to decide when I'm fuckin' cut off! I'm a big girl, I can decide for myself."

"Like hell! You'll end up bedding half the guys in this place with the way you been shootin' back tequila!"

"Fuck you, Brantley," Kels cried out and shoved at his chest, the momentum forcing him to stumble back a step or two. That's when she made her move to exit. She wasn't as quick as he was though and once again his long fingers gripped her forearms hard and pulled her back to him.

"You settle down, Kelsey Boyd. Or I'm gonna have to take you in."

To hell with him and his cocky cop attitude. What a prick!

"Brantley, let her go!" Dallie's voice grew louder and she stepped closer to them.

Kels gasped in horror as Brantley shoved Dallie's shoulder and she stumbled back, almost falling.

"You son of a bitch!" Her heel hit the top of his boot with force, but it didn't dispel him as he always wore steel-toed boots, even in the dead of summer. "She's pregnant. How *dare* you?"

"Then she can stay the hell out of my business."

Kels snarled as rage took over her and she fought to pull herself from the unrelenting grip he had on her, his nails digging into her arms. She cried, "Get your fucking hands off me!" and unsuccessfully struggled against the hands that imprisoned her wrists. He was undeterred, for he was tall and big, and she was too petite to even put up a worthy fight, but her words had the intended effect for they'd drawn an audience. He couldn't continue to bully her without someone seeing.

Just as Kels had given up on anyone intervening though, she heard a deep voice. "Brantley, let her go." It was Morgan. She'd recognize that deep, sexy voice anywhere. Her head whipped around to her left where he stood, his arm securely around Dallie's shoulder. He whispered into Dallie's ear and she nodded. She moved off, and Morgan stepped forward. "I said to *let* her go."

"Mind your own business, Butler."

"I'd like to, but you're making that increasingly difficult. Look at her arms. You're hurting her."

As if Brantley was stunned by Morgan's words, he looked into Kelsey's eyes, then to her arms where he held her in a death grip. He suddenly released her and took two steps back.

Kels felt the pressure lift, but her skin burned where his hold had chaffed and bruised her. She rubbed her arms absent-mindedly and frowned up at the breath-taking man of her heart. As much as she'd tried to erase him from her memory, his tall, dark and handsome profile had always lingered there, just a heartbeat away. His heated gaze gave nothing away before he settled it back on Brantley. The look he gave him was murderous, but Brantley didn't like being shown up. He had a reputation to uphold.

"Kels, outside."

"Like hell," Kelsey retorted. "I'm not going anywhere with you, you possessive asshole."

"Kelsey." Brantley took a menacing step forward towards her, and she literally recoiled. "I said *outside*."

Just before Brantley reached her, Morgan stepped in front of her, blocking him. His back hit her chest and his bottom hit her pelvis. She sighed, in love with the feeling of his comforting, familiar frame pressed so intimately to her. His strong, masculine scent filled her nostrils, not changing at all in the last twelve years, bringing all sorts of delicious and exciting memories in its wake. Having him so close after all this time filled her with a longing that made her entire body ache, and she couldn't help but lower her hands to his hips and lean her face against the curve of his shoulder blade, inhaling him deeply. For whatever emotions she'd felt for him up to this point had paled in comparison to having him, here and now, protecting her, coming between her and harm's way. Her heart overflowed with love, a love she'd had for him since she was merely twelve years old, a love that had only grown more profound over the years, even if she'd spent as much time without him as she had with him.

"That's enough," she felt his rough voice rumble deep in his chest, against her cheek, and despite their predicament, she knew it was all going to be okay because he was there to take care of her. "It's time for you to leave."

"Butler, I suggest you move the hell away from my girlfriend before I knock your ass out."

"I'm not your girlfriend, you sick fuck," Kels retorted back and tried unsuccessfully to look over Morgan's big shoulder to Brantley.

She felt Morgan pat the hand that gripped the left side of his polyester polo shirt.

"Now, that sounds to me like she doesn't want anything to do with you, Brant."

"I said to mind your own damn business, Butler. Or maybe you wanna go to jail tonight." Ah, Brantley Burgess and his idle threats.

"You'll be the one in jail. Or have you forgotten that I'm not the only one to witness your assault and battery charges?" Morgan let that comment linger for a moment before adding, "Now, let's call it a night, shall we?"

With that, Brantley finally looked around, Kels taking a slow step to the side to see around Morgan's arm. All eyes were on Brantley, and Barney was heading over, his head indicating to Brantley that he needed to head out. Brantley's brown eyes burned into hers and he narrowed them and pointed to her.

"This isn't over, Kelsey. Not by a long shot."

"Did you just threaten her?" Morgan growled and stepped forward. "I would advise you to reevaluate your situation here, Burgess. You may be a cop, but that doesn't mean you're above the law. Perhaps you should remember that."

Brantley grimaced and gave Morgan a shoulder bump as he walked past. Kels visibly relaxed, exhaling the breath she felt like she'd been holding the whole time. Morgan turned then, cupping her face as his entrancing blue eyes looked her over.

"Are you okay?" he asked tenderly, his hands falling to her wrists and forearms, lightly touching the red marks that had formed from Brantley's hold on them.

Any response she could've had died on her lips. Her flesh sizzled from his touch, and not in a bad way either. She gulped as his eyes looked back into hers. God, how she'd missed him. His thumb grazed her cheekbone, soft and gentle, and she literally felt herself melting, like a Hershey's Kiss in a jeans pocket on a hot summer day. She'd only *thought* she was in love with him at eighteen years old; at thirty, she was completely head over heels...despite that he'd just walked away after she'd lost their baby. The sudden memory cut her to the core as it always had, and he must have sensed it too as he said, "Let's get you and Dallie home."

He stepped away then, and she felt bereft without the warmth of him beside her. She solemnly followed him, all eyes on her as she and Morgan approached the table Dallie sat at. She stood and looked Kelsey and Morgan over, scowling.

"Well, I'm glad that didn't turn into a fight."

"It about did when I saw him shove you. Lucky for him you didn't fall, Dallie," Morgan stated angrily. Kels knew if it had come to blows, Morgan would probably have taken Brantley down, no problem. For one, Brantley had been wasted and two, despite Brantley's training and stature, Morgan was taller and more muscular. And he was Nathan Butler's son; he could pack a mean punch!

Apart from the striking physical resemblance to his father—eyes, skin, hair *and* lips—Morgan Butler was as different from him as night was to day. Morgan was soft-spoken, easy-going, and wasn't one for drama. He had a charitable heart and held a seat on the town council. He was an upstanding citizen of Abundance and an entrepreneur. He'd started his own construction business when he graduated from college and was doing very well.

Dallie spoke then as they headed toward the door of The Rusty Spur and took one of Morgan's elbows he'd extended to them both. "Thanks, cuz. I owe you."

Morgan scoffed. "You don't owe me a thing, Dallas. No man's gonna treat women like that while I just stand and watch." After all, Morgan had been raised by a hard-working, single mother whom he'd absolutely worshipped. Even in death, he revered Joanne Dean and spoke of her as if she were akin to Mother Theresa, despite that in her youth she'd been a practical rodeo groupie.

"Shit!" Dallie cried out, and all three of them stopped before the dark-tinted glass doors. She turned and looked out over the crowd, who no longer showed any interest in them.

"What?" Kels asked, her eyes attempting to ascertain what had upset Dallie so.

"Savannah! Where is she?" Dallie's eyes searched for their dark-headed compadre, but Kels noted she wasn't on the bull that the blonde man had accompanied her to not long ago.

Kels shrugged and smiled. "Last I saw, she was enjoying herself with an attractive cowboy at the bar."

"Great!" Dallie huffed and dug into her crossbody purse to locate her cell phone. She began punching numbers into it when she found it and held the phone to her ear. Morgan and Kels waited as the phone rang but went to Savannah's voicemail after five rings. "Dammit! We can't just leave her here. I have no idea where she is or who she's with." Her blue eyes pleaded with Kelsey.

"Oh, c'mon now, Dallie. We were the ones encouraging her to enjoy herself tonight. I'd say by the smile I saw on her face, she was accomplishing just that."

"Kelsey Jean Boyd! We can't just leave her with some stranger to do God knows what with. As much as I want to say, 'It's a small town, we don't have to worry,' we both *know* that isn't true." The concern that hit Dallie's face then stymied any response Kels might have, for both their families had been hit with devastating tragedies at the hands of men of this "small town". Kelsey gulped, trying hard not to let panic rise in her stomach.

Morgan reassured them then, patting Dallie's shoulder. "It's alright, Dallie. She's with Austin Montgomery. She's fine."

"What?" Dallie hissed out. "Are you *kidding*?"

"No. I saw them leaving together just a few minutes ago."

Dallie sighed. "No. We have to warn her."

"Relax, cuz. He may have a reputation, but he's harmless. He's not gonna hurt her. Trust me, she'll be just fine."

"And that *reputation* is what worries me… Daddy is gonna throw a shit fit."

"Oh, just take a breath, Doc," Kels contended. "We both know Savannah, our little genius. She'll just bore him to death with trying to explain string theory." Kels rolled her eyes, and Morgan gave a deep, sexy laugh.

"Kels *does* have a point, Dallie." His eyebrows shot up. "As beautiful as my little cousin is, she's a total dork."

Kels smiled fondly at that. Savannah was amazing- truly. Passionate. Loving. Kind. Generous. But damn, she was a complete space cadet, and when she got in the mood to talk about her work, she left them all feeling like a bunch of primitive-brained cave dwellers. But Kelsey hoped that whoever this Austin guy was would at least boost her ego and make her laugh before the night was out. Savannah deserved that much, at the very least, after the degrading rejection she'd received this morning.

And maybe, just maybe, one of them would get laid before the night was over. Kels would put her money on it being Savannah, for as much as Kelsey wanted Morgan Dean Butler, he was a complete gentleman in every sense of the word...and Vanna *had* looked smokin' hot tonight in that expensive dress of Kelsey's. Any man would be an utter fool to let Savannah's big brain threaten the prospect of getting her naked and into his bed.

Dallie hesitated for another several moments, eyes searching for her missing sister before she relented, nodded, and headed out the door. She didn't like it, but what could they do? Kelsey didn't know Austin, apparently Morgan and Dallie did, but Morgan didn't seem too worried by the fact that his younger cousin, by less than two years, had ran off with the guy, so why should Kels and Dallie be? It was out of Vanna's character, but then again, Vanna deserved to lose herself to a handsome cowboy. Kels, again, hoped he was giving her best friend a good time. She was gonna find out about it come tomorrow and *all* the juicy details. She couldn't wait to squeeze the info out of Vanna and tell her about Brantley's brutish behavior and Morgan's daring rescue. It had been the highlight of her week. God, she needed to get a life...

"Dallie, leave it. Let me drive y'all home. You're too shaken up." Morgan noted as he and Kels watched her keys shake in her hands as she attempted to unlock her driver's side door.

Dallie just sighed and took Morgan's offered arm, Kelsey bringing up the rear.

Once they were seated in Morgan's brand-new roomy Dodge pickup—Kels offering shotgun to Dallie—they rode silently to

Dallie's house. Dallie was probably mulling over the lecture she would be getting from her father about not keeping tabs on her sister, and Kels was swooning over Morgan's chivalrous bravery in the face of Kelsey's drama. She wasn't quite sure *what* Morgan was thinking but would give anything to be able to read his mind at that very moment as his eyes sought hers in the rearview mirror.

As they pulled up in Dallie's driveway, and Morgan put the truck in park, he turned to his older cousin and gave a terse grin as he patted her arm. "Please don't worry, Dallas. She's fine. I promise you. Ok?"

"I sincerely hope you're right, Morgan." Dallie's brows went up.

"I am. I know I am. Despite what your dad thinks, Austin isn't a bad guy." His eyes held Dallie's until finally she huffed and nodded, then looked back at Kels, the worry starting to dissolve a little. "I'll bring you your car in the morning. Get some rest." He kissed her cheek and leaned over to open her door for her, taking her hand as she stepped onto the nerf bar. Dallie looked back at Kels, holding the car door. "I'll walk her in in a minute. Kels and I need to talk." Morgan's deep voice grew wistful, and Kels felt her heart jump up into her throat.

That talk that she'd warned Savannah she wasn't ready for was about to happen.

Kelsey watched as Dallie's blonde eyebrows went up, once again, in surprise. She said nothing but gave Kelsey a firm smile and shut the car door, leaving Kels and Morgan alone in the truck.

Kelsey's heart slammed violently into her ribs as Morgan turned in his seat to face her.

"Will you come up here so that I can talk to you?"

Kelsey knew that all the blood had drained from her face. She simply nodded, willing her rubbery legs to move as she stepped up and slid, legs first, over the large console. She tried to gracefully cover her thighs with her short silk dress as she moved her body into the passenger seat. Morgan took her hand to help her into the bucket seat and pulled it back as she got settled, as if her touch had scalded him.

Morgan gave a long sigh, moving his big palms over his face. When he looked back at her, he looked incredibly displeased. *Great! Now I'm in for a lecture*, she thought, but couldn't hide her surprise when Morgan said, "This shit has gotta stop, Kelsey. I don't know what the hell you were thinking when you started dating Brantley Burgess, but I can't do this anymore." Kels knew her expression appeared baffled for that's what she was in that moment. "I can't keep pretending that I'm ok with all this because the truth of the matter is that I'm not...I haven't been and dammit, I never *will* be." What the hell was he trying to say? "Kelsey...we only have one life to live and I don't wanna waste another moment of mine without you." *Wait. What?*

"Morgan!" Kels scoffed. "You left *me*, remember?"

"Yes, of course I do. And it's haunted me every day since."

"Look!" Kels felt the bittersweet tears hit her eyes, the salty taste of her saliva filled her mouth as her mind raced back to that horrible day twelve years prior.

The hospital bed had been hard and unyielding to the pain of both her heart and body as the doctor explained to an eighteen-year-old girl and her twenty-year-old boyfriend that she'd miscarried their child. She'd never forget how her heart broke into a million pieces and how lost she'd felt in that moment. She'd also never forget the relief on Morgan Butler's face as he'd turned to face her.

"Oh God, Morgan. I'm so sorry. I don't—"

"No, it's alright. It's not your fault. These things happen. It's not without its reasons."

Her heart, which was already shattered, felt like it had just imploded into itself. He was happy about this, for now he was free. Free of her. Free to do as he wished. Free from the bondage she'd had him under when she'd become pregnant with his child.

The pain that had hit his face shocked her then. His beautiful sapphire eyes had burned deeply into hers and he looked her over, not unlike he was looking at her now. He'd grimaced and dropped her hand, covering his face as he pitched forward, suspended on his thighs. He'd rocked back and forth and breathed heavily. All the while, Kelsey's stomach had burned with bile and her throat felt like it was closing up. She was losing him, and there wasn't a damn thing that she could do about it. When he'd finally pulled himself upright, his face was as stern as she'd ever seen it and he stood, wiping the tears from his cheeks.

Kelsey'd swallowed hard, knowing the words that were coming before they smeared her hope across the floor, just like the first drop of blood that had ended her baby's life.

"You deserve better, Kelsey." His chin had tilted up and his lips had quivered. "I'm so sorry."

And with that, he'd walked out on her.

He walked out of her life. Out of her heart. And out of her future.

But he'd *been* her future, and she'd never known exactly what to do after that. For she'd never truly gained her footing back to reality. She'd tried, but loving Morgan Butler had been as easy as breathing had been and living without him had always felt rehearsed, like she was living a lie, living a life of someone else, never truly able to be complete. He'd taken the very breath from her body when he'd left her, and she'd not fully breathed again since.

"You don't get to just wipe the slate clean like nothing ever happened. It doesn't work that way, Morgan," she suddenly sobbed as the anguish overcame her.

"I know." He lowered his head then. "You don't know how much I regret what I did to you. I was young and stupid and I didn't realize what I was walking away from until it was too late. But you *did* deserve better. You still do."

"What does that even *mean*?" she screamed. "How can I deserve more than what I want, more than what I *love*?"

"You deserved to have a man who was happy that you were carrying his baby. And that wasn't something I could give you at that time."

"What?" Had she heard him correctly. "What are—"

"Kelsey, darlin'." He took her hand in his, tears falling down his cheeks, her heart hovering in her throat as his eyes looked into hers, opening a window into his very soul. "I have never stopped loving you."

"But you didn't *want* me! You walked out on me," she countered, daring him to deny it.

"Honey locks, it wasn't *you* that I didn't want. I never stopped wanting you."

Realization seized her as his words struck a chord, first in her brain then in her heart. "The baby?" He nodded, grimly. "You were *glad* I lost it." It wasn't a question. She'd known he was happy about it, but she'd always just assumed it was so that he could be free of *her*, not because he was actually happy about the baby dying. Again, he only nodded in response, squeezing his eyes closed. She said nothing for a moment, letting her emotions settle in some before she asked, "Why?"

"I lived half of my life believing that my father didn't want me. Believing that he'd wronged my mother. She never discussed it with me and if I ever brought it up, she dropped the subject. I was led to believe, in my mind, that he knew about me, but that was a lie. Nathan Butler didn't even know I existed until I came knocking on his door that day. He was completely oblivious, and there's a part of me that always wondered, if he'd been told about me on the day of my birth instead of when I was almost fifteen years old, would he have chosen to *remain* oblivious?"

"Oh, Morgan," she huffed out, on another sob. "Your father loves you but even still, you're not your father." She pulled his hand to her cheek then to her lips and kissed it.

"I know that now," he confessed. "But at almost twenty-one years old I wasn't so sure. I feared resenting that child like I always believed my father resented me and I can't describe how elated I was when I knew I wasn't going to have to face that dilemma." He buried his face in his hands and sobbed then, pulling raw pain forth from

Kelsey with each whimper. She sobbed in silence herself, staring out her window into the night, for she couldn't let him see her grieve. She'd grieved enough over what had happened, and it appeared that Morgan had to, despite what she'd thought all those years ago.

She let him cry; cry for himself, cry for her, cry for the infant's death that had torn them apart for long moments before his grief was spent. He sniffled and wiped at the tears with the back of his hand, trying to figure out what to say next. She had no words herself, for once in the span of her life, Kelsey Jean Boyd was speechless.

"Kelsey," he called to her, a desperation in his smooth voice that she'd never quite heard before, and she looked over at him, despite that she knew his piercing eyes were going to tear her heart right out of her chest. "Forgive me, honey locks. I'm so very sorry."

She watched his Adam's apple bob in his throat and looked him over. The man she'd given her heart and soul to long before she'd even been old enough to know what the hell love was. He was beautiful, every rugged inch of him, from the top of his shiny raven black hair to the soles of his long feet. He was tan, and handsome, and he belonged solely to her, she saw in that instant.

When he reached for her, she melted into his arms and his lips planted softly on hers and slanted, his tongue plunging into her waiting mouth, searching for absolution. Her moan was equal parts desire and bone-satisfying comfort. Her body was home in his warm embrace, back home where it belonged after twelve long years away. His hands shook as he gripped her hips and pulled her onto his lap and the rock-hard erection that grew there, solid against her inner thigh. Her hands immediately went at his sex, stroking him to his full potential as her mouth returned to his, her tongue eliciting moans deep in his chest.

"Oh, baby, yes. God, I want this, I want you," Morgan groaned as he gripped the strings of her thong panties with his fists and literally ripped them off her hips. She couldn't have said it better herself for it was exactly how she felt about him. After years of pent-up desire, her body ached to be filled by his sex again—his and his alone—unlike anything she'd ever felt before and nothing else mattered in those moments, not the truck still running or her backside hitting the edge of the steering wheel, for his hands cupping her bare breasts as he peeled the silky fabric off her shoulders could possibly be her undoing. His mouth moved from hers to the aching nipple he pulled into his hot mouth and his hand slid up her sweaty thighs, over the budge of his restrained erection, and into the nakedness between. "Oh fuck, Kelsey, you're so wet." He groaned again as his fingers pressed into her, sliding as easily inside her as her nipple did into his mouth. His tongue assaulted the pebbled peak and she whimpered his name, writhing on his hand, even as she groped for his fly and zipper. She needed him inside her for she was about to lose herself; she'd waited so long to be reunited with her one true love.

"Morgan, please, please," she begged even as his fingers thrust harder into her, giving her more, but she wanted his sex, not his fingers and she told him so. "No...I want your cock." She freed him from his jeans and took his hard, bare sex in her hands as his head flew back on the seat and he swore. She worked the length of him in her palm, showing him no more mercy than he'd shown her and after a minute or so, he was readjusting her on his lap as he pulled his jeans down his hips and sat her down upon him. She cried out in orgasm as the tip of his thickness entered her and within three thrusts, he himself was climaxing, but they didn't stop there. They hadn't filled the void, and God only knew when or if they ever would, for his hips continued to lunge, his thighs continued to hit hers, thrust after thrust he sought completion and forgiveness inside her. She met his resolve and gripped his shoulders as his mouth claimed hers once again. His thumb moved between her thighs and began to stroke her there. She cried out and his mouth moved to nibble her neck, his other hand cupping her breast, fingers pinching her nipple.

"God, I don't know how I've lived without you," he said breathlessly in her ear. "I've dreamed of this moment so many times. You, just like this." He moaned aloud as her sex clenched him.

"Is it how you dreamed it would be?" She arched a brow and looked him in the eyes as the hand at her breast moved to her lower back, pressing her further down onto him. She cried out as he thrust harder. He looked down, watching his body mating hers and gave her a sexy grin that almost made her fall over the edge again.

"It's even better, darlin'. If only I could see you, I would be fully satisfied."

She reached up absent-mindedly and searched sightlessly for the overhead light, fumbling for it even as she felt herself slipping closer to the edge once again. Impatiently, her finger pressed the button, and they were momentarily blinded with light from above. Her eyes easily adjusted and she looked at her lover, grinning contentedly at her. She watched him thrust into her, biting into his bottom lip as he had when they were younger, holding himself back as he waited on her to finish first. He'd always been such a gentleman, even in the bedroom, despite that his mouth had gotten dirtier and his demeanor kinkier.

If she'd thought he was handsome in his youth, he was gorgeous now. The lines of his face more defined by his age of thirty-three. Where once he was a boy, he was now a man and this man was fucking her like his life depended on it. She whimpered as his mouth took her nipple again, pulling, sucking and licking her into sexual stupor as his thumb gingerly caressed her exactly where she ached the most. She felt her breathing accelerate and the tingling begin deep within her core as she breathed out, "Oh, Morgan."

She watched him smile against her breast, his lips barely moving off her as he murmured, "Yes, my love, I wanna see you come for me again."

Her cries superseded her orgasm as Morgan arched his hips and pounded into her with no pity, throwing her into sexual bliss. She moaned and gasped, looking into his eyes as he watched her fall apart to his sex, his touch, her body clenching his cock in shuddering spasms. She saw his resolve waver as he too, started to fall. "Oh fuck, baby, you're so fuckin' sexy. I'm gonna come. Oh shit!"

His beautiful mouth opened in roars of pleasure and he thrust higher and harder, gripping her hips in his big palms and kneading her ass as his hips hit hers again and again, riding his orgasm for all it was worth. Finally, his thrusts began to slow and his breathing began to calm; their sexes still pulsing as he continued to move inside her.

"I love you, Kelsey Jean," he said softly, cupping her cheek. She smiled. He'd always called her that, especially when he'd gotten sentimental, like when they made love. She didn't even have to say it, for he knew that she loved him. She kissed his palm and moved it to her chest where her heart was. "You're achingly beautiful when you fall apart, you know that?" She stifled a giggle. God, he was such a horn dog. No one would guess it by looking at him, but he'd loved to fuck and apparently still did. He'd almost never wanted to do it from behind or with her facing away from him because he couldn't see her face when she orgasmed. It was one of his biggest turn-ons he'd told her one day when she'd asked a long time ago. "I have a lot of making up to do, I know that. And I plan on doing so for the rest of my life. If you'll find it within yourself to give me another chance."

Even as much as she wanted to tell him yes, her heart wasn't mended from the true knowledge of his rejection. It was like a scabbed-over wound that had just been ripped back open; the pain flooded her chest. They'd just had earth-shattering sex, but she wasn't sure they could earnestly have a future together. What would happen if their past simply repeated itself? Could she live through his rejection twice? And how dumb was she to have just let him take her without using protection?

As if sensing her hesitation, he sighed. "Oh, Kelsey. I know what you're thinking. But I'm not the same person I was. I want babies. I want to get you pregnant...right now in fact. I hope I just overloaded your womb with semen. I hope they swim and—"

"Stop," Kels commanded as if talking to one of her students. Morgan looked at her as if she'd slapped him.

With his sex still softening inside her, the talks of having another baby was too painful, too sharp, too soon. He must have recognized this, as he swore and pulled her into his arms, her bare chest smothered by his and she sighed as once again she felt as if she were home. He stroked her hair and cooed to her, kissing her temple as bittersweet tears fell silently down her cheeks.

"I'm sorry," he murmured and pulled back, wiping at her cheeks.

She wanted to explain to him that she wasn't sure she could give him another chance. She wasn't sure that her heart could withstand it. She'd distanced herself, and it was going to take time for her to heal. Hell, it had been twelve years and that amount of time hadn't been enough. She wanted to say so much, but her eyes just looked his achingly handsome face over and she shook her head, rapidly, sorrowfully. He seemed to understand because he was her soulmate and they'd been able to read each other's thoughts and hearts and finish each other's sentences upon their first meeting.

He sighed heavily and gripped her shoulders gently, placing her at arms-length, still seated on his lap, as his sex fell from within her. He dropped his hands and lowered his head for a moment, in deep contemplation. Then he chuckled easily and pointed to the dress that clung only to her mid-drift, it was covered in the stains from their sexual liberation.

"I believe I've ruined your dress, ma'am," he admitted and looked up bashfully at her. "I reckon I'll have to take you to buy another one." Kelsey's response was slow to follow as she just stared at him, unsure how to proceed. "I don't believe I introduced myself before we started." His grin was devilish as he continued. "I'm Morgan Dean Butler. I own my own construction company, and I'm chairman of the town council. What was your name?"

Kelsey couldn't help but be touched by his thoughtfulness and found herself smiling back at him as she took his offered hand. Her chin went up as she said, "Kelsey Jean Boyd. I'm a second-grade teacher here in Abundance."

"It's truly been a pleasure, Ms. Boyd."

Kels shivered at the way Morgan said the word 'pleasure' as he looked back down at her exposed sex, pulling on his bottom lip as he did so. Damn it, if she wasn't soaking wet all over again. She gulped, loving how dark his eyes got as he watched her getting aroused from his words. She wasn't sure exactly *who* this new and improved Morgan Butler was, but she was going to enjoy getting to find out.

CHAPTER 3

They had barely gotten out the door of the Rusty Spur when Austin grabbed Savannah and pulled her stark against him, kissing her with a possessive passion she'd never felt before. She felt licking flames that started in her lower belly and spiraled out to the rest of her and moaned unabashedly as Austin's tongue plunged into her mouth again. It was more vigorous than it'd first been, greedier, and erotic as it explored her mouth with an unrestrained curiosity that had her entire body humming. His beard tickled her, for she'd not kissed a bearded man before, but the new sensation was welcomed. One of his hands planted into her hair, holding her head in his big palm, the other hand was at her waist then splayed on her back. He pulled back for a breath, his arousal solid against her belly.

"Your place or mine, darlin'?" he asked and looked at her with hungry, dark eyes.

This was really happening. She was going to have her first one-night stand. Could she actually go through with it? This was totally not like level-headed, intelligent, well-put-together Savannah Kinsen. At any other time, her big brain would be alerting her to the dangers of casual sex and reckless behavior. It was numb from all the alcohol though and wouldn't be of any help. Her heart, as pure and optimistic as ever, was melting at the sexy cowboy that held her tightly against him; it wasn't going to be the voice of reason either, and her sex, well, it was reveling in the overpowering carnal allure that Austin exuded from every pore of his gorgeous golden-tanned skin.

He must have sensed her questioning herself, for the hand in her hair came down to her cheek, and he grinned. "Hey, no pressure, Savvy. I just want to spend some more time with you is all."

They both knew that wasn't entirely true as their bodies threatened to be consumed by the overwhelming lust that crashed violently between the two of them. She looped her arms around his neck and took his lips again, her final restraints buckling as she basked in the dangerous taste of him. He groaned. His hands moved down her hips and he pulled the fabric up just enough so that when he lifted her up, her legs could go around him. Austin walked forward, surprisingly easily, towards the parking lot as she continued to ravage his mouth like a crazed banshee, then he dropped her down as he fished for his keys in his back pocket. Savannah turned to look at his shiny, white, soft-top Jeep and admired it for only a moment before he pulled her in and a straddle of his lap, angling his head as his lips covered hers once again and his bulging sex pressed into her soaking wet panties. His hands gripped her hips and he ground himself against her even as he swore, his tongue striking hers impatiently.

"Fuck, Savvy. I want you bad, baby girl."

She sucked his tongue like a wild woman, feeling the pulsing ache within her, screaming to be quieted. "I want *you*," she whimpered as his left hand cupped her breast.

"Fuck *me*, you're so damn hot. But, not here. We need somewhere more private."

She could only nod as he shifted her over the console and into the passenger's seat. Austin cranked the Jeep and shifted it into drive.

Savannah's mind reeled from the alcohol and the manly scent of his cologne. She watched him as he drove out onto the road, silently wondering where the hell he was going to take her and if she'd made a grave mistake leaving a bar with a total stranger. She'd read papers, seen TV shows, heard tales of girls who'd disappeared this very way. What the hell had she been thinking? "We must be going to your place, huh?"

Austin's hand on her upper thigh stilled her thoughts, and he grinned over at her, that sexy dimple at the side of his mouth begging to be explored with her tongue.

"We don't have to, if you're not comfortable with that, darlin'."

"I think neutral would be best, don't you?"

"I got a neutral place we can go. Just down the road a-ways."

She nodded, but stopped as the motion made her dizzy. She settled her head into his neck, wanting to indulge in the wonderful smell of him again. Leather, fresh laundry and a musky, woodsy scent that reminded her of Irish Spring. She inhaled him and moaned in his ear, licking his neck and exposing her teeth to his flesh. He gripped her thigh and swore again, making her feel unabashedly sexy. She moved a hand down his chest, feeling the hard muscles tighten beneath her palm, and slid it down slowly to the bulge between his legs. She cupped him there and gave a teasing squeeze.

"Jesus, sexy lady. You're in for it. Let me go ahead and warn you." The arm he was holding her with tightened around her and his hand squeezed her bottom, making her gasp. He practically growled in response, and Savannah giggled. "Go ahead, have your fun." His eyes roved over her. "I'm gonna have mine here in two minutes."

Savannah wasn't aware of where they stopped or when, for her hand became fascinated with the thick, lengthy protrusion inside his jeans that extended down his inner thigh. She could see how big he was, and it both intrigued and intimidated her, but she couldn't—for the life of her—stop stroking it.

Suddenly, she was grabbed and pulled out of the vehicle, hearing the door slam as his lips made love to hers in a tangling of tongues that left her breathless. She moaned as he carried her a distance into light and pulled back as she smelled a familiar scent: hay, horse manure, and livestock. She opened her eyes and looked around. She was in a barn and not just any barn, her family's barn. She furrowed her brows and looked into Austin's tan face as he laughed at her expression.

"It's not fancy, I know, but I was trying to hold with the cowboy theme here, so I thought I'd go with it. Plus, your hand was about to do me in and this is the closest place I could think of."

"It has potential," she stated, gazing around. "Perhaps the hayloft."

He looked disinclined as he sat her down on the ground and pulled his lips from one side of his mouth to the other. "Are you sure?"

"Why not?"

"Well, I mean, I really wanna see you nak—"

Savannah had already made up her mind by that point as she moved to the rack of saddle blankets, grabbing up ones that looked to be freshly laundered and softer than the others. Austin smiled as he took her by the hand and led her to the back of the barn and up a ladder. She went first at his insistence; she wasn't sure if it was because he wanted to look up her dress or if he was simply being chivalrous.

He lit an LED powered lamp and flooded the ceiling with a blue-hued light. He took the saddle blankets from her and laid them down, arranging them like a make shift pallet, and sat down on a bale of hay, looking up at her.

"Show me how gorgeous you are, Savvy. Take that dress off."

"Ladies first? But I thought you supported women's rights." Her hands went to her hips.

"Yes ma'am, I certainly do." He chuckled. "Show me yours and I'll show you mine." He leaned forward and propped his elbows on his knees, licking his lips as her hands went to the hem of Kelsey's tight lacy dress. She had to shimmy it delicately up her thighs and hips, but when she got to her midriff, it stuck. She attempted to wriggle free but wasn't successful in her drunken stupor. She heard Austin chuckle again and felt his hands at her bare waist. He whistled. "My my, Savvy. These panties are mighty sexy." She gasped as she felt a finger trace the lace front of her underwear. "Mmm, they smell good too."

"Austin," his name was a breathy groan as she felt his nose at the lip of her panties. His lips kissed at the fabric that covered the delta of her thighs and she felt his tongue darting at her most sensitive spot. She whimpered as she felt a big hand grip her bare bottom and squeeze.

"Damn, woman. You were prepared to get fucked tonight. Thong, huh? Even better." His finger slowly traced the thin thread of silk between her cheeks and ever lower. "Hmm, this reminds me. I owe you a spankin'."

Savannah squealed in protest as she was upended and brought down on her belly, across his thighs, feeling a hand curve seductively over her butt cheek. "Austin, don't you dare!" she cried even as she felt gushing arousal rush from her womanhood at his intimate touch. She'd never been spanked, not even as a child, and the thought suddenly turned her on as much as it infuriated her.

"You asked for it, you naughty girl. And honestly, how can I resist a moment like this?" He laughed again, a cocky bastard satisfied with himself. She squirmed, trying to peel herself from the confining dress that pinned her from the breasts up. Then she felt a swift smack on her bottom and gasped as her body reeled from the audacity and her butt cheek tingled with a combination of pain and arousal. "That's for being so damn sassy this morning."

Savannah grunted as he gave her butt another sharp whack and then stroked the flesh he'd just struck with the utmost tenderness; she moaned.

"Is this turning you on, Savvy?" Austin's rough voice dripped liked warm honey, and she felt her center pulse achingly with longing. "Let's find out, shall we?" She felt his finger fiddle with the thread between her legs, touching the skin between her crack and her sex, and gasped as his finger gently entered her soaking wet center. He moaned—pleased with her response to his lashings—pushing his long, thick finger inside her. "Fuck, angel, you're so wet. God, you got me bustin' out of my pants." His finger withdrew only to plunge again, deeper, exploring her. She cried out as her sex clenched around him and he swore again. He began to thrust his finger into her, eliciting whimpering moans from her as her body lost itself to his touch. Suddenly, his finger was no longer filling her and she felt bereft, only to be blindsided once again as she felt another singing smack to her bare rear-end.

"Ouch," she protested more from the shock of it than the actual pain, "what the hell was that one for?"

"For torturing me all night with this sexy as hell body of yours."

"Well, if you'd assist me out of this dress, I can help end the torture," she established, feeling the blood rush to her head.

"Who said anything about wanting to *end* it?"

With that, she was lifted off his lap then lowered onto the hay bale, feeling the prickling of the dry grass as it touched her bare belly and thighs. Austin leaned down over her, and Savannah felt the weight of his body as he moved atop her in a reverse 69 position; his chest resting on her lower back, his cock at the back of her shoulders. She was slightly confused as to what the hell he was doing until she felt his hot breath on her bare flesh. His lips touched her bottom and he sunk his teeth gently in to bite her. She gasped again, feeling a wave of scorching pleasure roll over her. His kiss moved over her butt cheek, soft, sexy, gentle kisses then in between her thighs to settle over her center. "Oh, Austin," she whimpered again and moaned hungrily as his mouth began to lick and suck at her aching flesh. His fingers joined in on the exquisite torment and took turns, two fingers would thrust deep inside her then his tongue, his mouth would suck then his fingers would plunge again until she was begging and reaching and whining for the release that came suddenly and violently upon her. She cried out as her body shuddered and her sex clenched tightly around his fingers until finally she lay spent, trying to catch her breath. She felt his lips on her bottom then her back and he chuckled.

"Damn, you're hot as fuck, Savvy."

Once her orgasm had subsided, she noticed that the itchy hay had scratched up her belly and her ribs were protesting; she squirmed to get out of the dress she was still wrapped up in.

"Here, let's get this off 'a you." Austin moved off the top of her, and she felt his restrained erection rock-hard against her thigh as he pulled her off the hay bale and into his embrace. He peeled the dress from her midriff, freeing her—*Finally!* Vanna scowled at him and crossed her arms as a playful grin curved at his mouth and that sexy dimple popped back up. "Can you stop messing around now and give me that striptease I wanted?" Austin teased.

"Oh, I don't think so. This isn't a strip club. This is show and tell, you said, and I've not been shown anything yet. My head was stuck in a dress."

"Well, you *did* let me spank you, so I reckon I can show you my goods now."

"*Let* you? O-K."

"Hey, you weren't complaining just seconds ago." His sexy eyebrow cocked up.

He had a point. She wasn't complaining at all. In fact, she felt more alive in this moment than she ever had in her whole life and she wanted anything Austin was throwing her way, especially when the mouth he was suddenly kissing her with was melting her panties right off. Savannah could taste herself on his tongue and wasn't sure if she should be embarrassed or turned on again. Her body chose for her as her hands came to the buttons on his shirt, tearing at them, so that she could see how muscular he really was. She was rewarded with a broad chest, chiseled abs and large, inked biceps. She went at him with her fingertips first, then smoothed out her palms, admiring the indention of his sculpted muscles and the tattoo that spanned over his heart—a cross and horse shoe. He gave a ragged breath as she traced the faint dusting of golden blond hair that ran down his beautifully tanned torso, following his happy trail to the fly of his jeans. She was hungry to see all of him and quickly unbuttoned and unzipped him, shoving his jeans and boxers down with one good heave. Her eyes took the size of him in and she was equal parts aroused and worried. His member was girthy and long, bigger than she'd guessed, and she wasn't sure she would be able to accommodate him.

Only one way to find out for she wasn't backing down now.

Savannah went to her knees then, all the alcohol she'd consumed making her braver than her usual self. But the words that Sidd's mistress had said slaughtered her ears and insides-*You're boring...and mousy.* Sidd sure wouldn't think that if he could see her now. She was a wanton sex kitten who'd only just discovered her sexual prowess. She took Austin's steely erection in her hands and stroked him in her palm, pumping gently as her tongue shyly licked at the head of his sex.

"Oh, Savvy, baby..." Austin trailed off on a groan as she slowly sucked the tip into her mouth. She looked up at him, using his body language to gauge her next moves, his gorgeous amber eyes burning deep desire into hers. They held her, suspended in time. She was his sweet torture and fulfilling release all at once as her mouth gingerly moved on his rock-hard flesh. His palm gently cupped her head, fisting her hair; not forcing her down on him but letting her find her own rhythm...and she did so with a confidence the alcohol had created, his moans and head-lolling feeding her inexperienced ego. "Damn, baby girl, your mouth is fuckin' exquisite." He huffed out as her fist squeezed and twisted, coming up to meet where her mouth loved him and he growled his pleasure.

Soon, his choppy breaths were turning into grunts and his hips were thrusting as she explored the side of sex she'd not tried but a couple times before. Austin quickly pulled her up and into his embrace as he began loving her mouth all over again, his tongue plunging desperately in to stroke hers as his hands went to her bra clasp. He freed her from it and tossed it aside. He did the same with her thong before scooping her up and laying her down on the saddle blankets beneath his big, muscled body. His golden-tanned biceps were inked in various colors, tattoos her blurry eyes would have to assess later for he moved and tugged at his boots, freeing his feet from them and his legs from his jeans.

Austin grabbed something from his back pocket before his mouth came back to hers and his hands moved over her naked breasts and torso. She moaned as his kiss moved to her neck, her chest, her breast, his hot mouth settling over a nipple, pulling waves of pleasure from her lips as his tongue brought it to a pointed peak. He didn't forget the other one as her hands found his thick sex in her fist. He parted her with his fingers then sheathed his member with the condom he'd grabbed from his jeans. Thank God one of them was still lucid enough to think about *that*. Savannah would kick her own ass tomorrow, but tonight she was getting pounded by this rough and sultry cowboy, for at this moment his seductive eyes caught hers. They were open pools of yearning as he gazed at her. One last moment to back out before it was too late. He waited, wanting her full permission before advancing. With her nod, she granted it.

Gently, he guided his massive manhood to the entrance of her body. He was thick, thicker than she'd ever had, and the pain of the initial penetration she felt startled her. Her head fell back as she tried to relax and succumb to his dominance. He swore, pulled out and replaced his sex with his fingers, preparing her further. She grunted, eager to have him buried deep inside of her, and gripped his erection, centering it over herself before arching her hips to meet his slow lunge. She whimpered as he began filling her, inch by inch, her body acclimating to the stretch in glorious agony.

Austin's eyes closed and he gripped her thighs, moaning as his shaft settled inside her. "Mmm, Savvy...God, you feel *so* incredible."

Savannah answered him with a soft cry and wrapped her legs around him as her core fully encompassed him. He sighed as he began to pump inside her, bringing his body down over hers, closing the slight distance that'd been between them. He kissed her lips and stroked her curves with his hands, moving them over her as if he were trying to memorize every inch of her skin.

Austin thrust deep and slow and close to the hilt of her, further inside her than anyone else had ever been. Having his hefty sex buried so deep felt utterly amazing, and soon the mounting pleasure began building within her as she gripped his shoulders and met his lunges, her breath coming in short gasps. It was as if his cock knew the exact spots to hit as she started to fall and suddenly, the skies opened up and the stars shot out in a supernova around her. Her head flew back as she cried out once again in orgasm, her woman-hood clenching around Austin's erection as he continued to thrust inside her.

"Fuck, you're so damn tight, baby girl," he grunted and kissed her cheeks as she quaked and spasmed.

"Mmm, yes... Austin, pound me," Vanna growled as she came back to earth with renewed willpower. He smirked even as he moaned, her heels digging into his ass as her hips arched up against his.

"Let's just keep the pace we got now. I'm close. No need to *pound* you."

"But I want you to. Please?" All she wanted in those moments was to be claimed by this unruly relentless force of passion that had overtaken her. She was a naughty girl tonight. Not mousy and not boring and not just some dork who stared at the stars and thought of formulas all day. No, tonight she was a sex-crazed banshee. She was 'Savvy', and she wanted to forget all about Sidd and his betrayal. Right now, she was Austin's, her golden-muscled cowboy. And she wanted him to ride her with all his might. "Ride me, Austin. I want it *hard.*"

"Savannah," he protested, giving her a half-frown.

"You *said* you'd ride Sidd out of my system," she countered. Austin ceased his sensual thrusts and gazed down at her, moving her hair off her face. He sighed heavily. "Well..." Her brows went up. "Then *fuckin'* do it!"

Austin hesitantly leaned back on his haunches, pulling her hips towards his as he did so. He angled them up, gripping her ass, and lunged hard. Savannah gasped at the force. "Is this what you want?" he asked.

She gulped and nodded. He thrust again, his flesh hitting hers with a violent smack. She whimpered but held her ground even as her womanhood protested. He frowned as he noted her obvious discomfort. He then pulled out, flipped her over on all fours, and was pushing his shaft back inside her before she even knew what happened. His big palms gripped her hips and he gently pushed her upper body down as he began pumping into her from behind, driving fast and deep, but not quite as hard as before. Savannah moaned as wave after wave of pleasure hit her.

"Touch yourself, darlin'. Come for me again."

Savannah hadn't ever done that, so she wasn't sure what to do exactly, but she moved her fingers in between her legs and began stroking her wet folds where Austin had earlier. She moaned aloud as the pleasure from the caresses both inside and out began to unravel her. She felt the stirrings hit her and suddenly she was falling again as she sailed through the cosmos, crying out and bucking against the body that was adoring hers in that moment.

"Austin. Mmm. Yes. Yes."

"Oh fuck, Savvy. I'm gonna come. Oh...oh, baby," he cried as he arched and slammed his hips against hers, his climax assaulting him as violently as Savannah's had her. He moaned and gasped as he rode his orgasm out. After several minutes, his pulsing into her ceased then he leaned against her for momentary respite.

When Austin withdrew from her, he pulled her down to the blankets with him and gathered her into his arms. He held Savannah tightly there for a long time, her head resting on his pec, his hands stroking her back. His lips moved to her temple and he kissed her there, his hand cupping her cheek. He angled her face up to look at him and gave her that heart-stopping grin that had been her sinful downfall. "Did I hurt you, sweet angel?"

"No." Vanna shook her head, reassuring him, kissing the thumb on her face.

"You're sure?"

"Positive."

"Good. Because I'll be ready for round two here soon." Austin winked, and Savannah paused, unsure what to say. Surely he was kidding, *right*? He had worn her out. Completely. How could he possibly have anything left? He kissed her then, slow and sexy, and it took her breath away, his hand cupped her breast and his grip around her waist tightened. "Savannah." He murmured against her lips as he pulled back.

"Yeah?"

"I wasn't kidding when I said that I'd make you regret every lover you ever had before me." His grin could have been likened to the cat that ate the canary as Savannah's eyes widened in surprise.

"I assumed that was just a figure of speech…to try and get me into bed with you."

He smirked again. "Not entirely. It worked though, didn't it?" She narrowed her eyes at him in response and he laughed. "I gotta say, you're even sexier in bed than I ever expected, Savvy. You are like opening that coveted present on Christmas Day."

"Glad you enjoyed it." Savannah blushed.

"*Enjoy*? That's a bit of an understatement. If you're an addiction, I don't know that I'll ever quit you."

With that, he flipped her over onto her back and began releasing that inner banshee again.

~

*A*ustin Montgomery woke to the sound of a horse whinnying, the smell of hay and manure, and felt the gorgeous little sex goddess he'd made love to all night long stir next to him. He pressed his body against the back of hers, pulling her further into his embrace, and nestled his nose into her thick dark hair. He breathed her floral and spice scent in and smiled. God, she was stunning, every inch of her five-foot five-inch frame. And every bit of her had felt utterly incredible.

Yesterday's meeting of the maple-headed brunette with sea green eyes, olive-toned skin, and the most perfect set of DSLs he'd ever seen at the toy store had been both comical and audacious, and it had given him a hard-on he'd carried from Houston all the way back to Abundance. He'd not been able to get the fiery-tempered sass pot out of his mind. He'd come back home, unpacked his duffel bag from the trip he'd taken to his parent's, and then headed to the bar later for a cold beer. As fate would see to it, she'd been dropped right back into his lap...figuratively and literally. To say Austin had been surprised to see her there at the bar—and in that sexy as hell dress of hers—was the understatement of the year. It was as if the gods of sexual bliss had decided to bestow their blessings upon him. Her sultry attitude had done him in and it was all he could do not to grab her up, haul her to the bathroom and show her what her feistiness had done to him all day. He'd always loved a woman with an attitude, and he'd always enjoyed fucking that attitude right out of them too. For she'd been putty in his hands from the moment he'd suggested she ride the bull. There was just something about a woman on a mechanical bull that got them all wet and horny. It had never failed to work thus far.

But when he'd been lucky enough to get Savannah to leave with him, he'd received the whole package. She was smart, funny, sexy, *and* great in bed; he felt like he'd just hit the jackpot of a lifetime.

He nuzzled her neck, kissing her pulse point, and pressed his growing erection into her bottom as she sighed and stretched her arms. He took that moment to cup those full breasts of hers she arched out; they were too tempting to resist, covered in his big shirt. She jutted her plump bottom into his pelvis, and he groaned, eager to have her once more.

"Mmm, I see you haven't had enough just yet, huh, Savvy?"

He moved his nose to her jawline and heard her gasp and shudder but not from his mouth or his hands.

He gulped as he saw two sets of boots in front of her and his eyes raised to a scowling Jack Kinsen and Nathan Butler, both with their arms crossed over their chests, looking as if he'd just walked across their ancestors' graves. Savannah shot up from his arms and pulled her knees beneath her, trying to pull his shirt down over her naked thighs.

Yup, sure as shit, Austin was once again *back* in the hayloft with a half-naked woman after being caught similar to this merely a week ago. But it wasn't like he'd really done any damage. They were men too; surely they could understand why he would wanna spend a night with this enticing little vixen. He gave them both a knowing smirk and shrugged.

"I would expect this from your brother...maybe even your sister...but not from *you!*" Jack ground out. Austin scoffed. What the hell would he know about Austin's sister? "Savannah Grace Kinsen, get your bottom up and get it *out* of this hayloft. Right the hell now!" Jack's firm voice grew a smidge louder. *Kinsen?* Had Jack just said, 'Savannah *Kinsen*'? *No fuckin' way!* She was Jack Kinsen's daughter? *Sonovabitch!*

"Daddy! I'm perfectly capable of making my own decisions, thank you *very* much. I'm a grown woman and I don't recall needing to ask your permission who I end up in the hayloft with." Did she really just say that to the six-foot two giant growling down at her?

Jack Kinsen might be sixty years old, but he certainly didn't look it. The man was big, muscular, and intimidating. He ran a tight ship, had a no-nonsense policy, and the demeanor of a drill sergeant at times...or he did where Austin was concerned.

"Montgomery, I'd like a word with you in my office. Now!"

Savannah's head whipped around to look at Austin. "Montgomery? As in—"

"Oh, he didn't fully introduce himself? First name basis...well, ain't *that* convenient?" Nathan mumbled.

Savannah huffed and pointed up at her father and uncle. "Dammit! The two of you do *not* get to lecture me about who I sleep with."

The deep rumble that came from Jack Kinsen's chest could have started an earthquake as he stepped forward, his narrowed eyes burning into Austin's. Austin braced himself for battle, but Nathan's hand hit Jack's back, stilling him as Savannah shot up, fists clenched at her sides.

"Daddy, this is *none* of your business."

Jack's jaw ticked and he looked from his daughter to Austin; a mixture of disgust and contempt flew from his boss's eyes. "The *hell* you say!" Then Jack smiled, the grin of victory. "Savannah, why don't you ask Austin here where he was around this same time hardly a week ago?"

Dammit! Of course Jack had to bring that shit up! Austin had been new to town and had been a bit tipsy when he'd left the bar with the busty blonde. She'd given him a sloppy, unimpressive, half-assed blow job before passing out not far from where Savannah had rocked his world last night, which was one of the reasons he'd not wanted to end up back here in the hayloft. Austin didn't have sex with the blonde girl—she hadn't even gotten him off—and he hadn't heard from her again, but that hadn't mattered. He'd not been able to redeem himself, for they'd both awoken to Jack giving them a look pretty similar to the one he was giving Austin now and it had looked bad—of course it had. He'd been on the job just two weeks. Wyatt had been furious with him.

Looked like his brother would be pissed again...

Savannah turned and looked him over then, her beautiful face showing such disappointment that Austin actually winced. The pain in her gorgeous eyes quickly turned to scorn, and she simply arched a brow, pursed her lips, and shot him a bird as he reached out to her. She walked away, her long legs—beautifully olive-toned and flawless—stirring him in amazing ways. She was heading down the ladder, Austin left to deal with her father and uncle who glared at him, when Jack growled and stalked away after Savannah, calling for her to, "Hold up." Austin jumped up, grabbing his jeans and pulling them on, all too aware of Nathan Butler's laser-like glare on his back.

When he turned, zipping his fly, Nate's nose was within inches of his.

"Let me tell you who the hell you're dealing with, so there's no confusion. You know I pack a mean punch and well, so does my brother-in-law. I might be twice your age but that don't mean I can't still kick your ass from here to Birmingham, boy. You'll do well to remember that! Now, I'm gonna ask you one question and you better shoot straight with me, 'cause I'll know if you're lying... Did you take advantage of her?"

Austin quickly shook his head, not for fear that Nate would hurt him; Austin had served in the Army for almost a decade after all and could kill a man with just one strike of his hand, but he knew Nathan wasn't simply bragging about packing a mean punch and hell, let the old man make his threats if that made him feel better. He simply wanted her uncle to know that his intentions with Savannah weren't what Jack thought. "No sir. It was all consensual. I swear it."

Nate's grim face seemed to relax some as he digested Austin's words. Before Austin could continue, Nate said, "Now you need to stay the hell away from her. For your own sake as well as hers. Jack don't care for you, in case you ain't figured that out yet, Austin. He thinks you're bad news. Savannah's his baby girl, and if he doesn't fire you, that will be the only condition he'll have to keep you on."

Austin should've known Nate would say that...and hell, Jack too, if he were being honest. He hadn't exactly been the model employee

—or model civilian—as of late. But after having Savannah only one night, the thoughts of "staying away from her" didn't even seem possible. All he could think about was being buried inside her again. He could still feel the softness of her lips on his, her breasts against his chest, smell her sweet fragrance on his clothes, taste her sex on his tongue.

In less than twelve hours, she had invaded his mind and body in a way that rattled him to the core. He'd never had a woman do that to him before. And it both shocked and amazed him, but he was going to savor every second of it.

After the tragic death of his team member and best friend, Jerome Howard, in Afghanistan—and his own debilitating injury— not much in Austin's life over the last two and a half years had given him hope or happiness, or excited him, like meeting Savannah yesterday morning had. She'd been fierce and sassy as Hell, and he'd wanted to feel that fire of hers infect every cell of his body.

He'd sought purpose in every way he could following the devastation in Afghanistan. After officially retiring from the Army just months ago, he'd searched but hadn't had any luck in finding a career that fit him, until Wyatt had begged him to come to Abundance and try his hand at horse training. It had been a casual interest he'd picked up from Wyatt as a child, after all his big brother was ten years older than him and Austin had always wanted to be just like him, especially after Austin had seen Wyatt's incredible gift first-hand. Growing up in Alabama on a small farm had made it easy, but when his parents had moved to California, because of his dad's military career when Austin was ten years old, things changed. He'd gotten wrapped up in the surfer's lifestyle in his teens before enlisting at twenty years old, while Wyatt flourished here in Texas.

Austin had served first in the cavalry, then spent four tours in Iraq as a combat engineer before heading to Afghanistan as a team leader, where Jerome had been blown away by an IED right in front of him. Austin's knee had been riddled with so much shrapnel from the blast that he thought his leg had been blown clean off. The first week had been critical as they'd tried to salvage it. He'd needed a knee replacement at the age of thirty and countless hours of PT. His healing had been complicated by a staph infection and his hospital stay had nearly tripled in length. He came close to losing his leg, but amazingly could now do almost everything he used to. But the memories and nightmares of that horrific day had never left him.

Jerome had been like a brother to Austin; they'd gone to boot camp together and had formed an ever-lasting bond that had persisted through their tours together. They'd laughed together, cried together, killed their first man together, grown into men together. They'd been just kids when they'd begun their Army careers. Jerome had been his comic relief when times had gotten tough, the positivity he'd needed in the darkness, the faith that kept them all stable. And in the blink of an eye, he was gone.

Austin still stayed in touch with his widow, Laquanna, and his little son, Andre. He made sure they'd been taken care of and knew he shared their pain and grief.

After he'd healed up, Austin had been utterly lost. Not sure where to go or what to do. He'd gone to Houston to stay with his parents during his difficult rehabilitation and attempted to continue the life he'd had before going into the Army. But it hadn't been easy. He was former military and transitioning back into the civilian lifestyle had been difficult, especially following the tragedy...and his PTSD from it. The Army had been supportive and encouraged he stay on, but after a year and a half of teaching new recruits in weapons training and taking various courses to see what else might interest him, Austin had still felt something was missing and had wanted a change of pace and a fresh start. Most places didn't want to hire him due to his "disability," although they'd used some other bullshit excuse, so he'd started talking to his brother, and Jack, about going into horse training. Wyatt had been eager and excited to bring him into the fold, so Austin had moved here, with his dog, Caesar, to Abundance to work alongside his brother, the horse whisperer, trainer, and foreman of Kinsen Ranch.

"Austin, go shower and get to work. I have a feeling it's gonna be a while before Jack makes it back to his office." Nate motioned to the raised voices coming from just outside the barn doors, sighed heavily, and headed towards the ladder.

Austin shook his head and cussed himself out silently.

So much for a good first impression!

~

"*H*ey, I said to wait up!" Her father called to her as Savannah came to a stop just outside the barn doors, fighting the stinging tears at her eyes. He gripped her shoulders and turned her around. "What the hell was that back there, huh? And just who the hell do you think you're talking to like that?"

Savannah looked down, ashamed at herself for how she'd spoken to her father and uncle in the hayloft, but dammit, she'd been mortified. As if it wasn't bad enough to have to tell her father she'd been dumped by her fiancé, now she'd just been caught red-handed messing around with his employee.

"Savannah, I'm waiting." Her father was usually as patient as a saint, but his anger was mounting, she knew. He had every right to be angry with her, every right to want to throttle her. He deserved an explanation.

"I'm sorry, Daddy," she huffed out, tears springing to her eyes, as she looked up at him. He crossed his arms over his big chest and scowled.

"What in God's name were you doing half-naked with Austin Montgomery?"

Did she really have to tell him that? He didn't want to know the specifics, she knew for a fact, but just the memory of Austin's hand spanking her bare ass made her cheeks flame in further embarrassment. Her dad growled as if he could read her mind, and she pulled her lips in, waiting for the lecture to come.

"Jesus, Savannah. Aren't you *supposed* to be engaged to another man? What the hell are you doing in the hayloft with that rough-neck? Explain yourself, *now!*"

His green eyes burned into her own and she gulped, the tears flowing like a river down her face. She lifted up her left hand and pointed to her ring finger, the mark of the former ring still visible in her indented flesh. Her father's brows drew, confused. "He dumped me and kicked me out," she murmured on a sob. "I came home yesterday morning to my bags packed and a demand of my departure. He's got a new woman now…Apparently."

"Oh, baby," he replied and pulled her into his arms. "I'm sorry."

"No, you're not," she said even as she reveled in his comforting embrace, taking solace in the strength of his frame. "You hate Sidd." Her dad gave a humorless laugh in reply and shrugged when Savannah pulled back, wiping at her nose.

"Well, as much as I hate him, I hate that he's hurt you all the more." He cupped her cheek and his eyes softened. "Vanna, honey, but sleeping with Austin isn't going to change what Sidd did to you. That was a pretty irresponsible thing to do…especially coming from you."

Savannah pulled his hand away and pursed her lips up at her father, anger streaming through her veins. "I don't need to be preached to like I'm a child."

"You're *my* child and when you do something so out of character, I'm gonna call you out for it, whether you want to hear it or not is beside the point."

"Dammit, why is it that I can't have one-night stands if I want to? Just because I'm a certified genius doesn't mean that I can't enjoy myself too. I have needs and desires just like everyone else." She sounded like a pouty child now, *God bless!* She needed some pain killers, a bottle of Valium, and a month of sleep.

Her father covered his face with his big palm and stroked at his forehead with his thumb and index finger, as if he were trying to conjure every ounce of patience he had. After all, she and her father never had conversations like this. Of course, it wasn't like an occurrence like this had ever happened before.

He looked away before sighing once again, the look of the disciplinary figure returning. "Savannah Grace, answer two questions for me before I decide whether I'm gonna let that son of a bitch live or not."

Savannah crossed her arms over the shirt of Austin's cloaking her and frowned at her father.

"Did he hurt you?" Her father's eyebrows drew.

"No! Of course not. Why would he—"

"Did he use protection?"

"Dad!" she huffed out, embarrassed but understanding why he would want to know that, especially after catching him with that other girl just last week. Suddenly, Savannah felt pain rip through her chest at the thoughts of Austin with another woman and the realization of what she'd done assaulted her with overwhelming force. She felt herself breaking down and covered her face in her hands, giving into her anguish. She was sobbing and sputtering as her father pulled her back into his arms, his big hand stroking her back as he walked her towards the house.

She didn't remember the distance or the stairs even, all-consumed with the guilt, hurt and embarrassment of yesterday's break-up, last night's fall from grace, and being caught with her lover by her father of all people. She sniffled as the door opened and the familiar scent of home filled her nostrils. She dropped her hands and saw her mother, beautiful dark locks down and curled, standing in the kitchen, hands on her hips, her blue eyes full of both alarm and surprise.

"Vanna, baby, what on earth?" her mother took in her pitiful, half-dressed state, and Savannah felt humiliation ravage her guts again. The sobbing picked up where it had left off and she moved forward, arms extended, towards her mother, who looked apprehensively up at her father. "Are you alright, honey, what—"

Her father must have mouthed something because her mother

grabbed her and held her with the understanding and grace only a mother can possess. "Oh, honey. Tell me everything."

Savannah sputtered as her mother ushered her towards the breakfast table and sat her down. "Jack, grab her a wet rag," her mother called to her father and stroked her hair and back.

"Sidd dumped me yesterday. And Daddy found me in the hayloft with Austin this morning."

Her mother looked taken aback then recovered as she gave a terse laugh. "Well, you didn't waste any time, huh?"

"God, I'm so stupid." Savannah covered her face with her hands.

"The stupidest smart person I know," her father said, and she frowned up at him as he gave her a joking grin. He handed her the rag, and she brought it to her eyes, reveling in the warmth on her swollen eyelids. She heard him laugh and brought her head up to look at him. "Oh, c'mon, Vanna, I'm only kidding." He moved to the coffee pot and began pouring some into a mug. "You think you're the only person whose lost their inhibitions after a break up?" He lifted his eyebrow at her as he sat the coffee down in front of her, along with some cream and sugar.

"You?"

"Oh, hell yeah! I went into the rodeo, remember?"

She shook her head and gave him a confused look.

"We never told you that story?" her mother asked. "Your father was drunk the night your grandfather hired him."

As straight-laced as her father was now, she couldn't see him wild and shit-faced like that. He must have sensed her analysis, for he grinned. "Yes, I too, was once young and reckless. Following a break-up, no doubt."

"How'd you meet Austin?" her mom asked after Vanna just quietly absorbed what her father was saying.

"I met him in Houston, actually. I took an antique rocking horse away from him on my way out of town." The amused look her folks gave her made her groan in mortification. She looked down as she continued. "Then Kelsey, Dallie and I went out to The Rusty Spur last night to cheer me up and Austin was there, so I felt it only necessary to apologize for my earlier behavior. We ended up hitting it off and left the bar together not long after that." She blushed as her eyes met her dad's.

Her father's frown had returned, and her mother just gazed back at her in astonishment.

"Are you gonna fire him, Daddy?"

Her mom looked to her father then, assessing him as his brows drew at Savannah. "Why do you care? He's just your *one-night stand* after all, right?"

"Because he didn't know who I was. He didn't know I was your daughter. Please just let it go, alright?"

"We'll see," he said and huffed before getting up and heading out the back door.

Savannah pouted and looked back at her mom. "Do you know how horrible it was being caught getting felt up in front of Uncle Nate and Daddy?"

Her mom laughed. "Oh, I can only imagine."

After all, Savannah Grace Kinsen was a fairly private person and having her dirty laundry aired in front of her father and her Uncle Nate was one of the most uncomfortable things that had ever happened to her.

"So, tell me what happened with Sidd."

Savannah filled her mother in on what had occurred when Savannah had gotten to the apartment yesterday morning, about Sidd's new "bimbo", how she'd met Austin, what she'd said to him, her conversation at Dallie's with Kelsey, their trip to The Rusty Spur, and her love-making with Austin last night.

"Wow, Savannah, I have to say, I'm stunned. All this is completely out of character for you." Savannah just frowned. Her father had said the exact same thing. Her mom patted her hand, sensing her discomfort. "Oh, honey, I understand completely, don't get me wrong. I'm just surprised is all."

"Well, I haven't slept more than a few hours at a time for weeks now. I'm over-worked. I'm stressed. My filter has dissolved and my ego was damaged by Sidd and his new bitch girlfriend, so I wanted to go out and have some fun for a change. Sue me."

"Well, you're home now, so take all the time you need to rest, relax and find yourself again. You're welcome to stay as long as you need to." Her mom stroked her hair away from her face. "I'm glad you're here, even if the circumstances are less than desirable. Sidd didn't deserve you and well, Austin is sexy as hell."

"Mom!" Savannah laughed for the first time all morning.

"Well, he is. Do you know he rides a motorcycle?"

"Is that why Daddy doesn't like him...and because he has tattoos?"

"Oh, just one of many reasons I'm sure. I think he reminds your father of that younger, reckless version of himself." Her mom winked. "Honey, let me fix you something to eat. Are you hungry?"

"No, more sleepy than hungry. Maybe I'll go shower and take a nap."

"Absolutely. Go. Do that and I'll make you something when you come down later on."

Savannah just nodded and moved to stand up.

"Oh and Vanna? Don't worry about your father, alright." Her mother winked at her.

Vanna just nodded and headed upstairs.

Her room was just as she left it on her last visit home. All her paintings hung in frames around the room—landscapes, sunsets and portraits of her family—her easel sat in the corner with an unfinished work atop it, her violin was in its case on the shelf next to it, glow-in-the-dark stars were stuck to the ceiling and her bed was covered in a lavender quilt comforter. It was as if she'd stepped back in time and was a little girl again, not a grown woman with a bruised ego and a broken heart. She felt tears in her eyes form as she tried to dampen down the shame of having her dad and uncle see her at her most vulnerable. Savannah had always considered herself grounded and practical, intuitive, not apt to flights of fancy, but the last twenty-four hours had been a whirlwind. It was as if she'd been pulled from her stable, routine life and thrown into the mouth of Charybdis. As if the heavens had been bored with her predictable existence and forced her to adapt into some type of chimera; a skin-walker whose skin she was enjoying being masked by, for she could get a taste for the passion she'd been missing for some time now.

She turned the water to her shower on and removed Austin's leather, sex, and sandalwood smelling shirt—and her thong—and entered. She let the water wash her sins and cares away as she shampooed her hair and soaped her body up, remembering the night of unrestrained and unadulterated sex she'd had with Austin Montgomery. Her body and mind had never felt more alive than it had in his embrace. He'd taken lust and romance to a whole new level as he'd adored her—all her curves with his eager tongue, hands, lips and cock—as Sidd never had. His rough voice and sexy words filled her head, his smell and taste overpowered her senses and his enthusiasm to pleasure her touched more than just her insides. Their time together had been incredible. Savannah couldn't help but moan as her hands moved over all the places Austin's had recently been. When she moved to wash between her legs, her sex sore from Austin's love-making, she shivered as her fingers imitated the stroking his had done and soon, she was panting and crying her release into the spray of the water. But then her moment was ruined as she remembered the words her father said in the hayloft—Austin had been with another woman just a week prior to her. She wasn't any more special to Austin than she'd been to Sidd.

Why was life so damn cruel?

She rinsed and turned the shower off, dried herself, and combed out her long, thick hair. She dressed herself in an old tee shirt and cotton bikini panties from her dresser and climbed into her bed. She stopped pouting about the imbalance that was life, the angst of love, and the uncertainty of the future and closed her eyes to the sound of rain falling heavy on the roof.

CHAPTER 4

*A*ustin sighed as he made his way back from the shower room to Jack's office. He'd donned an old black Nirvana t-shirt, jeans, and his well-worn Justin boots, his hair still damp from his shower. He wasn't looking forward to what the owner of Kinsen Ranch was going to tell him and worried if Jack would still *be* his boss after this conversation was had.

Talk about awkward—Austin had never been more surprised in his life to learn that the sexy woman he'd bedded last night was his boss's daughter. The anger had been so evident in both Nathan and Jack's faces, he should have picked up on it immediately.

He was glad to see that Wyatt wasn't around yet nor Jackson. This was going to be uncomfortable enough without anyone else around.

Jack was sitting at his desk when Austin came to the open door and knocked. Jack motioned for him to enter and he came in, shut the door, and took a seat across from him.

Jack eyed him with an unnerving stare that had to be akin to being stuck under a microscope. Finally, Austin spoke. "Jack, I swear to God, I didn't know Savannah was your daughter."

"Do you honestly think you'd still be sitting there if I thought you did?" Jack retorted, his eyes narrowing.

Austin sighed—not knowing what to say, how to make this better, how to make Jack understand that he wasn't the person he thought he was. His first impression to his boss had been fucked up more than once now. And there was nothing he could do to fix it.

"Are you *trying* to get fired?"

"No sir."

"You've disrespected me. You've disrespected my property. You're constantly late, unreliable. Dammit, Austin, you're a waste of God-given potential and now you've disrespected my daughter too. Give me *one* good reason why I should keep you on."

"I can't," he answered honestly.

"You know you're only here because of your brother, right?"

Austin nodded and frowned. He'd been a terrible excuse for an employee. Much to his brother's dismay, the last two weeks, Austin had been late, hungover, cocky and even disrespectful, as Jack had put it. He didn't deserve another chance—even the military would be gravely disappointed in his behavior—and he wouldn't say that he did for it would be untrue.

"Do you enjoy what you do here?" Jack's scrutiny was turning into an analysis, something only an abundance of experience and wisdom could activate.

"I've always enjoyed working with horses...and with my brother," Austin answered truthfully.

"And do you enjoy it *here,* on my ranch?"

"Yeah."

"Am I fair?" Those piercing green eyes burned into Austin's, but he didn't waver. He'd stared into the face of evil, Jack Kinsen was a walk in the park compared to terrorism.

"You're a good boss, Jack."

"Then why are you such a bad employee? Doesn't attitude reflect leadership?"

That was the saying anyway, but it wasn't why Austin's attitude sucked. "No, sir. My attitude has nothing to do with your lack of leadership skills."

"Then what does?"

Why does he care? was Austin's original thought, but Jack *had* hired him on, flaws and all. "I guess I have my own short-comings." *To put it lightly.*

"We've all faced some form of tragedy in our lives, son. Unfortunately, everyone has a cross to bear it would seem." How could Jack say that? How could he possibly know what Austin had been through?

"I'm sorry you had to find me with your daughter like that, sir. I truly am," Austin said, trying to get this conversation away from the past.

"Thank you for saying that. But I want you to stay away from her."

As if he hadn't known *that* was coming! "I can't make any promises, Jack."

"Excuse me?" Jack's tone deepened.

Again, Austin didn't waver. "I can't guarantee you that I can do that. With all due respect, sir, it *is* a free country." *Thanks to guys like me!*

Jack growled and his fist clenched on the desk. "You're treading on thin ice, Montgomery. You know that?"

"Savannah's a grown woman, if she wants to see me, there's really not much you can do to stop her." Austin's brow went up.

Jack laughed humorlessly. "You must think you have some pretty big balls, huh, tough guy? Screwing your boss's daughter in his barn then throwing it back in his face. You're a real piece of work, Montgomery! Let me make myself clear, however. If you *don't* keep your distance from my daughter, you won't *have* a place to work. So, put that in your pipe and smoke it, asshole. Savannah's on the rebound and in a delicate place right now. As her father, it's my duty to protect her, and I will enforce my right to do so—by whatever means necessary. Now get the hell out of my office before I knock you senseless," Jack's jaw clenched as he growled again and crossed his arms over his broad chest—a chest slightly broader than Austin's own.

Well, that went well, Austin, you idiot, he thought to himself as he stood and turned. *Fuck your boss's daughter then antagonize him. That'll win him over real fast!*

"One more thing," Jack said as Austin was halfway to the door. "I should warn you, I'm not a man you wanna fuck with. With your retirement from the Army, your PTSD, and your injury, it must be tough finding work...especially work that satisfies you." Austin turned, surprised by Jacks' words. So, he *did* know about Austin's harrowing past. "Yeah, Nate told me. Plus, I do background checks on all my employees, no exceptions, so I know everything there is to know about you. Just keep that in mind if you decide not to heed my advice. I didn't get where I am today by being a pushover. Nothin' personal."

Austin stared hard into Jack Kinsen's face, the face of a man who was—apparently—as cunning as he was brawny, with newfound respect. He nodded. "I'll give Savannah the space she needs, sir," he replied with tight lips then turned and walked out the door.

He let his breath out once he stepped into the center aisle of the barn and headed toward their latest newcomer, Powhatan. He was a beautiful dark bay gelding with a fear of loud noises following a highway accident. Austin cooed to him and stepped forward. Austin rubbed his muzzle and spoke softly to the steed.

"You wanna go for a walk, boy?" he asked and opened the latch on the stall.

Austin placed a halter and lead on the horse and walked him out to the corral to begin the day. He knew he shouldn't be as angry as he was, but his anger was directed mostly towards himself and not at anyone in particular. He couldn't be mad at Jack for wanting to protect his daughter and after the last three weeks, Austin had done nothing but proven himself unworthy to even be in the same room as a woman like Savannah Kinsen, let alone be bedding her.

No, he was just gonna have to win them both over. With a clean slate. Starting today, he was going to start acting grateful to be here and *happy* to be here because where would he be if he wasn't? Back in a classroom, bored to tears? In IT working on computers? Neither of those things suited him. He was made for the outdoors. He was made for hard labor. He needed to keep this job. And he was going to do everything in his power to make that happen.

He began ground-driving with the young gelding and the horse easily took to Austin, much to his delight and surprise. They'd gone in many revolutions at a jogging pace before Austin saw his dog approaching, alongside his brother, who had a stern look on his face. Great! Jack must've told him. Austin greeted his German Shepherd with a pat on the head and braced himself for yet another lecture as Wyatt closed the distance between them.

"What the fuck did you do *this* time?" he asked.

Austin sighed and slowed the horse into a walk. "He didn't tell you?"

"No, but I know by the look on his face you did something to piss him off. I've worked for the man for the last seventeen years, I've learned to decipher his scowls…What'd you do *now?*"

"I slept with Savannah last night…and Jack and Nate caught us in the hayloft this morning," Austin said softly, almost inaudibly.

"Jesus Christ, Austin, you fuckhead!" His brother swatted him hard on the back of his head.

"Ow, dude, that hurt." He shoved at Wyatt. "I didn't know she was Jack's daughter. I met her yesterday mornin'. We didn't give each other our last names."

"What the hell year is this-1960? Why didn't you fully introduce yourself?"

"I don't fuckin' know. It didn't seem necessary at the time." He shrugged.

"How is it that you just keep fuckin' this job up, little brother? What's your damn deal?"

"I'm sorry. I just—" Austin searched for an excuse beyond his tragedy in Afghanistan but nothing came out. Maybe he needed to go talk to someone. He wasn't too good to admit that he needed help.

"You should be surprised your nose isn't smeared across your face. I'm shocked he didn't fire you on the spot."

"Yeah, well, that makes two of us." Austin's foul mood was back. "Now if you don't mind, I'm working here." He motioned to the restless horse attached to the lead.

"Fuck off, Aus. You're such a miserable bastard sometimes, I swear to God." Wyatt huffed off and Austin watched him leave, knowing his words rung true.

Wyatt had always been the golden child, he was first born and had always gone through life with his goals set and his head straight, despite his wacky sense of style. He'd married at age twenty-three and had three daughters. Sierra, their sister, was the princess, never doing any wrong. After finishing college, she'd married her high school sweetheart and had two boys.

Austin was the late bloomer, the screw-up, the baby of the family, who'd been the hell-raiser in his youth. He'd been caught smoking cigarettes at ten, then pot, drinking by the age of twelve, having sex at fifteen, skipping school and getting after school detention constantly, gotten tattoos by seventeen; he'd been trouble with a capital T. So, he'd shocked them all when he'd enlisted in the Army and his sergeant father couldn't have been more pleased. Austin finally had grown-up, finally had a path to follow, finally gotten his shit together. Then Afghanistan happened and he'd gone right back to his immature ways.

Well, now, he had a good reason to get his shit back together... her name was Savannah Grace Kinsen and she'd made him feel alive again.

"*S*avannah," a soft voice called to her from the doorway.

Savannah opened her eyes and looked up at her mother. "Mom?" She groaned. "How long was I out?" She turned to her nightstand to grab the phone that she suddenly realized wasn't there. Damn! She'd left her purse in the hayloft. "My phone—"

"That's what I came to tell you. It's literally been blowing up. Kelsey's called you about thirty times and Dallie—"

"Shit. What time is it?"

"Three o'clock."

"Three? Holy crap!" Savannah bolted upright.

"Honey, it's alright. I talked to your sister and I texted Kelsey and told her you were fine and sleeping. I'm sure she's dying to know what happened last night though. According to your sister, you just left without telling them where you were going," her mom scolded.

Hadn't that been obvious after she headed to the bar? Kelsey had seen her. But damn, she'd been so drunk when she left.

"No, I guess I didn't tell them..." she trailed off, hoping she wasn't going to get read the riot act from her mother at thirty-one years old.

Her mom just sighed and walked forward to hand her the cell phone in her hand.

"Vanna. I know you already know this, but you acted very carelessly last night. I'm sorry for how Sid treated you and I'm upset by it, but I'm also upset at you for the way you handled it. After what happened to your sister and your best friend's mother..." her mom trailed off. Savannah knew exactly what she was saying. It was how people got raped and murdered, going off with strange men from a bar. Savannah sighed and took her mother's hand in her own. "I'm just glad it was Austin you ended up with. That could have gone a lot worse."

"I know, Momma. I'm sorry. It won't happen again."

Her mom leaned in and kissed her forehead.

The devastation that had plagued her family before she was born couldn't be overcome no matter the amount of time that had passed. Jack and Natalie Kinsen had been overly protective and sheltering of their girls and with damn good reason. Savannah knew the dangers of being irresponsible and she suddenly thanked God she'd been just a victim of embarrassment and not something much worse.

"Your sister is coming over for dinner and she's bringing your bags."

"Oh, good."

"I'm making one of your all-time favorites-salmon patties, rice and gravy."

Savannah couldn't remember when those things had last been her favorite or the last time she'd had salmon croquettes. Living in Houston, she rarely cooked, and when she did, it was mostly organic and clean foods. She knew her mom had only made it for her comfort; her parents ate as healthy as she did usually.

"Here. You should call Kels." Her mom handed her the phone and kissed her cheek before getting up and leaving the room.

Savannah looked down at her phone and balked at all the messages from Kelsey.

Kelsey: OMG, Vanna. Where the fuck are you?

Kelsey: S-A-V-A-N-N-A-H

Kelsey: Oh God, you better be in a ditch somewhere, I swear to God.

Kelsey: Savannah, you NEED to call me, I'm freaking the fuck out.

Kelsey: Don't make me call your momma.

There were thirty messages from Kelsey and about ten from Dallie, not to mention all the missed calls.

"God, I messed up so bad," Savannah whined. She was sure she'd worried Dallie immensely and hoped that worry hadn't affected the baby.

She called Kelsey then and smiled when her indignant voice came on the line.

"Jesus, there you are, you evasive bitch. You better have gotten pounded by that sexy cowboy last night. I will *hang* up this phone if you say that you didn't."

Vanna couldn't help but giggle. "Yes! I did."

Kelsey laughed big. "OMG, I'm so dang proud of you, girl. How was it? Tell me everything."

"Wow," Savannah responded, flashing back to her night of gratuitous sex with the gorgeous, tattooed, golden-muscled cowboy. "It was sooo damn hot, Kels."

"Details! I need details, Vanna."

And Savannah gave her details. About him, his beautiful body, his words. His insatiable appetite for her. She'd never had such gratuitous sex in all her entire life. She told Kelsey everything, then her stomach pitched as she explained how her dad and uncle had found them and about the girl from last week.

Kelsey laughed. "Damn Vanna, talk about a buzz kill. I bet Uncle Nate and Uncle Jack were about to tag team his ass."

"I don't know who was angrier, me or them," Savannah admonished.

"I bet, but it sounds like it was well worth worrying your sister and best friend all night for."

"I don't know. After what Daddy said about the other girl I—"

"Oh c'mon, Vanna. We all have a past. Give the guy a break. Besides, you left with him from a *bar*. What'd you expect?"

The truth of that statement hit her like a ton of bricks. What *had* she expected? That she was special? That she was different than any other woman Austin had taken home from that bar? How many women *had* he taken home from The Rusty Spur? She wasn't sure she wanted the answer; the thought made her nauseous.

"Earth to Vanna. Oh, space cadet...I have something to tell you."

"I'm sorry. I'm listening." Savannah swallowed down the lump that had grown in her throat and tried to focus.

"I have some news of my own. Your night wasn't the only one that was exciting."

"Oh? You got 'pounded' too, huh?" Savannah laughed at that ridiculous word of Kelsey's.

"Indeed, I did. And it was fuckin' incredible. Guess who rescued me and your sister from Brantley Burgess?"

"Who?" Savannah's curiosity was now piqued.

"Morgan."

Savannah squealed. "You're back with Morgan? Oh, Kels. I'm so happy for you guys."

The line got quiet as Kels's muffled tears came over the line. "He told me why he left me that day."

"Oh, Kels. What did he—"

"He didn't want the baby, Vanna. He was glad I lost it."

Vanna gasped audibly, surprised that her sweet and caring cousin could be so callous. Morgan was anything but heartless. "Oh, I'm sure he—"

"No, he explained it all. He just didn't want to be like his father... Savannah, he still loves me."

That didn't come as a surprise, Morgan had seemed completely empty since he and Kelsey had broken up twelve years ago and he'd not been the same himself after Kelsey had lost their baby. He hadn't really dated much over the years and just when her Uncle Nate was convinced he was ready to come out of the closet, Morgan had gotten drunk and confessed to them all one Christmas that he'd only ever loved one woman and always would; it didn't take a rocket scientist to figure out who that was.

"I just don't know if I can forget and forgive so easily. My heart can't take his rejection again."

"But don't you love him too, Kelsey?"

"With everything in me."

"And y'all had sex?"

"A-MAY-zing sex. In his truck. In your sister's driveway." Kels giggled.

Savannah smiled. "That's wonderful. Y'all will work it out. I know you will."

"I just want to take it slow."

"Of course," Savannah agreed.

"He sent me a dozen roses," Kels confessed in a sing-song voice, and Savannah could practically see her smiling behind the phone. "And he's taking me out on Tuesday night."

Savannah listened intently to her best friend's excited rambling, glad that, finally, Kelsey and Morgan were working their heart-breaking past out.

~

*J*ax Kinsen smiled at his parents smooching in front of the stove as he entered the back French doors of home. He'd been gone most the day hauling horses back and forth from Eli Coleman's ranch in Tyler. It was pouring out, and his clothes were saturated as he swiped his boots over the rug and shucked the water off his wet hat before hanging it on the hat rack on the wall.

"Oh my baby boy, you're drenched." His mom pouted as she approached him, and he smiled into her upturned face as he loosely embraced her. Even at fifty-eight years of age, she was the most beautiful woman ever, outside and in, but he might just be biased since she was his mother and all. Her hair was dark and long and her eyes were a dazzling blue, her smile was infectious, and her passion for her family and life oozed from her very pores. He kissed her cheek and pushed her gently back from him so as not to get her as soaked as he was.

"Careful, Mom. I don't wanna get you all wet." He chuckled as she looked in surprise at her sopping hands. "Course it looks like Dad was doing a good job of it himself."

His mother gaped at him and his father gave him a withered look as he crossed his arms over his chest.

"Jackson David Kinsen! You're as bad as he is." His mom swatted at him as her cheeks flushed.

One would think, after thirty plus years of marriage, that his parents wouldn't still act like they were on their honeymoon. Hell, he *should* be used to it by now. They'd been like that his whole life. He wasn't, by any means, complaining. It sure as hell beat hearing them fight like cats and dogs like some of his friend's parents did.

"Go on down and get a shower. We have company coming for dinner, and I have a surprise for you." The twinkle in his mother's vibrant eyes had him smiling again. He wouldn't ruin it for her and tell her that he already knew the news; he wouldn't do a single thing to take the happiness away from her in those moments. He simply nodded, grinned and slugged his dad playfully on his big bicep before heading down to the basement.

He peeled his wet clothes off and threw them right into the washing machine before he hopped into a scalding hot shower. Despite that it wasn't that cold outside, even though it was early March, being soaking wet had made him bone cold and he savored the warmth on his skin. That and the fact that he'd been both surprised and angered by what he'd heard regarding his sister, Savannah.

He and Jacob, a fellow ranch hand, had pulled in about thirty minutes ago to a solemn group surrounding the circular corral, and Jackson had immediately known something was amiss. Usually, they were all joking and light-hearted. Today, there had been visible tension between Wyatt, their ranch foreman, and his brother Austin, so much so that it could have been cut with a butter knife.

He'd looked around to see Craig and Pete looking anxious and Tanner and Matt appearing amused. He'd approached Tanner then, the only other hand closest to his age. Tanner was holding Austin's dog, Caesar, by his collar as he barked and growled. Jax whispered as he stopped beside him, "Dude, what's goin' on?"

"Uh, you might wanna ask your buddy Austin over there. He and Wyatt are fightin'." He'd motioned into the corral where Austin and Wyatt faced off.

"Fighting? Why?"

"'Cause he was caught in the hayloft…again. Only this time it was with someone you know." Tanner had shaken his head, flabbergasted, and looked away.

"Who?" His gut reaction had been immediate. Who the hell could it possibly be?

"Go ask him," Tanner insisted, and Jax felt uncomfortable. Perhaps he didn't want to know. His stomach had roiled, but he couldn't stop himself from walking over to the guy he'd grown close to in the last couple weeks.

"'Sup, J.D?" It was another nickname for Jackson. Several of his friends called him J.D.

When Austin had turned to him, Jackson noted that his nose was bleeding. Damn! Tanner wasn't kidding. He and Wyatt were *literally* fighting.

Wyatt walked away from his brother. "Get your fucking head out of your ass, Aus," he'd muttered as he passed Jackson.

Austin wiped his nose with the back of his hand and approached Jackson then, reassuring his dog with a pat on his head.

"What was that all about?" Jax had asked.

It looked as if Austin hadn't even fought back or that perhaps it had been one hit that had busted his nose and then they'd been interrupted by the truck pulling in.

"My brother's not a big fan of mine today." Austin had smirked.

"Ya think? What'd you do?"

"If I tell you, you're liable to pick back up where he left off."

"Who'd you end up in the hayloft with?"

Austin had sighed and planted his hands on his hips, squaring his jaw as he looked into Jax's eyes and answered him. "Your sister."

Jackson had been taken aback and literally started. His first thought was Dallie. But the thoughts of the two of them hooking up together seemed completely wrong. Dallie loved Cole, Dallie was pregnant…and Austin wouldn't do that. Would he?

As if reading his mind, Austin huffed. "Savannah," he murmured.

Savannah? What? When? *How?* Savannah was in Houston. Savannah was engaged.

"Savannah?" Jax croaked out. His brainy, spacey, astrophysicist sister had slept with *Austin?* Bearded, tattooed, cocky Austin! No way! "And I'm sure she'd just *love* it if she knew that the whole fuckin' ranch knows now!" He yelled to Wyatt, who'd stalked angrily off. "I swear to God. This day has turned out to be much shittier than it started, I assure you." Austin smirked again and suddenly, anger boiled in Jackson's blood. The thoughts of that rowdy rough-neck man-handling his gentle sister made his fists clench at his sides and his lips purse. "Whoa. Easy there, cowboy." Austin put his hands up. "Wyatt got his free shot in; I'm done for the day. I'll fight you if that's how you wanna play, but keep in mind that I was in the cavalry before I was a corporal, I'll have your ass on the ground in three seconds flat."

Cavalry? *Corporal?* Austin had been in the Army?

"It was completely consensual. Don't look at me like that. I may be a lot of things, but a damn rapist ain't one of 'em," Austin reassured him.

Jax had felt himself relax some and dropped his arms down as a thought occurred to him. "Does Dad know?"

Austin had scoffed at that. "Hell yeah, he knows. He's the one who caught us—he and your Uncle Nate."

Boy, it had just continued to get more and more interesting. The questions continued to build as Jax got more answers, instead of vice versa.

Finally, Austin had said, "Truce, Jack Jr. I'm done being everyone's damn whipping boy today. I'm going back to my bungalow. Think it over. If you still wanna fight, you'll have to catch me after I have a cold beer. This day can kiss my ass. C'mon, Caesar, let's go home, boy."

With that, Austin Montgomery had huffed off, Caesar on his heels, pushing past Jackson on his way out of the corral, and Jax had been dumbfounded. He'd stayed only long enough to find out that

Wyatt and Austin had been working together with one of the new mares brought in when their raised voices had drawn a crowd and Wyatt had punched Austin. No one could tell him why, but Jax knew Wyatt wasn't one for getting physical with anyone. Wyatt had worked for his father for as long as Jackson could remember and he'd never needed to punch somebody. Jax was positive it had been some smart remark from Austin that had gotten Wyatt riled up; Austin was good at being a wise ass. Despite his smug attitude—and the fact that his father appalled him—Jax liked Austin. He was funny and well, he was cool. He rode a motorcycle, had various tattoos covering his arms, sang in a local rock band, was a surfer, and could shoot a gun with ridiculous accuracy. Well, now Jax knew why *that* was.

Jackson was twenty years old now. And as one of the future heirs to his family's multi-million-dollar horse ranch, he couldn't be happier. He had a girlfriend he absolutely adored, a bright future as an owner and trainer, and a home he would soon begin building with the help of his cousin Morgan on the Butler/Kinsen land they all owned. Jax had gone to college only long enough to get a two-year degree in business management because unlike his genius sisters, he had no desire to become a doctor or a rocket scientist. Jackson David Kinsen was his father's son and he worked hard doing what he loved. He didn't need college to make him feel worthy. He had all he'd ever wanted or needed right here at Kinsen Ranch.

And as he climbed the stairs to boisterous laughter coming from the dining room, his heart overflowed with it—Love. His family. His sisters. His niece, giggling at her grandfather as he tickled her.

"Paw-Paw Jack," Lily squealed, trying to catch her breath as his father sat her down. Jax smiled big at her darling little cherubic face and light brown curls before turning to see his sister, Savannah, smiling up at him from an easel.

He laughed. He loved seeing her in her element again, and ran to her, hugging her to him, delighted to see her beautiful face.

"Oh, baby brother, you look so handsome," she said as she pulled back and took his face in her hands, giving him a soft peck on the lips. "I've missed you."

"I missed you." He squeezed her again and murmured into her ear. "We'll talk later." His eyebrows went up and Savannah's olive skin flushed red.

Jax then turned and patted his brother-in-law's arm and squeezed his pregnant sister, Dallie, before grabbing up his niece, kissing her plump cheek and spinning her around.

Lily was adorable and at four years old, just kept getting bigger each time he saw her. Her sister, Gracie Marie, would be here soon.

Jackson smiled as Dallie placed a hand on her big pregnant belly and sat down.

"Alright y'all, let's eat. I'm starved," Dallie pleaded.

"You don't have to tell me twice," Jax concluded and sat down by Savannah, giving her a peck on the cheek.

Everyone else followed suit; Lily plopping down between her grandparents, and Cole said the blessing. Plates were passed around as they dined on salmon croquettes, rice, gravy, English peas, carrots and homemade yeast rolls.

They dug in and Dallie discussed her Saturday rounds at the Binx's farm and a duck with a cold, getting Lily to cackling, thus cracking up the whole table. It was good to have the whole family under one roof again. It had been a while—months since Savannah had been home—and as Jackson's eyes fell on his mother, he knew she was thinking the same thing. She grinned sweetly at him.

"Aunt Vanna," Lily asked slurping a pea into her mouth. "What does it mean to 'get weighed'?"

"Weighed? Like someone weighs you?" Savannah asked, cocking her head.

Lily shrugged. "I dunno, Momma told Daddy that you got weighed last night."

Dallie almost spewed the drink in her mouth and their mother gasped. Jackson started cracking up as their father huffed and cleared his throat, giving Dallie the mother of all looks. Dallie's porcelain skin turned beet red, and Cole began coughing as Savannah practically slunk down in her chair.

"Dallie," she hissed and looked around.

"What? I didn't know that she *heard* me." Dallie shrugged, helplessly.

"Well, perhaps you should be a bit more discreet." Vanna scowled.

"It's not my fault," Dallie countered.

"It's not your business to be telling." Vanna scoffed and threw her napkin down onto the table as she stood. "Anyone *else* wanna get a laugh at my expense tonight?" The hurt was so plain in her eyes that it made them all wince.

"Vanna," their mother pleaded and reached for her hand.

But it was a wasted gesture, for Savannah was already walking off. They heard the French doors to the back porch open and slam shut again after a moment.

Dallie sighed and looked apologetically to their mother and father. "I'm sorry. I didn't—"

"Did I hurt Aunt Vanna's feelings?" Lily asked, innocently.

"Oh no, sweetie. She's just not feeling well is all," their mother answered her granddaughter.

"Getting weighed is no fun, huh, Nee Nee?"

"Nope, those darn scales are a nightmare," Jax answered and winked, getting up from his seat. "I'm gonna go check on Aunt Vanna, alright, squirt?" He gave his niece a little tickle and walked out of the dining room.

He opened the French doors and firmly shut them behind him. He moved to the Adirondack chair adjacent to his sister's and watched her face staring off into the distance towards the bright glowing orb that was the moon. It was a new moon tonight and appeared to entrance his sister. He was sure she was contemplating its celestial alignment with the earth, not even aware of his presence there beside her, until she spoke.

"Sidd broke up with me yesterday morning...right beside his new girlfriend."

"I'm sorry," Jax responded and took her hand.

"I don't know what was worse, being kicked out and losing everything I've ever known in Houston or being caught half naked in the hayloft this morning by Daddy and Uncle Nate."

"Sounds like it's been a rough twenty-four hours." Jackson laughed humorlessly.

"God, I'm so completely mortified, Jax." She leaned her head over onto his shoulder.

He and his middle sister were eleven years and five days apart. They were both Pisces and were highly in tune with each other's emotions. Jax had always been close with both his sisters, although the vast age gap had—of course—affected their childhood relationships growing up. When Jax had turned fifteen, and was approaching adulthood, the breach hadn't seemed quite so wide. His sisters had taken him under their wings as a baby, coddling and protecting him, rightfully so, then telling him all about girls, the birds and the bees, and how life worked when the time came. He'd considered it invaluable and inside information and felt it had truly prepared him for dating and the opposite sex. After all, he was getting advice that most guys would kill for; he had the inside scoop on all things woman. And when he'd come into his own as a man, he'd felt he'd had a clear advantage when it came to the female gender and sex, for Dallie and Savannah had coached him on the ways to a woman's heart.

"So, how does Austin fit into all this, Vanna?" he asked softly, easing the truth from her as his hand stroked the top of hers.

She looked up at him. "I met him at an antique toy store yesterday morning on my way out of Houston."

"Oh, that's right. He was visiting his parents. They live there."

Savannah just gave him a nod and continued, "I was such a bitch to him. I haven't had a decent night's sleep in weeks, I was reeling from my break up, and he was arguing with me over a damn rocking horse I wanted for Lil."

"Yup, that sounds like him." Jackson chuckled.

"God, he's so cocky," she huffed out and wiped a tear from her eye. "I literally took it away from him and went straight to Dallie's. She, Kelsey, and I went to the Rusty Spur later that night and I ended up seeing Austin again at the bar. I got pretty drunk, and we ended up in the hayloft together last night."

They were quiet for a time, and Savannah shivered from the chill in the air. He pulled her into his arms and felt her tremble as she began to cry.

His sister wasn't one to air her dirty laundry and having everyone know her business was difficult for her. She'd been reserved her whole life and expressed herself and her passion through her music and in her artwork. She wasn't necessarily timid or self-conscious even, but having the entire family, and ranch, see her vulnerabilities in this way was incredibly problematic for her, he knew. Savannah was vastly intelligent and that's where her confidence lie, this side of her was a side no one had ever seen before. Vanna didn't go around half-cocked, every decision she made was made with calculated precision. She was highly organized and her life revolved around order and routine...and right now her life had been hectically crammed into two suitcases that sat in the living room foyer.

Jax's heart went out to his big sister, his systematic, logical sister in her highly chaotic and ungodly embarrassing torment, and he smiled big at her as he pulled back and wiped at her tears. "Hey. It's been a while since you and I went riding, ya know? How would you like for me to saddle up Amadeus and we take a ride together tomorrow?"

She gave a little giggle as she wiped at her eyes with the back of her hand. "I would like that very much." She nodded and kissed his cheek. "You're the best little brother ever, you know that?"

He just gave her a crooked grin and nodded. "Let's go in and get you up to bed. I know you're exhausted. You're not one to give compliments."

She scoffed as he laughed and pulled her up, hugging her to his side as they walked into the house.

~

*J*ack sighed deeply as he pulled his wife into his arms and kissed her temple. They lay on the bed, naked, wrapped in each other, their skin damp from their love-making. He buried his nose into her freshly cleaned hair and inhaled deeply. His heart continued to hammer as he came down from his sexual high, and she gave him that sultry little knowing giggle of hers, happy with herself and the hold she had on his mind and body.

"What?" he asked, even as he knew her line of thinking wasn't far from his.

"My sexy hubby still has it."

"As if there were any doubt." He grabbed her breast, giving it a squeeze and moaned aloud.

"I'm just *glad* you still have it."

"*It* being the erection you bring on or the ability to blow your mind like I do."

She giggled. "Both."

Jack grinned and shook his head, bringing her further into his embrace. He stroked her back lovingly and let her hands excite him again as they moved over his biceps, shoulders and chest. He knew he was lucky. He was approaching sixty years old and most men his age had all sorts of health issues and couldn't even get it up without some drug to help them. He didn't have any significant health problems nor an issue with his dick not working like it was supposed to either. He'd taken care of himself over the years. He ate healthy, he exercised, he wore sunscreen, and took his vitamins. He tried not to stress too much over things he couldn't control, he had three healthy children who were his pride and joy, and he went to church like he was supposed to. Life was good. And right now, he was grateful that he could still make his wife happy and that he could still rock her world as he just had moments prior.

But his mind flashed back to an image he couldn't get out of his mind- his daughter's misery. Finding her in that hayloft this morning had been shocking. Jack had been disappointed, angry, and ready to kill Austin Montgomery. Savannah was mortified he knew, but after seeing Austin's hands groping her in a way that was a bit too familiar for comfort, Jack couldn't see beyond the fury he felt and he'd lashed out. After she'd explained her breakup with her longtime fiancé, Sidd, and what had happened that night, Jack hadn't been quite as angry but that didn't mean he approved of his daughter being with Austin Montgomery, of all people.

Austin was bad news. He was rude, arrogant, and was headed nowhere fast. He cared for no one but himself—from what Jack had seen—and had heavy, invisible baggage he lugged behind him that was liable to drown him if he wasn't careful. And Jack didn't want his daughter to be dragged down with him. Savannah was too brilliant for a scumbag like Austin. He would do nothing but break Savannah's heart, and Jack couldn't allow that to happen again, so he'd threatened him. It wasn't how Jack liked to play, but he would do whatever he needed to keep his girls safe. Austin wasn't like his brother, Wyatt. It was as if they came from two different families, but then again, Austin had been to war, and war changed people. Jack hated that Austin had been through literal Hell and almost lost his leg in the process, but that didn't give him a right to use people. Jack would be damned if he stood by and watched Austin use his daughter for pleasure or fun or whatever the hell he'd used her for. And he had indeed used her—for what other reason would a man like Austin need with a woman like Savannah. He wasn't one for commitments and stability. He thrived on chaos and unpredictability, and Vanna didn't do either of those things.

As if reading Jack's mind, his wife of thirty-two years kissed his nose and smiled into his eyes. She could see the wheels turning in his head for she knew him all too well. "I didn't realize how much like me our daughter really is."

"It shouldn't surprise you." He gripped her bottom and squeezed. "She's always been more like you than the other two are. I swear, seeing Savannah all agitated this morning was like going back in time over thirty years ago, to that day when we met on Hopewell Road. I was staring into the eyes of the same feisty woman."

Natalie moaned and kissed his lips longingly before pulling back to look into his face. Her blue eyes sparkled, and he found himself lost in their sapphire depths. "I meant in her passions." She said the word 'passions' erotically, and Jack grunted. He didn't want to think of his daughter's passions, especially not when they involved Austin Montgomery. "Oh, my love, don't be like that. She deserves to know what it feels like."

Jack rolled his eyes. "Nat, I don't need to know these kinds of things. This is what girl talk was invented for. That's my little girl you're talking about; I don't need gory details about what kind of *love* life she needs to have."

"She wasn't happy with Sidd, and you know that."

"Sidd was a complete douchebag, but she ain't gonna be happy with Austin either. She has no business having spontaneous one-night stands with hooligans like him."

"Oh, honey, she's never done anything like that before, and I highly doubt she'll ever do it again."

"Well, thank God! I'm getting too old to find my daughter in predicaments such as that. I mean what if they'd have given me a heart attack? Isn't that how shit like that happens?" He said it to be funny and sarcastic, and Natalie laughed as he'd hoped she would.

It wasn't far from the truth though. He knew his blood pressure had to be through the roof when he and Nate had found them. And to think they'd only gone up there for inventory and because they'd heard rustling. Nate had swung by last minute. What were the odds they'd both be there when they had? For Pete's sake! Jack hoped he never had to see something like that ever again. Of course, it could've always been worse.

"Do you think Austin will ever recover from what happened to him?" Nat asked, absent-mindedly stroking his arm.

"I don't know, darlin'." He pulled her head down to his chest as he continued to stroke her naked back and tucked her head beneath his chin. "Only time will tell."

CHAPTER 5

*J*ackson woke Savannah early so that they could watch the sunrise, much to her delight. At first, she'd regretted not getting to sleep in, but as they rounded the hill and that beautiful, burning, heavenly star kissed the horizon and the colors melded into something one of her paintings couldn't dare replicate, she laughed, really laughed, for the first time in a long time.

"Glad I woke you up so early now, huh?" Jax asked.

"I am. Thank you, little bro."

"Anytime." Her handsome brother winked at her and gave her a stunning smile. God, he was growing up so fast. When had he gotten so dang handsome? He was wise beyond his years. The best of both their parents. Soon, he would take over the ranch when their dad decided he'd had enough, although if Savannah knew her father, it was still years from now. Jax and Dallie would be the ones to head the business. And Savannah would be back in Houston... the thought suddenly depressed her. As if sensing her sudden unease, Jax asked, "What's the matter, Vanna?"

"Oh, nothing," she dismissed, not knowing how to explain it

herself. "So, I forgot to ask you last night. How are you and Cassidy doing?"

"We're good. Well, I mean, from *my* viewpoint anyway." He laughed. Vanna could see his mind going to Luther and Bella Boyd's baby girl of eighteen ripe years old. A beautiful, curly-haired, strawberry-blonde with hazel eyes and tan skin; the sweet, nurturing young woman who'd stolen her brother's heart when they were merely babies.

"I'm glad to hear it, brother. She's good for you," Savannah said earnestly, knowing that Cassidy had been destined for the nursing lifestyle as she'd always been so caring and compassionate. She and Jackson had dated from the time she'd been old enough to know the difference between boys and girls, much to their parent's dismay and delight, equally.

"She's amazing. I absolutely adore her."

Savannah knew he was telling the truth. He'd been smitten with the sweet girl for as long as Vanna could remember and he'd always treated Cass like a princess. They would be married one day not too far in the future, she knew, and she was happy for them. At least Savannah's siblings knew what love was. Savannah wasn't so sure she would ever truly know it, herself. Her track record didn't leave much probability.

"Has she chosen a college yet?"

"No. She's still getting acceptance letters in. Still hasn't made her mind up yet."

"You seem apprehensive." Savannah could sense the unease emanating from him.

"She's set to graduate as salutatorian. She pretty much has pick of the litter like you did. You know how passionate she is about becoming a nurse. I'm just afraid she'll pick somewhere far away."

"And if she does?" Savannah asked as they turned their horses around at the edge of the property.

Jax shrugged and cleared his throat, looking ahead, trying to appear unaffected by their conversation. Vanna could see that she needed to back off a little as her brother's demeanor had changed completely. He dreaded Cassidy leaving, for fear that their relationship wouldn't survive, she wasn't sure, or fear that Cass would be too far from his protection perhaps. She didn't want to push him though and knew it was a sensitive subject.

They walked their horses in silence back across the east pasture, hearing the birds chirp and feeling the sun warm them as it penetrated the cold surrounding them. Savannah lifted her face, shaded by her hat, and smiled as the rays hit her face.

When they came to the clearing where four bungalows sat, Savannah's heart leapt into her throat as Austin's bare chest came into view, his arms covered by a green button-up shirt that he'd yet to button. His damp curls were wet and steaming around his head, his tan hat atop it, thighs covered in a pair of well-worn jeans and the same snakeskin boots he'd worn the night they'd slept together.

"Mornin', J.D.," Austin said as Jax closed in and Vanna hung back some, stunned to see him there as nervousness overcame her.

"'Sup, man? You look better than yesterday, although your eyes are black." Jax laughed.

Why would Austin's eyes be black? She gasped as she came to the other side of Jackson then and looked over at Austin, whose eyes were indeed dark and his nose bruised.

Jackson cleared his throat and motioned over to the fence. "I'm... uh...gonna go check the fence."

Savannah rolled her eyes at her brother's departing back, but another look at Austin and her heart hammered uncontrollably in her chest. His amber eyes were moving down over her as if he knew exactly what she looked like beneath her flannel shirt and jeans— and she suddenly remembered that he did. He knew very well!

She reminded herself to breathe and tried to regain her composure.

"Hey there, gorgeous," Austin's deep voice held her captive as his eyebrow went up and he approached her horse.

It took her a moment to be able to respond, for her voice was stuck as his hand came to her ankle and he squeezed lightly, looking up at her.

"Why don't you come down off 'a that horse so I can greet you properly?" he murmured, giving her that sexy grin of his, and she gaped at his black and blue face.

"What happened to your nose?" she asked, and he immediately frowned.

"My brother."

"Why?"

"Let's just say he wasn't real happy with me yesterday." He shrugged nonchalantly.

"Perhaps he's tired of you bringing a different woman to the barn every week," she smarted back.

Austin's eyebrows narrowed, making him look even more menacing, but Savannah wouldn't be deterred, he needed to know she wasn't going to be swayed so easily with his charm—not today anyway. She hadn't had anything to drink since Friday night; she had *no* excuses this time.

"Do I sense jealousy in your tone, darlin'?" he asked, his grin becoming devilish. She was the one frowning this time.

"Don't flatter yourself into thinking there was more to Friday night than there was, Austin."

"Oh, I know *exactly* what it was, Savvy. The question is- Do you?" His grin returned, but the conviction in his words cut deep, and Savannah swallowed down the hurt that they caused. She looked away, begging her backbone to hold out for a few more minutes. When she didn't respond immediately, Austin gripped her boot-covered ankle once again and squeezed gently. "You and little bro out for a ride this morning?"

"It doesn't take a rocket scientist to figure that one out." She glared down at him.

"Man, it looks like someone needs yet another spankin' to fix that sassy little attitude of hers, I see." His gorgeous eyes were practically predatorial when they looked into hers, and she felt her center clench at the thought of having his hands on her bare ass once more. "Were you sore Saturday morning?" His brows went up again. *Fuck*, his cockiness was stunning.

"Is that some macho ass thing men ask women? Does it make you proud to know that you fucked me so hard that I couldn't walk straight yesterday? I'm riding a horse today, aren't I?" The audacity! Even though her vagina *had* been sore as shit the day prior, there was no way she was letting him know that.

Austin's hand began to move up her leg and she smacked it hard. "Don't touch me."

Austin practically growled up at her. "That wasn't what you were sayin' Friday night, *Savvy*."

"Stop calling me that!" she cried, and Amadeus jerked beneath her at the shrillness of her voice. She patted her horse's neck, soothingly, even as Austin looked suddenly hurt by her spontaneous outburst.

"Savannah, I—"

"Everything alright over here?" Jackson asked, his tone harsh as he looked over at Austin, his brows drawn.

Austin immediately moved his hand off Vanna's leg and stepped back, looking forlorn as his gaze burned into hers. Why was he looking at her with such hurt on his face, as if she'd just taken something from him?

Austin lowered his head. "No problems, man. Y'all have a good day. I'll see ya around, Savannah." He winked and grinned again, although he didn't look as confident as he had upon their arrival.

When they were out of earshot, Jax moved his horse beside her and reached out, gripping her bicep. "Do I need to head back to that bungalow and make the rest of his face look like his eyes do?"

Savannah smiled over at her protective little brother, glad he was willing to go to bat for her. She shook her head. "No. I was just overreacting."

"Are you sure? Because it sure sounded like—"

111

"He didn't hurt me, Jax. I swear. He didn't call me names. I just…" Savannah trailed off. Her pride more hurt than any other part of her.

"If he did, Vanna, so help me God, I—"

"No, Jax. I appreciate you defending me, but it's fine. I promise." She reached over and took his hand, willing him to understand without making her relive the biggest mistake of her life.

He gave her a big smile. "Army or no Army, I'll still fight him. I don't care. Nobody runs over my sister and gets away with it."

"You're adorable, do you know that? Cass should feel lucky to have you in her life," she said, as much for the truth as to distract her baby brother from the topic so uncomfortable for her. But in the back of her mind she was asking, "Army? What is he talking about?" She would have to remember later to ask him.

~

"*K*nock, knock," Morgan said as he came through the door of his parent's home on Monday night.

"Come on in," he heard his mom say and smiled as the smell of sautéed onions and garlic hit his nose as he came through the kitchen door. "*There's* my boy," Jordan Butler cooed as she approached and opened her arms to him.

Morgan embraced the woman who'd welcomed him into the Butler home some eighteen years ago and had become his second mother, loving him like he was her own since she'd first had knowledge of his existence. The woman whom he in turn loved with all his heart, who listened to him and gave him advice when he needed it and scolded him when he deserved it.

"Hey, Momma." He kissed her cheek as he pulled back, giving her a big grin.

"You look wonderful, son. What's changed?" she asked, evaluating him as she took the bottle of red wine from his hands.

"Well, I do have some good news. Where's Dad?"

"He's in the living room, watching basketball. It *is* March madness, you know? Go on in, I'll have dinner ready soon." She winked at him and nodded for him to go on in and talk to his father.

He moved through the door and into the dining room, smiling at the three place settings there.

"Hey Dad," Morgan said as he approached the recliner his father was sprawled out in, his feet up on the footrest.

"Howdy, son. How are ya?" He took Morgan's outstretched hand in his own and shook it, patting it easily with his other hand.

"I'm good. Good. You?"

"I can't complain too much. Still ticking. Only the good die young they say," Nate winked back at him. "I reckon your momma and I'll live forever."

Morgan just shook his head at his old man, his once raven hair now silver, his dark beard full of gray too. He had some crow's feet around his eyes now in his sixty-third year, but all in all, Nathan Butler had aged well. Morgan only hoped he was so lucky.

Morgan took a seat on the couch next to the recliner and settled in, relaxing.

"You want a beer or somethin'?" his father asked, raising his own.

"Nah, I brought some wine for dinner. Thanks though."

"You're in a good mood, Morgan. What's up? Something new going on at work?"

"Well, I do have some good news. I wanna tell you and Mom at the same time though. It's not work-related but just as exciting." Morgan couldn't hide the smile on his face as he thought of Friday night with Kelsey. How sweet and sexy and amazing she'd been. How vulnerable, how raw, how emotional. It had been a pivotal moment. A moment that marked a future for the two lovers that had been destined for one another that magical day at a barbecue some eighteen years ago.

"Well, you've got my curiosity piqued, son. But I'm happy for you. Whatever it is." Nathan raised his beer again and tilted it at Morgan. "To you, Morgan Dean Butler."

"Thanks, Dad." Morgan couldn't help but blush.

"So, speaking of work—"

"Dad," Morgan warned, his hand going up. "Let's not do this again, please? I'm in a good mood and I don't want it ruined by talks of—"

"Why the hell can't we talk about it? What's the big damn deal."

Morgan internally sighed. It was like this now every time he came over. His dad was pushing him to take over the ranch, insisting that it was his. His heritage. His legacy.

"Dammit, Morgan. Why don't you want it?" his father asked for the umpteenth time.

"Because I already have my own company. I can't get things done as it is. What am I supposed to do with a ranch?"

"Hire a foreman and let him run it. It's yours by right. By name. Hell, you have a house on the land. Now take the ranch to go with it. It's an investment. It's your legacy." There he went again with that damn word. Morgan was starting to hate that freaking word.

"Dad, please, I don't—"

"I don't understand why you would balk at such a gift!" Nathan was yelling now. This was the way it got every single time they talked about it.

"I'm not balking at it, but come on, you throw it on me every single—"

"Your mother and I are going to be retiring soon. We're gonna travel. I need you to step up."

"I don't want it."

"It's yours. Whether you want it or not is beside the point."

"Give it to Dallie, Savannah, and Jackson."

"You're the last Butler. It goes to you!"

Morgan sighed heavily and pinched his nose.

"Dammit, Morgan. Just fucking take it. I'm signing it over to you."

Morgan looked up, a withered look on his face. "You know how I feel about this."

"And you know how *I* feel. If you really don't want it then *you* sign it over to the Kinsens." With that, Nate leaned up and slammed the recliner footrest down with his feet. He stood and pointed at Morgan. "I'm done fighting about this. It's your land. You do with it what you see fit. But you're my son and your name is the one on the deed." His father threw his beer back and drained it then swiped at his mouth with the back of his hand and moved away, out the back doors to the porch, leaving Morgan to feel like shit.

It wasn't that he didn't want the ranch, not really. He wasn't sure why he fought with his dad about it. He knew he was the last Butler. It was a heavy burden to bear, knowing that unless he had children the name would die with him. That thought had kept him up at night as of late, which was why he'd finally had a "come to Jesus" with Kelsey Friday night. The realization of his mortality had begun to plague him, urging him to act. His heart tired of living without its other half, seeking its mate unsuccessfully over the years, yet knowing it lie in only one woman. The woman he'd loved with his entire heart from the moment their hands touched. It had been a physical shock to his system and he'd known he would never be the same. He'd given her up years ago, thinking he was doing her a disservice by being with her, as he'd never felt worthy of her. And felt even more unworthy of her when he'd been glad that their child had died. The sting of it still burned his heart like hot flames as he recalled the look on her face as he told her goodbye. He'd never forget it as long as he lived.

"Morgan," his mother's soft voice called to him. "Baby, why do you get him so riled up?"

"I'm sorry, Momma. I should go." Morgan scowled as he stood.

"Honey, he doesn't want you to go and neither do I. Baby, you're home." The pain of that word hit him hard and he felt tears come to his eyes as he just stared back at his beautiful red-headed step-mother. "That's the real problem here, isn't it, son?"

Jordan approached him and took his shoulders, looking up into his face. He took in her high cheekbones, her honey-whiskey eyes and her plump lips, and he felt the first tear fall down his cheek. He shrugged. "I dunno, Momma. I just—"

"Morgan, son, you have no reason to feel unworthy of it. It's yours. It's *always* been yours. It's always gonna be yours too. You are Nathan Butler's only child. And this ranch and land are as much yours as they are Dallas, Savannah, and Jackson's. Do you hear me?"

He nodded even as he cried and felt his mother's arm come around him. She rubbed his back and sat him back down on the couch, cradling his head to her ample chest.

"My son, don't you see that you belong to us? All of us. We love you so very much. We missed so much of your life. I know your daddy hates that as much as you do. He regrets it as much as you do, but we only have the here and now. I may not be your biological mother. I know you miss her somethin' fierce, but I'm your momma and you are my son. Blood isn't the only thing that matters, Morgan. Haven't you seen how much that matters to Jack and Dallie? Lily doesn't even share any Kinsen blood, but try to tell that to them. It doesn't matter! You hear me! Nothing matters but love." Jordan continued to stroke his hair and reason with him, until his head came up and he looked into her eyes.

He nodded, grinning. "You're right."

"Of course I am, honey." She winked at him and wiped at his tears. "You take what's yours. Ain't nobody gonna be upset by it. I know Jax and the girls will be thrilled and so will your dad and I for that matter."

"You're just sayin' that because you want Dad to take you to Italy."

"Well, that too," she said with a giggle, "but honestly, baby. He really wants you to have it. So very much."

"I do," came a deep voice from the other side of the room. "Please? Don't make me beg my son to take his own land."

"Ok," Morgan said. "Sign it over to me. I'll make you proud, father."

"Son, what you don't understand is that I've *always* been proud of you." Nate walked back over and took his son's hand, pulling him to his feet. "I just wished I hadn't passed on the stubborn Butler gene to you is all." He laughed and patted Morgan's back. "Now, let's eat. Go pour your wine. We got something to celebrate."

Jordan laughed and hugged them both before they all three moved into the dining room. His mother began bringing out serving dishes, and Morgan poured them all some wine. They sat down to the table and began passing around the platters of Salisbury steak, mashed potatoes, English peas, rolls and salad before saying the blessing and digging in.

"Mmm, Mom, this is delicious as always," Morgan complemented as he took a bite of steak.

"I'm glad you're enjoying it, hon," she said as she winked over at him. "Now, are you gonna leave me in suspense or tell me this big news of yours?"

"Ah, yes. Well, I, uh—"

"Spit it out, kiddo. I ain't gettin' any younger," his dad laughed and patted his back.

"Kelsey and I are getting back together," he stated proudly.

Jordan's eyebrows went up in surprise and Nathan's fork froze mid-bite.

"Wow, I—I don't know what to say," his mother broke the silence first.

"Say that you're happy for me, Mom," Morgan insisted, his apprehension growing with the awkwardness suddenly surrounding him.

"Well, of course we're happy for you, Morgan. I mean, it's just— well, that was twelve years ago that y'all split and we didn't even know y'all were talking again," his dad stated.

"Well, it was a bit abrupt, that's for sure. But, well, we have a date tomorrow night."

"Oh, good. I hope it goes well."

"Wait. You guys, what aren't you saying?" Morgan asked, dropping his fork to his plate.

"Oh, honey, it's nothing—" Jordan waved her hand, nonchalantly.

"You broke her, Morgan. Don't you remember how hurt she was when you left her in the hospital all alone?"

"Y'all knew about that?"

"Of course we did, honey. We're best friends with her parents… and hell, we live in a small town. People talk. You know that." Jordan gave him a look of pity, and his stomach hit the floor. "Oh, sweetie. Don't look so upset. We're not mad. Just surprised is all. Y'all loved each other so much, and if you worked your problems out then good for you. Many people don't get that chance." She reached out across the table and took his hand, giving him a big smile. "It's brave of you to go after what you really want. You haven't been happy for a long time, Morgan. Go. Make yourself happy, sweetie."

"Son. We only have one chance at this life. If Kelsey is your future then you fight for her." His father patted him on the back again.

Morgan sat there and sighed, smiling into the love that reflected back at him from their eyes, and knew they were right. Kelsey was his future. Kelsey was the love of his life. Where he'd only been going through life, aimlessly without her these past twelve years, he now had purpose. She was his purpose. His and his alone. And tomorrow he was going to show her that, no matter what or how long it took. Kelsey Jean Boyd was Morgan Dean Butler's, by right and by name.

~

Kelsey rang the doorbell at 6:58 sharp. Kelsey had always been punctual. All her life. She might be a lot of things but late was never one of them…well, except once. At the age of eighteen.

The beautifully carved mahogany wooden door opened quickly with a "whoosh" as if he'd been standing there waiting for the bell to ring, and Kelsey smiled as she looked up into the handsome face of the man whom she'd loved from the minute she'd first seen him.

Morgan Butler looked incredibly sexy tonight in a black button-down dress shirt that hugged his chest tightly, two buttons undone, a dark tuft of hair peeking from the V in it, grey slacks that hung low on his narrow hips and shiny black Oxfords shoes. His thick black hair was styled with gel, combed over to the side, the top longer than the shaved sides. He looked like a CEO wet dream she'd had recently.

"My God, Kels," Morgan said as his eyes roved down her body slowly. She gulped. "You look amazing. How on earth am I supposed to focus on anything beyond your gorgeous figure poured in a dress like that?"

Kels gave a little giggle as his eyes returned to hers. She knew she looked good tonight. She'd primped for hours, trying to get her hair and makeup just right and then inched herself into the slinky fitted red dress.

"You look pretty good yourself, Mr. Butler." She arched a brow as she stepped forward across the threshold and his hand moved to her waist as he leaned in, kissing her cheek.

"Please, come in," he recovered as he extended his hand. "Welcome to Butler manor." He gave her a big smile as she looked up at the twenty-five-foot ceilings with dark wood beams and chandeliers of cascading hammered bronze with exposed lightbulbs. Morgan's home had both a rustic and industrial feel to it as she looked past the foyer into the great room and a huge floor to ceiling stone fireplace.

"That looks just like Uncle Jack and Aunt Nat's."

"It was inspired by it, honestly."

She smiled as she remembered their conversation on Sunday. He'd asked her where she would like to go eat; he'd been planning to take her to a five-star restaurant on the river in Denton when she'd suggested simply staying in would work for her, seeing as it was a work night for the both of them. That's when Morgan had stated that Kels should come to his house and he would cook for her. What girl didn't want a man cooking her dinner? It sounded terribly romantic.

She stepped into the foyer, following Morgan's lead, and rounded the corner to see a huge open kitchen with dark granite countertops, a stainless-steel hood, white cabinets with dark wood grain accents and white subway tile backsplash with a mosaic of landscapes from around the world.

"Did Vanna paint that?" Kels asked as she approached a leather bar stool and put her purse down, pointing to the backsplash on the wall behind the stove.

"Indeed, she did."

"She's amazing," Kels stated, proud of her best friend.

"Wanna see my bedroom?" Morgan asked as she had just turned to look around the room. She instantly froze and whipped her head around. His sexy blue eyes burned into hers as red hit his cheeks. "I —I mean. I—" he stymied.

"Sure." Kelsey cleared her throat and nodded, not wanting him to know how rattled his question had made her.

He simply looked away and gestured toward the stairs in front of them. She took the beautiful dark wood stairs slowly, admiring the black metal railings and dark wooden bannisters.

She stopped at the landing and let him lead her through the French doors of the large master suite, his hand coming to rest at the small of her back. It had a wall of floor-to-ceiling windows, a comfy-looking King-sized sleigh bed with a grey comforter, and a flat screen TV mounted to the wall adjacent to it. There was a large mahogany dresser, matching the bed, beneath the TV, a couple of abstract paintings, and a large oriental rug that gave the room a pop of color.

She smiled at Morgan who ushered her to the entry of the giant master bathroom that looked more like a spa than anything she'd ever seen in a home before with its stark white-tiled ceilings, walls and floor. A crystal chandelier hung over a gorgeous claw foot tub, and he'd built a shower fit for a king with what appeared to be three oversized shower heads.

"Man, living in the lap of luxury I see, huh, Morgan?" Kelsey's whistle echoed in the large room as she looked over at the double vanities where her eyes briefly gazed over his toiletries there. One of those must be the delicious cologne he wore that wafted up her nostrils as he stood next to her, making her want to literally tear his clothes off and devour him. That stuff really worked, the commercials weren't lying.

He seemed to be momentarily thwarted by their closeness as his eyes roved her face, and she subconsciously gulped. "I—uh—I wasn't tryin' to brag, honest," he admitted.

"Oh, I know. If I was a contractor, I'd have the best of all this stuff myself. I'm sure you get a deal too." She winked and elbowed him, trying to comfort his unease.

He gave her a weak smile and looked down before he cleared his throat. "Are you hungry?"

She only nodded and turned to go back downstairs, hearing music waft through the built-in speakers, smooth jazz met her ears. She smiled, surprised that he listened to something other than country or rock. Morgan moved towards the stove, donning a glove on his hand, and her sense of smell was overloaded with the scent of garlic, parmesan and almonds as Morgan pulled a baking dish from the oven.

"Wow!" she murmured, peering over the bar to see what he'd made for them. "That smells absolutely delicious." Her belly grumbled for good measure, and they both laughed.

"I hope you like sea bass."

"Sea bass? Are you kidding! I freakin' love sea bass."

"It's parmesan and almond crusted."

"Damn. So, you're a contractor *and* a chef. Did I die and go to Heaven since stepping through your doors? I didn't realize I was getting the red-carpet treatment. A girl could get used to this, Mr. Butler."

His eyes sparkled as he looked over at her, and he moved to the wet bar to the east wall of the kitchen. "Let me guess...white wine?"

"Well, you had a fifty-fifty shot, but you guessed wrong. Guess you're not Mr. Perfect after all." Kelsey feigned exasperation, getting a laugh out of Morgan.

"Red, huh? Well, at least you *like* wine, but I also have beer and liquor if there's something else you'd prefer." He looked back over at her, awaiting her answer as his hand stilled on a red wine glass.

"No, no, whatever red you have is fine."

"How about a blend? I have a great Cabernet/Shiraz mix that I got from the local vineyard."

"Ah ha, seducing me with your sophistication, I see."

She watched as Morgan uncorked a large bottle of wine and poured it into a funky, twisty aerator/decanter. He then took the decanter and filled two wine glasses before bringing them over to Kelsey, who by then had taken a seat at the barstool. He handed her one of the glasses and clinked his own against it, his sultry gaze burning deep into her. She felt her body flush as she thanked him and brought the glass to her lips, inhaling the delicious sweet scent of the wine before taking a sip.

"Seducing you has been all I've thought about all day, honey locks."

Kelsey could do nothing but lick the lips Morgan was fixated on as she swallowed the smooth dry wine down with nostalgia. That had been the name he'd chosen for her, back when they first started dating; 'honey locks' for the color of her hair.

"Having you here, in my house, seeing you in my room...I would love nothing more than to peel that dress right off of you, carry you to my bed, and run my tongue over every inch of your gorgeous skin, darlin'. I haven't been able to think of anything else since Friday night. I want you screaming my name as I pommel that head-board of mine into the wall."

Kelsey felt her entire body tingle with anticipation. She'd been unable to think of anything else herself, but how incredible he'd felt inside her again. How her body had responded to him, absorbed him, as if her sex had muscle-memory and wallowed in the pleasure of being filled by him for the first time in over a decade. She'd felt sheer pleasure, she'd been home. But the doubt was still there, the fear of him leaving her again, to the point where she'd had a panic attack last night and woken in a cold sweat. This was too unbelievable to be real. She'd longed for him for so very long and felt the pain of his abandonment in every corner of her soul. The agony of losing him had nearly killed her. It had been as painful as losing their baby.

For the last three days, she'd read and reread his text messages and the card from the flowers he'd sent her on Saturday. He'd also sent her flowers to work. Just as she had started to wonder if she were crazy, wonder if she was making a huge mistake, and the awe of what she was doing started to take over her brain, he was messaging her or contacting her. It was almost as if he knew when her uncertainties were surfacing. She'd been so excited to see him once again, she'd not been able to contain herself. She'd simply gone through her Monday and Tuesday, teaching her class, and counting down the hours. Now here she was—in his home, on his territory, in the mouth of the beast. And she wanted that beast with a hunger she'd never felt before. She wanted him, her man, Morgan Butler. The man who'd taken everything from her. But she'd known she had to keep her head about her, had to ease into this, had to learn to trust him again... and crawling right into his bed was *not* the way to do it.

He seemed to sense her hesitancy as he cleared his throat and looked down, tucking away his desire for the time being. Refined Morgan took over once more. "It's good, right?"

"Delicious," Kels agreed, glad her voice hadn't caught.

"Are you hungry?" He stepped away and subtly adjusted himself as he moved to the fridge. "I made kale salad with a delicious peach vinaigrette."

"Morgan, you are just full of surprises." Kelsey grinned as he pulled two salad bowls out of the fridge.

"Nothing but the best for my lady."

If she hadn't been so cautious about jumping his bones right off the bat, that would have been the clincher. *His* lady. *His*. And she *was* his, his and only his. She'd always been his. But was he hers? Really and truly, when it came down to it?

Only time would tell. Morgan had said he was and he'd never

married. He'd not even really dated. He'd not had a real girlfriend since her. Perhaps they were just simply picking up where they'd left off. As if the miscarriage hadn't happened. As if he hadn't broken up with her. As if he hadn't walked out and ripped her heart right from her chest as he went. But he had. And the stigma was still there. Would she ever be able to forgive him? Forget what he did?

"Kelsey," he stepped forward then and took her hand, helping her off the stool. As she eased down she fell forward and bumped his hard chest, feeling heat engulf her as she looked up into his eyes.

Morgan pretended not to feel it too, but she knew he did, for she could feel his hard-on pressing steadily into her thigh.

He took a swift step back and smiled, pulling her hand as he led her to a glassed-in outdoor patio. It overlooked the Butler/Kinsen land that surrounded them, the back pasture of Starlight Valley not too far from their view. A horse grazed in the pasture in the early twilight and Kelsey gasped at the beauty of the grass covered hills.

"Beautiful, isn't it?"

"It's gorgeous, Morgan."

"I eat out here a lot, especially when I need a mental break. The view helps put it all into prospective for me."

"You truly have a beautiful home here." Kels said as she sat down in the high-top chair facing him.

"Thank you. My own blood, sweat, and tears went into this place." He looked around proudly.

She picked up her fork and began eating her salad and Morgan followed. The conversation was light and easy as they dug into the beautifully golden fish fillets accompanied with wilted spinach and basmati rice.

"Oh my God, Morgan. This is delicious. I'm seriously impressed."

"It's one of my hobbies, honestly. Momma taught me...well, both of them did." He gave her a rueful grin.

"You've been blessed by two amazing women in your life."

"Three," he corrected and raised his glass. "Here's to you, Kelsey Jean Boyd. For giving this wrecked soul another chance. A refuge from the Hell he's been living in." The sorrow in his eyes brought tears to hers. "To the woman I love, the one who holds my heart in her hands."

Kelsey looked down. Perhaps she wasn't the only one with all these doubts and hesitancies. An unbidden tear ran down her cheek when she looked back up at him.

Morgan looked as if she'd slapped him and his eyes followed the tear that fell down her cheek. He reached out and swiped it with his finger, his frown deepening. Then suddenly, he bolted upright and came to her side.

"Forgive me, Kelsey. I—"

"No. Don't, Morgan. I can't—"

"It's my fault. I—"

"Morgan, please stop." She held her hand up. "I'm trying so very hard not to throw myself into your arms. I already doubt my strength. When I'm with you, I'm literal putty. Please don't force me to crumble because I'll end up in bed with you again and I really don't think that's what we need to do right now."

Morgan sighed heavily and just scowled into her face. "I meant what I said, Kelsey. I don't want to live without you anymore. I just want to love you. The way I should have been loving you these last twelve years. The way I've loved you all along."

"And I want to love you too, Morgan." She took his face in her hands and he sighed as if she'd just given him the keys to Heaven. "I just need some time. I'm still so frightened."

"Baby, I swear, all I want to do is prove myself to you. I'll do anything it takes. Whatever it takes. Just tell me and I'll do it." He'd stepped closer, peeling her hands from his face, planting himself in between her thighs and gripping her hands in his. "I live to worship you, my goddess."

She gave him a big smile then. "You've gotten a bit dramatic in your old age."

"I've just wizened up, is all." Morgan blushed. "I know I fucked up, Kels. But we've punished ourselves enough for what happened.

I'm ready to live again. Tonight. Right now. Let me worship you. Let me show you how much I've changed. How very much you mean to me. How much I love you...I'm not the kid I once was."

"I can see that." She grinned, looking him over. No, he wasn't the boy she'd fallen in love with. He was all man now. Taller, broader, the boy she'd fallen for...only now more muscular, with a beard. And an ass of steel, she noted as her hands came around his waist and lowered to his bottom, squeezing.

"Kels," he warned, and she could feel his erection growing into her thigh once again.

"What'd you make me for dessert, Mr. Butler?" She arched an eyebrow and let her eyes fall to his open V of his shirt.

He smirked. "Dessert? I thought *you* brought the dessert, Ms. Boyd."

She gulped as she moved a hand up, letting her fingertips tickle at the chest hair that peered out of Morgan's shirt, looking up into eyes that darkened with desire. Would having sex with him again really be so bad? After all, they'd done it on Friday. Why was she waiting? She'd gone long enough without his touch. It was all she'd wanted, all she'd dreamed about for twelve long years. Having his arms around her, his hands on her body, his sex buried inside her.

He stood, patiently waiting for her to make up her mind, until finally he pulled back and moved her hands back to her lap. He turned, his back to her as he walked toward the railing and gazed out into the darkening night.

"You can't know how sorry I was. The minute I stepped out of that room. The minute I realized I'd lost you, Kelsey. I might as well have died too. It's like I've been going around in a fog these last twelve years. Aimless. Not really fulfilled. A ghost of a man. Until I saw you Friday night...and Brantley's disgusting hands on you." He growled. "I wanted to kill him. Do you know that? I wanted to beat him bloody. My whole body was itching for it." He turned, his sapphire blue eyes flaming. "I realized then that living without you is something that I won't do anymore. I can't. Because I'm not alive until I'm with you, Kelsey." He walked back over, stopping to stand in front of her again. He leaned in, his nose almost touching hers. "I don't care how long it takes or what I have to do. I'm never going to let you out of my sight ever again. You'll have to pry my cold dead fingers from yours because I'm not letting you go, not now, not ever."

With that, he leaned in and kissed her. She moaned as her arms went around his neck and her thighs wrapped around his waist. "Oh, Morgan." She pulled herself to him as his arms went around her. He deepened the kiss and lifted her, his tongue plunging into her mouth, and she heard herself whimper, clinging to him like he was her lifeline, for he was. She was alive. Fully alive in his arms, his mouth on hers, his frame pressed against hers. "Take me. Make me yours. I want to scream your name as you break your damn headboard."

Morgan laughed even as he moaned and she lost all her inhibitions. He took the stairs quickly, bouncing them both as they held onto one another and tried not to break their kiss.

Within minutes they were stripping each other naked and Kelsey was beneath him, writhing as his thick sex filled her. She cried tears of joy and love with each thrust of his hips. "Oh God, Morgan. Yes. Oh yes, baby." She gripped his shoulders, kissing his bare skin as his desperation to fill her took over him.

"Oh, my sweet Kels, I love you. I've missed you so much, darlin', your sweetness, your hands, your moans, your lips." He kissed her passionately and thrust his tongue into her mouth. "You're so beautiful, baby," he murmured as he stroked her naked flesh with his hands and his head bent to take her nipple in his mouth.

She screamed his name as she climaxed within minutes and his pace increased, rocking the bed and hammering the headboard against the wall as he'd assured her he would do. She would've laughed had she not been overcome with yet another orgasm as he came, roaring at the top of his lungs as his back arched and he spilled himself into her.

They both moaned and gasped as they rode out their mutual euphoria together, gazing into one another's eyes and continuing to touch each other as if they were making sure the other was real.

"Did you break your headboard, my love?" Kels asked on a laugh.

"If I did then so be it, it was worth it to hear you calling my name like that in the throes of passion."

"If not, we'll keep at it until we do."

Morgan laughed big. "Damn right, my gorgeous honey locks." He cupped her cheek and kissed her sweetly on the lips. When he pulled back, he had a devilish smile on his mouth and Kels shivered in anticipation. "Now, about that dessert..."

"Oh, Morgan. You didn't tell me to bring a dessert. I—"

Morgan's smirk said it all before he answered with, "Darlin', *you* are dessert."

She stopped laughing as he moved his head down her body, between her legs, and he began nibbling at her inner thighs.

"Mmm, Morgan," she moaned, and he chuckled. He wouldn't be chuckling for long because soon, she would need to be telling her father that she and Morgan were back together, and Luther Boyd wasn't going to be handling that quite as well as Kelsey had.

CHAPTER 6

"*J*ax, please?" Austin pleaded. He hadn't seen the gorgeous brunette who'd blown his mind that incredible Friday night for over a week now and he was dying to see her, hear her beautiful voice once more, know how she was.

"She doesn't want to talk to you, dude. Let it be," Jax answered and threw the saddle he was carrying over the mare's back.

I can't! Austin wanted to scream. He needed to gaze upon her face, talk to her, be inside her again. His nightmares had returned with a vengeance and he knew it was because he was super stressed out, stressed knowing that she was upset with him. "Jax, I just want to talk to her."

"You had your chance and you blew it!" Jax turned around and heatedly shoved at Austin's chest, the younger man stronger than Austin had realized. "What did you say to her Sunday? What did you *call* her?" Jackson's angry face was inches from his and although he wasn't quite as big as Austin, he was almost as tall.

"What?" Austin balked.

"Don't deny it! I heard her tell you to stop callin' her something.

What was it you called her, Austin?" The murder in Jax's eyes surprised him.

For a minute Austin had no damn idea what he was talking about. He tried to recall the exact conversation in his head...then he remembered. By then Jax had ahold of his shirt collar.

"Whoa, easy up, J.D. I didn't call her a dirty name, man. I would never."

"Then why was she so freakin' upset after she talked to you, huh?" Jackson shook him, and Austin winced as his hung-over head throbbed violently.

"Savvy! I called her Savvy. It was a nickname I gave her on Friday night," Austin caved.

Jackson looked at him confused and let him go, not sure what to say at that point. Austin continued, "I swear that's all I said to her. I don't know why she's upset with me, honest."

"Because she thinks you're a player. And you are! She was the second girl you brought here in the span of a week. Why wouldn't she see right through you? She's fucking brilliant, in case you haven't realized that!" Jackson slung over his shoulder as he walked back to the brindle mare he was getting ready to ride.

She is *fucking brilliant, and I want her with a hunger that won't wait,* Austin thought to himself. But instead said, "I'm not, I swear to God. I want to date her, take her out and court her." *And fuck her sexy, brilliant brains right out of her gorgeous little head,* he thought, but didn't say it out loud.

"Save it. You already know what my dad thinks of you, and right now, I'm not too fond of you either," Jax grumbled.

"Come on, dude. You know that I didn't know she was your sister...or my boss's daughter." He ran after Jackson.

Jackson turned again and growled. "Would it have mattered, Austin?"

Hell *no!* It wouldn't have. He would have taken that delectable little morsel no matter who she was. He'd been starving for someone with her passion and since Friday night, she'd awoken something deep inside him that simply couldn't be contained. He had to have her again...and again...and again.

"Is this all for the chase of it, the thrill? Because you can't have her, you want her all the more?"

Austin didn't really have an answer for that. He didn't think so. But then again...

"Stay the hell *away* from my sister. You've been warned once already." Jax mounted the mare and grabbed the reins, turning the horse in the opposite direction.

Finally, Austin's voice took hold. "Jax, it's not like that I *swear*." Austin ran to catch him before he bolted. "I'm not the guy that you think I am," he cried, knowing it was true. Deep down, he wasn't a bad guy. He wasn't a player. He wasn't a trouble maker. He was a military man stuck in a civilian lifestyle that he couldn't quite fit into. He was a PTSD victim. He was a survivor. He was a drowning man in a body of water he didn't quite know how to swim in, and Savannah had been his lifeboat. He needed her. To continue to live and breathe. She'd brought him to life again and he couldn't give her up. He wasn't going down without a fight. "Please Jackson?" He knew he was begging now, but dammit, he didn't care. "You said she's upset...so she must feel *something* for me."

When Jackson scoffed, Austin threw out, "At least give me the opportunity to apologize to her, make things right. Can I have her number so I can call her?" Jackson shook his head incredulously; he wasn't giving Austin her number. On to plan B. "Fine then. Here, give her *my* number." Austin took the piece of paper he'd written his number on from his back pocket and handed it over to Savannah's little brother, who gave him the once over before taking it. "Tell her that I want to speak with her. I *need* to speak with her."

Jackson raised his eyebrow. "Fine, I'll give it to her, but if she doesn't call you, don't be shocked," he grumbled. "Now get back to work."

With that, Jackson walked the horse some distance before he dug his spur into the horse's flank, signaling her into a canter and he was gone, leaving Austin to once again feel hopeless about his situation.

Austin ambled back out of the back pasture, towards the barn, wondering where the hell Savannah had been and what she'd been doing since he'd seen her last Sunday. Over a week had passed since their incredible night together and not more than an hour went by that he wasn't consumed by thoughts of her sweet body against his, the taste of her lips on his, the smell of her invading his nostrils. He'd felt incomplete the past week and three days, going through the motions of his daily routine, waiting for her to come to the barn, to see her in passing, in town, *anywhere*. But he hadn't seen her at all, and inside, he was aching.

They hadn't parted on the best of terms last Sunday; he'd clearly upset her, but he hadn't understood exactly what he'd said that would cause her to be so despondent with him that day. Ok, so he'd brought her to the hayloft after he'd brought a different girl there the week before, it didn't bode well. He understood that. But surely, she'd felt the same things he did after their bodies had clashed together in the unbelievable harmony they had that night. He'd never experienced a sexual union quite like that before. He'd never felt so in tune with another human being like he'd been with her, so at peace in a woman's body, in her presence, so at *home*.

Austin headed to the corral to see where Wyatt wanted him today, glad to avoid his boss at all costs. Jack still looked at him as if he wanted to literally skin him alive. He would've made a great Roose Bolton in the *Game of Thrones* series. Jack Kinsen's sigil would have been the flayed man for sure, although he'd been more of a Ned Stark type before he'd found Austin in bed with his daughter. Ah hell, who was Austin kidding? After the way he'd acted the first three weeks of his employment, he couldn't say he wouldn't feel the same way about his own employee had the roles been reversed.

The last seven days though, he'd been a saint compared to those first two weeks. He'd been on time, stayed late, volunteered to help out in any way necessary, and his brother had seemed proud of him.

It made Austin happy and despite how much he missed Savannah, he'd felt joy for the first time in a while.

Just then his phone rang in his back pocket and he stopped dead in his tracks to answer it, although he knew Jax hadn't had time to give the piece of paper to Savannah.

Austin smiled anyway, when he saw Trevor Bishop's name on his caller ID. "T-man! How the hell are ya, brother?"

"I'm good. How about you, *Mustang*?"

Austin laughed heartily as he propped himself against the fence post, glad to hear from the man he'd lead—and fought beside—the last two years of his military career. "Damn, it's good to hear your voice! How you been? Whatcha been up to?"

Trev had been injured in the same assault that Austin had; Trev's face had taken the shrapnel and after multiple surgeries for facial reconstruction, he'd recovered, received his purple heart, and gone to work for the FBI. He had excelled as a field agent and intelligence analyst; he was smart as fuck and had been their coms guy when they'd run their missions together in Afghanistan.

"I'm well. Just working and playin', you know how it is. I heard you're living in Abundance now, Corporal. How are you liking it there?"

Austin proceeded to tell him about coming to work at Kinsen Ranch, about training horses with his brother and how he enjoyed small-town living—leaving out his piss poor attitude in the beginning...and Savannah.

Trev congratulated him on his new job and wished him well. "Hey, do me a solid and keep an eye out. You ever heard of a Max McClintock?"

Indeed! The man was already becoming a nuisance to Abundance after being here for just a couple months and no one liked him. He was an up and coming land shark who seemed to have his sights set on the small town. Austin told him so, and Trev gave a smirk, "Yeah, he's a fuckin' gangster, to say the least. And we're keeping a close eye on him. We've heard rumor Brody Sims has been his gofer for the last several years now, you remember him?"

Austin's stomach took. Brody Sims. He was the epitome of the word bad—in every sense of it. "Yeah, I remember that sleaze-ball."

"Yeah, well, you see him around and you call me right away. I'm afraid these two are bad news with a capital B, my friend. Hey, you don't sound like yourself, buddy. How are you, *really*?"

Austin didn't wanna lie to his friend. After all, they'd shared the same tragedy of losing Jerome and the stressful wake that only combat vets can comprehend. "I'm hanging in there, man."

"Hey, you know I'm in Dallas, right? There's a MOPH chapter in Denton and we actually got a meeting tonight. Why don't you join me? I'd love to see you! You know, the guys have really helped me a lot. It'd do you some good to connect with those of us who understand, Corporal."

Austin smiled. He'd thought about talking to someone about his issues, knew that he probably needed to. Now, here was his chance. To connect with other purple heart recipients, soldiers who'd been in the same situations he had, who'd lost something in the line of duty—a limb, a friend, their path—like he had.

"I appreciate that, Trev. I'll give it great consideration and let you know. I think I'd enjoy that."

Trev encouraged him to come once more and they talked for another few minutes before Wyatt motioned for him to join him in the corral.

He and Wyatt had never really seen eye to eye and they'd fought over the years as much as they'd gotten along, but they were brothers and loved one another immensely. Austin had always looked up to Wyatt, admiring his gift, his persistence, and was essentially glad he'd moved to be closer to him.

As if sensing his thoughts, Wyatt gave him a big smile and patted his back. "Still chasing tail, I see, little bro." Wyatt gave him a laugh and Austin frowned, remembering the awkward conversation with Jackson. "I haven't seen a woman do quite the number on you in a while. You look downright depressed. She must be one hell of a woman." Wyatt winked at him and patted his back hard again.

Wyatt knew Savannah better than he did and knew exactly what kind of woman she was. But Austin gave him a grin in return, agreeing with him. "You know she is."

"Well, I'm glad to see you fighting for her, although I think you're in over your head here." Wyatt laughed again as Austin's smile faded. "You don't know the Kinsens like I do, A.J. You've got your work cut out for you." He shook his head. "Hey, you wanna have dinner with us tonight?"

"I would, but I'm gonna go catch up with an old friend—at the military order of the purple heart meeting. Can I take a raincheck?"

Wyatt gave him a grin. "I'm glad to hear that, brother. And you absolutely can."

~

*A*ustin enjoyed having a good amicable dinner with his brother, sister-in-law, and nieces the following evening at a local burger joint in town. Although what Wyatt said and Austin's own thoughts on Savannah weren't far from his heart and mind. Perhaps he did have his work cut out for him. But he didn't care. He was going to keep fighting to win her over. If Austin could do anything in his life, it was fight. He was a born warrior. It was in his blood.

He'd smiled over at his niece, Ashlynn, as she recanted a funny story from her college philosophy class. Austin couldn't get over how grown his three darling nieces were: Ashlynn, Katie, and Rachel. Nineteen, seventeen, and ten. Man, how time flew. Ash and Kate knew Jackson and Cassidy well. Both girls and Jax had attended Abundance High together and they'd all hung out periodically. Jax and Ash's boyfriend, Ben, were best friends. What a small world! But Abundance *was* a small town after all, Austin remembered.

Ashlynn's sandy blonde head had tilted back in laughter, and

Austin couldn't help chuckling right along with her. She was so much like her father. Wyatt had always been such a jokester too. Although Ashlynn and Katie looked more like their mother, Angela, with their hazel eyes and freckles. Rachel had taken more after Austin and Wyatt with her tan skin and chocolate brown eyes, her hair a bit darker than either of her sisters.

Angela Lowndes Montgomery had been the best thing that had ever happened to Austin's brother. They'd met young, married young, and started making a family by the time they were twenty-two years old. They had always been happy from what Austin had seen. They were the exception to the rule, he knew. He had far too many friends who were divorced or in the process.

Now Austin understood how a man could be so smitten by one woman. A woman whose aura sung to him, as Savannah's sang to Austin. Speaking of singing, Austin, who'd gotten home barely an hour ago, was now strumming his guitar on the front slab of his single bedroom bungalow. It was one of four on the property. It was small but large enough to house a king size bed, dresser, wall-mounted TV, a kitchenette, spacious bathroom with a stacked washer and dryer and a closet. It had all the amenities one would need for minimalist living and he was only one of three hands in the bungalows. The last one down sat vacant.

"Savvy, oh Savvy, I can't get you off 'a my mind. Savvy, sweet Savvy, I aim to make you all mine." He sang in his raspy voice as Caesar howled along with him. The ladies had always swooned over his singing and strumming. *What's not to love about a cowboy/biker/musician after all?*

It had started back in high school, during his teen surfing days in California. He and his buddies would head to the beach on the weekends by ten, hit the waves and surf until dusk then build a big bonfire at night. Austin would sit with his guitar across his legs on a log they'd rounded up, singing and strumming, sounding like Chad Kroeger from Nickelback, and he'd watch as the girls practically creamed their panties over his vocals. It was how he'd gotten many of them into bed. He smirked, remembering his time in the Army when they were stuck in Afghanistan on the cold nights with only their memories to keep warm. He and Jerome would sing to them all as he played his harmonica, for they'd harmonized well together. They'd sing songs they knew, alternative and country, for Jerome was surprisingly a big fan and when they'd been sick of those songs, they'd made up their own. Austin recalled the night, Carmen, the only woman in his regime, had laughed after they'd made up a vulgar song about needing some "pussy". Some of their songs weren't meant for civilian ears but the boredom was all-encompassing at times as they did recon.

"Well, you sure won't be getting any tonight after that brutish display." She'd shaken her dark head in disgust. They'd apologized for being such scoundrels, laughing. "No need to apologize. I already know you boys are dogs, I didn't need a song to confirm it." She was right, for she'd seen them at their very worst. Cussing, pissing, farting and being average All-American men at times. In their small group, they'd seen and done it all together, living in such close quarters. Carmen had been the first one to assist him when the explosion went off.

Austin squeezed his eyes, needing to think of something else. It had been good to reconnect with Trevor last night and shoot the shit with fellow veterans, young and old alike. Knowing he wasn't alone in his grief had been good for his soul, but he still felt hollow without his sweet Savvy. She'd grounded him.

"Dammit, Caesar, this sucks, buddy." The dog whined back at him and laid down. "Fuck this!" he yelled and picked himself up of the steps of the front entry to his bungalow. "I'm gonna go see her. You stay here and hold down the fort." He replaced his guitar in its case and walked over to his black Harley Heritage. He strapped the case to the back and hopped on, pushing his cowboy hat down tighter on his head.

He started the bike, and revved the throttle, taking off at a low speed down the dirt road toward the house. He was going into recon mode. He was literally dying to see Savannah and since she hadn't called him, he'd deduced that she was A.) not planning to or B.) Jackson hadn't given her his number, so now it was time to act. Austin had gone long enough without taking action. He didn't wanna push it with his boss. He knew that Jack despised him, but perhaps he could get close enough to see her, maybe pull an old-school and throw a rock at the window or something. Of course he had no idea of knowing which room was hers, and just his luck he'd throw a rock at the wrong window or worse, break a damn window.

Austin parked his bike not far from the back gate as he saw a dark-haired female silhouette on the back porch. Could his luck really be *that* good? His heart hammered in his chest as he got off the bike, slowly walked towards the gate, and stopped—for it had a big deadbolt on it. He easily climbed over the top and jumped down, his boots hitting the ground hard.

The porch was dimly lit, sparse light coming through the thick curtains behind the window, and he heard nothing as he closed the distance, thinking perhaps the silhouette had been a figment of his imagination as his eyes adjusted to the darkness of the night and the porch. He could see the outline of a figure in the rocking chair before him and his breath took, it had to be her- Savannah.

Austin said the first thing he thought of, "What light through yonder window breaks? It is the east and Juliet is the sun[1]."

He heard a gasp and joy flooded his heart. It was her. *Oh, thank God.* She could hear him, see that he was standing there, see that he'd come to her. He only prayed she was swooning on the inside and that she would answer him, for he longed to hear her beautiful voice.

He waited endless moments in silence, awaiting some response, some acknowledgement of his presence, his blood pounded in his ears as the night sounds of crickets grew around him.

Just when he thought she wasn't going to respond, Austin heard a giggle, but it didn't sound like Savannah's, it was deeper but still feminine.

"I don't believe I am a Capulet or you a Montague for that matter, sir." The voice that graced his ears was just as attractive as he remembered. God, how he wanted to climb those stairs and pull her into his arms, feel her sweet, soft frame against his, but he held fast.

Oh God, Savannah. How I've missed you, he longed to say. He grinned and replied with, "What's in a name? That which we call a rose by any other name would smell as sweet[2]."

Austin thanked his wonderful high school Lit teacher, Mr. Roper, who'd encouraged him to play the part of Romeo in the play that year, embedding these Shakespearean lines deeply into his memory. He hoped his romantic side was winning him some killer points right now; he had more where that came from if need be.

He heard a throat clear and a muffled sound as one dark head turned to another. Oh, fuck! She wasn't alone. *Son of a bitch!* But Austin quickly saw that it was two female silhouettes on the porch and thankfully, not a male.

The figure he assumed to be Savannah stood and came to the railing. He wished he could see her beautiful face, but it was shaded. "Austin, what are you doing?" she asked softly, sounding far more serious than she had but a moment ago.

"I brought back-up. One moment," he stated before turning and running back to the gate. He hopped it and jogged back to his bike, removing the guitar from its case and throwing it over his shoulder, laid it across his thighs and sat down on his bike. He strummed the first song that came to mind, wanting her to know how he really felt deep in his heart. Austin began strumming the chords to "To Be With You" by Mr. Big. The words flowed strong and true, and he hit the guitar riff with a passion he hoped emanated to her from his perch on the bike. Was she digesting his bravado in coming to sing to her tonight, were the words seeping into her heart as they echoed through the pasture, were his emotions being emitted through his vocal cords as he called to her through the lyrics of the song? He could only hope as the song came to an end and the tune died, reverberating off into the night sky. He sighed and looked up, unable to see her, but knowing she was there and heard every word.

All was quiet on the porch, one could have heard a pin drop, and Austin held his breath, waiting for some response to his unspoken question.

Suddenly, the overhead porch light came on and the door opened quickly, but Austin's eyes were on his prize. Savannah stood at the railing, gazing out at him with awe-struck eyes, and his heart soared. For the first time in over a week, he felt hope, strong and true, swell within him. He beamed brightly at her, nodding his head at her.

"Montgomery, what the *hell* are you doing?" Jack's gruff voice pulled him out of his reverie.

Austin looked over at his boss. Jack's eyebrows were raised in equal parts annoyance and amusement, his big arms folded over his chest.

Austin shrugged and gave a light chuckle."Just serenading the ladies on this beautiful evening, boss."

Jack smirked and looked over at Savannah and Natalie, who sat in one of the six rocking chairs. Natalie was grinning at him, stars in her eyes. *Yup, my song had the intended effect, I see.*

He'd not lost his touch after all. *Score!*

"Well," Jack looked down at his watch, "it's after ten, so let's call it a night, shall we? Work comes early, after all, huh?" Jack gave him a subtle nod. He wasn't quite as mad as Austin was anticipating.

Austin relaxed some and smiled back at him. "Right. Concert hours need to be re-assessed, got it!"

Jack just gave him a laugh and shook his head, heading back inside after he looked over at his wife, who smiled big back at him. Austin's gaze flew back to Savannah, whose face was unreadable now. Uh-oh! He'd been so close, close to breaking through to her, close to a reconnect with her. Why was she giving him such a sad look? He hesitated in speaking, suddenly wanting to kiss that pout off her sexy lips.

"Good night, Momma." She whipped her head away sharply from his gaze and looked at her mother before turning on her heel and heading inside...before Austin even had a chance to talk to her, his whole reason for being there gone in an instant. He hadn't even gotten to apologize.

Austin sighed heavily. Had he gotten through to her? Had his song penetrated her big brain? Or had he given this performance in vain? His head fell.

"You're quite the charmer, Mr. Montgomery," Natalie's voice called to him from the porch.

He looked up and gave her a sweet smile. "Thanks, Mrs. K. I hope y'all enjoyed my performance."

"Oh, was that what it was?" Natalie grinned knowingly back at him and gave him a wink. "Good night, Austin. Sleep well." She waved before heading inside, leaving Austin to ponder his quandary once more.

~

Savannah smiled as she got ready the next morning. She thought of Austin's smooth voice singing the '80's hair band song to her the evening prior. Seeing his tall, manly, muscular frame clad in his skin-tight jeans, a fitted t-shirt, and his tan cowboy hat atop that bike with a guitar across his thighs had done incredible things to her body. And when his sexy voice had belted out in song, she'd felt her womanhood literally oozing lust, causing her breath to catch and her thighs to clench.

And he'd known Shakespeare. Leo DiCaprio, eat your heart out! Who *was* this guy?

He was a diehard romantic. And a charmer down to his core. Perhaps he wasn't the man she'd originally thought he was. Or perhaps he was stepping his game up...or perhaps...*Stop!* Savannah screamed at her over-analytical mind. He's a player. A womanizer. *You don't need to let him get to you. He's only gonna break your already broken heart*, she told herself.

But damn he was so flippin' gorgeous. His unruly, curly, sandy blond hair that came to his chin and curled up underneath his cowboy hat. His deep amber brown eyes and golden tan skin. His big biceps and forearms inked in an array of black and colored tattoos that the artist in her longed to evaluate with both her eyes and fingers. He was Sidd's polar opposite in almost every way. Maybe that's why she'd been so drawn to him. That and he was eloquent with his words…and tall and cut like an athlete and hung like a—

"No! Stop," she said aloud even as she looked out the window to find him. She inhaled a sharp breath and turned away, looking over at her easel that sat in the corner. She'd been hanging out with Dallie, Lily, and her mom the past week and a half. They'd been shopping, gone into town several times, made dinner together, played games, strung peas, and just enjoyed their un-rushed time together. They'd visited her grandparents yesterday, and Savannah had tried to call Kelsey but she hadn't answered, only texted her that she was "Fine" and they would "Talk later".

She walked to her nightstand and picked up her phone to call her again. When Kels didn't answer, Vanna huffed, shoving her phone into her back jeans pocket, and grabbed her canvas, easel, and paint kit. Today was a great day for painting. It had been a while since she'd done any, and she felt the incessant itch stir in her fingers.

Yup, I'm painting today. Savannah walked gingerly downstairs with her awkward load, heading towards the best morning painting spot and pulled a chair away from the breakfast table. She set her easel in the corner of the bay window and set her kit down on the table. She grabbed her earbuds out of her purse that sat in the living room on the coffee table. She opened the curtains, angling her easel to catch just the right amount of light, then she chose a relaxing, classical music station on her Pandora and began to immerse herself in the unfinished landscape before her as time stood still.

~

"*T*hat's a good boy, Hollis," Austin cooed to the fifteen-year-old gelding he was training today. Hollis was a rescue an old man had brought over from Lubbock. He would be headed to a children's therapy camp once they'd finished with him. Dallie had already gotten her magical mitts on the sensitive horse earlier that morning. He'd been the victim of abuse and neglect, and Wyatt had wanted Dallie to "read him" before they agreed to donate him to the popular children's camp that Wyatt and Dallie had opened three years prior.

Austin had believed in horse whispering once he'd seen what his own brother could do, but Dallie was a true miracle worker. It was as if she could actually talk to them and hear what they were "saying". He'd heard talk of Dr. Dallas Kinsen-Callahan for years before he'd had the pleasure of meeting the beautiful blonde-haired, blue-eyed "Dr. Dolittle of horses". The minute she touched the horses, she knew what was ailing them. It was the damndest thing Austin had ever seen. He remembered meeting the stunning vet that day a month ago.

"She's amazing, right?" Wyatt had asked him after Dallie'd "read" a mare who'd just been brought in.

"Fuckin' A, brother. She's the real deal alright." Austin had smiled and shaken his head in awe.

He'd been slightly disappointed to see her pregnant belly and wedding band, seeing as she was even more beautiful than Wyatt had led on, but Austin was still happy to finally meet the woman he'd heard so much about over the years.

His service in the Army had prevented him from coming to visit his brother here in Abundance, as his free time had been scarce and coming home for the holidays wasn't always a guarantee. Plus, Austin had literally gone from mission to mission over the years, not necessarily because he wanted to but that was just how it had panned out. He was glad to be here now—and glad to be working alongside his brother, the famous Doctor, and on Kinsen Ranch to boot. Austin had been excited to make the acquaintance of David Butler, another man he'd heard of for years, growing up in the horse world. To think this had all started over sixty years ago from a dream and inherited land. This family had a legacy—a solid, unshakable foundation. And Austin was now a part of it. He let that thought sink in as his mind drifted back to the gorgeous maple-headed beauty he'd crooned to last night. He was finally taking pride once again in his work. Proud to be a part of something big, bigger than himself. And he was no longer having to kill people to make a difference.

"Hey, big boy," came a feminine voice, and Austin turned to see Mrs. Kinsen walking up to the horse that Austin had pulled to a stop for a water break. Her soft, small hand came to rest on the gelding's throat latch and she looked up at Austin with a gorgeous smile. He saw right away where Savannah got her looks from.

He gave her an equally beaming smile and tipped his hat at her. "Howdy, ma'am. To what do I owe the pleasure?"

"Ah, I was just checkin' in on things, making my rounds." She winked. Austin remembered Wyatt telling him that Natalie Butler Kinsen had been a big name in the horse world herself, winning many competitions back in her teenage years. No wonder their children were equestrian gurus, the Kinsens knew their craft and knew it well. "I've been meaning to ask you, Austin, how are you getting on here on the ranch?"

"Oh, I'm enjoying my work here a great deal, Mrs. Kinsen. Thank you for asking."

She waved her hand. "Call me Natalie, please?"

"Why, yes ma'am."

"You have quite a voice. I must say, I didn't know you were a musician."

"I've played guitar now for a long time. I used to play gigs periodically with some friends of mine back in the day. Still do every now and again," Austin stated with pride.

"How fun." Natalie grinned, a mischievous look in her eyes that he couldn't place. "When was the last time you had a good home-cooked meal?"

The question took Austin off guard and he smirked. "Oh, wow. It's been some time, I would say. I'm a terrible cook, myself. I think even my dog would agree," he admitted with a shrug.

"Well, you've been on the ranch now for almost a month, and we haven't had you up to the house for dinner. Would you like to join us tonight?"

Boy, would *I?* he wanted to shout, but instead said, "Why, yes ma'am, I'd be honored."

Natalie grinned again, raising a dark eyebrow at him. "You're quite a charming, young man. I can see now why my daughter was immediately attracted to you."

Austin gulped and felt his cheeks flush. He was glad it was the heat of the day and he could use the sun as an excuse. He tried to recover, but Natalie had seen his eyes change and only looked down, giving him that mischievous grin of hers. Damn, she was beautiful, even if she was in her late fifties. Savannah favored her so much; her dark hair, light eyes, and sexy mouth all came from her mother. No wonder Jack Kinsen was so protective of his family. He had every right and reason to be—his ladies were drop dead gorgeous.

"Do you have any food allergies?" Natalie asked as her head came back up.

"Oh, no ma'am. I'll eat anything that doesn't eat me first."

Natalie laughed. "Well, come on up to the house around five. I'll teach you a few tricks in the kitchen, so that you won't be such a bad cook." She gently patted his bicep then pulled her hand away, smiling. She turned away, and Austin internally rejoiced, turning back to the horse. "Oh and Austin?" Natalie looked back over her shoulder.

"Yes ma'am?"

"You can use the *front* door this time." She gave a cute little giggle, and Austin chuckled.

"Yes ma'am, I certainly will." He beamed brightly and tipped his hat at her once more.

His luck was turning around; he was going to have dinner with the Kinsens. He had a second chance at a first impression.

But as he turned to lead the horse out of the corral, he caught Jack Kinsen's eye as Natalie walked past her husband. Jack's arms were crossed and his eyes had narrowed beneath his black Stetson. He wasn't happy.

~

*M*organ Butler looked over at his unwelcome visitor, Maximillian McClintock, and scowled.

"No, I'm sorry. I've explained to you that my plot, Terra Viridis is not for sale."

"Mr. Butler, I don't think you quite understand—"

"No, it's you, Mr. McClintock, who doesn't understand." Morgan cut him off.

He'd be damned if this man continued to bully him about the piece of property he'd purchased specifically for community development and green living. He knew Max McClintock and he knew of his intentions. If the notorious "land shark" thought for one moment that he was gonna bribe Morgan into bull-dozing the 120 acres of land he'd purchased last year and allowing McClintock to turn it into a big strip mall or some other commercial infrastructure, he had another thing coming. The town didn't want that and they didn't want *him* for their mayor. The old man was a business tycoon out of New Mexico and he'd gotten lucky in the world of commercial real estate when he'd begun building large strip malls and selling them for twice what he'd built them for. He'd made a fortune overnight, turning a small town into a big city within a short amount of time... and under sketchy building permits at that. Yeah, Morgan knew Max. He knew that the man was a crook and a swindler. And he didn't want anything to do with him.

Abundance wasn't Prospect, New Mexico, and it didn't want to be like it. Abundance was a community of founding and new families that enjoyed still having that small-town feel. There were no malls, no theaters, no shopping strip malls and no mixed-use developments. There were hardly any subdivisions even and the people of Abundance liked it that way.

Morgan's idea for Terra Viridis was a wholly eco-friendly, community-supported idea. He'd even had to speak about it six months ago at a town council meeting to get the approval needed, but it was something he was passionate about. Terra Viridis encouraged sustainable living with solar panels for power, all eco-friendly building materials and lights, tankless water heaters and energy efficient appliances. It was the wave of the future, and the entire town had been behind it when he'd pitched the plan to launch the initiative. It would be three divided subdivisions amassing 400 units, with a mix of housing types from townhomes to double-family occupancy homes. It respected the principles of new urbanism and would have biking and walking trails, a centralized park, and eventually a ten-acre organic farm with a water conservation irrigation system that the community would maintain and locals would be able to grow and sell the produce within the entire community. A man like Max McClintock couldn't possibly understand or respect that concept and could furthermore care less because it wasn't quite as profitable as turning the land into yet another business-aimed venture.

"Morgan, don't you dare underestimate my reach, son."

"And don't you underestimate *mine!*" Morgan was yelling now, but he didn't care. He'd had it. This was the second time this man had come here to harass him and it was high time he learned that Morgan Butler wasn't one to be bullied, not even by a man like Max. He didn't intimidate him in the least. He was an old man with new money, and Morgan was a young man with old money. But money didn't mean shit to Morgan. Not when the integrity of his town was at stake.

"I think you need to reconsider your aim," Max stated, a little too calmly for Morgan's liking. "There's a lot at stake here." Max looked around the conference room. "You have a lovely office building. A lovely home. A lovely...girlfriend." He looked up and out the tinted conference window to Kelsey, who'd just come in from outside, her slender frame stopping in front of the reception desk.

Morgan scoffed. "Are you threatening me?"

He shouldn't have been surprised. After all, men like Max McClintock were dirty, taking what they wanted with force if necessary, but the audacity of his words still shook Morgan.

"I'm just sayin' that it would be quite unfortunate if something were to—"

"Don't you *dare* finish that statement, McClintock. Let me tell you something right here and now. If a war is what you want, then so be it." Morgan growled, unable to restrain his anger. "But you're barking up the wrong tree. You don't know who you're messing with. This isn't Prospect, sir. Abundance takes care of its own. You'd be wise to remember that. Now, once more, my land *isn't* for sale. Now get out of my office before I call the police!"

CHAPTER 7

The day had gone by achingly slow as Austin mentally prepared himself for his dinner with the family he worked for and the woman he'd missed like crazy the last week and a half.

Now, he was knocking on the front door, all clean and showered and clad in a pair of new dark denim jeans, a navy blue polo shirt, and his newest tan Resistol hat. He held a bouquet of white calla lilies in one hand and a bottle of Pinot Noir in the other. He took in a deep breath as footsteps approached and tried to wipe the nervousness from his face. He'd been to war, this should be a walk in the park!

"Austin, you're punctual," Natalie Kinsen said with a smile.

"Why, yes ma'am. I don't like to keep lovely ladies waitin'." He winked, getting a sultry laugh out of her.

"You are such a flirt, Mr. Montgomery."

"I aim to please, ma'am." He tipped his hat at his boss's wife, and she blushed.

Natalie Kinsen was a highly attractive woman. Even on in her years, her face and skin still glowed with a youthful beauty. Her shining blue eyes and dark hair with wisps of inescapable grey, her lean, curvy body and bright smile—again, he could see some much of her in Savannah.

"Please, do come in." She took the flowers and wine from him as she stepped aside and opened the door all the way to let him through. "These are gorgeous, how thoughtful."

He smiled then looked out into the large open living room. "You have a beautiful home, Mrs. K."

"Thank you. My husband gets *most* of the credit for it." She winked.

Austin took in the lovely stone fireplace, high ceilings, and wrought iron staircase before him. Natalie led him into an equally large kitchen with granite countertops and an island. She dug out a vase and attended to the flowers as Austin looked around, taking in the comfortable and homey feel of the big house. It was a perfect family home, roomy with leather and dark wood furniture, earthy colors and gorgeous paintings of landscapes. Pictures of the Kinsens and Butlers were everywhere. It reminded Austin a lot of his own childhood home. There was love here, and it made him smile.

"Well, I hope you like fried chicken," Natalie offered, tilting her head quizzically at him.

"Are you *kidding*? It's one of my all-time favorites! What a treat. I never get homemade fried chicken."

"Well, roll your sleeves up and dig in because today, I'm gonna teach you how to make it." She gave him a stunning smile, and Austin couldn't help but laugh at her enthusiasm.

Why Natalie Kinsen—of all people—had taken a sudden interest in his well-being was beyond his understanding, but as they washed their hands, got out the big pieces of juicy bone-in chicken marinating in buttermilk, prepared the different bowls for dunking, dredging and dipping, Austin found himself super glad she did. He was in even brighter spirits as they conversed, laughed, and she instructed him on the art of frying chicken. She taught him how long to cook it, how to know when the next piece needed to go in and at what temperature to make it crispy and done to perfection.

While the chicken was fried to a gorgeous golden brown in the deep cast iron skillet, they began preparing the sides to go with it: fresh green beans, coleslaw, and a squash casserole. By the time all the food was almost ready, Austin's belly rumbled hungrily, getting a laugh out of Natalie.

"You've worked up quite an appetite, I see."

"Yes ma'am. This chicken looks incredible." Austin admired their work as he gripped the last piece of chicken with the long tongs in his right hand.

"It does. You did a fantastic job."

"Well, thank you, Mrs. K. But I'll be honest." He sat the big, juicy thigh down on a plate lined with paper towels and turned. "I don't know if I'm gonna be able to remember all these steps or further-more, if mine could ever turn out as beautiful as this right here." He pursed his lips.

Natalie gave him a knowing grin. "Now, Austin, you had a great teacher...but if you need some more lessons, I guess you can come back, and we'll do it again."

With that, they both laughed heartily. Man, Savannah obviously got her sense of humor from her mother too. What a lucky S.O.B. Jack Kinsen was.

Speaking of Savannah, he thought. "So...where's Savannah?" Austin couldn't help the blush that spread across his cheeks, and Natalie's brow went up as she grinned at him. Again, with that mischievous, fox-like, sly grin of hers. What was she up to?

She propped her elbows on the counter as she said, "Why don't you go into the dining room and grab my big serving platter from the china cabinet for our chicken? It's on the bottom right side." She gave him a wink, and he, again, just gave her a funny smirk as he moved into the dining room she suddenly pointed out to him to do as she'd instructed.

He stopped dead in his tracks as he entered the door frame. Savannah sat there, her back to him, gazing into a canvas rich with color, paint brush in her hand. How had she not heard them in the kitchen? Or perhaps she had heard them and was still ignoring him. Either way, he couldn't stop his feet from moving forward towards the entrancing painting of a sunset landscape with dark silhouettes of horses with riders on green rolling hills. He came to stand directly behind her, taking the realistic looking artwork fully in. It was breath-taking. And Savannah had painted it? Wow! Did her talents ever end?

"It's gorgeous," he stated loudly, in surprise.

Savannah gasped as if he'd materialized out of thin air and turned her head sharply to look up at her intruder. Her mouth opened into a shocked O. She sat silent like that for a few moments as he took in the beauty of her stunned face. She then seemed to come to and pulled an earbud from her right ear.

"What…" she began. "What are you doing here?"

"You painted that?" Austin pointed to the painting, and Savannah finally turned her chest back to her work, looking it over.

"Well, it's not finished. It needs—" She sounded unsure of herself.

"Savannah, it's amazing. It looks like a…like a picture!" Austin couldn't contain his astonishment, his awe at how incredible her talent was. "It should be in a gallery somewhere."

"That's what we keep telling her too," came a gruff, deep voice.

Austin turned to see his boss, eyes unreadable, approaching from the door frame. He took an instinctive step towards Jack and away from Savannah, distancing himself from the man's daughter.

"Welcome to my home, Austin." Jack shook his outstretched hand as Austin came closer.

"Thank you, sir. You're truly surrounded by beauty." Austin said the double entendre before thinking, attempting to keep his eyes fixed even as Jack's narrowed suspiciously. His grip tightened on Austin's before he released his hand.

Jack's eyes changed as he looked back over to Savannah. "Darlin', that's incredible." He moved up behind his daughter and took her shoulders in his big hands. Jack's large frame hid Savannah from Austin's view, but he could still hear the doubt in her voice.

"I don't know, Daddy. I've worked on it all day. I just—"

The basement door opened then and Austin heard scuffling and moved out into the living room to see who was coming in. Jackson popped out of the door and grinned as he saw Austin. "Well, look what the cat drug in! Sup, Mad Max?" Jackson greeted him and shook his hand, smacking his arm as he laughed, the tension from days ago seemingly gone. Mad Max was one of several nicknames Wyatt had given Austin long ago when he'd started riding motorcycles. Jackson had picked it up just recently.

"This your crib, huh, J.D.?"

Jackson nodded. "Home sweet home." He opened his arms in a showcasing gesture.

"Now, I know why you're not eager to get a place of your own."

Jackson winked and pointed an index finger at him. "You got it, Aus." He patted his back as he moved away into the kitchen. "Damn, Momma. It smells like Heaven in here. I'm freakin' starving."

"Language, young man," Jack called back as he shook his head and moved out of the dining room towards the kitchen. Austin quickly moved through the other door frame, back into the dining room to see Savannah.

She had turned away from her easel and was pulling the other earbud from her ear. When she caught sight of him, she froze. She looked utterly exquisite, as always. Her shiny, thick, maple-colored hair cascaded down her back in wavy curls, her eyelids were covered in brown and pink hues, showcasing her stunning green eyes. She chewed her plump bottom lip with her teeth as her eyes fell down his body, and it was all he could do not to pull her slender frame against him and consume those pouty rosebuds with his own hungry lips; he wanted to lick the sweetness right off of them. His eyes fell down over her pink and white V-neck cotton dress, a vintage Victorian pastoral pattern. Her arms were bare, her olive-toned skin radiant in the sunlight that streamed in through the windows, and Austin gulped at the sheer beauty staring back at him. He'd never wanted anything more in his life than to scoop her up and make her his all over again. She completely overwhelmed his senses, and he found time stood still when he was in her presence.

She finally looked down, gulping. "I, uh…"

"You look gorgeous, Savvy," the words were out of his mouth so quickly that he didn't have time to consider how much she'd scoffed at that name when he'd last called her it. She didn't like it, but he didn't care, it suited her, and he couldn't stop calling her that. It was his name for her; she was his sweet, sexy, Savvy. But instead of being angry, she seemed even more ruffled as she blushed. "I've missed you," he whispered as he came closer, wanting to touch her. But he stopped when he was within inches of her, afraid that if he didn't, he'd kiss her breathless, right there in front of her family, in front of her belligerent father who despised him with a passion. He watched her eyes as they stared back into his. God, she was the most gorgeous thing he'd ever looked at in his life, her sparkling Caribbean blue-green eyes burning into his soul, fueling him with a desire he'd never felt before.

"Momma needs that platter," Jax said as he swooped in and opened the china cabinet, digging for the dish Natalie wanted.

"Shit," Austin mumbled, embarrassed that he'd gotten so side-tracked and left Mrs. K waiting on him. "I'm sorry."

"No worries." Jax winked as he turned, pulling the large silver platter to his chest.

Savannah seemed to regain some of her composure then. "I—I need to see if Momma needs some help." Her beautiful cheeks turned crimson, and Austin grinned at her and gestured for her to go in front of him.

He followed her as she moved slowly towards the door frame. His eyes fell down her back to her plump bottom and back up. He longed to bury his nose into her dark hair and inhale her sweet, floral scent, to let his lips nibble at the crest of her shoulders and back—bare where the dress didn't touch—to move his hands up her enticing body and cup her breasts in his palms, make her moan his name as she had so many times almost two weeks ago.

Austin attempted to still his thoughts as they moved from the dining room back into the kitchen where Natalie began passing dishes off to her family members.

"Austin and I made that gorgeous chicken," Mrs. K bragged as she moved the chicken pieces to the serving tray and looked up at him, smiling.

"Hopefully it's up to par," Austin added and picked up the large bowl of coleslaw from the countertop in front of him.

"You're our guest, Austin. Let the kids set the table," Natalie scolded.

"Nonsense, Mrs. K. I'd be remiss to forget my manners. My momma would have my head." He just gave her a wink as he turned, not looking where he was going, to move back to the dining room, running headlong into a turning Savannah. He had just enough time to raise his arms over his head with the big bowl as she crashed right into his chest, her head hitting his collarbone and her hands gripping his back. She gave a surprised, "Oof," as he attempted not to dowse them in coleslaw and his breath whooshed out of his chest.

"I got it," Jax cried as he quickly took the bowl from Austin's extended hands.

Austin's arms instinctively went around Savannah, and she looked up at him in horror. He couldn't tell if she were more embarrassed by being so clumsy and colliding with him or by the hard-on now digging into her lower belly. He swallowed hard as he tried to regain his composure and his breath. "Are you alright?" he finally asked.

She simply nodded, her hands moving off him, scorching his skin in liquid fire.

"Jeez, Vanna," Jax laughed as he looked her over. "Still as spacey as ever."

Vanna blushed and moved off to grab silverware from a drawer as Austin watched her from the corner of his eye, her face beet-red.

Natalie handed Jack the heaping platter of chicken—Man, they'd made a lot of it. And Nat began to pull the casserole from the oven.

"Need me to grab that, Mrs. K?" Austin asked as she straightened and set it on the stovetop.

"You're a doll. Thank you." She nodded and let him take the mitts and lift the casserole. He made sure to look where he was going this time and cautiously moved into the dining room, leaning in to set the casserole down on a placemat someone had placed there.

"Excuse me," came a hushed voice as Vanna's hand softly touched his shoulder and she reached in to place a large spoon into the casserole, avoiding his eyes.

Once again, her touch scorched his skin and he internally groaned. *Damn, this is fuckin' torture.*

Savannah moved to sit across from where he was, probably purposing getting as far away from him as she could. But Mrs. K's subtle match-making schemes suddenly came to light as she came through the door and said, "Austin, honey, why don't you sit over there next to Vanna? Jax, you sit next to me, baby boy." Natalie kissed her taller son's cheek as he beamed sweetly down at her and hugged her to his side. Austin nodded and rounded the table to do as she'd suggested, both eager and anxious to be so close to Savannah once more.

Austin cleared his throat as he pulled the chair next to Savannah out and slid into it. He pulled his chair up to the table, glancing at a nervous Vanna out of the corner of his eye.

The tension in the room mounted ever so slightly as Jack came in and took his place at the head of the table. All was quiet as he looked around with scrutinous eyes; the authoritative demeanor of King Arthur in the midst of his court. His no-nonsense green eyes hit Austin's, and Austin held his stare for a moment before Jack's gaze moved to his son.

"Jax, say grace?"

"Yes, sir," Jackson replied and somberly began a solemn prayer of thanksgiving to their Lord and Savior.

Once the blessing was said, the atmosphere became more jovial as the food was passed around. When everyone had their fair share, Austin dug into his chicken thigh and moaned aloud.

"Man, Mrs. K, we did a fantastic job on this chicken! It's delicious."

"I mean," Jack agreed, biting into a chicken breast, and nodded his head to the chefs, who sat adjacent to one another.

Austin laughed back at his boss, "Perhaps, I can add more skills to my resume now." He joked.

"Don't push it, Montgomery. We all know you had a great mentor." Jack smirked, getting a laugh out of his wife. "Don't be taking *all* the credit."

Austin was taken aback. Had his serious-as-hell boss actually just joshed with him? No way!

Savannah seemed to find her voice then. "Momma, I'm sorry I didn't help out with dinner." She sounded so forlorn that Austin looked over at her, his brows drawn at her distress.

"Oh, hon, don't even worry about it. I knew you were painting today. That's why I asked Austin here to help out." Natalie winked over at Austin, who gave her a big grin.

The table grew loud as the laughter continued, and everyone began recanting the events of their days. Austin found peace with this remarkable family he'd come to work for as he listened intently to them and their easy conversation.

"So, how long have you been painting, Savvy?" he heard himself asking when there was a short lull in the conversation.

Austin noticed how bright red Savannah's cheeks were once again, and she looked over at her family bashfully before turning her head to look at him. It was the first time he'd spoken directly to her during dinner, and he suddenly realized he'd just called her the name that she'd asked him not to...and in front of her father no less. *Dammit, Austin*, he thought to himself, *Way to go, asshole.*

"Uh, since—since I was little actually."

"That painting up there is hers." Jack pointed to the wall behind him, and Austin turned to look at it.

"Holy crap, Savannah," Austin murmured as he stood to take it in. It was a beautiful replica of the three-story home they were in with a bay quarter horse grazing out front at sunset—She sure loved her sunsets—but it was the absolute elegance and subtle brushstrokes that blended together seamlessly that had him reeling. Again, the utter skill of her hands and eyes bringing the painting to life was astonishing. "Please tell me that you don't just do this for fun?" His gaze fell on her surprised face, and she looked down, hiding behind a shy little giggle.

"I do."

"No. You're simply too talented. I don't believe that for one second. Tell me that you have your own art gallery in town or something?"

She shook her head.

"She's put a few pieces in that boutique on Main Street, but she won't sign them," Nat stated ruefully.

"What?" Austin balked as if Savannah had just confessed to murder. "Why on earth would you *not*?"

"She doesn't want anyone to know," Jax smirked.

"Savannah, this...well, it's simply incredible. You *have* to show-case your work for all to see."

"Not gonna happen," Jack stated, shaking his head.

"Why?" Austin's voice grew soft as he moved back to his chair and sat down. His hand fell to Vanna's and he stroked it softly as he looked deeply into her eyes. "You're amazing. Why not share your gift with the world?"

"She's like Cass, she doesn't like the spotlight," Jax said, breaking Austin from his reverie. He moved his hand from Savannah's then, all too aware of Jack Kinsen's eyes boring holes into him.

Seeming to know that she needed to steer the conversation in another direction, Natalie asked, "Speaking of Cassidy, where the heck has she been? I haven't seen hide nor hair of the girl in weeks. And you haven't even mentioned her. Is something going on?" Mrs.

K poked her son's bicep and he avoided her eyes, looking down as his hand moved to rub the back of his neck.

"Well, she—she's been busy with school and that externship she's doin'," Jax responded uncomfortably.

"Uh-huh," Nat said and crossed her arms over her chest. "You wanna shoot straight with your mother or am I gonna have to call Bella to find out?"

"It's nothin', Mom, I just—We've both been busy lately. She's been waiting to hear back from her college applications and I know...I know I need to go see her. I'll call her tonight and take her out somewhere romantic tomorrow. Will that make you happy?" Jax offered with a crooked grin.

"Jackson David, you're my only son. Don't be goin' and lettin' the Kinsen charm die like that. I raised you better," Jack said with raised eyebrows, making Austin laugh.

"You need some pointers, Casanova?" Austin offered and pointed at Jax.

"Ha! He doesn't need *any* pointers. He was taught well by his two big sisters." Savannah crossed her arms over her chest and scowled over at her little brother, clearly disappointed that he wasn't wooing his girlfriend like he should be.

Come to think of it, Jax hadn't mentioned his girlfriend but once or twice, which made Austin wonder just what was going on. Was he bashful about it? After all, Austin hadn't hung out with Jax much. Or was it just mere coincidence? Were he and his girl fighting and he didn't want his family to know? Austin would get it out of him.

Either way, his family didn't look real happy with Jax on the matter as they all continued to assess him with their wandering gazes. Austin decided to rescue his boy. "Well, anyone up for dessert? I'm sure Mrs. K and I here are ready to move on to the next stage in our culinary delights." He winked over at Natalie, who beamed at him then.

Score! *You owe me one, kid.* Austin winked over at Jax before moving to stand.

"Dishes are on me and Jackson," Savannah said as she took the dirty plate Austin lifted.

Austin tipped his hat at her, suddenly realizing he'd left it on at dinner. *Sonovabitch.* His eyes looked over at Jack, who smirked as if to say, "*Idiot*," rolled his eyes, shook his head and stood. *Great second impression, Austin.* His mother would have smacked him on the head after throwing his hat onto the floor.

"Austin?" Savannah asked, her gorgeous blue-green eyes looking into his. He melted for the three-thousandth time that night.

"Sorry." He shook his head and smiled. "Food coma. What were you sayin', darlin?" His hand moved to cup her bare arm and he stroked her there tenderly with just his thumb. He heard her sharp intake of breath and felt his body tingle, his sex growing hard as it seemed to do as of late in her presence.

"Uh, I, uh, I said…" She blinked a few times, trying to regain her composure, which only fueled his intense desire for her. He grinned into her tortured face, his stroking growing lighter, more sensual. He could hear her choppy breathing and the internal battle going off within her. He could sense her arousal and almost smell it; his salivary glands going into overdrive. Fuck, he wanted her so badly. His mouth was literally watering for her. To taste her lips, her sex, her lust for him.

She seemed to sense it too as she froze and began to tremble under his gaze and his touch. "Thank you for helping make dinner," she squeaked out. And he smiled, satisfied that she was practical putty in his palms. He wanted to have her beneath him, begging, writhing, moaning and falling apart to him as she had in the hayloft.

God, he needed to get her out of this house before he grabbed her up, laid her atop the table, shoved her panties aside, and thrust all nine inches of his raging boner into her.

"Any time, *lover*," he whispered into her ear as he leaned in so that only she could hear him, although now they were suddenly alone in the dining room. She gasped as his hand moved to encircle her waist and he pulled her hip softly into his erection, moaning as the outline of it brushed her thigh. "Fuck, angel, I can't wait to be inside you again." His nose brushed her jawline and she whimpered, her fist tightening at her side. His cock leapt in his jeans and he growled. "I swear to God, Savvy, if you make that noise again, your father will bear witness as I plaster you to that wall right there and slake every *ounce* of my overwhelming hunger for you."

Savannah seemed to come to then as if she'd been in a trance. She gaped up at him and took a step back, gulping as she closed her mouth. Austin arched his brows in all seriousness, promise echoing in his eyes. She looked around, frightfully, and smoothed her dress before her eyes fell down to the erection she'd brought on. She couldn't dare hide the surprise that hit her face and if his cock wasn't so swelled to bursting, Austin might have laughed.

Instead, he took in a deep breath and gave himself a few moments after Savannah walked out of the room to let his hard-on wane, trying to imagine everything he could to get it down: puppies, cold weather, vomit—anything but Savannah's sweet, sexy naked body on his. It took time, but finally he was able to adjust himself and walk out of the room, grabbing some food bowls left behind and carrying them to the sink. He avoided Savannah's gaze as Jax splashed and joked with her as they loaded the dishwasher. He moved to head outside to the back porch, where Jack and Natalie sat in the rocking chairs. The same venue where he'd sung his heart out to the woman who was slowly driving him mad in every wonderful way possible.

~

Savannah smiled over at Austin, whose sexy amber eyes burned straight through her. "Bullshit," she called back. That devilish grin of his might just end up being her undoing, she decided once more.

Following dinner and watching the sun set out on the back porch next to him in a rocking chair, they all came inside, made a pot of coffee, had some cookies her mother had made earlier that day, and proceeded back into the dining room to play one of their favorite family card games. It had been her mother's idea—no surprise there. Her mother had been the one to invite Austin to dinner that night and the one to ask him to help her cook. How on earth Savannah hadn't known he was there before he'd happened upon her in the dining room was still a mystery to her. When Savannah was painting, it was as if nothing else existed and she were in another world, where her imagination took her away. It didn't matter though, it'd still been embarrassing and his surprise and words had completely taken her off-guard. The way he looked at her made her insides quake. As if he knew exactly what he was doing to her poor attention-starved body. And he did. He had to. Didn't he? *Of course he does!* Her pissed-off brain retorted indignantly. *He's playing you. Stay on your toes.* But her womanhood wasn't listening. It was swooning, off in some corner, jumping for joy. *Stupid cunt.* This internal battle of hers was taxing to say the least, especially when the object of her lust licked his full lips at her like that, like she was some delicious treat he couldn't wait to indulge in.

Her breath took even as she arched her brow, trying not to let him see how much he affected her.

"Well, only one way to find out," he said and flipped the discarded cards over, indeed revealing the two sixes he'd claimed to have. Savannah huffed and smacked her hand to her head.

"Man...that's twice in a row, sis," Jax stated and laughed, scooting the card pile over to Vanna to pick up.

"*Someone* is skilled in the art of deception," her dad said, giving Austin a look that if looks could kill...

"Now, darling," her mother scolded. "Austin's only playing the game as it's meant to be played." She winked over at Austin, who gave her a panty-dropping grin.

If Savannah didn't know any better, she'd think he'd gotten to her mother now too. This man was on a roll.

Her dad coughed into his fist with a grumbled, "Bullshit," of his own, getting a laugh out of Savannah and Jackson.

"Well, I never was really good at this game anyway," Vanna offered.

"That's because you're too distracted," Austin smirked.

"Don't flatter yourself, Montgomery. Not *all* of us are deceived by your bribery. Some of us *know* you're nothing but a bullshitter," her dad stated.

The tension was rising in the room, and Vanna gulped as she watched her dad's eyes narrow at Austin. Austin didn't seem to be the least bit deterred though. There weren't many men who Jack Kinsen couldn't intimidate, but it seemed Austin Montgomery might be one of them. Savannah didn't know if that made Austin incredibly brave or incredibly stupid.

"Alright, it's my turn," Savannah's mom said, pulling the attention from the men to her.

Savannah looked over at her beautiful mother, the one who'd orchestrated all this, and wondered what she'd been thinking. After all, it was apparently no surprise that Vanna's father disliked Austin immensely. Obviously, Austin was cocky, arrogant, and a bit on the reckless side compared to her father, but he wasn't a criminal or anything...was he?

Vanna remembered back to her brother saying something about the Army and realized how little she knew of the man seated across from her. She felt guilt tear at her. She'd spent the night with a man whom she knew practically nothing more about than the fact that he was A.) excellent in bed and B.) wanted to get her there once more, apparently. She also knew that he was Wyatt's brother, former military, and currently employed by her father, who seemed to despise him for more reasons than just the fact that he'd slept with Savannah. She *needed* to know why.

"Vanna...Earth to Miss Space Cadet." Jax waved his hand in front of her face. "Your turn." He laughed and elbowed her as she blushed.

"Three fives," she huffed, exasperated, and planted her cards face down on the table.

"Bullshit," Austin stated, far too confidently, and Vanna picked her cards back up again, feeling like a blasted idiot. He laughed, pleased with himself, and she shot him a go-to-Hell look, of which his brow cocked up again. God, he was sexy...even if she knew nothing more about him than that. He was certainly nice to look at.

When the game was over, Austin winning for the third time in a row, Jax took up the cards and Savannah's mom feigned a yawn, winking over at her. "Mmm, it's getting late, Jack. Let's head on up to bed, don't ya think?"

Her dad balked, looking over at her mom as if she'd lost her mind then he glanced at his watch and sighed heavily before he shrugged.

"I'll take care of the mugs," Savannah offered and stood along with her parents. Her father leaned in to kiss her cheek and she smiled up at him. "Love you, Daddy."

"G'night, baby doll. Get some rest. I love you." He gave her a big bear hug and turned to Austin, who'd ambled over next to Savannah by then, and shook his hand, giving him a tight smile. "Austin."

"Thank you for a wonderful dinner, Mr. and Mrs. Kinsen. I enjoyed it." Austin nodded, seeming genuine, although what did Savannah know?

"It was fun. Thank you for helping with dinner. I hope I was a good teacher," her mom said as Austin hugged her.

"The best. We'll tackle something more difficult next time." He gave her a big grin and a wink, and she giggled. Savannah couldn't help but laugh even as she saw her father's eyes roll and he turned to leave the room.

"Goodnight, sweetheart." Her mom pulled her into her then for a tight hug. "You're welcome," she whispered into her ear before kissing her cheek.

Savannah gave her a sly grin and watched her walk out of the dining room. She then slugged her little brother's shoulder lightly after he hugged her and bid him a goodnight as well.

When she heard the basement door shut and her parent's foot-falls on the wooden steps, she turned to Austin. "Would you like more coffee?"

"Sure. 9:30 is early for me. I don't head to bed before midnight usually."

"Me either," she admitted and felt her cheeks flush as she turned to head to the kitchen, their coffee mugs in hand, feeling his eyes roving her body once more.

"Hazelnut creamer, right?" he asked as he opened the fridge while she poured more coffee into their mugs.

"Yes, please?" She turned. "Wait. You remembered?"

"Of course. I have an eye for details. Although, not quite like *you* do. I had no idea you were an artist."

"And I had no idea you were in the Army," she blurted out just as he sat the creamer down on the counter. His eyes changed then, looking sorrowful as he froze before her.

His face paled as he looked into her eyes, but soon he was giving her a weak smile and a terse nod, answering her with, "Corporal Austin Montgomery, at your service, ma'am." He saluted. She gulped and stilled for a moment, surprise seizing her.

She was all too aware of her shaky hands as she poured the creamer into their mugs, remembering that he too took creamer in his coffee. She handed him his mug and said, "Let's go out onto the porch."

He moved in front of her to open the French doors. She cursed, hearing the door chime on the house alarm system, and moved to turn it off before joining him to walk out onto the porch, choosing a rocking chair mid-way down. He sat down next to her.

He looked out over the dark pasture to the motion light that went off on the barn as one of the tabby cats scurried beneath it and grinned to himself.

She didn't think he would say anything until she surprisingly heard him clear his throat.

"I was in the Army for over ten years. I served first in the cavalry, then I became a combat engineer and served four tours in Iraq before making corporal and being sent to Afghanistan for two years as a team leader for an elite recon squad to gather intel. It's all highly classified, but needless to say, we were plunged into some pretty dangerous territory. On my last mission, there were seven of us in my unit, we arrived by parachuting into the desert in the middle of the night trying to stay under the radar."

He'd jumped from a helicopter into the pitch-black darkness? *Holy shit!* This guy was an adrenaline junkie for sure.

"We'd only been there a few days when we headed through one of the towns we'd been told was highly suspect for illegal military-grade weapons, so we were on high alert, watching our backs and each other's carefully. The place seemed abandoned, but I had a bad feeling as we split up and two of my team members and I headed down an alleyway. We heard a car alarm go off and a literal millisecond later, Jerome was vaporized right before my eyes. The heat and blast were so intense that I was blown several feet into the air."

By now, Savannah was staring at Austin in awe, her mouth covered with her free hand.

"I thought my leg had been blown off. I was down for only a few minutes before my team came to my aid. It wasn't good. I had so much shrapnel embedded into my knee that I ended up losing it and having to have a replacement." Austin took a breath and looked over at her then, his face solemn. How had she missed the scar on his leg? Which leg was it? Had she been *that* drunk that she would miss something so major? Or had he hidden it from her purposefully? Even when she'd gone down on him she hadn't been aware of a scar. But then again, she hadn't really been looking at his knee. Now that she thought of it, he did favor his right leg a bit...God, she felt so shallow!

"Even after the replacement set up staph infection and I was at risk of losing my entire leg, all I could think about was Jerome. He wasn't just my team member. He was my best friend." Austin sighed again and looked away, back out at the barn. "We'd gone through training camp together, served in each unit together. We made one hell of a team." He grew quiet then and Savannah thought he'd finished speaking. She said nothing, just tried to absorb his mindset, his story, his tragedy.

She was grateful she'd never seen war, not even been around when all the horrible things had happened to her mother and sister. The worst thing that she could ever remember happening in her life was when Dallie was taken that day some seventeen years prior. Cole had gone to jail for it and remained apologetic to the whole family about his wrong-doing, but that hadn't taken the stigma completely away. It had been traumatic for the thirteen-year-old girl Savannah had been at the time, for she'd had to run to the barn with her squalling baby brother, her heart pounding, praying the whole way there, seeking out a surprised Wyatt and telling him to call the police as she cried hysterically. She'd even been put in therapy for a time in the weeks that followed as nightmares plagued her. Not many people had known how badly it had affected Savannah, but she'd practically forgotten all about it in her older years. Hell, she must not have been too horribly altered by it, she'd left a bar with a total stranger and ended up in bed with him!

"I wasn't able to fulfill my field duties, so I went into teaching, but things just weren't the same without Jerome, and I lost my motivation. I received a purple heart last year and retired from the Army three months ago. Wyatt persuaded me to try my hand at training horses, so here I am."

"It's your left knee, right?" she asked. He simply nodded, looking embarrassed. "Oh, Austin. I'm so very sorry that happened to you."

"It's been a difficult transition, to say the least." He gave a humorless laugh.

"I'm sure." Vanna shook her head, in empathy. "Does your knee still bother you?" she blurted out.

He nodded. "Sometimes, if I ride too long or stay in one spot for extended periods of time. I'm just glad to be alive, it could've been much worse."

Savannah gave him a sad smile, and he gave her an equally weak one back, looking back out into the darkened fields for a time.

"So, you've been a brilliant artist your whole life, huh?" he asked, nonchalantly.

She gave a short laugh. "My family calls me a prodigy."

"I'd say that's a fair assessment." His smirk was back, the serious Austin gone now. "Genius, rocket scientist, artist... Am I missing anything?"

"Doctor," she mumbled and blushed deeply when his head whipped back around to look at her.

"No fuckin' way? You're a doctor *too*? Damn girl, you're the whole enchilada!"

She wouldn't mention she was also a master violinist and composer, for Savannah simply wasn't a braggart. She'd tell him...in her own good time.

"No wonder your father hates me." Austin scoffed.

"Why *does* my father hate you?"

"You tell me, darlin'. He's *your* father after all."

Savannah just shrugged. He hadn't told her, so it was anyone's guess. The tattoos, the bike, the cocky, indifferent attitude... She didn't know for sure.

"I have a feeling he'd hate any man you're with."

"Why do you say that?" she asked, not liking his condescending tone.

"You're his baby girl, Savvy. I bet he hated Sidd too."

She shrugged again. It was true, but her father didn't like Austin *before* they'd slept together, so his estimation was wrong. If Austin were more like her father, she had a feeling they wouldn't even be having this conversation. Austin was careless, after all, and her father was the epitome of responsible and Jack Kinsen was also a gentleman, whereas Austin was a downright scoundrel in his eyes. And Savannah suddenly remembered *why* he was.

"He probably doesn't like the company you keep," she quipped, her tone smart, and he picked up on it, looking her over.

"C'mon now, Savvy, that was before I met you. Don't be jealous." He sipped at his coffee and gave her that Cheshire cat grin of his.

"Ha! So, you *don't* make a point of taking different women home from the bar when the opportunity serves you?" She looked down at her hands to keep her gaze from his.

"In case you ain't figured it out yet, baby girl, I haven't so much as glanced at another woman since I've been with you."

She gulped as she looked up into his piercing amber eyes. They seemed so deep and sincere that she had a hard time concentrating. What was she saying again? Oh yeah, the other woman.

"It still doesn't change the fact that you brought *me* back to the same spot where you bedded another woman just a week prior to being with me." There. She'd said it.

He pursed his lips and looked back out at the barn once more. "Savannah, did your father witness me fucking her?" Savannah balked at the word fucking...the mere thought of Austin with another woman made her blood boil. She shook her head. Her father hadn't said that—had he?

"Sweetheart, that's because it didn't happen."

Vanna glanced up sharply at him.

"That's right. I didn't fuck 'er." God, could he please stop saying that *blasted* word? "I was pretty drunk that night and neither of us should have been driving really, but the truth is that I didn't wanna take her back to my bungalow. I mean I didn't know the girl from Adam, so we ended up in the hayloft. She was equally as drunk as I was, and no sooner had I gotten my pants down and she'd put her lips around my cock, she was passed out cold on the damn floor. I was so annoyed that I didn't even finish myself off, I ended up falling asleep beside her and that was that."

As happy as that should make her, it didn't. He'd still taken a random stranger home to "fuck".

As if sensing her dismay, Austin brought her chin up with his thumb and index finger. "It was a mistake. It shouldn't have happened. I'm glad it didn't go any further to be honest." He smiled. "I wanted to take *you* back to my bungalow, but you didn't wanna go there, remember? The hayloft was the only other place I could think of, sweet angel. I would have taken you in the backseat of my Jeep as much as I wanted you, but I thought that would've been disrespectful."

Were all men as dumb as he was? *For God's sake!*

"Disrespectful?" Savannah tried to force the tears back. "So, taking me back to the place where you were planning to bone another stranger seemed like a *better* idea?" she scoffed.

"Now, darlin', don't be like that. I was only thinking with one of my heads. The other one was lacking proper blood flow." He chuckled lightly, seemingly unaware of the fury blossoming just beneath the surface of her skin.

Savannah gaped at him. "I guess that's just what happens when you're drunk, huh? Any old excuse will do for you men? Especially ones that pardon you for a being a total dickhead. Pun intended!"

Austin was full out laughing now, and Vanna's veins hummed in rage. Her slight scowl was transforming into a full out frown when he looked back at her with amused eyes.

"Aww, now, Savvy. I wasn't drunk the night you and I had sex." He reached out to take her hand, but she pulled it away as if he'd just scalded her. She gasped, and he looked over at her, startled.

"What?" she ground out.

"I wasn't dru—"

"I *heard* what you said...but how is that possible?"

"Baby, I only had two beers."

Surely, he was mistaken! Surely, she'd misheard him. Surely...

"Sav—"

"Don't call me Savvy...or...or baby...or darlin' or *any* of those words. Just—I want you to leave. Now!" She shot up from the rocking chair, feeling equal amounts nauseated and furious as she sought the railing to keep from falling, the emotion building within her like the pressure inside a volcano.

"Savannah?"

"No, Austin. You've worn out your welcome. Now, it's time for you to leave. Don't make me call for my father or my brother because you won't like what follows when I do." She turned, daring him to defy her, her entire body shaking in fury; she wanted to claw his eyeballs out.

He came forward gingerly, palms out to her, as if he were calming one of his horses—or facing a rabid animal. "Please?" The sincerity in his tone disarmed her, and she tried to calm her pounding heart. "Whatever I said I'm sorry. I wasn't trying to offend you. I was only trying to lighten the mood, I swear." His eyes held the same look they'd had when he'd told her the story of his injury in Afghanistan, and for a moment, she was taken off-guard. Perhaps she was simply overreacting, once again. Damn, she was doing that a lot lately.

"So, *I* was the one making a complete ass of myself that night, it wasn't the both of us, like I'd originally assumed?"

"No." Austin shook his head. "You didn't make an ass out of yourself."

"Didn't I? I mean I get myself good and hammered and end up going to bed with a man whom I'd known for mere hours. I'd say that counts for making a total ass out of oneself." She harrumphed.

"You were hurt. You needed—"

"Needed to what? To *fuck* my cares away? Is that what people do, Austin? Just relinquish their responsibilities and throw their moral code to the wind after they get their hearts broken? Because *I* don't do that. I am not that girl, dammit!"

"*What* girl, sweet angel?" His voice softened and he stepped closer, taking her hands in his and squeezing them lightly.

She could feel the panic rising in her throat once more, threatening to overtake her. "That girl." She started to snivel. "The one who has one-night stands! I don't do that. I'm not—"

"Shh," he crooned and pulled her into him, his hard frame comforting her as his arms encircled her. "I know that. I know it, baby. You're so much more than that. I know." His strong hands stroked her back, and she felt the moment that her anger turned to raw lust and hated herself for it.

"I'm not a tramp. I'm not a slut. I'm not a skanky blonde *bimbo* who tells other girls they are mousy and boring to make myself feel better about taking their men away from them," she sobbed into his shoulder, letting her angry emotions out.

"You're none of those things, Savannah. None. Do you hear me?" He pulled her head from his shoulder and took her face in his hands. His amber eyes burned into hers. "Baby, you aren't just a one-night stand. You could *never* have been. Can't you see that? One night with you, Savvy, would never be enough." He grinned easily, but his words stuck in her craw, the pain still as sharp as it had been that next morning.

"No? But you sure made me feel like one." She pulled his hands down off her face and stepped back from him. His face was ghastly, as if she'd just pulled his still-beating heart from his chest. But he'd hurt her, whether it had been intentional or not, it didn't matter. He'd *made* her his one-night stand. He'd shamed her. He'd made a fool out of her and set her up to be caught once more by her father, his boss, on the morning after his rendezvous with her. Intentional or not-it made no never mind.

Austin took a step toward her and stared hard into her eyes, his face serious once again. "You can't possibly know how sorry I am for how much that hurt you. Now, I can only apologize for the wrong I've done. But I won't apologize for that night because I'm not sorry. I'm *not* sorry for meeting you, I'm *not* sorry for bringing you back to that hayloft, and I'm *not* sorry for spending one of the best nights of my life with you, Savannah Grace Kinsen. So, take that to the bank, Doc. I'm done apologizing for one lifetime. The last two and half years, I haven't even lived! I lost all hope and self-worth in

Afghanistan…until the day I met you. And I'll be damned if I let another second go by regretting what it is that I'm about to do."

With that, he closed the distance between them, and Savannah watched helplessly as he pulled her back into his strong, solid arms. His head fell and his lips took hers, kissing her with an urgency that both aroused and frightened her. She literally melted, feeling like she was soaring on a fluffy cloud of desire as his taste, feel, and smell overwhelmed her senses. Suddenly, all her anger was spent and nothing else existed but this rugged renegade and his hunger for her. His tongue was eager yet languid as it expertly invaded every inch of her mouth as well as her inhibitions. She felt it unraveling her with each leisurely stroke over her own. It was as if they were back in the hayloft and she was falling into a sea of bliss with him all over again. She heard herself moan wantonly as his hand splayed across her back, and when he gently pulled back, every cell in her body tingled. She licked her lips, tasting his fiery flavor on them as she looked up into his smoldering eyes. They were dark with desire and his groan was equal parts animal and human.

"I'll let you sleep on *that*," Austin said, rubbing his nose softly against hers before he released her and turned, leaving her a quivering bundle of damp, wanting flesh. He grinned as he looked back over his shoulder. "See you around, Savvy." He arched an eyebrow in challenge.

CHAPTER 8

*J*ax sighed heavily as he heard the ringing of the phone in his ear. He was calling his girlfriend, Cassidy, his girlfriend of three years. The girl he'd adored for as long as he could remember. The girl he'd given his heart and virginity to. The one who was currently breaking the heart he'd given her so freely and pulling away from him as surely as the sun sets and the moon orbits. And there wasn't a damn thing he could do about it. For she was the one who'd slowly started becoming aloof. Not him. And that's what he couldn't tell his family. He could feel it— had *been* feeling it for some time. Her slipping away from him. It had started with their kisses, then their love-making and finally their time apart.

She hadn't said it, but she didn't need to. He could see the doubt in her mind, taste the hesitation on her tongue, and the last time they'd had sex, she'd been miles away. He'd pretended to finish, but his heart had been breaking too much to find any satisfaction in her intimate embrace. That had been almost a month ago.

Her sweet voice stated as the voicemail kicked on, "Hi, it's Cassidy. I'm busy at the moment, so leave me a message and I'll get back to you. Kisses."

He listened to the prompts, his heart ripping in two as he waited for the beep to tell him it was time to leave a message.

"Hey darlin', it's me." No need to say his name for she knew who 'me' was. "I was hoping I'd catch ya before your shift started. Listen, uh, I was wondering if you were free tomorrow. I'd really love to see you. I miss you so much, hummingbird." His voice cracked a little when he called her the nickname he'd given her when they were just kids because she always went around singing and humming all the time, for she'd not hummed much lately and he didn't really know the reason why. "Call me back. I love you, Cass." His voice dropped as he said those three little words he'd been saying for years now only starting to ponder their true meaning as of late. He ended the call and set his phone down on his nightstand as he fell onto his bed and looked up at the ceiling.

Could this really be the end for them? He didn't want to even think about it. Jackson David Kinsen and Cassidy Jane Boyd had been inseparable even as young children. Hell, they'd cried just when their parents had taken the other out of the room let alone to another house. A mere eighteen months was all that separated their ages. They'd played together as children, spent countless weekends together, almost every holiday. Had their first kiss when Cass was ten, their first French kiss when Cass was fifteen, and lost their virginity when Cass was sixteen. Everything had just clicked into place without a ton of effort on either of their parts. She was as constant as the air he breathed. She'd always been there to experience life's ups and downs with him. She was his heart, his other half, his soulmate. And he was somehow losing her.

He wasn't even sure when it had started to happen, but something had changed. The look in her eyes, the sway in her hips, her warmth towards him. It had slowly started to grow cold, her eyes hollow, her touch platonic. And he'd ignored it…for perhaps, he'd not wanted to acknowledge it in the beginning, give it a host to breed in. But day after day that passed, it started to become blaringly apparent that Cassidy wasn't happy with him. Was she no longer in love with him? Could people even fall out of love? He knew so many happy couples around him that the thought perplexed him. Could two people who were meant to be together somehow fall out of love with one another? *Impossible!* The only people who fell out of love were people who weren't in love in the first place…right?

Jackson knew he wasn't like other guys his age. Hell, he was twenty years old. He was supposed to be raising hell right about now. Drinking too much. Partying with friends. Having meaningless sex with tons of drop-dead gorgeous women. Being reckless and doing stupid shit that might land him a night in jail or wake up in the bed of a truck, buck naked and not remembering who and where he was… But Jax had known for a long time that he was an old soul trapped in a young man's body. His old man had been the first one to be surprised by his accountability and restraint. He'd even encouraged Jax to date other girls, ride a bucking bronco, and go away to college. Jax had done none of those things. And he'd only wanted one girl. The only girl who warmed his heart as much as she did his bed. A gorgeous petite strawberry blonde with lightly tanned skin, freckles, eyes that were the color of a Ponderosa pine tree in full bloom and breasts that were bigger than the rest of her.

He'd fallen in love with her slowly over time but knew it after he'd finally gotten the guts to kiss her that hot July night in the cab of his truck. It was their third official date and she'd been the one to coax him to do so. He remembered how stifling the air had been and how hard he was just looking over at her smooth thighs bare where her short shorts didn't cover.

"Well, are you gonna stare at your steering wheel all night long or are you gonna kiss me, Jax Kinsen?" she'd said, far more confident than he'd ever been.

And he had, with a bravery he'd suddenly unleashed. He'd grabbed her and laid one on her, releasing all the pent-up desire he'd felt for months of her flirting with him, looking at her sexy body clad in such revealing clothing, pursing her lips, and leaning her breasts down so he could get a look at that full cleavage of hers. He'd been literally mad with lust, had day-dreamed and night-dreamed and woke up with raging boners for her, and suddenly, her lips and tongue were his to command. He'd been drunk from the taste and touch and feel of her skin on his and he'd fought everything within him not to claim her that night, but she was so young. Fifteen. Far too young. He had to wait. Needed to wait. But that hadn't stopped his hands from grabbing the breasts that had teased him so, hungrily kissing the lips that had tormented him, pumped at her writhing hips as she'd moved to straddle him. He'd been like a ravenous animal before she'd finally pulled back to answer her cell phone, jerking him away from his fantasy only to see how close they'd been to having sex, for his hands were beneath her shirt, clasping her lacy bra, his jeans were undone and his shirt unbuttoned. He'd been shocked and amazed and…in love. In love with the idea that she was his. Or soon would be.

And the night he'd finally taken her. It had been amazing, in every sense of the word. He'd known the first time would be awkward, he'd been warned, he knew it would be silly and clumsy and over quickly. But their union had been anything but that. It had been sweet. It had been soul-rendering, it had been the most incredible thing he'd ever felt in his life. Claiming her for his, entering her, having her wet silky heat squeezing around him had been the most delicious and wonderful thing he'd ever felt. She'd been so eager, so giving, so completely his in that moment. And his heart had tumbled along with his body as she'd milked him into mind-blowing satisfaction of his entire being. Her hands and lips and moans had only driven him crazy with the need to drive hard and deep and validate his stake on her. She was his then. Fully and completely. And he was hers. His heart, his body and at that moment, his soul.

But that had been two years ago, and apparently something had changed for her that hadn't for him. Was it something he'd done? Something he'd said? Had he not done something he should've done? Had he not been as good to her as he'd known how to be? What was it?

As if reading his thoughts, the phone rang loudly beside him and he started then grabbed it up, seeing her name and number come over the screen.

His heart galloped in his chest as he swiped the answer button, both nervous and eager to talk to her. "Cass?"

"Hey, Jax." The tone with which she said his name annoyed him—so nonchalantly, like she hadn't screamed and whimpered it hundreds of times in the throes of passion. "What's up?"

He could feel his face fill with blood as a blast of anger shot through him. How could she act like it hadn't been two weeks since they'd last spoken? Dammit, she was his girlfriend.

"How are you?" *First and foremost*, he wanted to smart off, but held back.

"Fine." There was that fucking word again. She'd said it at their last conversation, and he knew she was anything but.

He took in a deep breath and counted to five. "Listen, I wanna see you. I was thinkin' that we could—"

"Yeah, I need to see you too," she cut him off. "I wanna talk about some things."

His heart froze. There it was. The admission. The promise of impending doom to come. He gulped as his heart sank. "Ok. Want me to—"

"I'll come there. Tomorrow. I'll be there by lunchtime."

"Alright," was all he could say as sorrow filled his core.

"See ya then. Bye, Jackson." It was the softest her voice had been in their last three phone conversations he'd had with her, and he felt as if his soul was being torn into a million pieces.

He didn't even have a chance to say goodbye before she hung the phone up.

He didn't sleep that night, he tossed and turned, heartbreak blurring his vision and eating into him as night turned into dawn and his alarm went off at 5:30 AM.

He groggily rose from the bedsheets, and robotically showered, dreading the conversation to come. He knew Cassidy was breaking up with him as sure as he knew anything in the world. She'd been too distant with him lately and now there was nothing he could do about it. He was too late, he'd dragged his feet too much, not been a good boyfriend. He was ashamed; he'd known better. But it had been easier to ignore the detachment in her eyes than to acknowledge the problem.

He'd gone about his usual routine, day in and day out, waiting for what he didn't know exactly. He'd been inattentive, unmindful of her needs, ignorant to the requirements of his relationship. But, in truth, he'd not been ignorant at all. Deep down, he knew what all this was about. And Cassidy would soon be putting words to the thoughts that had plagued him for some time now. Thoughts he'd suppressed because he believed that despite the differences between them that they could make it work.

He yawned, feeling as dog tired physically as he was mentally as he clomped up the stairs, waving to his dad in the weight room as he passed. He needed coffee before he did anything. He'd only recently discovered it, recently understood why his parents needed it on a daily basis. That brown liquid charged him especially on mornings like this.

He felt even more morose as he caught sight of his mother humming softly in the kitchen, cooking some scrambled eggs. He cleared his throat gently, so as not to startle her, and she turned and smiled at him only to frown as she took in his blood-shot eyes.

"Oh, baby, you look awful."

"Gee, thanks, Mom," he grumbled as he moved toward the coffee pot.

"Did you not sleep well?" she asked as her concerned face tilted up to look at him, grabbing his arm as she came closer.

"No, I didn't sleep for shit," Jax admitted and wouldn't divulge why.

His mother's frown deepened. "Well, why don't you just take the day off and try and sleep. I'll give you some melatonin or—"

He shook his head. She knew him better than that. He wasn't one for laziness or sleeping in. He was like his father. He was up at the butt crack of dawn and went to bed no later than ten, usually.

He gave his sweet mother a smile. A smile he couldn't make as big as he wanted to, for his heart wasn't in it, his heart was breaking at the moment.

She seemed to know something was amiss—as all mothers do when their children aren't well—as she closed the distance between them and pulled him in for a hug. Her lips softly hit his jawline and he closed his eyes, feeling like a kid again needing a boo-boo kissed by his momma. He held her close, inhaling her scent and drawing comfort from her.

"It's all gonna be ok, sweetie," she murmured as she rubbed his back.

Jackson towered over his mother by almost a foot and had for years now. He was as tall as his father but wasn't as broad as he was, although he was broader than most his friends. But no matter how much bigger he was than her, he would never stop needing her strength, her hugs.

"I promise you that whatever happens, life will go on," she stated solemnly as she raised up on her tiptoes to speak into his ear. "Remember, I was twenty-eight when I met your father, and that's when my life really and truly began."

He knew this. He knew the entire story, every gory detail of it, but his life had *already* begun. It had begun the day he'd fallen for Cassidy Boyd, and he was sure no woman—no matter how amazing she was—could fill that void, should Cass not be in it. She was the only woman he wanted. The only woman he needed. She *was* his life.

But Jackson didn't say all that, he only said, "Thanks, Momma," and kissed her on the cheek as he stepped out of her embrace and moved to the cabinet to retrieve his thermos.

The morning went by achingly slowly as he mindlessly did his chores: feeding, haying, watering, checking shoes, shoveling out stalls, and finally training. It was getting close to noon and his fears filled his mind as he led the filly he'd been halter-breaking into the pasture to graze with her mother.

He headed back into the barn, as much for the A/C as for anything else. He removed his hat from his head, swiped at the sweat accumulating on his brow and replaced it. He was moving towards his stallion Drogo's stall when he caught sight of her and his heart leapt up into his throat. How had he missed her car pulling in? He was sure he'd been watching for it, but then again, his mind wasn't entirely present. His nerves jangled and his stomach fell as he closed the distance between them and she turned to face him, her eyes red and swollen.

Why? Why was she doing this? If they were both upset about this break-up then why in hell was it even happening in the first place?

He tipped his hat to her and tried to grin, but he couldn't. "Cassidy. You look beautiful."

Despite her red face with no makeup on, the statement was true. She was clad in a pink cotton and lace dress with three-quarter length sleeves and her usual pair of brown leather cowboy boots. She was a cowboy's dream and always had been and his heart hurt at the sight of her.

"Jackson." Her head fell as she said his name and his stomach clenched. He awaited the blow, awaited the searing pain in his already splitting heart. "I—I don't know how to say this," she began. "I—"

"You're breaking up with me." It wasn't a question and her head shot up. As if she were shocked to hear him say it, although they both knew it to be true. How could he not know? "That's why you're here. That's what you wanted to talk about, right?" he asked, his steady tone giving nothing away.

She gulped and slowly nodded. *Fuck!* "I got an acceptance letter... from Emory University."

"Emory? All the way in Georgia?"

Again, she nodded. "It's one of the best nursing schools in the nation. I got a full ride and—"

"Cass, you can go to nursing school *anywhere*," he smarted off but was so numb at this moment in time, he couldn't feel beyond that.

"I know but—"

"That's almost a thousand miles away."

"I know, Jax. But I need to go."

There it was. The other piece of the puzzle he'd put together recently. She'd said it before on multiple occasions.

That was one of their biggest differences and probably the one that was most difficult to overcome. Her desire to go and his to stay. He was a home body. Always had been. Here in Abundance was where he belonged, on the ranch, doing what he loved.

"But that doesn't mean that we have to breakup, Cassidy," he was trying to convince himself as much as her, but she was shaking her head. "I can still come see you on occasion and you'll be home for holidays. It's only four years."

Four years. God, what a short and painstakingly *long* amount of time.

"I need to be free, Jackson." Tears fell from her cheeks and her lips quivered.

Free? If she hadn't been free then what did that make him? Her captor? He faltered, stepping back as that thought clenched his heart in a cold grip. Had he held her back in some way? Had he made her feel like a prisoner? What the hell?

His brows drew as anger hit him full force. *"Free?* Of me? Of the heavy chains of our relationship? Is that really how you feel, Cassidy?"

She only looked up at him, tears filling her hazel eyes, as his already breaking heart split open at the seams.

He scoffed. He couldn't believe this. It was like some horribly bad nightmare he was startling awake from. "Then by all means!" he haughtily remarked, crossing his arms over his chest. "Don't let me stop you from doing what you need to do. Since I'm such a heavy burden on you then go. Do whatever it is that you wanna do. Be free from me. Free to do as you please." He leaned in closer even as she began to sob and the sounds ripped his soul apart. "Fuck who you wanna fuck." After all, that's what she wanted right? Since he was the only man she'd been with thus far. Being free meant she wanted freedom to have other partners, other dates, other relationships, right? The mere thought made him want to hurl.

"Jax," she sobbed and reached out to him. He recoiled from her touch, for if she touched him, he too would crumble into a heap of tears. She gasped, surprised by his reaction and stepped closer to him even as she swiped at her tear-stricken face. "It's not like that. I just need space. I need to see what's out there beyond this tiny ass town."

"Yeah, that's the problem, isn't it, Cass? You've *always* wanted out. It's not ever been enough for you. *I've* not ever been enough for you." He swallowed down his pride even as it hurt to acknowledge, but he'd known it all along. She'd said it for years, dreamed of going away, seeing more of the world. And who was he to stop her? If that's what she wanted then he wouldn't stand in her way. Not any longer.

But she was shaking her head and sobbing again, moving closer, and he couldn't take that. He couldn't stand to be so near to her and not be able to hold her in his arms, bury his face into her hair, kiss her beautiful lips. He stepped back again and held his hands out, stopping her like she was one of his horses.

"No. It's over. You're right. We're obviously just too different. That's fine. Have a safe trip to Georgia."

With that, he turned on his heel and stalked away, not daring to look behind him.

~

Savannah held her breath. What had she just bore witness to? She watched her little brother walk away and exited Amadeus's stall to see Cassidy literally crumple to the ground in sobs. Her heart went out to the young girl, the sister of her best friend, her brother's now ex-girlfriend. They'd been together for as long as Savannah could remember, not officially but still. Now, Cassidy was in a heap, getting her dress dirty as she covered her sobbing face. Savannah moved towards her and gripped her shoulders. Cass's head snapped up and her sobs grew louder when she realized that Savannah wasn't who she'd wanted to comfort her, but instinctively her arms went around Vanna's neck and she buried her head into Vanna's hair.

"Oh, God, what have I done?" Cassidy murmured, her sobs stifled amid Vanna's thick hair.

Savannah soothed her even as they got looks from the fellow hands that Cassidy's sobs and Jax and Cass's breakup shouting had brought forth. Vanna motioned to them that everything was ok as she moved to escort Cassidy to the bathroom to get her some tissue.

She'd been down at the barn in hopes of running into Austin. After last night's confession and kiss had stirred her in many ways, she wanted to see him, let him flirt with her, give him another opportunity to— Hell, who was she kidding? She'd started painting after her morning workout and her mind kept drifting back to him, so she'd dressed and come down to the barn.

She sat Cass down on the bench in the locker room and ran to grab a roll of toilet paper. When she returned, Cass was hunched over, hands covering her face as her sobs continued. Vanna unrolled a good bit of tissue paper and handed it over to her, stroking Cassidy's hair.

"Emory, huh? That's quite an accomplishment, girl. You should feel honored."

"Well, right now, all I feel is like a raging bitch," Cass grated and took the tissues, blowing her red, running nose.

"It was the right thing to do, I guess," Vanna fished.

Cass shrugged. "I know he thinks there's someone else but I swear there isn't. It's just—"

"You don't have to explain yourself, Cassidy. You're eighteen years old. I was there. I know what you're feeling. I went away to college and I'm so glad that I did."

"Yeah, but you didn't have a boyfriend back home who wanted to turn you into a wife and a mother as soon as your college degree is given to you."

She had a point. No, Savannah hadn't even had a boyfriend until college. And God, that sounded like a damn nightmare when she put it that way. Savannah hadn't really even imagined herself in a white gown or with a bundle of joy in her arms. No, the call of a career and learning about the stars that she was fascinated by was far more appealing to her than being a stay at home mom had been. Although now, she was starting to like the idea of having a baby.

"He's just so—" Cass began only to look over at Vanna. "Sorry, he's your brother so I—"

"It's ok. You can speak candidly with me, Cass. I won't say a word, I swear."

"I love him." Cass sobbed again and buried her face back into the tissues. After a moment, she spoke. "I do! I mean, what's not to love, right? He's handsome and sweet and so very loving…he's everything a girl could want and then some, but I just don't know if the ranch life is what I want. Is that so terrible? Does that make me a bad person?"

Savannah shook her head.

"I mean, I've lived it my *whole* life. I know what it entails. He'd be married as much to the ranch as to me and I don't know if I wanna compete with it or not. I mean, I want to travel. I want to see the world and he wants to be here. He loves it here. And who am I to ask him to choose between me and what he loves to do, where he loves to be." She broke into another bout of sobs.

Savannah just pulled her into her chest and stroked her hair and back and let her cry until the sobs finally turned to whimpers and sniffles. "You know," Savannah began. "He's a young man but he has an old-fashioned soul. He's always been that way, even when he was little.

186

And there's nothing wrong with you wanting to go out and see the world, even if it's not what Jackson wants. Look at me." She pulled Cass's face up so that she could look into her eyes. "Wanting to explore isn't a bad thing, just like being passionate about what you love isn't either. No one can be upset with you for doing the unselfish thing of stating how you feel and releasing yourself before it's too late."

Cassidy broke out into sobs again and Savannah once more, held her, feeling her body quake as the tears overcame her.

"There, there, you never know what life has in store for you," Savannah murmured, knowing what Cassidy was probably thinking. "This may not be the end for you two. Love is funny like that." She thought of her mother and father. Of her Uncle Nate and Aunt Jordan. Of Morgan and Kelsey, who *still* hadn't called her back. Their lives together hadn't even begun until their late twenties/early thirties. "You're still so young. You have a career ahead of you. And you'll do yourself and Jackson a huge favor by finding out who you are...*without* one another before committing yourselves to each other. You know?"

At her words, Cassidy's head came up and she looked at Savannah like she'd just said something brilliant. Well, she was, after all, a certified genius.

"You're so right, Savannah," she stated. "Even if you haven't had many boyfriends of your own."

Savannah scoffed. "Boyfriends or not, I'm still a deep thinker and I see below the surface. Besides, I have a few years on you, kiddo." She winked and chucked her chin, getting a little giggle from the freckle-faced Cassidy. "Speaking of which, where in the world is your sister? Have you talked to her?"

"Don't tell Daddy, but she's been at Morgan's since last Tuesday," Cass admonished, pulling her lips in.

"And what do you think of that?"

Cass shrugged. She'd been just a young girl when Kelsey and Morgan had dated back in the day. She'd been smitten with Morgan almost as much as Kelsey had been. "She loves him. Always has. Always will."

Savannah gave her a big smile back. "I'm glad she's happy. She deserves it after all these years...but she still needs to call me back. If you talk to her, tell her to call me. Or I'll have to head over to Morgan's and interrupt their sex-capades just to check in on her."

Cassidy laughed big and nodded.

"Now, you head on home. Are you ok to drive?" Cass just nodded in response. "Alright. I'm gonna go find Jackson. Don't worry. Everything's gonna be fine. Ok?"

Cassidy's hazel eyes filled with intensity and she gave another terse nod before hugging Savannah. "Thank you. I'm glad you were here."

"Me too, flossy." She gave Cass's hot forehead a kiss and stood with her.

Cassidy might be glad she'd been there, but Vanna rather wished it had been her mother instead. Still, she was grateful Cass had a shoulder to cry on even if it'd been hers.

She walked Cassidy out to her car and watched her peel out. She was grateful that Austin wasn't around now, he would have only distracted her, for now she had to go hunt down her brother and God only knew where his brooding self would be.

❧

*J*ackson had never been a drinker. Not even close. Savannah had rarely even seen a beer in his hand— despite that he wasn't even *officially* old enough to drink —not at family functions or parties or anything else. So needless to say, when she finally found his drunk ass, shit-faced and leaning over the bar at The Rusty Spur, she was taken aback.

"Da fuck, you doin' here?" he slurred as she took a seat beside him and nudged his shoulder.

"What d'ya think I'm doin' here, lil' bro? Someone had to hunt you down. You sure can't drive like this. How did you even end up —?" She didn't finish her statement as she looked to a shrugging Louise. "Never mind."

She'd called and searched all day, reassuring her concerned parents that she and Dallie could find him and for them not to worry. It had been Dallie's idea to check the Spur before she got called to an emergency situation, leaving Savannah to fend for herself.

She was glad now that Dallie wasn't here to witness the spectacle that was their little brother's self-pity; her pregnancy didn't need any more drama right now.

"She doesn't love me, Vanna. She said I held her captive."

Cassidy had never said those things; she knew, she'd bore witness to the whole conversation, unfortunately, but she let him continue.

"I fuckin' love her so much, and she doesn't want a life with me. She wants to go away to college and *fuck* other dudes." He waved his hands dramatically, yelling the word 'fuck' and drawing more attention to himself.

Savannah looked around and grinned apologetically to the wandering eyes of their audience.

"Jax, let's take this conversation home, why don't we?" She began pulling on his arm, realizing how limp it was as it fell like a heavy dumbbell to his side.

"Home? Home isn't good enough for that selfish bitch."

"Whoa, now. Don't be calling her names, Jax. There's no call for that." Savannah went on the defense. Just because he was her brother didn't mean he got to badmouth Cassidy Jane Boyd, who was one of the sweetest, most caring people they knew. Hell, she was gonna be a nurse after all. She'd always been one to take care of those around her. It was the perfect profession for someone with a heart as big as hers was.

"I'm sorry," he whimpered as he began to pout, tears coming to his eyes. "I'm a bastard who doesn't deserve her and I know it. I'm just drunk."

You can say that again, Savannah thought, for she'd never seen her brother so unlike himself. He was so much like their father—responsible, protective, steadfast. A younger, light-hearted, more immature version of him...but still.

"I'm not like you and Dallie, I'm the outcast of the family."

"Outcast?" Savannah scoffed. "I don't think so, Jax."

"I am!" he practically shouted. "You and Dallie are doctors for God's sake, and I barely have an Associate's degree in Business Management. Morgan is a fuckin' contractor and what am I?"

The heir to a multi-million-dollar horse ranch? she wanted to say but held her tongue for she had a feeling he needed to get this out.

"I'm not smart like y'all. I'm just a simple hick who barely got through school."

"Oh, Jackson. C'mon. Since when does a degree make someone deserve more than a man like you who works his ass off for a living?"

Jax just looked up at her for the first time since she'd walked in and sat down beside him. His jade green eyes were blood shot and he reeked of booze. Savannah would be sure to have a talk with Louise later. What the fuck had she been thinking? And why had she given Jackson so much liquor? She knew about alcohol poisoning and the dangers of it, especially for someone like Jackson who never drank.

"I can't think about life without her, Vanna. I don't want to."

"Jax, y'all are still so young. You don't know—"

"Yes, I do. I'm in love with her, dammit. I've been in love with her for years. The thought of being without her is ripping me apart."

She shut her mouth then for she didn't know what being in love felt like, and he damn well knew it, which was why he was scowling at her now.

"It's not like you know what I'm even talking about anyhow. You weren't in love with Sidd. You've never even been in love, sister. You love your paintings and your music and yourself."

Ouch. That cut deep. But it was kinda true. She hadn't loved Sidd. Not fully. For she'd never lost herself to him. She'd not loved

Paul either, the man she'd given her virginity to in college. Savannah enjoyed her solitude, she enjoyed being at peace in her own mind and those two had been mere pawns in the game of life. No, Savannah had yet to find her life partner. Sidd would have worked, but Savannah wanted a man who ached for her like her brother was aching for Cassidy right now. A man who couldn't live without her. And that hadn't been Siddharth Bhushan.

"Go home, Vanna. Leave me alone. I don't wanna talk anymore."

"I'm not leaving you here for Louise to poison, and they don't have Uber out here in the sticks, lil' bro. So, I'm your ride tonight. Unless you wanna sleep in a booth?" she sassed and planted her hands on her hips as she stood.

He looked around, his eyelids heavy. Her tall, still handsome brother, even in his inebriated state. His full lips pouted back at her as he pursed them out.

"I don't wanna go home."

Savannah huffed and looked at her watch. It was already past nine now.

"Jackson, don't make me haul you outta here. You're heavier than me. You'll give me a back problem."

Jax laughed even as he laid his head back into his folded arms across the bar counter.

He began to sob and Savannah sat back down in the stool beside him and rubbed his broad back. She remembered him being a baby and how much she'd adored him from the moment she'd laid eyes on him. She'd vowed to protect him and love him, even if his crying distracted her work and his clumsy fingers ripped her pages of music.

His sobs tore at her heart strings as he held nothing back and she looked up at the bartenders who finally looked like they felt bad about what they'd done. They should! She could have this bar shut down for serving an under-aged kid. But she gave them a weak grin and gripped Jackson's big bicep. She rested her chin against his shoulder and began murmuring into his ear. "Jax. Please come home with me. This isn't the time or place. Ok? Mom and Dad and Dallie, well, they've been through enough for one lifetime. You know that. Let's not worry them anymore today, ok?"

After all, Savannah was spent playing negotiator for one day; she needed a reprieve. And maybe a drink of her own.

Jax finally looked up at her, his long dark lashes wet like his face. He swiped his nose with the back of his hand and looked down before nodding and moving to stand. He faltered and would have fallen, but a set of golden-tanned, inked arms moved forward then and strong hands gripped Jax's bicep and waist.

Austin. He was there, in the bar before her, and had stepped in to assist. He gave Savannah a soft sexy smile before letting Jax lean on him, and they moved toward the exit.

Savannah's gaze burned into Louise's then and she pulled some money from the back pocket of her jeans. "Here. This should cover what he drank tonight, but if he comes back in here, you are *not* to over-serve him. Am I clear? I'm sure Sheriff Kilmer would love to have a reason to close the doors of the Rusty Spur once and for all."

Savannah met the guys outside and moved to the driver's side of her dad's truck that Austin was pushing Jax into.

"We'll grab my jeep tomorrow," Austin murmured as he opened the back door and hopped in.

Savannah only nodded and looked over to her brother, who'd propped his face on his elbow against the window. She peeled out of the dusty gravel lot and drove ahead at a leisurely speed, grateful Austin had decided to ride with them, when not just two minutes in, Jax was grabbing for the door handle.

She panicked and grabbed for his arm. "Jax, what are you doing?"

"I'm gonna be sick," he whined and opened the car door.

She barely had time to hit the brakes as he began to literally fall out of the truck even as she reached for him. Once again, Austin was miraculously there to assist and held Jackson upright as he puked his guts out violently in the nearby ditch.

Savannah pinched her nose and sighed heavily, grateful for once that they were in a small town and on a deserted road so that her brother hadn't been hit by a car in his necessity to evacuate his booze-filled stomach. Soon, Austin was helping Jackson back into the truck and they were headed down the road once again, Jackson's head resting on the headrest.

All was silent for a little bit until Jax murmured, "You're the best big sister ever, Vanna."

Vanna smiled over at him, amused. "I won't tell Dallie you said that."

"She is too...but...you...you're special. Anybody can see that."

"Well, I don't talk to horses like Dallie does. I would say that's pretty amazing." She smiled back to Austin in the rear-view mirror, who grinned big at her. Damn, he looked good tonight. Fresh, like he'd just showered, and his cologne captivated her mind, like it did on their intimate night together, as it wafted through the enclosed cab of the truck.

"No, but she can't play a violin and piano like you can either. Or compose a piece of music...or paint a masterpiece. Vanna you're a true prodigy."

Vanna looked over at her brother as his hand fell towards hers and she grasped it tightly. As much as he loved Dallie, Vanna had been closer to his age than Dallie had and he'd bonded with Savannah in a different way than he had with Dallie. Even though he and Dallie worked together now and had the horses as their common ground, he and Vanna shared many memories that occurred in Jax's childhood while Dallie was in college.

"Thanks, lil' bro." She smiled even as she blushed back at a surprised Austin, whose eyes burned admiringly into hers, reminding her of their intimate night together.

"But then there's me," Jax stated, looking over to her. "What do I have to offer someone? I'm nowhere near as smart as y'all are, nor as talented."

"Yes, you are, Jackson. You're talented in your own ways. Remember what your teacher said about your writing skills that time back in third grade? You take after Momma, you have a gift with words."

Jax grunted, after all he was like their father in that he didn't sit still for long either. He wasn't like Savannah. She could literally paint for days on end if it came right down to it, but Jax and Dallie needed to be outside. God forbid there be too many rainy days in a row. They got as frazzled as a mug full of Alka-Seltzers.

Jax seemed to drift off as his head fell to the side, and she looked down at his chest to see if he was breathing.

Austin reassured her. "He's ok." His amber eyes held hers in the rearview mirror once more as she looked back at him. "But I should probably keep an eye on him tonight, just in case."

She nodded and took the road off the long driveway, towards the cottages. She shut the engine off when she pulled up front of Austin's and cut the lights. The flood lamp located just fifty yards to the left of the first bungalow gave them ample lighting as they moved to the passenger seat to assist Jackson. Vanna heard a bark and glanced over to see a German Shepherd wagging his tail, seated at the stairs.

Vanna took Austin's keys from him and unlocked the door as Austin lugged a drunken Jackson up the steps and through the doorframe. He sat Jackson down on the bed and removed his hat as Jax fell to his side, head hitting the pillow as he succumbed to slumber. Savannah moved to help Austin take Jax's boots off and pull his heavy legs up on the bed. The dog sat next to the bed and whined at Jax, and Savannah realized she'd seen the canine around the barn lately; was it Austin's dog?

"Is this your dog?" she asked.

"Yup. Savannah meet Caesar. Caesar, Savvy." The dog barked again and approached her. Vanna gave him a pat on his head.

"Hi Caesar, aren't you a sweetie?" she murmured as he leaned his big head into her thigh.

"Jax?" Austin stated and shook Jax 's shoulder.

"Hmm," Jax murmured, his eyes widening for a moment before closing again.

Savannah realized she was fisting her shirt, pulling it taut across her breasts, as Austin approached her and took her hand in his own. "He's alright. I was just testing his responsiveness." He gave her a slow grin, looking her over. "I missed seein' you today. Your dad had me runnin' errands."

She faltered, for she started to say she'd missed him too, but then she didn't want to admit to it. He seemed to sense her hesitancy and laughed.

"Well, I've been putting out fires today. Although, I could never be a firefighter, it would seem. I was slow on the uptake on this one." She motioned over to Jackson and got a laugh out of Austin.

"You're pretty funny, Miss Prodigy." His eyes held that admiration once more, and Vanna didn't know whether to be embarrassed by it or to swoon, although she was far more tempted by the latter of the two. "I've got a running list of nicknames for you now, Ms. Kinsen, and it seems to be ever-growing." He gave her a crooked grin, and she felt her sex begin to tingle. She gulped. "Do your talents truly have no end?"

"Nope. They certainly don't." He was good for her confidence, she saw right away as she smiled back up into his gorgeous face.

"Mmm, I'd love to get acquainted with each and *every* one of them then." His eyes fell down her body, and she was so grateful she'd put in those extra reps of squats and ab curls earlier today.

The hand he held hers with interlocked their fingers and he took a step forward, separating the distance between them. God, he smelled incredible. All man, leather, sex...and was that danger? Was it possible that danger could have a smell? He laughed as she sniffed sharply again, noticing that she was inhaling his cologne. She blushed.

"Like that, huh?" he asked and took her face in his big palm. She practically whimpered as his thumb brushed across her bottom lip and her sex clenched hungrily. "It's called Danger."

Dammit, she knew it. Danger *did* have a scent, and it was Austin Montgomery's fuckin' signature.

"It's supposed to attract the ladies. I'd say by your reaction, the little tagline on the container wasn't lying." His blond eyebrow went up, making his tanned face even more handsome than she'd thought could be possible.

He'd trimmed his beard since she'd last saw him, it was cut close and framed his square jaw and his big plump lips. His unruly waves were hidden beneath his ever-present tan Stetson and he was clad in a body-hugging t-shirt and jeans that he could have been poured into. God help her, she was practically drooling. She bit into her bottom lip to try and keep her wits about her.

"You're talented too, Austin," she croaked out.

"I am, huh?" his cocky look, at any other time would have her scoffing, but his intoxicating scent held her captive.

"Guitarist, singer, horse trainer, motorcyclist, former military…"

"Only a few of those are really talents, per se."

"Depends on who you ask, I guess." She tried to calm her nervousness, so as not to show him how rattled his closeness was making her. "Now, I'll have to add rescuer to that list after tonight." She nodded her head over towards her sleeping brother.

"I used to be a lifeguard, back when I was a surfer. I guess it stems from that." He winked.

"Oh, you surf too, huh?" she grinned, surprised once again to learn more about this mysterious rambler.

"Indeed, I do. I have great hand-eye coordination. But then, you already know that, don't ya, darlin'?"

He tilted his head and her heart rate doubled, slamming her heart hard against her ribs. She fought everything within her not to whimper, for she'd remembered his comment yesterday about what her whimper did to him and she had a fleeting vision of him gripping her bottom, slamming her to the wall they stood just a few feet from, and taking her right there against it as she cried his name in passion.

She shivered, and he grinned, as if he could somehow read her thoughts.

Just when she assumed he was going to kiss her, for his amber eyes were fixated on her lips, he asked, "You want somethin' to drink?"

She blinked a few times, trying to awaken her brain and quiet her yearning womanhood. She shook her head.

"I think I'll make some coffee. Looks like I'm in for a long night." He looked back over at Jackson, who slept peacefully now, and Caesar who'd curled up not far from Jax, at the foot of the bed.

"Oh my gosh, where will you sleep tonight?" she asked and looked around, finding the oversized microfiber arm chair and ottoman Austin pointed to.

"That's about as comfortable as a bed on the nights the nightmares get to me." His eyes were intense as they looked back into hers. Once more, she felt he was sharing something with her that he hadn't with anyone else. She frowned up into his face. "And don't worry, I can stay up all night. I've done it many times before."

"Oh, Austin. You can't do that. You have to work tomorrow, don't you?" *What day was it?* She'd lost count of the days since she wasn't working herself. "He's *my* brother. I—"

Austin shook his head, as if she were being silly. "Savvy, I got this." He winked again and leaned in to kiss her cheek, his lips pressing softly on her flesh, a stark contrast to his scruffy beard and mustache.

"Well…let's at least take shifts, at least," she stammered.

"And where, my dear, were *you* gonna sleep?" His eyes fell down her body once again, licking at her, and that sexy, cocky ass grin of his—God, it was gonna be her damnation.

"I'll lay with Jax—Wait! Austin, this isn't fair. He's taken your bed and now you have to stay awake all night? No. That's not right. This is my business to deal with. Not yours."

"Doc, I made this my business the minute I walked into the bar," he answered and tapped her chin lightly with his index finger as he turned towards the kitchenette across from the bed. "Coffee?" he asked as he looked back at her, reaching over his head into the cabinet.

She nodded and moved back over to where her little—albeit bigger than her—brother lay and ran her hand through his sweaty light brown hair. He stirred slightly and moaned as he inhaled deeply. He'd always loved to be touched in his sleep, have his back rubbed, and his hair played with. Her mouth lifted into a smile as she looked at him and leaned down to kiss him on the cheek, glad he was safe and sound.

She looked back over at Austin, who smiled big, those sexy eyes of his burning deeply into hers.

"Once a big sister, always a big sister, huh?"

"Oh yeah. I was eleven years old when he was born, so he was as much *my* baby as Momma's—mine and Dallie's." She smiled at the memory. "He was the sweetest little thing. Sweetest kid, even in his teens." She recalled what an easy-going child Jackson had been. So agreeable and down to earth, just like her dad. Until someone threatened his family.

"I wouldn't know. I'm the baby of the family; the spoiled one." He laughed as he filled the Keurig with water. "Wyatt and Sierra never saw me comin'."

"That's right. I forgot you and Wyatt have a sister. How far apart are y'all?"

"Wyatt's ten years older than me. Sierra's six years older. My parents thought they were done." He looked back at Savannah then. "I got dark or medium roast. Which would ya like?"

"Dark." She smirked, waiting for a smart remark.

His hands went up as he laughed, shrugged, and continued the previous conversation. "Sierra wasn't real fond of no longer being the baby." He winked over at her as he popped the pod of dark coffee into the Keurig.

"I'll bet. I myself had my reservations about this one." She plopped her butt down in the small space between Jackson and the edge of the bed, resting her hand on Jackson's back so she could feel him breathe. He wasn't snoring and damned if she could remember whether he did or not, but weren't drunk people supposed to snore?

"He's ok," Austin stated, calming her even as Caesar scooted closer and licked her hand.

She realized she was frowning down at her little brother and her head shot up to Austin, who brought her a delicious-smelling mug of coffee. "Thank you."

"My pleasure, darlin. Don't worry," Austin reassured her once again. "He vomited, so a good bit of it is out of his system now. He's gonna be alright. I figure he'll sleep it off and not have too much of a hangover come tomorrow...well, hopefully. Nothing a few ibuprofen and some greasy food can't fix." He pointed to Vanna's mug. "It's not hazelnut creamer, it's almond milk and raw sugar, hopefully that's alright."

Savannah just nodded over at him, and he returned to the Keurig to make a cup of coffee for himself. She took a sip from the Superman mug in her hand then a thought occurred to her. "Wait, you drink almond milk?"

Austin smirked. "You don't look like *this* eating McDonalds every day, darlin'." He winked again. Damn him, he was so freakin' cocky. But he had every right to be as she remembered him naked—his broad build and perfectly-sculpted muscles. When she scoffed, he added, "I eat clean for the most part. I wouldn't have your momma know it for nothin' in the world, but I hadn't eaten fried chicken in *years*. Damn, it sure was good though."

Vanna smiled over at him. It *had* been good, but she knew what he meant. The last few gluten and sugar-laden meals she'd eaten had left her stomach in a world of hurt.

Austin doctored his own coffee and came to sit in the big arm chair across from the bed. Savannah turned her body to face him, still keeping her left hand over her baby brother's broad back. She jostled him slightly, and he sniffed and grunted, much to her relief.

Savannah took in the small bungalow that her cousin had built, unsure if she'd ever even been inside one of them until now. It was spacious for a little cottage and had a queen-sized bed, two night-stands, a closet, a large kitchenette with an island and a small pantry, a high-top breakfast table with four chairs and a decent-sized looking bathroom she could see into from the door that was ajar. Perfect for one…or even two for that matter.

She looked back over at Austin, sprawled out in the over-sized chair with his feet propped up on the ottoman, a large flat screen TV above his head on the wall behind him. He sipped his coffee then with his other hand pulled his hat off and tossed it on the hat rack closest to the door. He, of course, nailed it and grinned over at her knowingly. He looked far too comfortable in his skin but in all seri-ousness, he should. As good as he looked with his cowboy hat on, he looked just as scrumptious with it off, his wavy blond curls tucked behind his ears, halfway to his shoulders. She longed to run her hands through them as she'd done to her brother just moments ago, but for a very different reason altogether. She cleared her throat, trying to tear her eyes off of him, finding the task practically impos-sible even as he seemed amused by her unease.

His face grew serious then as if a lightbulb had switched on inside him. "So, Cassidy broke up with him, huh? That the reason for all this?"

Savannah nodded solemnly and ran her hand down Jackson's back, feeling the muscles of his back expand and contract as he breathed once more. "They're just babies. So young and unsure. But try telling Jackson that. He's had his future planned out for them for so long. He'd have already had her barefoot and pregnant I'm afraid, if it weren't for her ambitions of being a nurse."

"Ah, young love. So enviable and unsuspecting. I only had one steady girlfriend back in high school, but it wasn't quite *that* serious, then I went into the Army at his age."

"So, you're sayin' you've never been in love, huh?" Savannah grinned.

Austin eyed her suspiciously before saying, "You neither?"

She blushed even as she shook her head.

"Well, isn't that quite the conundrum? Perhaps our meeting in the same places twice in one day was kismet after all." He gave her another wink and sipped at his coffee, looking all the world pleased with himself. She envied him. Him and his easy-nature, but even as confident as he appeared to be, she knew he'd had a hard past—he'd been through pure Hell not so long ago half a world away.

Her phone rang in her pocket, pulling her from her inner monologue and she rushed to answer it, seeing that it was her mother.

"Momma?"

"Baby, please tell me you've found him? Your father—"

"Yes, yes, I did. He's fine. He's resting now. We're here at Austin's. He's had a little too much to drink, but we're keeping an eye on him."

"Oh," her mother's surprised voice said back. It took her a moment before she asked, "So, he's ok?

"Yeah, he's ok. Just gonna have a hangover tomorrow. But I promise he's ok."

"How bad off was he, Savannah?" her father's deep voice asked into the receiver.

"Pretty bad, Daddy, but he vomited a good bit."

Her father sighed heavily before asking, "Where'd he end up?"

"The Spur."

"Dammit, I knew it! We should have checked there first."

"Well, he wasn't there earlier because we went by there. I think he might've went to Jared's first."

"Hell fire. That's probably where the drinking started."

That was more than likely true. Jared Campbell, one of Jax's best friends, drank like a fish. She could see Jared cursing Cassidy to Hell and back, as he'd never been a fan of hers in the first place, and encouraging Jax to shoot all kinds of shots back with him. But there was no sense in crying over spilt milk as her mother and grandmother always said.

"Alright, well, so you're staying over there tonight, I assume?" She heard the bite of anger in her father's tone.

"Well, I mean, I—"

"Do, whatever you need to do, Savannah," her mother said. "Just —make sure my baby boy is ok."

Savannah frowned. As much as her father disliked Austin, which made Vanna doubtful of his sincerity coming to their rescue as he had tonight, her mother's concern alone was enough to keep her vigilant for her brother's sake—despite that the man in question made her want to rip her clothes off and let him have her in any and *every* way he wanted to. No, tonight she was taking care of her brother and her dad would just have to be displeased with the decision. After all, Austin surely wouldn't try anything with Jax in the same room, would he?

"I will, Momma. I promise." With that, Vanna said her goodbyes and told her folks she loved them before hanging up. Then she looked over to Austin—golden-tanned, hard-muscled, tattooed and bearded Austin—and prayed that she hadn't just shut the gate to the lion's den.

CHAPTER 9

Savannah awoke to the sound of voices and felt the sun warming her skin as it leaked in from the window beside her. She groaned and raised her arms up in a stretch, yawning as she did so. She opened her eyes to see Austin at the kitchenette island and Jax sitting on the edge of the bed, head down, an apprehensive look on his face.

"Mornin', darlin'." Austin was the first to greet her and did so with the same smug look he always had. Dammit, how did he look so renewed after the little sleep they'd had last night?

They'd not talked long about their jobs, lives, and favorite things, Austin flirting with her like always as they sipped their coffees— maybe a couple of hours—before Savannah had started yawning, and Austin had patted the chair beside him, a playful look in his eyes. It took only a few seconds hesitation on her part to get a withered look out of him.

"Oh c'mon, Savvy. You know I don't bite...well, not *too* hard anyway." He'd raised a sexy eyebrow then in challenge. Again, she'd resisted, only to be rebutted with, "I promise to be a gentleman tonight. After all, what kinda man would I be if I cheaply copped a feel with your little brother right there next to us?"

So, she'd acquiesced and checked Jax once more, patted Caesar's head, then moved to sit next to Austin in the oversized chair he filled like a king on his throne. She'd gingerly sat down beside him, her hip and side aligning with his, and stretched her feet out on the ottoman, her leg bumping his. His arm had settled around her shoulder, pulling her ever closer, and he'd leaned in slightly, his nose brushing right above her ear. She'd literally tingled as her body became once again engulfed in his smell and touch and the overwhelming presence that only Austin exuded.

"Comfy, right?" he'd whispered and kissed her there before pulling back a little, all her nerve endings rapidly firing off at one time. He'd looked down into her eyes and gave a sly grin, happy that she'd caved, she assumed. "Are you warm enough? Want a blanket?" She'd had him dig one out already to cover Jackson and hated to ask for another, plus the fact that her body had been *literally* on fire with raging lust for him so she hadn't needed one. She'd shook her head and hadn't been able to contain the yawn that came once more. She'd shyly covered her mouth and he'd given a low chuckle. "Sleep now, Doc. I'll take first watch," he'd said before he began to sing, low and melodic, a gospel hymn she knew well.

Austin had pulled her against his chest, and she'd settled herself there, resting her head on his shoulder. She'd loved the security of his strong arms around her, his solid frame against her own, as he'd languidly stroked her back and hair. Had she ever felt so safe in Sidd's embrace? She didn't think so. She'd closed her eyes and let his sexy, raspy voice lull her to sleep, all the while realizing that it was the second time they'd slept together, and it had yet to be in a bed.

Now, as he stepped forward with a mug of coffee, she noticed he'd showered, for his curls were still wet.

"Thank you," she stated and took the mug from him, looking over at her brother as Austin nodded, grinned, and moved back to the island. "How do you feel, Jax?"

At the sound of his name, Jackson's head came up and he frowned. "You mean other than like a royal asshole? I feel like I was hit by a Mack truck." He grimaced even as Austin handed him his coffee and told him not to worry, that it wasn't a big deal. "But it is. I had you guys running all over hell's half-acre to find me, worried Mom and Dad, and ended up stealing your bed, dude. I'm really sorry, Mad Max."

Savannah looked over at Austin in both confusion and amusement. Had Jax just called him 'Mad Max'?

"It's a nickname the guys have for me. It was a movie with Mel—"

"I *know* who Mad Max is," she admonished with a giggle. "I just took you for one of the biker gang members instead."

"Oh?" Austin looked thoroughly nonplussed by her comment.

Jax scoffed. "That's because she doesn't know you, Aus. Don't take offense."

"None taken, J.D. Looks like I'll have no trouble in bringing her to the dark side." At that, Jax busted out into laughter.

He was referring to *Star Wars*. Now *there* was a true surprise. Savannah would have never taken either of them for fellow fans. She shrugged and sat up, straightened her shirt, and sipped her hot coffee.

"I reckon you can do my chores for the next week and we'll call it even, huh, buddy?" Austin teased.

Jackson sighed in frustration and ran a hand through his hair. "I shouldn't have drank that much. It was a mistake."

Caesar whined at Jax's anguish and licked his cheek. Jax threw his arm over the dog.

"Stop beating yourself up, kid. You got your heart torn out and stomped on by the woman you love. A weaker man would've done a lot worst, believe me."

"I'm just glad you're alright, little brother." Savannah came to sit beside Jax and nudged his shoulder with her own. "I was so worried about you!"

"Wait—you stayed the night here?" As if this thought just

suddenly occurred to him, Jax huffed and swore. "I'm sorry, Vanna. I was really selfish."

"Well, I *had* to stay, just to make sure you didn't have alcohol poisoning," Savannah offered sympathetically.

"It all worked out." Austin ambled over and patted Jax's shoulder. "You made out okay, and I got to spend another night with your sexy sister. I consider this a victory in any case." He shrugged then laughed. "Ah, I'm only kiddin', but seriously, next time, Sav, you might not wanna volunteer for second watch if you can't stay awake for it." With that, he winked, and Jax burst out laughing again as Savannah blushed, feeling like a heel.

After coffee and profusely thanking Austin for all he did last night, Vanna and Jax left, and got into her dad's newest duelie, a beautiful cherry red F-350. Not many girls could drive a truck this big with comfort, but her dad had put her behind the wheel of his big trucks—him *and* her Uncle Nate—from the beginning and she'd gotten used to it. Even though she used public transportation back in Houston and she and Sidd only had his car because the parking spot for an additional vehicle was simply "too much money" each month. Again, proof of the man's never-ending selfishness.

"I hope you're not mad at me, sis," Jax mumbled under his breath, his hat hiding his eyes. "But you *did* get to hang out with Austin, so hopefully it wasn't too bad." He smiled weakly over at her, and she returned it with a big one of her own.

"Jackson, you were hurt yesterday. I'm not upset at you, I'm upset *for* you." Savannah sighed and took his hand. "I guess I should tell you that I heard the entire conversation between you and Cass in the barn."

"You did? But how?"

"It wasn't intentional, mind you, but I was in Amadeus's stall and heard what transpired."

Jax was quiet as Savannah slowed her pace up the rutted gravel road. "I love her so much, Vanna." A lone tear fell down his cheek and her heart ripped in two at her brother's pain. "And I know you're supposed to let what you love go and it'll come back to you if it was ever really yours…but I can't even think about being without her. It hurts so much."

"Then, little bro, that's what you need to do. I know this is the hardest thing you've ever done. But she needs to go out, be on her own, and find herself. You don't want to start a future with someone who's unsure of what she wants, unsure of how she feels, do you?" she asked, and Jax just shook his head in response. "By traveling and seeing other places, who knows, she may just realize that there's no place like home and see what she's missing from her life by being so far away from you."

He nodded and swiped at the tear on his face. "Is that what happened with you?"

Savannah was taken aback by his question. She wasn't actually talking about herself. And she hadn't really traveled much, per se, although she and Sidd had been to Europe a couple times and they'd all taken a family trip to Hawaii years back. No, she'd actually only been referring to Cassidy, but as she sat in the idling truck looking at her baby brother she realized in just the 13 days since she'd been back how good it felt to be home and just how much she'd missed it while she was busy busting her ass in Houston.

She pulled into the driveway and parked the truck. She gave Jackson another smile and pulled him to her for a hug. He held her tightly and inhaled sharply. He blew his air out slowly and pulled back.

"Thanks, Vanna. For being there for me. For talking some sense into me. I realize I just need to be patient, give Cass the space she needs, and wait for her to see that this is where she belongs. I'm gonna let her know that when she decides to come home, I'll be right here waiting for her."

"That sounds like a great plan, Jackson. You're a good man. She'll see it, in time. She loves you. She told me herself."

He gave her a terse nod and took in another deep breath before he laughed a little under his breath.

"What?" she asked, amused.

"Austin is sure crushin' hard on you."

"Why do you say that?" Vanna's brows drew and she felt her heart sputter.

"Isn't it *obvious*? He makes any excuse he can to see you and he flirts with you like crazy."

Savannah waved that off. "I have a feeling he flirts with anything with a pair of boobs."

"Yeah maybe, but he looks at you like he's certainly enjoying what he's seeing."

And talks about consuming me like I'm a damn dessert, she thought but just shrugged, trying to hide her blush.

The minute they walked into the house, their mom ran up and grabbed her baby boy.

"Oh thank goodness, Jackson. I was so worried, honey." Her mom squeezed Jax in a big hug as her father scowled over at Savannah. He took her elbow, leading her into the kitchen.

"He ok?" he asked. Vanna just nodded. Her father crossed his arms over his chest and looked her over, as if assessing her for any sign of corruption. "Did Austin behave himself?"

"Dad, seriously?" Vanna gave him a withered look. "Our focus was on Jackson not on sleeping together...again." She looked away, embarrassed.

"That's not what I asked you, Savannah Grace."

"Yes, Daddy. He did. He stayed up all night to make sure your son didn't choke on his own vomit and was responsive enough for us not to have to call an ambulance. So, yes, I'd say he behaved himself *well*. Well enough for you to take your proud ass down there and thank him for it and perhaps even give him the day off since he didn't sleep a wink!" she exclaimed and crossed her arms over her own chest; she was his child after all. She had as much sass as her Momma and could be just as defensive as her father, even if she wasn't quite as intimidating as he was.

Her dad seemed to see this and tried to hide behind a sly grin.

Savannah rolled her eyes and huffed off. "I'm gonna go take a shower now."

*A*fter a nice hot shower, Vanna brushed her teeth and dressed in a pair of khakis and mint green top that complemented her eyes. She blew her hair dry and ran a straightener through her thick locks. She then applied some lip gloss and mascara. Vanna wasn't one for wearing a ton of makeup and was grateful for her olive-toned skin so that foundation wasn't something she had to wear to hide redness that she didn't have.

She was heading down the stairs when her cell phone rang and she grabbed it from her back pocket, swearing as she saw that it was finally Kelsey. She stopped midway down the staircase and answered it.

"You bitch, I've been trying to call you for over a freaking week! You had better have some *damn* good excuse for not answering your phone."

Kelsey purred, "Oh I do! His name is Morgan, sooo…sorry, not sorry. I've been spending every waking hour that we're not working in his bed." She cackled happily.

"Please, spare me the details." Savannah made a fake gagging sound, getting another laugh out of Kels. "I'm glad he finally loosened the cuffs long enough to allow you a phone call. Y'all freaks! I mean, I know y'all have some making up to do but damn. "

"Right? And holy shit-balls, have we been making up for the last twelve years! It's been fuckin' amazing."

"Well, I'm glad you two have rekindled the old flame at last. It's about damn time." Savannah took a seat on one of the stairs, looking down into the living room below her as she smiled at Kelsey's amorous tone.

"Well, last Tuesday night was super emotional, and I wasn't gonna sleep with him originally, but God, he was being all swoony and I couldn't resist. Then, well, you know how it goes."

Vanna giggled, knowing her BFF was—and always had been—a sucker for Morgan. "So, where is he now?"

"He's gone to check on his site, but he's coming back shortly. I—"

Savannah heard glass break loudly on the other end of the line, and Morgan's house alarm go off, shrieking jarringly into her ear.

Kelsey screamed. "Vanna, oh my God! There's someone breaking in!"

Savannah ran as fast as she could down the remaining stairs and into the kitchen. Her mom was there and she yelled, "Momma, call 9-1-1, send them over to Morgan's, there's someone trying to get in the house with Kelsey."

Her mom looked horrified as she ran to do as Savannah asked. Vanna continued out the French doors, onto the back porch, and down the stairs.

"Kelsey?" she called, but all she could hear was muffled footsteps and heavy breathing. Vanna's feet flew as she ran towards the barn, screaming for Austin. All the hands in the pastures and surrounding the barn looked at her as if she'd lost her mind, but she needed Austin. His bike and his gun...shit...hopefully he had a gun. He'd been in the Army. He *had* to have one. "Austin?" she cried again, out of breath as she closed in on the barn entrance. Wyatt gave her a confused look. "Where's Austin?" she asked breathlessly.

Wyatt pointed over to the corral beside them to a dumbfounded Austin, who approached her as she ran to him.

She tried to hold onto her composure as she reached him and grabbed his shoulders, feeling like she might faint. His hands immediately came around her protectively.

"Austin. It's Kelsey. She's at Morgan's. Someone's breaking in," she ground out, pleadingly. His gaze held hers for but a moment then he went into action.

"Take me there." He grabbed her arm and steered her towards his bike. "Caesar, stay," he called to the dog, who'd started to follow only to sit at his master's command. What a good dog!

Savannah muted her phone and stuck it in her back pocket,

hoping her panic hadn't given Kelsey's position away to the intruder. Austin started the motorcycle and revved it up, assisting her on behind him and they were off. Fence posts and trees flew by as he accelerated.

Savannah pointed towards Morgan's house just two miles due west, beyond the scattering of trees on the hill before them. She held Austin tightly around his waist, her heart pounding out an erratic rhythm as he reached a speed that at any other time would terrify her, especially atop a metal death trap, but all she could do was pray that they wouldn't be too late in getting to Kelsey before the burglar did.

Morgan's two-story log house came into view. "That's it!" Savannah yelled over the roar of the loud engine.

Austin accelerated again, and Vanna felt her stomach pitch as much from the speed as from the situation then she gasped as they came to a screeching halt, the bike tires stopping so fast that her brain rattled.

Austin reached down beside them into the left saddle bag and pulled out a revolver. He cocked it and turned to Vanna.

"I need you to stand behind me and not make a sound. Can you do that?" His amber eyes were hard and no-nonsense as he held her gaze. She nodded, and they got off the bike, Austin moving in front of her. He looked around before taking the steps softly, picking his heels up so as not to make any extra noise despite that the alarm was busting their eardrums with its incessant screeching.

Vanna stayed right behind him as Austin came around the porch to the broken window. He nodded to it and stepped through first then she did, being mindful of the glass. She took solace in his tall, muscular frame in front of her, burying her nose in his shoulder, stifling a whimper, as he stopped and looked around. He had both arms up, gripping the gun, moving from the living room to the kitchen, glancing left and right. This was as close to a crime scene as Vanna had ever wanted to be, but she focused on simply getting to Kelsey and prayed the assailant wasn't armed, but knew she was being naïve. They saw the back door ajar, but Austin kept moving, looking in Morgan's downstairs office and dining room before coming past the front door.

Austin gave her a quick nod as he motioned to the stairs and she returned it, staying close on his heels as he began the ascent. He took the wooden stairs one at a time, stealthy and smooth, and her heart beat in a cadence that frightened her as the anticipation mounted.

He entered Morgan's master bedroom first, gun up and ready, his head darting around for the intruder. He motioned to the closet and Vanna again nodded. He opened it slowly but it was empty—no Kelsey. Savannah's stomach sank. Had the intruder taken her? Was that why the back door had been opened? Had he kidnapped her? Savannah gulped and gripped Austin's black t-shirt with both hands as he led them into the large tiled master bathroom. She heard a whimper and her heart stopped.

"Kelsey?" she cried and tried to step around Austin, but his arm held her back.

"Just a second, darlin'," he murmured and stepped forward to open the door that was shut. It was locked, so Austin gave two knocks.

Savannah heard Kelsey scream and she gasped in relief. "Kelsey! Open the door. It's ok."

She felt Austin's shoulders relax as he lowered his gun and stepped aside to let Vanna through.

"Savannah?" Kelsey cried in relief and opened the door. She launched herself into Savannah's arms as she came up off the toilet lid.

"Oh, thank God," Savannah cooed and stroked Kelsey's blonde locks as tears came to her eyes.

"Oh, Vanna. I was so scared. Oh my God. It was so horrible!" Kelsey exclaimed as she pulled back, her red tear-stricken face pouting up at her friend.

"Kelsey," Austin said and looked at her. "Is he still here?"

"I—I don't know. As soon as he started to come into the window, I ran upstairs, here to the bathroom, and locked myself in."

Austin scowled. "You two stay put. I'm gonna check the rest of the house."

Savannah watched his retreating back before her eyes came back to Kelsey, who wiped her tears with her hands.

"Oh, I'm so glad you're ok," Savannah whined and grabbed Kelsey again. "That was so scary."

"I know! I was sitting there on the couch talking to you when this guy—" She stopped talking as Savannah pulled her to the bed and they both sat down. "Shit. I guess I need some pants." They both looked down at Kelsey's bare thighs then. She was dressed only in a big shirt of Morgan's and a pair of lacy black panties. "Not a great first impression meeting your new beau in my undies, huh?"

"Classic Kelsey," Savannah remarked and got a laugh out of her BFF, who was shaking. "I'll grab you something." Savannah moved to the dresser and began searching for sweat pants and quickly found some. She grabbed them up and brought them over to Kelsey, who'd literally just stepped into them when Austin came back in, a hard frown on his face.

"Well, the house is empty. Can you shut that fuckin' thing up?" he asked and motioned to the alarm.

A frazzled Kelsey quickly moved to the keypad near the bedroom doors and clumsily punched in some numbers. She had to do it a few times, but finally, silence met their battered ears.

Austin tucked his gun into his back pocket, and looked Kels over. Vanna joined Kelsey, who smiled ruefully up at Austin. "Tha—Thank you."

Austin gave her that sexy smile of his and approached. "Austin Montgomery, ma'am. I do apologize that we have to meet under these circumstances." He extended his hand and tipped his hat at her —if Savannah hadn't been so rattled by all that had happened in the last eight and a half minutes, she might have swooned at how heroic he'd been in playing the knight in shining armor. Damn, he was so completely fine.

"Kelsey Boyd. I've heard a lot about you." Kelsey grinned and her brow went up as she shook his hand.

"Only the good stuff is true, I'll have ya know." He gave her a wink and took his hand back. "Morgan's got a pretty sweet pad here." He looked around admiringly then his hand came to his bearded chin and he looked back at Kels thoughtfully. "Wonder who would wanna break in?" His eyes changed then, the no-nonsense Austin was back.

When Kelsey shrugged, he motioned for the girls to sit down on the bed and he moved to the wall, propping himself against it as he crossed his inked arms over his broad chest, the sleeves of his dark shirt pulling taut across his biceps. What was it about a dangerous situation being such a turn on? Savannah could have launched herself at him at that moment.

Austin pursed his lips and rested his chin on his fist. "Kels, did you get a good look at this guy?"

Kelsey shook her head. "He had a black ski mask on. I—I didn't see his face."

"Could you tell if he was white, black, pale, tan?"

Kels pulled her lips in and looked down. "Tan, like deeply tanned."

"Ok, good. What color were his eyes?"

Kels took her face in her hands, trying to think back. "Dark eyes. Not brown, but like hazel maybe, not light for sure though."

"Any distinguishing marks? Tattoos, piercings, scars you saw?"

Kelsey closed her eyes and Vanna rubbed her back, noticing that she was still trembling. "He had a—a tattoo on his forearm, I believe."

"Can you describe it?"

"Like an arrow maybe, or a triangle, black and thick...oh, and he —he had an infinity symbol on his...thumb. I saw it as he was breaking the window and his hand came up to open the—" she paused and shuddered. Vanna moved closer and took her hand.

"It's ok, Kels, he's gone now." She looked up to Austin then whose frown had deepened as he looked back at her. "Do we even know if he actually got inside?" she asked.

Austin nodded but didn't say it out loud. Probably to save Kelsey any more trauma. "Kelsey, one more question, darlin', did he have a deep voice and was he stocky in build?"

Kelsey, with her eyes still closed, shook her head, unsure. "I—He didn't say anything. I don't think. He was stocky though from what I could tell. He broke the window with a crowbar. And as soon as he reached in, I got up off the couch and ran upstairs. I didn't hesitate. I didn't look back. I—" Kelsey began to tremble again and her breathing increased. "Oh God, I'm so glad you guys showed up." Her lips trembled as she looked over at Vanna and tears ran down her cheeks. Savannah pulled her back into her embrace, soothing her as Kelsey began to cry.

Savannah looked back up at Austin. He looked angry now, angrier than he'd been, and he moved away from the wall.

Just then they heard loud footsteps on the front porch, and the door open downstairs. "Kelsey?" came Morgan's deep voice.

Kelsey gasped. "Morgan?" She got up and ran to the doorframe. "Morgan?" she called loudly.

"Oh Jesus, baby. Thank God you're alright." Savannah heard Morgan say as she followed Kelsey out to the top of the landing. Kelsey ran down the stairs as Morgan ran up and they grabbed one another midway, kissing after they embraced. "Oh, my honeylocks. I'm so sorry. I got the call from the alarm company and— Are you ok?" He pulled back just enough to look her over before pulling her back into his arms and kissing her forehead in relief. He stroked her hair and back and finally looked up at Savannah, giving her a funny look. Vanna felt Austin's hand come to the small of her back then as he stepped up next to her.

She looked over at Austin, who gave Morgan a terse wave. "Hey, man. Looks like you pissed somebody off good and well?"

The look on Morgan's face was murderous even as he held

Kelsey with all the gentleness of a lover. "Yup and I know exactly who the hell it was too."

"Yeah...well, I know exactly who it was that broke in."

❧

"*H*ey, thanks again, guys," Morgan stated as he shook Austin's hand and patted his bicep then moved to Savannah and gave her a big hug.

"I'm just glad we were close enough to help," Vanna said as she pulled back.

Austin nodded in agreement as Morgan's gaze moved to him. "I appreciate all the info and collaboration, Austin."

"No worries, man. We'll get this all squared away. I'll be in touch."

With that, Austin took Savannah's elbow and escorted her back to his bike.

It had been an eventful day to say the least, and after talking to the cops, calling Trevor, making plans with Morgan for security measures, talking with Nate and Jack, and finally having dinner with Morgan and Kelsey since everyone had missed lunch, Austin was beat.

He assisted Savannah onto his bike after he was astraddle of it and handed her a helmet this time.

"Can we go a little slower this go 'round?" she asked over his shoulder, and he grinned at her, loving the feel of her arms around him as he started the bike and revved it up.

"Absolutely, darlin'," he yelled over the roar of the engine.

He pulled the kickstand up with his boot and settled his legs on the ground. He backed out of the driveway before gripping the handlebars and giving the big Heritage some gas. Night had fallen some time ago, as he and Savannah had been at Morgan and Kelsey's for hours, now he was ready to kick his feet up and relax.

The ride back was peaceful save for the humming of his Harley across the dark pastures and groves of trees. In less than five minutes, he was pulling up to his bungalow, dropping the kickstand, and cutting the engine. He could feel the tension from Savannah as she took the helmet off and her arms dropped from his waist.

"Uh, aren't you gonna take me home?" she asked.

He couldn't help but smile as he turned to look at her. "What's the matter, Savvy, you afraid of the big bad wolf?"

"Well, I—"

"I was gonna have a few beers with you and do some star-gazin'. It's been a chaotic day. Let's sit for a spell."

After all, it was a gorgeous night without a cloud in the sky and the stars out here did seem brighter than they had in California, Afghanistan, and even Houston. Crickets, cicadas, and tree frogs sang out at them, bringing the darkness to life. Savannah shivered as he helped her off the bike behind him and gently handed him the helmet.

"That helmet's meant for a woman, huh?"

"Yup."

Savannah blushed brightly, and Austin laughed as he dismounted and placed the helmet onto the handlebar.

"Sav, I originally bought it for my nieces so they could ride with me. Honest." He winked even as she gaped up at him. "You're the first woman who isn't family to ride with me."

He left it at that and took his key, moving towards the door of his bungalow. The other cottages sat quietly, and he assumed his coworkers were either gone or sleeping. It was getting close to ten after all. He was grateful that the bungalows weren't on top of one another. They were separated by enough distance that one couldn't hear the neighbor fart.

Once he unlocked the door and turned on the lights, he moved over to the fridge and watched a bashful Savannah hugging her arms at the doorframe.

"I got Yuengling or Red's. You got a preference?"

"Umm, I'm not really a big beer fan...maybe I'll just stick with water."

"Here," he said, grabbed up a Red's Apple Ale, and twisted the top off it, "try this one. It's sweeter than regular beer. Wyatt's wife, Angela, likes them."

Savannah took the glass bottle from him and gingerly brought it to her lips. She took a swig then looked back at him as she swallowed.

"It's pretty good," she admitted and gave him a smile. Damn, she was gorgeous, standing in his doorframe looking so uneasy. He wanted to scoop her up and kiss her breathless. But he turned back to the fridge and grabbed a Yuengling for himself. He closed it back and noticed once more that Savannah was shivering.

"You cold, baby girl?" he frowned and came to a stop in front of her. He set his beer down on the small table near the door—it was the place where he usually threw his keys and mail—and took her biceps in his palms, rubbing them to try and warm her up. She wore a thin shirt and it *was* a bit nippy out. She looked up at him, her sea green eyes making his heart skip a beat and only nodded, seeming to be as rattled by his touch as he was by her eyes piercing his soul. "I'll grab you a hoodie."

He moved off to his closet then and took an old Texas Longhorns hoodie off its hanger; it was one he'd had forever.

"Oh, no," she harrumphed and shook her head. "You know my family is all Aggie fans. If they see me wearing that, I'll end up disowned for sure."

Austin laughed heartily at that. "Ok, first of all, Aggies suck, and second, your family would never disown their golden child."

"I'm not the golden child. That's Dallie…and Jax is the baby. I'm the one stuck in the middle."

"In your family, no one is stuck *anywhere*, but least of all you."

She just grinned and looked down.

"Besides, I'd love nothing more than to see the anger on your father's face at seeing you wearing this hoodie. In fact, I'll pay you money to wear it." Savannah scowled and shuffled her feet at that statement. It was only half true, Austin realized, and came forward, stopping in front of her. "Savvy, I was kiddin'. It would make me the happiest man alive to smell your heavenly scent when I wear my favorite hoodie again." His finger came to her chin and she gulped as she gazed back up at him.

"You're quite the charmer aren't you, *Mad Max*?"

"Well, I *am* a Libra."

They held each other's gazes for a moment, lost in the other's eyes. He'd never had a woman still his mind and heart and soul like Savannah Grace Kinsen did. She gave him pause, put him in awe, and made him want more all at the same time.

She was the first to break the silence. She set her beer down and took the hoodie from him, begrudgingly. "Only because I'm cold," she confided and gave him a look that dared him to say otherwise. He didn't say a word but grinned like the cat that ate the canary. "And *no* one ever knows that I wore this."

"Oh c'mon, Savvy, you went to Harvard, what do you care?" he scoffed.

"Wait a minute, you're *from* Alabama. How come you're not a Bama fan?" Savannah frowned up at him.

Austin gave her another grin. "Save for me, my family's all Texas natives… and Longhorn fans at that." He winked.

He grabbed an oversized blanket from the large ottoman and motioned for Vanna to grab the beers as he closed the door behind them. He moved a good-ways away from the flood light so that their view of the stars would be uninterrupted, and when he found a good spot, he laid the blanket down.

"Damn, if you don't look good in burnt orange though," he smirked as she sat down and made a face at him. He laughed and took his beer from her as he took a seat beside her.

"Where's your dog?"

"Wyatt probably took him home with him; he does that when I'm away. Caesar's like the barn mascot now, apparently."

Savannah grinned and looked up at the sky. "I'm kinda surprised that you're a stargazer, Austin." She nudged his knee with her own.

"Why?"

"Well, maybe I *shouldn't* be, I guess. After all you're a singer and guitarist, you quote Shakespeare, and you have a taste for art." She pointed down to his inked arms.

He grinned and shrugged. "Did you not hear me say that I'm a Libra?" He looped his arm around her shoulder. "I'm the most romantic sign in the zodiac, I'll have you know. And you should feel damned lucky about that too," he cooed.

"Speaking of Libras, there's Venus," she smirked again and pointed up at a brightly lit planet.

"Nice. It's so bright," he stated back and looked over at her, smiling at her beauty which the planet Venus couldn't even compare to, her eyes glistening up at the stars she studied for a living. "You know what it's like making love to an astrophysicist?" he quipped.

She smiled over at him, amused. "What *is* it like?"

"It's out of this world."

Savannah burst into a fit of laughter and the sound of it made him feel all mushy inside. Her throaty laugh was sexy, but the joke was completely true. Making love to her had been the best thing he'd ever done and he couldn't *wait* to do it again.

"Tell me about string theory," he coerced as she took a sip of her beer.

"You know about quantum physics?" Savannah gasped and pulled the bottle down quickly.

"Keyword, Doc, I know *about* it! I'm sure I can't quite hang with *you* though." Austin laughed and tilted his beer back, looking back up at the stars. They were so poignant and beautiful as they twinkled brightly, small to big, in different arrays, amid the onyx and indigo night sky. He took a sip of his Yuengling and gave a satisfied expulsion of breath after he swallowed it down. "But yeah, I've heard of the string theory, it's like the theory of everything, right?"

"Well, I won't put you to sleep with *my* personal take on the super string theory, astroparticle physics or string cosmology, which I personally believe *doesn't* entirely explain the 'theory of everything' as some of my colleagues would argue. Simply put, it leaves as many questions as answers. Although I would have to agree with Kaku when he stated—" Savannah paused as Austin's brow went up and he gave her a slow grin. "I lost you, didn't I?"

"Not in the least." He licked his lips, aroused by her boundless intelligence. She'd been so quiet until he'd brought up something that she was obviously quite passionate about.

"I know, I know, no one wants to talk about the cosmos, but it's all fascinating stuff really, to think that the particles that make up our universe could be produced of vibrating energy—like say when you stroke the strings of your guitar."

"It *is* fascinating when you put it that way." Austin swiped at a strand of her hair that the wind blew over her face.

"Essentially it all boils down to numbers."

"Numbers? Like one plus one equals two." He pointed from himself to her.

"Yeah, it's all math and formulas, really." She didn't seem to catch his meaning or maybe she did, either way, she was simply too enticing for him to resist any longer.

"Hmm," Austin murmured as he leaned into her, the nape of her neck beckoning to him. "You know what *I* find fascinating?" His lips fell to her throat and she shivered even as he smoothly took their beers, sat the bottles down on the flat dirt beside them, and easily laid Savannah down onto the blanket. "Is how," he paused as he kissed her neck and caged her torso in with his arms as he moved his chest over hers, "any man could have ever dared let you go." He opened his mouth and his teeth grazed her pulse point. He gently bit into her quivering flesh. His already stiffening cock jumped in response at her sudden gasp and moan as his possessive fake bite had the effect he'd intended. His tongue licked at the pulsing artery in her throat then he kissed her there softly, barely moving his lips over her skin, watching it break out in goosebumps. She tilted her head back as his hand moved over her side. "All I can think about day and night, every fucking waking second, is burying myself deep," he ground out as he fisted her shirt in one hand, moving the other to her hip, "deep inside your sweet, little honey pot over and over…and over again." He gripped her bottom in his palm and her thighs splayed as he pulled her beneath him. "But damn, am I glad that bastard dumped you, Savvy. He has no clue how much I've relished in what he *foolishly* gave up."

His mouth moved to her collarbone and teased it, continuing to get mewing sounds from Savannah's sexy throat as he did so even as his hands lazily skimmed her torso, moving ever slowly up her belly towards her firm breasts.

His lips had moved to her jawline and he was so close to kissing her lips when they heard a coyote wail off in the distance. Savannah jumped in his arms like a bomb had gone off, gasping loudly and grimacing. Her arms and legs gripped him like he was her lifeline, her head burying into his shoulder.

He gave her back a gentle pat and expelled a soft laugh. "It's alright, darlin', it's just a coyote. No need to worry. He ain't coming any closer."

Her worried eyes sought his as she pulled her head off his shoulder, and he couldn't help but grin at her fear, feeling protective and needed in that moment.

"Now, I know you've lived out here all your life and that ain't the first coyote you've ever heard," he snickered. "Perhaps, you're just finding excuses to hold onto me?"

"Sorry, I—" she looked around and gulped. "It's just, with all that's going on, I guess I'm more on edge than usual." She looked embarrassed, but he kissed her nose sweetly and shook his head.

"Hey, I'm not complaining." He winked and moved his hand down the back of her thigh.

"Do you think he's still out there?" Savannah's shiver that time wasn't from the cold, and Austin moved off her, realizing the coyote's cry had killed the moment. He turned and sat up, adjusting his uncomfortable crotch in the process and took Savannah's arm, helping her up. She scooted closer to him, and he wrapped an arm around her. "It's pretty ballsy, coming onto our land and breaking in like that."

Austin nodded. It had been incredibly ballsy and if he were being honest, worrisome…and in broad daylight to boot.

"Max isn't gonna stop, is he?"

Austin shook his head. "Which is why I'm gonna set up cameras and motion detectors around the perimeter. But don't you worry none, sweetheart. I'm on this first thing tomorrow. Your dad and Nate are on board too. We got plenty of guns and we aren't afraid to use 'em."

"So, you know the guy who broke in?"

Austin nodded. A dishonorable Army discharge, Brody Sims. Bad news with a capital "B". Austin hadn't gone on any missions with him but had gone through boot camp with the man whose reputation had preceded him. He'd had the darkest eyes Austin had ever seen, dark and cold. Austin had heard stories of Brody's bloodlust and uncontrollable violence. Violence that had eventually gotten him a court-martial. And now he was in Abundance, under the command of a man that both Trevor and Morgan said was equally as irreputable. What were the odds? Kelsey had been lucky, and Austin had been too, charging in not wearing a vest or protective gear of any kind.

Savannah looked down then, twiddling with her fingers. "I'm sorry. It's a sensitive subject, I'm sure."

Austin took her hand in his and brought it to his lips, shaking his head and grinning. "Savvy, you can bring up any subject you want to with me. I love talking to you," he stated earnestly. "I just don't want you stressing about this, alright? Today was simply for show. That's all. They were just rattling the cage, wanting us to take note that they're here. It's what bullies do." He began kissing her fingers, craving to make out with her gorgeous lips as opposed to talking. He'd thought of nothing but savoring her lips again the last 36 hours.

"What's that mean?" she asked as she pointed to his forearm

before he could pounce on her, and the numbers there, along with the dog tag replica for Jerome or J-Dawg as they'd called him.

"It was our squad name and number- Zulu Team 824."

Savvy gave him a sweet smile and the sincerity in it hit his heart, jolting him. "You have one on your chest too." Austin looked down and rubbed at where it was, across his heart. A Celtic type cross interlaced with a horseshoe, elements of his upbringing. He had two more decent-sized tattoos on either of his biceps. One was more tribal, the other a sunset scene reminiscent of his surfing life in California with a set of scales and an Army emblem below it. "I've been thinking of getting one…" Savannah trailed off.

"Oh?"

"Yeah, perhaps a planet or a galaxy—Andromeda maybe. I like the ones that look like water colors."

"Yeah," he agreed, "those *are* pretty neat, but I gotta be honest, darlin', I don't see you as the tattoo type."

"No?" Her face drew in a slight frown.

"Well, no one in your family has one…do they? And I bet your dad wouldn't be happy—"

"You know, I don't live to please my dad," she huffed and pulled her hand away from his. "I'm not Dallie."

"Easy there, princess."

"Well, I can get a tattoo if I damn well want to. I'm sick and tired of people stereotyping me."

"Whoa now, I never—"

"Just because I'm a *nerd* doesn't mean that I have to fit into a specific box."

"Darlin', you don't fit any box I ever saw. You shine as brightly as those stars you love so much," Austin stated and gently placed a hand on her knee. "I wasn't trying to offend you. I think a tattoo would be super hot on you. But you're simply gorgeous just as you are."

She gulped as she looked into his eyes. "You think I'm gorgeous?"

"*Fuck* yeah! Have you looked in a mirror lately? You're stunning."

She gave a little grin as she looked down bashfully.

"Savvy, you're smokin' hot. So hot that I get a raging boner just looking at you."

"You do?" Those blazing green eyes once again burned into his, and he felt heat spread through him.

"I'm getting one right now as we speak," his voice deepened and he grinned slyly at her. "Wanna take my word for it or would you rather *investigate*?" His brows went up at the word investigate, and Vanna paled. Austin couldn't help but laugh at her expression. For being such a sexy little minx that first night they'd met, she acted like little more than a virgin ever since. It was a huge turn on, and he fought the urge to grab her, pull her hand onto his raging boner and fuck her breathless right there on the blanket in his Longhorns hoodie. He realized he might be being too forward and should perhaps back off—for tonight anyway. He tore his hungry eyes from hers and looked back up at the stars. "So, where's Orion's belt?"

She pointed up at it, and he began asking her questions regarding the cosmos—the formation of stars, how a black hole works, planetary alignment—which led to more questions and explanations as he stepped into her realm. He learned how truly fascinating space was and how math really did play a major part in creation. And Austin found himself starting to fall hard for this gorgeous brainiac with an IQ as big as her passion for life was. She was captivating, everything about her, and the more he talked to her, the more he wanted to know—about who she was, what made her tick, what she wanted from life.

They'd laid down atop the blanket, their heads close to one another's as she pointed out all the constellations that were visible this time of year, including Ursa Major, of which he didn't know The Big Dipper helped to make up. He also didn't know that the Pleiades made up Taurus. She was like an endless well of information and he wanted to pick her brain until he knew and understood everything she did, even though he knew that it was probably never gonna happen.

Austin looked back over at Savannah, the night air had grown chillier as their star-gazing had turned into hours and their blanket had become damp, her eyes were closed. She'd surrendered to sleep under the stars she adored. She looked just as beautiful in slumber as she had charged with life, discussing her passions, and his heart did a queer jolt. He remembered how long he'd stared into her sleeping face just last night as he made sure her brother hadn't suffered from alcohol poisoning. What he hadn't told her, as he'd not been inclined to worry her any more than she already was, was that he was concerned for Jax too. They'd had no idea how much liquor he'd consumed in the hours he'd been gone and his vomiting had been a symptom of the condition and not the remedy for it. He hadn't told her that he'd awoken Jax in the middle of the night, sat him up, and forced him to drink water to help flush the alcohol out of his system and rehydrate him. Austin had kept an eye on his vital signs and his body temperature all night and hadn't slept a wink.

Now, he just grinned at how sweet Savannah looked as her long, thick lashes lay across her cheeks and her pouty lips puckered. She'd turned over to face him and tucked her hands beneath her head, her knees into her chest. She felt secure in his presence and the realization humbled and warmed him. Her long, dark hair cascaded around her head in swirls, her breathing deep and steady. She was the most beautiful thing he'd ever seen. She literally took his breath away and had from the moment he'd seen her in that antique store, hands on her sexy hips, sassing him with that sexy as Hell mouth of hers. He smiled to himself remembering how feisty she'd been—she had to get that trait from her father.

Austin frowned, remembering how much Jack Kinsen despised him. How on earth was he ever gonna get the man to like and trust him? Jack had already made his mind up about Austin. It was too late to change it. He was gonna have to do some serious groveling, and Austin wasn't one to grovel. But this gorgeous fox might end up being worth it in the end.

He moved to kneel on his left knee and bent at the waist, thrusting his arms underneath Savannah and scooping her up and to his chest. Then putting all his weight on his good leg, he stood up, his left knee protesting slightly—going from one position to the next as it tended to do at times. He walked towards his bungalow and twisted the doorknob with his hand, kicking the door a little to open it. Austin placed the still sleeping beauty on his bed and pulled her shoes off before pulling the comforter over her. He then went back out to retrieve the blanket and beer bottles. He looked around, wondering too if they were alone out here, but the night gave nothing away.

After coming inside and locking the door, Austin tossed the beer bottles into the receptacle and threw the blanket into the washing machine. Before coming to sit in his big overstuffed chair, he pulled his gun from its holster and checked the magazine, taking the safety off and cocking it.

He was ready should that motherfucker Sims come here tonight, and this time, the bastard wouldn't be so lucky to leave without a scratch.

CHAPTER 10

"*I*t is done, sir," Sims told his boss over the phone.

"Good. Did you have any problems?"

"Well, he has an alarm and—"

"You moron. Of course he does!" McClintock sighed heavily into the phone. "Please tell me that you were smart enough to be gone before the cops got there?"

Brody almost growled. Of course he was smart enough to do that. "Yes, sir."

"Good. But they got my message, I take it?"

"I would expect so." Brody couldn't help but laugh. The woman had been completely terrified. The look on her face was classic. Too bad he couldn't have had more fun with her, she had legs that went on for days...but his boss had said just to break in and make a statement, so he had. Maybe next time his 'statement' would include a good hard fucking.

"Well done, Castor." Castor was the code name he'd been given to cover his identity. McClintock was a smart business man. He'd even given Sims a burn phone so no one could trace him back to Max. So far, the last six years, their arrangement had worked seamlessly. "Keep a close eye on them and report to me next week."

"Will do, sir."

~

*J*ack Kinsen awoke pissed off as all get out the next day. Between the chaos of Cassidy and Jax's breakup, worrying about Jackson drinking too much, the break-in at Morgan's and now Savannah spending yet another night with Austin Montgomery, he was ready to explode. He'd went to Savannah's room first thing—he'd not heard her come home last night and dammit, she'd said at Morgan's that she was going to, until Austin volunteered to bring her home. Jack should have known that weasel was up to something. The bastard was defying him, on every front, and it was high time to let Austin know who he was fucking with after all. Montgomery had been warned but he'd not heeded it; now Jack wanted to draw blood.

It hadn't helped that Luther had called him all upset yesterday when Cassidy got home, before Jack had learned of Kelsey's brush with the intruder at Morgan's, to tell him that Dan Wilson was going to be released from prison that day. Had it really been thirty years he'd served? How had it gone by so fast? And how terrifying that a man like Dan was going to walk free down the streets? But Luther had worried Jack by saying the things he had. Like he was going to make sure Dan never hurt anyone like that ever again. Jack knew what he intended to do and Luth had every right to feel that way, but dammit, why did he have to tell him? Now if something happened, Jack would be a freaking accomplice.

He tried to calm his fury as he made love to his wife that morning, with a passion more intense than he'd originally intended, although she only reveled in it which turned him on all the more. But even as he climaxed and his release filled him with some sense of calm, the anger only returned once he started dressing into his gym clothes and headed down to the basement. He figured his workout might help blow off some steam. He started on the treadmill, running his usual four miles at a pace that had him drenched then he moved onto working out his chest and biceps. By the time he'd done his first three sets of each, his rage was spiking like the arc on a Jacob's ladder, and he made his mind up. He was pumped, charged, and ready to fight the son of a bitch who looked far too much like Dan Wilson to suit him. If Austin Montgomery thought he could continue to disrespect Jack Kinsen, he had another thing coming. Jack was going to beat the hell out of him and enjoy every damn minute of it.

~

*A*ustin smiled over at the dark-headed angel sprawled so comfortably atop his bed. He longed to crawl in with her and press his rock-hard cock into that plump, delicious ass of hers that jutted out at his gaze. Then he wanted to slip his hands beneath the hoodie of his she wore and squeeze her full breasts in his hands as he slid his thick shaft into her hot, dripping wet center. The thought was enough to make him moan aloud, but she was already turning over, yawning as she stretched, and he smiled as the hoodie rode up and gave him a shot of her sexy, slender belly. God, how he wanted to dip his tongue into her navel and make her squirm.

Instead, he stuck a pod into the Keurig so she could have some coffee.

She groaned and blinked a few times before looking over at him. He gave her a big smile, and she returned it.

"Did you sleep well, Sleeping Beauty?"

"I did. Although I feel bad that once again you were put out of your bed." She frowned as she pulled the comforter off herself and sat up in the bed, tucking her legs beneath her.

"Don't be. I had the most amazing view while jerking off this morning." Her gaping mouth made him laugh. "I'm kidding, Savvy."

SHANNA SWENSON

He chucked her chin as he sat down next to her and handed her the mug of steaming hot coffee. "But I could seriously get used to waking up to your gorgeous face and body in my bed every single day." His voice had dropped low and his eyes gazed deeply into hers as he moved closer to her. Her lips parted in surprise and his eyes fell to the juicy, tempting, little buds. He wanted to taste and torture them so badly, he ached with it. "I want you so much, Savannah," he murmured even as his hand moved into her mass of unruly curls and he brought her head to his tilting one. His lips gently fell to hers and he savored their sweetness as electricity spiked through him at the touch of her full lips to his. He moaned deeply, satisfied yet even hungrier for her than he already was—How the hell was that even possible? She moaned in turn and his cock pulsed with a desire that started to overtake him. He slanted his mouth across hers and deepened their kiss, his tongue dipping in to taste her.

Just then he felt a burning wetness dampen his shirt and he jumped up, yelping in pain as hot coffee scorched his skin through his shirt. He winced and began to pull his thin t-shirt off, wiping the remaining coffee from his chest and torso. He looked up at Savannah, who'd placed the offended mug on the nightstand and had covered her mouth with her hand.

"Oh my God, Austin," she whined and looked him over. "I'm so sorry. Did I burn you?" Her eyes filled with concern and he couldn't help but laugh at the humor of the situation.

"Damn, baby, I didn't realize quite how *hot* you really are," he smirked, but her mesmerizing eyes began to fill with tears, probably a combination of embarrassment and trepidation. Just as he was about to grab her and replace her tears with moans of pleasure, a pounding came at his door.

Savannah gasped loudly and looked at the door in apprehension. Austin checked to see where his gun lay, just in case he might need it. It was on the ottoman, cocked and ready, within an arm's reach. Savannah caught his gaze, and he moved forward to answer it as she pulled the comforter to her chest, lips pulled in.

He took a deep breath in and pulled the door sharply open.

His eyes fell on Jack Kinsen, clad in a muscle shirt, long shorts and sneakers—sans cowboy hat. That was new. Austin's relief was palpable as he leaned his hips back on the door and crossed his arms over his chest.

"Hey, Jack. What's up?" he asked casually.

But he wasn't prepared for the angry eyes that affronted him then, the deep growl that came from Jack's broad chest as his eyes looked beyond Austin to Savannah laying in Austin's bed. "I'm gonna beat the living fuck outta you," Jack stated with a snarl.

Oh shit! Austin immediately saw how this looked to his boss, after all he was shirtless now, and remembered that Jack had told him to stay away from Savannah just two weeks ago.

"Jack, I—" That's all he could get out before his arm was roughly pulled and he was thrown out onto the gravel. He landed on his side with an expulsion of breath then gripping hands began to pull him up by his bicep and shoulder.

"I hope you've made your peace with God, Montgomery," Jack grumbled as his fist landed into Austin's belly. The breath whooshed from Austin's lungs and he fell on all fours, but he'd prepared and had flexed his abs, so he was only momentarily thwarted.

Austin heard Savannah's shrill scream in the background. "Daddy, stop it! What are you doing?"

Jack ignored her and jerked Austin back up. "Don't cower now, son. Get up and fight like a man."

Austin's anger surfaced even as his mind tried to rationalize the situation.

Jack shoved his chest, distancing himself from Austin as he raised his fists in a fighting stance. "You were aching for a fight. Well, now you got one, you son of a bitch."

"Jack, you don't wanna do this, old man." Austin laughed humor-lessly, eager to spar—it had been so long.

"I'll show you an old man." He jabbed, but Austin moved quickly out of his way.

"Daddy!" Savannah screamed and moved to the doorframe, watching the scene unfold.

"I told you to stay the hell away from my daughter. You've defied me, disrespected me, and now you mock me. No more. I'm done with your bullshit. I'm gonna pound a big fat dose of humility into your sorry ass." Jack stepped forward then with a one-two punch towards his face. Austin moved back, missing the first punch, but wasn't entirely clear enough to evade the second as Jack's big fist caught him in the chin, busting his lip, and ringing his head like a bell.

Austin grunted and fell to his haunches, swiping blood off his lip. He steadied his reeling head before he stood, eyes taking in Jack's red face as he came back at him for more. Austin moved swiftly to his left, using his own fist to block and hit the side of Jack's jaw, throwing him off course, and he spun back around to face him. Jack was only momentarily taken off guard and he roared as he lunged again, his face growing even more red. As angry as Austin was, he really didn't like fighting his boss—his soon to be girlfriend's father—for as arrogant as Austin was he wasn't quite the asshole he wanted everyone to think that he was. He disliked Jack, but he respected the man, especially that he was so protective of his family. Austin swerved, missing Jack's bulky frame once again, and pushed him away from him and towards the door.

Savannah came forward then and tried to reason with her father. "Daddy, please stop this. It's not what you think. It's—" She grabbed for his shoulders.

Jack growled once more as he turned from her and raised his fists again. Jack was breathing hard and he shook—Austin couldn't tell if it was from rage or adrenaline—but he was bloodthirsty as he came back at Austin for more.

"Jack, let's talk this out. I don't wanna whip you in front of your daughter," he egged him on, getting a hiss out of Savannah, but Austin was eating this up.

Jack was about the only guy on the ranch he could tangle with in an equal fight. Sure, Wyatt had gotten his punch in week before last, but honestly, Austin could've taken his skinny ass down with one kick. Jack—now he was fair competition. The man was as tall as Austin and a bit broader, weighing a good two-sixty to Austin's two-forty. Jack worked out religiously, like Austin did, and he was fair game, despite that Austin was half his age. He had to give the man props!

"I'm about to make a fool out of you in front of your lover, Austin," Jack bellowed and lunged again, getting a good hit in at Austin's ribs before chucking his fist at Austin's jaw.

The hit rattled Austin's brain once more, but he shook it off and hit his boss back, a quick uppercut to Jack's chin sent him reeling backwards. Jack stumbled a step, but stayed on his feet and held his head in his hands for a moment, as jarred as Austin had been by the blow prior. Jack's look turned murderous as his hands fell, his brows drawing. He marched forward, palms flexing. Savannah jumped in front of her father then, stilling him momentarily. She whipped her head around, her eyes pleading with Austin to cease and desist, but Austin was too hyped up now to stop the antics. Savannah seemed to be aware of that fact and turned to face her father.

"Enough, Dad," she pleaded.

"Stay out of this, Savannah," he grumbled and moved her aside with a sweep of his forearm.

Austin gave a slow smile, the adrenaline coursing through his veins, his muscles rippling with the promise of physical conflict.

Jack huffed and took his stance again, but his face seemed to pale as he shook his head, his breathing grew more ragged. He took a step forward, stumbled. What the hell? Had Austin hit him too hard? *Nah!* It was a mere jab, not enough to be a knock-out shot. Jack's eyelids looked heavy though. He was about to pass out. Austin had seen it too many times.

Just as Jack's eyes began to roll back in his head, Austin ran to catch him as his big frame started to collapse to the ground. Austin made sure to cushion Jack's head as the momentum of his large body caused them both to fall.

Savannah screamed, coming to her limp father's side. "Oh God, Austin. What did you do?"

She looked over at Austin as he thrust two fingers into Jack's carotid artery.

"Fuck," he mumbled as he searched for a pulse.

Please God, don't tell me that I just killed her father?

~

"Well, I'm clearly fine now," Jack grumbled and attempted to cross his arms over his chest, but the needle stuck in his hand stymied that.

He winced as the plastic tubing pulled taut. The short young blonde nurse who was clad in black scrubs took his hand and looked it over but sat it back down as she realized he hadn't pulled the catheter out of his vein.

Jack's big frame took up most of the gurney. He sat propped up, shirtless with IV tubing running out of his right hand, multiple leads on his chest that monitored his heart rate and rhythm, a blood pressure cuff on his arm and a pulse oximeter on his left middle finger. Despite all that, he looked as formidable as a cornered steed ready to buck off its rider.

Savannah could have laughed at his expression if she hadn't been so shaken up still. She sat with her arm looped through her mother's, who sat in a chair beside her father, her hand squeezing his bigger one.

"Jack, honey. They're just making sure." Savannah's mother patted the hand she held.

"I know," he mumbled and gave the skinny blonde nurse a weak smile.

"The doctor will be in shortly to discuss your test results, Mr. Kinsen. Can I get you anything?"

"Can I have somethin' to drink?"

"Let me just make sure the doctor doesn't have you NPO, but if not, what can I get you?"

"A water would be great."

"Of course. Would anyone else like anything?" The patient girl asked.

Savannah, her mom, Dallie and Jackson all shook their heads and thanked the nurse as she exited through the curtain. Jackson had been the last to join them in the cramped ER bay. He was standing, propped against the wall, concern etched across his handsome young face. Dallie sat adjacent to their father's bed, looking bored. All this medical stuff was nothing new to her.

Vanna sighed heavily, feeling the strain of the last three days taking its toll on her mind and body. Her butt hurt from sitting so long in a horribly uncomfortable plastic chair. She stood and offered her chair to her brother who just shook his head, his dusty black cowboy hat followed. She looked over at her dad and felt her eyes sting with fresh tears.

Watching the big mountain that was her father slowly crumble to the ground like that had completely shaken Savannah to the core. She'd feared the worst when Austin's long fingers shoved into her father's thick neck searching for a pulse. Less than six seconds passed before Austin sighed in relief.

"He's ok," he stated and looked up. "Go call an ambulance."

And she had. And the wait had been nerve-wracking as she'd paced and awaited further instruction from Austin who'd propped her dad's head and feet up with blankets. Although it hadn't taken the ambulance long, Vanna was charged with the task of riding with her father while Austin followed in the jeep, grabbing her worried mom along the way.

Her dad had awoken with a start in the ambulance as the IV needle pierced his skin; he was quite disoriented. She'd grabbed his big hand, all the while tears falling down her cheeks like rain, reassuring him even as he looked more pissed off than injured, despite the lacerations and bruising that had started to pop up on his fist-battered face.

The police had been called—of course—once the nurse had seen her father's fists and face then Austin's after he'd joined them in the ER bay and her father had yelled for Austin to "get the fuck out of his sight."

Savannah had nodded for him to wait out in the waiting area out front, and the cops had come in to question her father then Austin after him. Neither of them were pressing charges. There'd been enough drama these past few days as it was.

The EMTS had run an EKG in the ambulance, then once he'd gotten into the ER triage area the doctor had come in and ordered a battery of tests, including a CT scan of his head to rule out a stroke, bloodwork to check his levels, an echocardiogram with a bubble study to check his heart and a stress test. All of which her stubborn bullheaded father had agreed to but the stress test.

"I run four miles every day, I'm not doing a stress test. I don't need that."

"Well, if you run four miles every day, you won't have a *problem* doing a stress test then will you, Mr. Kinsen?" the tall Asian cardiologist smarted off and left, leaving Savannah and her mom to laugh at his retreating back.

When Dallie came in, she immediately grabbed the nurse, asking all types of medical questions and talking jargon that Savannah didn't understand—what his labwork had shown, what his C&P levels were, what tests they had ordered, etc.

He'd had the stress test, CT scan and the bloodwork. Now, they were just waiting on another bag of fluids to get into his system and the echo, and if everything looked good, he was going to get to go home.

Savannah paced and sighed again. She could go for a stiff drink right about now and a long, hot bath with a good book, and a foot rub to top it off...or a butt rub at this point. She came to sit on the edge of her father's bed, letting the tears fall now as they may. He scowled over at her, his handsome face drawn in a deep frown. His head tilted and he reached out his hand to her. She took it and squeezed tightly.

"I'm fine, honey," he reassured her for the umpteenth time, but it still didn't take the worry away or the stigma of watching him collapse like he had.

The door opened then and the ER doctor came in with a laptop.

"Mr. Kinsen," she said with a bright smile. "Everything looks fantastic so far. Bloodwork is perfect. The CT scan was completely normal, no sign of any infarcts or hematomas. So, now we'll get another bag of fluids and check your heart with that echo. But I think it's safe to say that your blood pressure sky-rocketed along with you being dehydrated and it caused a syncopal episode."

Her dad just smirked up at the doctor as if he could have saved her all the hassle. "Doc, I told you. I take care of myself." He shrugged. It was true. He had for as long as Savannah could remember. He exercised, he ate healthy; he was the picture of perfect health.

"I can see by your physique that that's true, Mr. Kinsen." The brunette doctor blushed as her eyes fell over his naked, chiseled chest, and Savannah's mom gave a little giggle.

"If you think his body is impressive, you should see his stamina."

Savannah gaped at her mother as if she'd just confessed to being the devil himself and almost choked on saliva. "Mom!"

Dallie laughed out loud like a hyena and Jackson just shook his head, covering his face.

"What? It's true!" her mother confessed and raised her brows.

It was wholly embarrassing, but Vanna secretly hoped that one day she and her significant other would be exactly the way her parents were. It was like they just couldn't get enough of one another. Savannah thanked God that she'd been such a space cadet; having a room so close to her parent's bedroom had taught her at an early age to put her earbuds in at night before dosing off. They'd been discreet at least but still, she'd heard them on occasion.

Oh well, their love was real and ever-lasting. It was endearing, she supposed, and awfully romantic.

They waited another half hour before a knock came at the door.

A young woman clad in mint green scrubs entered, pushing a large machine on wheels.

Jackson moved forward and assisted her, looking out the door momentarily before closing it back. Savannah's heart went out to her little brother once again. Cassidy was on her shift today and had stopped in to check in on them. She'd blushed and hadn't been able to look Jax in the eyes, but she'd reassured them that Dr. Barton was fantastic and that their father was in good hands. She'd given Jax a regretful look before reluctantly leaving.

"Hi, you must be Mr. Kinsen." The tech said as she washed her hands upon entering and pulled the machine to a stop on the right side of the gurney. "I'm Nicole. I'm going to be doing your echocardiogram."

"Hi, Nicole," Vanna's father said easily and gave her a smile.

The tech had strawberry blonde locks, curly and long down her back. She was hazel-eyed and freckled with full lips and high-cheekbones, and a smile that lit up her face.

She leaned down to plug the machine in, pulled the screen upright and turned the power on. Then she donned a pair of gloves. "Can you just verify your name and date of birth for me?" she asked and checked the armband on Jack's hand as he corroborated what she'd asked. "Perfect. Have you ever had an echo before?"

"Nope. Never."

"Well, this is an ultrasound of your heart. I'm gonna smear some gel on your chest and take pictures with this." She pointed to a small transducer and smiled at him again. "Mind if I lower your bed?" she asked and Jack shook his head.

"No ma'am. Do what you need to do."

She pushed a button on the side of the bed and Savannah started to move.

"Oh, you don't have to move. You're fine where you are, if you wanna stay there." She motioned for Savannah to stay seated in her spot beside her father. Jack began to slowly recline from a seated position to lying almost flat.

"Can you roll over onto your left side for me and bring your left arm up under your head?" The tech helped Jack untangle the IV tubing and doubled his pillow up before raising the whole bed up and moving to dim the lights.

"Mood lighting?" her father asked and arched an eyebrow.

"Daddy!" Savannah huffed at him and swatted his knee. "Behave."

He gave a terse laugh and her mother moved to stand on the other side of him, facing his back as the tech giggled and grabbed a bag of electrodes and separated three from the row of five in the set.

"I'm gonna put three stickers on you so I can monitor your heart rate along with the test."

"Aren't I wired up enough already?" he grumbled and motioned down to the wires already on him.

"I wish I could somehow tap into those but I can't. I'm sorry."

She hooked the stickers to leads of her own and began placing them on his skin then she entered his information into the big machine. It was fancy looking with a flat screen, touch screen monitors and all sorts of buttons. It reminded Vanna of the control panels at Houston's space control center and she almost grimaced.

"What do I need to do?" Savannah's father asked the tech.

"You just get to lay there and I do all the work." She winked.

He smirked, "Sounds like a good time to me."

After the entire bay laughed, Dallie asked. "Daddy, remember the ultrasound we got on Wren when she was pregnant?" Her father nodded in response. "It's the same technology."

"She's a vet," Savannah stated when the tech looked over at Dallie with a sly grin.

"How cool. I wanted to be a vet when I was younger," she trailed off as she smeared some gel onto the probe and placed it in the middle of Jack's breastbone.

"Holy crap, that's my heart?" her dad asked, and they all looked at the screen in awe.

Sure as the world, a strange-looking image came up on the screen of his heart with two flapping pieces of tissue. Savannah could see what looked to be cardiac muscles contracting.

"Interesting," Savannah's mom said and leaned down to rest on her father's right arm.

"Here's his heart muscle here, his valves, and his chambers." The tech pointed out and began pressing buttons.

"Is it supposed to be flipping around like that?" Her father pointed to what the tech had stated were valves and she nodded.

"Yup. They're opening and closing like they're supposed to."

"Oh, good," he sighed in relief. "I was afraid something had broken loose."

She giggled again and began pushing more buttons. Color overtook the screen and Jackson's interest was piqued then.

"Whoa, what the heck is that?"

"It's color Doppler."

"Really? Like Doppler radar? Like the weather?"

"Exactly like the weather," Nicole confirmed. "Only it's tracking blood cells, not storm clouds."

"Cool, Dad," Jax said. "Does everything look okay?" he asked, concern darkening his eyes.

"Well, I'm technically not allowed to say anything about the test. It has to be officially read by a cardiologist."

"They know that," Dallie scolded her family. "She can't tell y'all nothing."

"But she sees them all day, she knows what she's looking at." Savannah's mom gave the tech a wink.

"I do. And I've perfected my poker face over the years too." She grinned and winked back at Natalie. "But it's always a good sign when I'm not running out of the room to find a doctor."

"Hopefully you won't be doing that today..." Savannah stated, hopeful. The tech just gave her a little smile.

They moved into a brief but comfortable silence as the beeping and swishing sounds emitted from the machine. Then Nicole said, "Ok, we're changing spots now, Mr. Kinsen. Cold stuff." She squirted more gel onto the probe face and stuck it to Jack's side. He took a breath in but didn't flinch as she moved the probe around and sighed heavily.

"Ah, Mr. Kinsen. You make my job look easy."

"I do?" he asked, confused.

"Yup, you have gorgeous pictures. They're so easy to see. I'm barely touching you."

"See, I told you that you have a beautiful heart, husband." Natalie leaned down and kissed her husband's cheek. He grinned over at the tech.

"I take it you don't see that often?" he asked and raised his brows.

"Let me put it this way, not everyone in our lovely state is what we call 'echo-friendly'."

"That machine is pretty advanced," Savannah said after a time.

"It is. It's top of the line. Fairly new."

"She's an engineer," Savannah's dad bragged. "She might've helped build it."

"That's ultrasound physics, Dad. I study astrophysics…but I'm sure our measurements and techniques probably coincide."

"Astrophysics?" The tech asked, looking impressed. "Wow. That's amazing."

"She works for NASA," Vanna's mom stated proudly.

"How cool is that? Aliens and cowboys, huh?" she nodded over to Jackson, who still donned his cowboy hat.

"We own a ranch," her father said, his deep voice laced with pride. "No aliens though, just horses."

The tech laughed. "A vet, an astrophysicist, and a cowboy walk into the ER."

"We're quite an entertaining bunch, huh?" Jackson chuckled. It was the first time Vanna had seen him really smile since he and Cassidy had broken up.

"A family of multi-faceted people, I can tell you that." Natalie smiled big and looked around at her children.

"I'd say so," Nicole said and gave them all the same admirable grin.

She continued acquiring images, loops and dopplers then moved the probe to Jack's belly, right at his diaphragm, and he laughed.

"I'm not pregnant...I hope."

"It would explain the fainting," the echo tech teased.

"Man," her father smirked.

"No, it's just another spot where we get more images. Here I can look at a bit of your thoracic aorta and see your inferior vena cava."

"Wow, look at that," Vanna's mom said in awe and pointed to the screen. "We're not bothering you, I hope. I realize we've asked you far too many questions and crowded you too much," Nat said regretfully and moved back a step.

"No ma'am, I enjoy talking about my work. It's good to have patients that are interested." She gave a soft smile, took another picture at Vanna's dad neck and excused herself to grab the nurse for the bubble study.

Dallie had tried to explain the bubble study to them all before the tech and nurse returned.

"So, your nurse, Tiffany here, is going to inject the bubbles into your IV, and I'm going to take a couple pictures while she does so."

"And what do the bubbles show?" It was Savannah who asked.

"Well, I'm sure your sister, the vet, is already aware of this but while we're in the womb, there's a little 'trap door'—so to speak—in your heart that shunts the blood away from the lungs...seein' as we don't need to use them just yet. And in about twenty-five percent of the population that little trap door doesn't close like it should. It's called a PFO or patent foramen ovale."

"Dang, I didn't realize the heart was so technical," Vanna's dad stated in surprise.

"The PFO is one of three shunts in the fetal heart. Pretty cool stuff." Nicole blushed. Clearly, she was passionate about her job.

Once the bubble study was performed and the final pictures were taken, the echo technologist thanked them and began removing her stickers and getting her equipment ready to depart.

Savannah waved at her and decided it was time for her to talk to her dad in privacy. Once the tech left the room, Vanna looked up to her mom, who seemed to sense her thoughts.

"Alright kids, let's give your dad and Vanna a minute to talk, alright? My legs need a walk and Jax you haven't had anything to drink since you got here."

Natalie corralled Dallie and Jax out, who both looked over at Vanna with a mixture of pity and sadness.

Dammit, she didn't want or need either of those things; she was a grown woman and she didn't need her family's approval of whom she decided to mess around with. Sure, she was the brainiac, level-headed, reasonable Savannah but that didn't mean she had to play by a set of rules or fit into a certain mold as she'd told Austin just the night before. She was free to make her own choices and her father needed to stay the hell out of it.

When her eyes lifted to his ruggedly handsome face, his look was a culmination of angst, shame, understanding and disappointment. It made tears leap into her eyes and she couldn't control them as they fell silently down her cheeks.

"I didn't sleep with him, Daddy," she blurted out. "But you didn't give me a chance to tell you that before you decided you wanted to kill him."

Her father took in a long deep breath and let it out slowly before he spoke. "He's not the type of man you need to be around right now, baby," he stated softly and reached for her hand.

She scooted closer to him and took it, squeezing it tightly, allowing her strong father's presence to comfort her even though she was still upset with him over all that had happened. If he hadn't have gotten so riled up, they wouldn't be here in the first place.

"Darlin', whether you realize this or not, you're in a delicate state right now. You're on the rebound and he—"

"I know I'm on the rebound." She rolled her eyes and gave him a retired look.

"He's going to take advantage of you. He's nothin' but a trouble-maker, Vanna. He was enjoying every minute of that fight. You saw it, yourself."

"Yeah, well, he wasn't the only one," she smarted back, remembering the smirk of pleasure across her father's face while the two men were tussling.

"He's disrespected the both of us, honey. He has no regard for anyone. He's a changed man. The Army—"

"He lost his best friend, Daddy," Vanna whispered, recalling the pain in Austin's eyes when he'd told her about what happened in Afghanistan. "He almost died himself."

"Yes, and things like that change people. You just need to keep your distance from him... I'm gonna have to let him go."

"No," Savannah gasped. "Don't fire him on my account. Please, Daddy? It wasn't his fault. I—"

Her father shook his head. "It's been a long time coming, darlin'. The only reason I've kept him on is because of Wyatt, but I'm too old for all this B.S."

"If I promise to keep my distance from him, will you give him a second chance?"

"You mean a fifth— No tenth— No *twentieth* chance? Hell, Vanna. Let's not kid ourselves, here. I told him to stay away from you and he didn't obey my wishes, as either a father or his boss. I can't have an employee who goes over my head like he does. He's too much like—" Her father practically growled and looked down, anger smearing his face.

Vanna's brows drew in confusion but before she could ask him who Austin was too much like, the door opened and the nurse poked her head in.

"Doin' alright?" she asked then blushed as she realized she was interrupting something important, taking in the tears that continued to fall down Vanna's cheeks. "I'll come back." She winked and exited.

Vanna's gaze returned to look at her father, who had a pained look on his face. She spoke before he could. "Daddy, he helped take care of Jackson that night when I fell asleep. He didn't have to do that! And *I* was the one who sought *him* out yesterday when Morgan's house was being invaded because I knew he'd know what to do. Maybe he's not the person you think he is. What if you're wrong? I know you think you have this sixth sense about people and can read them...but what if your radar is off on Austin?" she asked, knowing her father's radar had never been off before. But even a tracking dog could be wrong—couldn't it?

Jack sighed and shook his head as if she were being ridiculous but then he gave her a weak smile. "You're so much like your grand-mother sometimes." Vanna was taken off guard for a moment even as she loved being compared to her grandmother. "Corrine always sees the good in everyone. Nat can be that way sometimes too. And we all *know* Dallie only sees the good. I honestly pray I'm wrong about this guy. I do, Vanna. But tragedy does things to people...and sometimes what's done can't ever be overcome. Your momma was fortunate, your best friend's mother was lucky, your sister and Cole they were patient enough to finally get their happy ending too...but darlin', this ain't Hollywood, this is real life. And post-traumatic stress disorder affects everyone differently, and I'm afraid for Austin, it's going to be his downfall."

Vanna mulled that over for a minute. Austin really wasn't as bad as her dad thought. She knew it couldn't be so. Austin was romantic, he loved art and music and star-gazing on clear nights. He *had* a sweet side, despite his tough outer appearance. So, he liked to fight, he liked to ride motorcycles, but he wasn't dangerous. He wasn't! He'd come to her aid time after time. Austin Montgomery was a hero. And Vanna wasn't going to let his prior follies or the tragedy in Afghanistan cloud her father's views of him. She made up her mind.

"Give him just *one* more chance, please?"

Her father gave a soft chuckle and gave her hand a little squeeze. "Always the optimist."

"My head may be in the clouds, Dad, but my heart is still well grounded here on earth, and so is yours." She raised her eyebrows. Her father, intimidator extraordinaire that he was, had the biggest heart of them all, she knew.

He gave her a crooked grin and seemed to think it over for a moment. "Fine. But you keep your distance, and he keeps his." The last statement was a command; she felt it all the way to her spine.

She only nodded and leaned in to kiss his cheek, bringing her arms around his neck for a hug. Tears fell down her face once more, and she let them fall as his big arms came around her. "I love you, Daddy, so much. I was so scared." Her body trembled as she tried to hold the sob in that wouldn't be contained—all the awful things that had happened in a matter of days finally bringing her emotions to a head.

Her father held her tightly to him and stroked her hair as he let her cry it out. "I know, sweetie. I know. But everything's fine now."

She wasn't aware of how long she bawled in his arms, but having her rock of a father there to hold her up when her world had collapsed was what she'd needed all along, she realized. She and her father had never been quite as close as he and Dallas were—Vanna had always been a Momma's girl—but the love between them had always been strong and fierce, as strong and fierce as the love the entire family shared. She'd never doubted that, but as she pulled back and swiped at her face, she realized their relationship was going to be even better now.

He chucked her chin and kissed her cheek, feeling the shift himself. He might not understand her artistic and intellectual ways, and she might not understand his, but their differences made them as endearing as their likenesses did. And she was her father's daughter after all, she realized with a little giggle.

"Hey, that wasn't a *Longhorns* hoodie you were wearing this morning, was it?" Her father looked thoughtful as his brow raised.

Savannah gaped at him as if he'd lost his mind. "Daddy! I would *never!* Are you sure you didn't hit your head harder than you thought?"

With that, they both laughed heartily, and she embraced him once more.

The door opened then and the care tech entered to check his vitals. Vanna gave her dad's hand another squeeze as she stood. She needed to go talk to Austin.

～

*C*assidy cleared her throat as she approached Jackson— handsome, sweet, constant Jackson. The boy she loved. The boy she'd given everything to, her heart, her virginity, her life. The boy she'd recently freed herself from, although she didn't feel entirely free, any more so than she'd felt "imprisoned" by him as she'd made out to be on Thursday. But he wasn't a boy any longer, he was a man —a man she'd hurt deeply and he needed to understand why.

"Jax, can we talk?" she asked, and Natalie and Dallie gave each other looks before silently heading to the waiting room.

Jax's eyes took her in. He looked tired, solemn, and worried. He was tall like his father, standing at six foot two inches and broad with big shoulders. He was ruggedly handsome, his lips were the softest thing about him, plump with a perfect cupid's bow. His hair was a light brown and his eyes were a shade lighter than moss green. He was tan and utterly beautiful. He'd always been to her and even now in the distance she felt between them, he still stole her breath.

"I'm sorry," she said truthfully.

Jackson gave a nonchalant shrug. "You just stated the truth, Cass. No reason to be sorry."

"How's your dad?"

"Fine, it would seem. Stubborn as ever."

This small talk was enough to make her wanna scream. Why did he have to look at her as if she were a complete stranger now?

Couldn't they remain friends at least? This was hard enough as it was.

"What'd ya wanna talk about, Cass?" Jax rubbed at his neck, shielding his face with his cowboy hat. "Don't you have patients to tend to?"

"Please stop hating me, Jackson," she whimpered and tried to hold her tears at bay.

"Hating you? Is that what you think? Do you even know me at *all*?" The growl that hit his throat startled her, the conviction in his eyes made her tremble. "I don't hate you, not even an ounce. How can you not see that? This would be so much easier if I *did* hate you. I guess I'm a glutton for punishment." He sighed and looked down. "I'm still here, Cass. I'm not going anywhere."

"Do you understand why?" She took a step closer, longing to touch him, make him understand her plight.

"Not really, no. But I guess it is what it is. I'll be here waiting for you when you decide to come home, I reckon."

Cass shook her head. He hadn't understood at all, it would seem. "No, Jax."

He looked up at her, really looked, for the first time in a long time. His brows drawing as he searched her eyes. "What are you saying?"

"If I don't come home, I mean…" She gulped. It was possible she wouldn't come back to Abundance. After all, she had dozens of opportunities to have her life go where ever the wind blew her.

Suddenly, Jax stepped back and seemed to grasp what she'd been trying to say all along. It was why she'd had to let him go, after all. She loved him and had to be honest.

"I don't want you to wait on me. I mean, I can't ask that of you. It's not fair." She tried not to cry but it was no use, the tears fell despite her attempts to squelch them. "Find a girl who wants what you want, Jackson. I—I'm not that girl. And I don't know that I ever will be. I'm setting *you* free too. That's what I was trying to tell you the other day. I love you. I'll always love you, but I need to—"

He nodded, his jaw clenching. "You need to fly, hummingbird. You've always needed to fly. Well, you've broken out of your cage, so enjoy your flight, little bird. I pray it's as smooth a sailing as you think it'll be, darlin'. Who am I to clip those wings, huh? I won't bog you down any longer, Cassidy. Consider me as free as you are then."

Her heart bled at his words, for the look in his eyes had never been so hard, so cold, so unfeeling. There, she'd done it. She'd gotten her point across to him. But if it'd been the right thing to do then why did it still hurt so very much?

~

*A*ustin had never felt more like an asshole in his entire life than he had when Savannah's beautiful face had stared back at him as he'd searched for a pulse in her father's neck.

He'd found a good strong one in a matter of seconds, much to his relief. He'd known his hit hadn't been enough to hurt the mountain of a man that was Jack Kinsen, but watching his boss as he'd fallen at Austin's hand had been a real eye-opener for him. He realized what kind of damage he could truly do to civilians and the impact of what his actions had done. He'd been selfish, irrational, and a complete and utter son of a bitch. His parents would be so incredibly disappointed in him and God help, he didn't want to face his brother with what he'd done either. Wyatt already had him pegged as a loser; this would only be the icing on the cake.

So, he'd sat patiently waiting in the ER waiting area as people came and went—coughing, bleeding, and whining. He waited with the patience of Job for that gorgeous maple-headed beauty to come give him some sign that she didn't hate every fiber of his being. He'd had all the time in the world to think about everything he'd done in the last month of being in Abundance, Texas and he'd come to the conclusion that he was a lost cause. Really and truly. Jerome would take one look at him and give him a swift punch in the nose.

"Wake the fuck up, *Mustang*," he'd say. "What are you doin'?" Then

Austin would have gotten one hell of a lecture from the man who'd been his brother while they were fighting for their lives in the desert. Life was too short, he'd always said. "We have to make an impact. We are the ones responsible for our destiny. Us. No one else." J-Dawg had always been such a philosopher. Savvy would have loved him.

Austin felt guilty, alone, and disappointed with how he'd acted this last month on the ranch. He'd been a sour, cocky bastard who deserved to be fired for what he'd done and he'd known his brother would be firing him the minute he stepped foot back on Kinsen Ranch, which was why he'd continued to wait and ponder his life.

He'd never been good with people—not really. He'd been all about making himself happy, to hell with everyone else. He'd been reckless many times, arrogant most of his life, and downright irresponsible when it came to being an adult...until he gone into the military. Then he'd been in his element. Alongside his brothers, he'd had a purpose—a duty—and he'd taken that duty with great regard. But then he'd lost his footing and fallen, hard, into a dismal darkness where he felt once again like he didn't truly fit in. Austin was wandering, aimless, with no direction. He'd gotten so used to feeling aloof that he hadn't realized how much he'd warmed up to the Kinsens, the ranch, and working with his brother, until he was now, suddenly, in jeopardy of losing all of it.

Savannah. She was what was changing him. Awakening him. Bringing him slowly back to life. He hadn't really known when it had started to happen, but somehow, it had. He felt different when she was near him, in a good way. He felt more alive in her presence than he had in the two and a half years since his knee had been blown off. She was beautiful, funny, smart...and he wanted nothing more than to let her continue to invade his mind and soul and body in a way that only she had.

But now, she was in the ER with her father, whom Austin had practically knocked out hours prior. And she—more than likely—wanted to cuss him black and blue, as she had every right to.

Just as Austin checked his phone for the millionth time, he ran a hand through his long hair and looked up. There his sweet Savvy stood, red-faced and worried. He shot up off the chair and came to stand before her.

Her hands came up, palms out, and she gave a soft grin, her teary-eyes breaking the last of his resolve. "He's fine. All the tests are coming back normal."

"Oh, thank God," Austin stated with a sigh and a relief that went bone-deep. He wouldn't have been able to live with himself if the results had been anything different. It was bad enough that he'd put Jack here in the first place.

"I'm surprised to see that you're still here."

"Why?" Her statement had him reeling. Where the hell else would he be?

"I just figured..." she trailed off and looked down, pulling her bottom lip in and chewing on it.

He wanted to bend down and give it a soft kiss, a much-needed reprieve from her gnawing teeth. He even stepped forward as she stopped the action, as if reading his mind and licked them, enticing him all the more with that little pink tongue of hers. He almost moaned aloud remembering all the places her tongue had been on him; in his mouth, darting across his chest and abs, twirling around his rock-hard shaft. He licked his own lips and gave her a soft smile, stymying her thoughts. He took her hand and interlaced it in his own, loving how soft and delicate it was in his; a sharp contrast to his bigger, more calloused one.

"I'm really sorry, Savvy," he whispered and leaned his forehead to rest on hers, closing his eyes for a moment and breathing her intoxicating floral scent into his nostrils. God, she smelled so incredible. When he pulled back to look at her once more, she was crying, hard. "Oh, baby," he said on a sigh, his gut jerking in pain at seeing her so upset. He pulled her into his arms then, cherishing her slender frame pressing against his. She buried her face into his shoulder and sobbed. He stroked her back and hair, the curly tendrils flirting with his fingertips, making him want her all the more. He murmured to her and kissed her temple, hating himself so much as she expelled her pent-up emotions into his shirt. "I'm so very sorry, baby girl. Please forgive me? I've behaved badly."

She seemed to come to her senses then and pulled away suddenly, wiping her tears and nose, sniffling. She took a step back and crossed her arms over her chest then, shutting herself off to him, and he felt the blow as if it'd been a kick to his gut. "You should go now. I know you have lots to do to help Morgan."

He swallowed hard. She was dismissing him. He gave a nod, trying not to show her how affected he was by her obvious dissatis-faction with him. "Yeah, I need to get the perimeter secured, install some hidden cameras, and get the systems updated. The police were supposed to be informing us on how he managed to get onto the property in the first place, hopefully they've updated Morgan by now," he rambled. He did have lots to do but making sure his girl was okay was his number one priority. *His girl.* Was Savannah his girl? He sure as hell wanted her to be. In every single way possible.

"Sounds like you'll be busy then." She looked down, and the pain reflecting in her eyes gave him pause. What was she not saying?

"I'm never too busy to be here for you, Savvy," he stated softly, taking a step toward her.

She gaped as she looked up at him, those sexy green eyes scorching his soul into a smoldering pile of ash. She was the fire, he was the embers, set alight by her and her alone—a slave to her touch, coming to life by her spark, ablaze amidst her flames. Before he could stop himself, his palm was cupping her cheek and he was leaning down to kiss her sweet full lips, fanning the fire into a raging inferno. He deepened the kiss and felt the tension release from her as she kissed him back with a passion that excited every cell in his body, proof that he was *indeed* the embers. All too soon, she was pulling back again and he realized they weren't alone in the waiting room as a throat cleared loudly.

He couldn't stifle the laugh that built in the back of his throat and he murmured in her ear, "God, I can't wait to have you wrapped around my cock again."

She looked embarrassed as her head fell and she shifted uncomfortably on her feet. "Austin," she scolded on a whisper.

"I know. I should control myself, but you're just so damn irresistible." He longed to pull her into the erection that was beginning to grow uncomfortably in his jeans, but her stern look eradicated it as quickly as it had excited it.

"We need to back off now, Austin," she said firmly, crossing her arms back over her ample bosom.

He scoffed. Right! Like that was even a possibility. Especially after that flaming hot kiss. "We both know that's not what either of us wants, Sav."

"Regardless of what we want, it's what's best for everyone right now."

"Everyone" being her father. Anger clenched his heart and he wanted to go hit his boss in the face again. *Dammit!* "By 'everyone', I assume you mean your father?" He couldn't control the venom in his hiss.

"Things are just too tense right now, and I think it's best if we not add fuel to the fire." Her brows went up and the look she gave him dared him to argue.

There was the sassy little minx that stirred his blood in so many amazing ways. He gave her a crooked grin. She wanted to play coy. Fine. He was down for more of her games. It was so much fun to play with her after all. And his reward would be great, he knew. He looked her over, letting his eyes do all the talking as they licked her ever so slowly from the top of her gorgeous head to the bottom of those sexy sandals of hers and he tipped his head at her, sans his hat.

"Now may not be the time, but the flames burning between us *will* be fanned and I intend to let them engulf me."

With that, he ambled out of the exit and didn't dare look back.

CHAPTER 11

"You have some fuckin' nerve, Butler," Luther Boyd grumbled, pointing his finger at Morgan, who stood behind Kelsey on the front porch of the house.

"Daddy, stop!" Kelsey countered and stepped forward, placing her hands on her father's chest to push him back. "We're here to talk."

"Oh, I got *lots* I wanna say," he growled. "Like when the fuck did *this* happen?" Her father motioned between Kelsey and Morgan then added. "And why the hell weren't we called yesterday? Why did I have to find out about it from Peggy fuckin' Freeman at the Piggly Wiggly this morning for starters?" He sighed heavily then moved aside to let them through. "Get the hell in here!" he yelled.

Boy, her dad was really pissed; Morgan knew he would be. Yesterday had been so crazy and hectic following the break-in, and Kels hadn't wanted to tell her folks over a phone.

"Hey, baby," her mother stated and pulled her into her arms. Bella held Kelsey close and closed her eyes.

"I've a good mind to beat the ever-living hell out of you," her father continued to growl at Morgan, who lowered his eyes in shame.

"Enough, Daddy. It was me that he did wrong, not you—"

"*Not* me, huh? You really wanna go there? His actions affected us all, I'll have you know."

"Luther James Boyd." Bella's tone was calm, contrary to her husband's. "That was twelve years ago. And if Kelsey can forgive Morgan then so can we." She stepped forward and took Morgan's hands in her own. "Welcome back, Morgan." Her smile was big and she embraced Morgan, who patted her back in surprise.

Morgan had been the one to suggest they come and talk to Kelsey's parents about not only them but the break-in. He also wanted to get her out of the house for a little while, even though he'd known how difficult this was going to be, for both himself and Luther Boyd.

Luther had been ready to kill Morgan after he'd left Kels at the hospital that day. Good thing he'd gone out of town; Luth had carried a baseball bat over to Starlight Valley with a threat to beat him to death, much to Kelsey's displeasure. She and her father hadn't spoken for weeks after it happened, Morgan had later found out. Kelsey had drifted into depression and ended up having to go to therapy. Marking yet another apology Morgan owed Kels.

"Y'all want something to drink?" Bella asked, to which Morgan robotically nodded. "I'll bring out a pitcher of tea."

Kelsey smiled at her mother's retreating back and motioned for Morgan to take a seat on the couch, adjacent from her father who took the leather recliner across from them. Luther continued to eye Morgan like he would pounce at any second and Morgan's tense frame leaned down, propping his elbows on his knees. Kelsey put a hand on his back and crossed her legs. She was clad in a grey pleated skirt and black silk blouse, and Morgan had on a pair of dark khaki trousers and a light blue linen button down; they'd both just come from work.

"Luther, I'm sorry, but this is important. I—"

"Who the hell said that you get to go first?"

"Daddy! Now, dammit, we are all adults here. Let's fuckin' act like it," Kelsey yelled and gave her father a snarl.

He gave an equally murderous look back, cussed, and let his eyes fall back to Morgan. He waved his palm, motioning for Morgan to continue.

"Kelsey and I have been dating. We've reconciled, and she's been staying at my house this past week." In fact, Kels hadn't been home at all, save to put clothes in an overnight bag, but Morgan wouldn't dare tell her irrational father that right now. He continued, "We love each other." He straightened up a little and took her hand, her gorgeous hazel eyes holding him captive. "I've apologized to her, knowing there's no way to make up for all the wrongs I've done, not in this lifetime...or the next." Kels pulled her lips in, her eyes tearing up at his words, making his heart melt. "But all that matters now is how much we mean to one another and that we're moving forward despite our tragic past."

"Yeah, yeah, Romeo, I figured as much...now get to the part about some fucker threatening you, and in turn my daughter."

The threat hadn't been public knowledge. He must have heard it through the family grapevine- Morgan had told his father, who'd probably told Jack, who'd in turn told Luther.

"Max McClintock—"

That name was all Morgan needed to say before Kelsey's father was fumbling. "Jesus Christ. Of all the fuckin' people in this town you had to go and piss off, Butler."

"Daddy!" Kelsey scoffed. "Morgan didn't piss him off," she defended. "He's been harassing him for weeks about his land. Morgan isn't selling to that criminal."

Luther looked Morgan over once more, his anger seeming to soften some. "He's bad news, Morgan."

"I know that, sir. But I can't sell this town off to a rat like him. He'll corrupt Abundance like he has that town out in New Mexico. I can't let that happen. We can't just sit back and allow him to weasel his way in. He must be stopped."

Luth gave a nod but then smirked, "And how the hell are we supposed to do that?"

"I haven't figured it out yet." Morgan sighed and looked back at Kelsey.

They'd discussed it on the ride over. McClintock was a growing powerhouse but he wasn't all powerful just yet. He had money and he had intimidation, but he didn't have respect. There wasn't a single person in town who wanted him for their mayor but yet no one was brave enough to run against him either. Abundance needed someone stronger, more capable, with the town's best interest in mind, and money to back them up. But so far, there wasn't anyone who was willing to step up to that plate. McClintock knew his extortion was limitless which was why he was doing an early victory dance, but the fat lady hadn't sung just yet. After all, he hadn't officially proposed his intent to run for mayor, and the council hadn't approved it. There was still time.

"On a more personal note, what have you done to safeguard my daughter?"

"I'm taking care of that right now as we speak."

Jackson and Austin were going around the Butler/Kinsen property right that moment, putting up security cameras, securing the fences, setting up motion sensors, lights, everything. Morgan had spared no expense. His construction team had already started the building to house the control center for the monitors and Morgan intended to hire a security guard to monitor the cameras and a body guard for both him and Kelsey if need be. Austin had also recommended doing the same on his building site because he felt as Morgan did, that this thing had only just begun, but Morgan wasn't going to tell Luther Boyd that; he already wanted to kill him.

The police had found tampering at one of the fence lines where the intruder had gotten onto their property; the thought made Morgan sick to his stomach. The town he'd always felt safe in was already starting to become insecure at the hands of Max McClintock. If it weren't for him, they'd never have to do all this.

As if reading his thoughts, Morgan's phone rang and he grabbed it from his back pocket.

"It's Austin. I need to take this." He excused himself and stepped out onto the front porch.

"Yeah, give me good news, man," Morgan stated, answering his phone.

"So...I'm thinking we should hire *two* security guards," Austin proposed.

"Why?"

"Well, we need someone to run perimeter checks too. Let's be honest, this fencing back here is a joke! It ain't gonna keep anyone out, so I don't think being overly cautious is a bad idea here, do you?"

Morgan sighed heavily, of course Austin was right, but they could probably do their *own* checks and have one less person to deal with. "Well, I mean, we're all packing, even the girls. I don't think we need another security guard, hell, the one in the control center will probably be sleeping most the time anyway."

"Aye, aye, captain," Austin smarted back with a scoff. "Your call, buddy. I've placed the motion sensors at the fence line, so if anyone comes across, we'll know."

Austin then assured him that the cameras and motion sensors would be up and working by days end.

Morgan thanked him and hung up the phone. When he went back inside, he saw a rattled Kelsey crying on the couch. He rushed to her side and pulled her into his arms.

"What's wrong, my love?" he asked, his heart tearing as he pulled Kelsey's blonde head off his shoulder to look into her face.

She shook her head, sniffling. She couldn't answer him. Morgan then looked up to her father and mother and sister, Cassidy, who'd joined them and sat holding her mother's hand. The women were teary-eyed and Luth looked again murderous.

"The man who attacked and almost killed my Bella all those years ago is free to walk the streets now," Luth stated, deathly calm. "I'm keeping a close watch on him, but I intend to run him out of town... or make him disappear, whichever comes first." The brown eyes that studied Morgan were even darker than they'd been before and a shiver went up his spine at Luther's intentions.

He gulped and returned his gaze to Kelsey, who shivered. "I never knew what all he'd done...What he—" she sobbed again and looked back at her mother. "Oh, Momma. I'm so sorry."

"Oh, sweetie." Bella gave a smile even as big tears fell down her cheeks. "It all turned out alright. It brought me and your daddy back together and now I have you beautiful girls and two big strong boys, I wouldn't have had otherwise. I wouldn't change a thing."

Even as true as that statement might be, it didn't change the horror of what Morgan assumed the man had done, for he'd never seen this family so rattled. It had been a bad week for the Butlers, Kinsens, *and* Boyds. Morgan only hoped next week would be better.

They stayed for dinner and had an amicable evening, despite Luther's permanent scowl, which Morgan felt wasn't entirely directed at him now. The girls talked for a little while and Morgan stepped back outside once more to talk to Austin, who'd gotten the control center up and functional as he'd promised, which was impressive to say the least. Morgan thanked him profusely before hanging up the phone and coming to sit out on the front porch swing. He gave a heavy sigh and listened to the sounds of the cool spring night.

Would he ever stop wondering if someone were watching him? Have peace of mind to leave Kelsey home—or *anywhere* for that matter—alone? His stomach twisted violently at the thought of someone harming his sweet Kelsey as that man had harmed her mother. He would kill any man who touched the woman he loved. But they wouldn't have another chance, he decided. He would hire a bodyguard for her. Even if she knew nothing about it. She would tell him he was being ridiculous after all, or would she? She'd been completely rattled after the break-in and on into the night and they hadn't slept much, every sound outside keeping them restless, even with his rifle and pistol within inches of his grasp. It wasn't solace enough.

Last night, he and Austin had planned out where the cameras would go, the best type to use, where to hide the motion sensors, where to install the lights. It had felt like they were safe-guarding a fortress and for once in his life, Morgan regretted living on so many acres. There were too many places to hide, too many places that couldn't be covered by security, too much space for invaders to lurk.

He'd always loved the land he lived on, his family's land, his legacy, and the quiet of it all, but now that quiet had been tarnished. Tarnished by one violent man with cruel intentions.

Morgan looked up as the screen door opened, hoping it was Kelsey but almost groaned as Luther Boyd's big frame came into view. His brown eyes looked Morgan over as if he were nothing more than a pest, but softened as he came forward to sit next to him, pulling a pack of cigarettes from his back pocket and a lighter. He pulled out a cigarette and lit it, inhaled slowly, and closed his eyes, savoring it.

Morgan had smoked some back in college but hadn't gotten addicted somehow. It had been casual use, like his drinking.

Luth motioned for Morgan to take a drag, and Morgan immediately shook his head. "No, thank you."

"It's been one hell of a week. I needed it," Luth defended. He'd get no judgement from Morgan. It *had* been a hell of a week. "When my girls are hurting, it tears me apart," Luth continued, as if in a reverie. "First Cassidy comes home bawling her eyes out, saying she broke up with Jax, then I get a call stating Dan Wilson is going free on the same day I find out my daughter had an intruder...Fuck." Luth grumbled. "We have to shut this guy down, Morgan. I'm with you, whatever needs to be done, I'm in." The look in Luther's eyes might have scared Morgan had he not been thinking along the same lines.

When it came to keeping the woman he loved and his family safe, he would do whatever it took. Morgan nodded solemnly. He couldn't imagine what Luth had been through when Bella had been attacked and almost murdered. He'd not been told all the details, but he'd been told enough to know that she was lucky to even be alive. Morgan knew beyond the shadow of a doubt that if someone did that to Kelsey, he wouldn't be able to live until they paid for it with their life. But it wasn't going to come to that. He had his permit to carry, he was constantly packing heat now and he would continue to do so, and Kelsey wouldn't be in a position to have that happen to her—*never*.

"Swear to me that you'll keep my daughter safe, Morgan Dean Butler. Swear it on your life."

"I swear," Morgan stated with conviction as he looked into Luther's frowning eyes. "On my life, I swear it."

Luth held his gaze for a moment and nodded. "My family has been hurt enough. I'm sick of these bastards thinking they have a right to hurt other people. It's time for them to pay for what they've done," Luther said as he stared off.

Morgan had a sinking feeling that Luth wasn't talking about Max McClintock and wouldn't dare ask him what he intended to do, for Morgan understood all too well. "I love Kelsey, Luther. With all my heart. I've never stopped loving her. What I did as a kid was stupid and wrong and selfish. But I'm not a kid anymore. I intend to spend the rest of my life making my mistake up to her. She will never want or need for anything so long as I'm alive."

"Good."

"I mean it. I intend to marry her and make her mine, give her all the children she wants, make her the happiest woman I can."

Luth nodded, and they sat quietly, Luther continuing to smoke his cigarette. "That's all well and good, and you have my blessing to do so, son. But keep in mind, if at any time you hurt my daughter again, I will hunt you down and destroy every last shred of you. Like I said, I'm sick of bastards hurting my family. Sick to death. And I'll add you to that list if you give me any reason not to trust you. So, keep that in mind. I mean to clear the path. And if you aren't on the path with me, you're in my way."

With that, Luther snuffed out his cigarette and went back inside.

Morgan sighed, he didn't know what Luther planned to do to Dan Wilson and he wouldn't ask, but man, he was sure glad he was no longer on Luther Boyd's bad side.

~

"*B*uck Jenkins, as I live and breathe," Jack Kinsen stated and gave his old friend a half hug as he took his extended palm. "How the hell are you?"

"I'm doing good, Jack. Doing good. What the *hell* happened to your face, man?" Stella's father grimaced at the lacerations and bruises on Jack's face; he'd obviously been in a fist fight, and recently.

"Ah, just a little tussle, nothing big." He frowned before giving them a big smile, dismissing the subject.

"Dang, this place is bustling. Do y'all ever take a break?" Stella's father laughed and set his eyes admiringly on Jack's training facility.

"Don't tell me this little beauty you got here is your daughter all grown up?" her uncle Jack winked playfully and moved toward Stella.

"Uncle Jack," Stella scolded with a giggle and swatted his bicep before embracing her uncle's big frame. His arms came around her and she squeezed him, kissing his cheek.

"Stella Rose, you're as beautiful as your momma ever was, girl."

"They grow up too darn fast, Jack. It ain't fair, is it?"

"Not in the least," Jack gave her chin a little chuck, and she giggled again.

Stella looked over the ranch she'd always admired, and the family she'd always loved, as it'd been as dear to her heart as her own home was.

"Now, Nat's gonna be upset. Where's your wife, Bucko?"

"Ah, Viv's stuck in Miami on a set and couldn't get away, but she said she might be able to come in weekend after next. She's ready to be home after this one, I tell ya. It's been a little crazy."

Stella nodded. Her mom had been all over the place with this movie. They'd started in Montana, then gone to San Francisco, Maine, Costa Rica, and now finally Miami. Vivian had been exhausted with the film schedule, and Stella and her dad had followed as much as they could but had deadlines and obligations of their own to fulfill. Stella was due to head to Dallas in two weeks for a show she would be making a cameo role in, which was why she was here.

"So, what do I owe the pleasure?" Jack asked.

"Well, our little star here has a request. I hope we aren't intruding at the wrong time—"

"Are you kiddin'? Y'all are family. There ain't no such thing as intruding." Jack winked over at Stella, who gave him a beaming smile.

Even at sixty-one years old, the cowboy was ruggedly handsome, very much like his gorgeous son that Stella had always had her eyes set on.

"I have a role coming up. I'll be riding western and I wanted to look like a natural," Stella confessed. "Daddy suggested I come see you."

"Well, you're in the right place, darlin'." He took her hand and looped it through his arm, leading them into the huge training facility that they'd always just called a barn. If this was a 'barn' then a horse was just a pony, for this was the most extravagant barn she'd ever seen, and she'd seen a lot going back and forth from Texas to California over the years.

Stella Rose Jenkins was five-foot seven inches tall, blonde and hazel-eyed, and had a dancer's body with muscular legs, a slender waist, and medium-sized breasts. She'd just turned eighteen years old two weeks ago and was as free and easy-going as a girl could be. Today, in preparation for her lessons, she'd donned new denim jeans, a form-fitting white V-neck shirt, big belt buckle, authentic cowboy boots and hat, and had on a layered hemp necklace with a horseshoe emblem. Diamond studs shone in her ears, her hair was curled and long down her back, and she'd applied enough makeup to make her look like she didn't need makeup.

She was proud, like her father, talented like her mother, and had a gypsy soul. She loved Stevie Nicks and wanted to be like Julia Roberts when she grew up.

"Hey, Jackson. Come 'ere. Look who came to see us."

At Jackson's name, Stella's heart hammered in her chest.

They'd stopped in front of a stall, and Stella heard the Dutch door open. She watched as Jackson's tall, muscular frame came into view and felt her heart stop when she looked at him. God, he looked good, really, really good. It had been fifteen months since she'd last saw him, but he was more beautiful than she ever remembered. Tall, muscular, broad, handsome, tan, green-eyed and gorgeous, Jackson. His mouth fell open and it too was beautiful—like everything else about him. She couldn't help but blush as his eyes fell over her, so grateful she'd wore tight clothes to showcase the body she trained every day to be in tip-top shape.

His stunning green eyes came back to hers and she giggled. "Hey, Jax." She licked her lips involuntarily and sauntered forward to stop in front of him.

"St—Stella?" He said her name as if he couldn't believe it was her. "You—you've grown. Wow. You—you—" He was speechless, and she was on cloud nine. She giggled again and lowered her head, bashfully.

"I'm taller, huh?" her brow went up.

He gulped, his eyes moving down her body again, settling on her breasts. Suddenly, he blinked as if coming to his senses. "Uh, yeah, taller, that's it." She heard her dad and Jack snicker behind her and sucked her breath in, her confidence soaring.

"How are you?" she asked and closed the distance between them, leaning her body into him, and he froze. She wrapped her arms around his neck and gave him a kiss on his scruffy cheek. His strong arms came around her waist robotically and her skin felt as if it sizzled with a liquid heat under the surface; she could have moaned aloud.

Jax looked down into her face as she pulled back and grinned at him. "It's good to see you."

He smelled so good, like leather and sweat, livestock and spice, fresh laundry detergent and sunshine, sweet and potent, it made her want to bury her nose into his shirt and inhale him.

"You look beautiful, Stella," Jackson stated as he stepped back, shuffling his feet and looking down. When his eyes came back up they went to her dad. "Hey, Uncle Buck." He rubbed at the back of his neck and Stella practically swooned at how adorable he was with his red cheeks. She could kiss the blush right off of them.

"Jax, you've grown up, son. Getting a beard and everything." Her dad laughed and stepped up to shake Jackson's hand.

"Stella here needs some lessons. I figure you'd want to be first in line for that," Jack stated and cleared his throat.

Jax frowned for a moment before giving Stella a big smile that made her insides hum. "Of course! I'd be happy to help. Right this way." He led her from the center aisle of the barn to the outside where all the corrals were. She waved to her father and Jack, who looked incredibly amused, and followed Jackson.

Once outside, he approached a fellow cowboy who had a horse in tow, saddled and ready to ride. "Hey, Wyatt, can I borrow Hattie for a little while?" he asked, and Wyatt gave him a slow grin.

"Sure thing, J.D. I've got better things to do anyway." He winked and tipped his hat to Stella, who gave him a grin in return. "Well, howdy Stella. How are ya, young lady?"

"I'm good, Wyatt. How's Ash, Kate and Rach…and your wife?"

"They're all doing well. Thanks for asking."

Wyatt handed the horse's reigns over to an impatient Jackson, giving him a terse laugh. Stella came to Jackson's side and together they walked to a circular corral; one that was empty. He opened the gate and Stella and the horse followed him in. "So, you need to learn to ride?"

"Well, you *know* I can ride." She elbowed him, and he gave her a crooked smile. "I just need to know all the nuances, you know? I wanna be able to tack up my own horse and look like a pro. Like you do." She winked, getting a chuckle out of him.

"Well, I don't have *that* kinda time, but—" he teased even as he checked the cinch of the saddle and the bit in the horse's mouth, Stella assumed to keep his eyes off of her.

"Hey," she chided and poked him in the side. This was gonna be fun. Flirting with Jax Kinsen. *Be still my heart, he's fine.*

He chuckled again and looked her over before putting the reins over the horse's head and patting the saddle. "Let's see whatcha got, cowgirl?" His brow lifted and boy, did she want to show him what she had.

Game on, Jax! she thought and popped her foot into the stirrup, grabbed the horse's mane, and pulled herself smoothly into the saddle, taking the reins.

Without another word, Stella took Hattie for a spin around the corral, remembering how she'd been taught to ride, back straight, hips posting with the horse as she moved from a lope to a canter. She took a couple laps around the circular corral then came to a stop before she reached Jackson, the mare only slightly out of breath. "How was that, cowboy?" she asked and pursed her lips at his surprised look.

"Damn. You're a natural. You don't even need me." He shrugged.

Oh, but I do, she wanted to pout and throw herself at him.

"Nonsense," she said and dismounted. "That was just beginner's luck."

Jax scoffed and shook his head. "No. You've taken lessons before. It shows. Who taught you?"

"Your mom, don't you remember?" It had been Natalie Kinsen. Years ago, when she was still a young child.

Jackson shook his head again. "Nah, I guess not. I was too little."

But you aren't little now, are you, big boy? she thought. She bet there wasn't anything little about him. But there was a wedge in between them and always had been. Cassidy. Stella's heart sputtered at the thought of her.

"How's Cassidy doing?" she couldn't help but ask, for it'd been on the tip of her tongue for fifteen minutes now.

At her name, Jackson stilled, his brows drawn, eyes shaded by his tan Stetson. He gulped and just when she thought he wouldn't answer her, he said, "I don't know. She—she broke up with me."

Stella could have literally fallen out. Were those words just what she'd wanted to hear and she'd imagined them? She gaped at him as she searched his eyes, their light green depths were filled with sadness, and she longed to reach out and test the softness of his light brown hair, the tufts of which stuck out from his cowboy hat. "Oh, Jax. I didn't know. I'm so sorry." *Let me soothe your aching heart, you beautiful man.*

"It's all good," he looked away quickly. It must be a new break up. "No harm, no foul." His lips pulled up in a soft grin and her heart gave a little pitter-patter in her chest.

"She's missing out, Jackson. Truly."

He tucked his head, his cowboy hat shielding his gorgeous face with its square jaw and straight nose, his strong chin and high cheekbones. God, Cassidy was an *idiot*. What Stella would give to have a man like Jackson David Kinsen be hers. He was still in love with Cassidy, Stella quickly saw, and her chest hurt with the realization.

"Hey, uh, so, you can ride, obviously. Wanna see if you can take all her tack off, yourself?" he asked.

"So you can get rid of me?" Stella asked. "And move on to bigger and better things?"

"What, like cleaning out a stall?" he harrumphed, and she laughed big.

"You don't have anything bigger or better than *that*?"

"Not today, darlin'."

Damn, the way he said the word "darlin'" had her mind reeling and her heart skipping. "Man, I've missed being back home in Texas." She sighed with a swoon.

He laughed. "Folks back here have more manners than those yuppies out west, huh?"

"Well, those Californian accents sure don't melt panties off like yours does." Shit! Had she just said that out loud? *Oh my God!*

Jackson blushed even as he gave her a surprised laugh. She played along, screaming inside her head to control herself, even as her sex throbbed in unrequited agony.

"They can't fill out a set of Wranglers with the ease that you do either."

Jackson's gaze held hers captive for a moment as he fell still and silent once more, his eyes unraveling her insides.

"You're good for the ego, Stella. You know that?"

"Did Cassidy damage it badly, Jax?" *For God's sake, Stella, just shut the hell up already!* her heart begged, but her brain wasn't listening. He gulped, and she stepped closer to him. "I don't know what happened between you two, but I would be lying if I said I'm not glad you're single." *Abort!* her heart screamed even as her eyes focused on his lips once more.

"You're not seeing anyone?" God, his blush was so damn adorable.

Seeing anyone? She'd seen lots of people. But none quite like him. None with his swagger, his laconic nature, his ruggedly handsome profile and deep, soothing voice. None that had touched her heart like Jackson Kinsen did. She'd had a crush on him for as long as she could remember, but had only realized it two Christmases ago when she'd last saw him and his laugh had jolted her into her own private cowboy Heaven. That was until she'd seen him kiss Cassidy Jane Boyd and all her dreams burst in an instant.

Stella could only shake her head in answer, for his presence was all-consuming and the heat of his closeness set her on fire; she longed to be engulfed in those flames.

She watched him lick his lips again and wanted to beg for him to do the same to hers. God, this was torture. What had she been thinking when she'd come here? She'd known she couldn't be this close to Jax and not think of all the ways she wanted to be with him.

He took a hesitant step back as if a thought just occurred to him and he cleared his throat.

She took that as her cue to be indifferent, she was an actress after all; a trait succeeded to her by her mother. She gave him an easy smile and began removing the saddle and bridle from the horse as Jackson watched wordlessly. It wasn't as easy as riding had been, and she struggled a bit, but within five minutes had the horse bare.

She turned her head for Jax to assess her timing, and he gave her an unimpressed shrug. She balked. "What?"

"You'll get better as we go along."

At that, she smiled.

So, she *would* be seeing more of him then after all.

~

"*W*here you going, A.J.?" Jax asked Austin as he was leaving the barn and getting into his Jeep two days after Jack and Austin's fight.

"Gym, J.D." Austin motioned to his gym bag and workout clothes. "You wanna join me?"

"Dude, I got a workout room in the basement. It's got everything you need. Why don't you come workout with *me*?" Austin noticed then that Jax was wearing gym clothes too. *Great minds and all.*

Austin got out of his Jeep and followed Jackson as they walked from the barn to the back of the big, two-story house.

Jax used a key to enter the basement door and locked the door back once they were through it. Jackson led him to an oversized weight room with two treadmills, a stationary bike, three ellipticals, two full sets of dumbbells, barbells, and rows of free-weights. There was also an array of benches as well as weight machines, exercise and medicine balls, and kettle bells.

"Nice," Austin grinned over at Jax and set his gym bag down in the corner, not failing to notice his girl was running on one of the treadmills. Lady luck was shining down on him today.

Savannah looked put out and scowled over at her brother.

She was gorgeous today, not unlike any other time he'd seen her, and he smiled at her as he took the elliptical right next to her. She was dressed in black yoga pants that flattered her sexy ass and a snug top that left her midriff bare and her breasts peeking out of the top. This was going to be an enjoyable work out, Austin realized.

Heavy metal played over the overhead speakers, and Jax cranked it up before joining them on the stationary bike. A flat-screen TV in the corner had the news on and was muted, but Austin was oblivious as he glanced at Savannah out of the corner of his eye.

He was well into his cardio, sweat dripping from his hairline and back when Vanna stopped the treadmill she was running on and moved in front of him, taking a bench and a set of twenty-pound dumbbells.

Austin watched her trim muscles flexing as she did various curls for her biceps and triceps before moving on to rows and dips. He admired her seriousness and focus on her work out.

Soon, he was stepping off the elliptical and taking a bench next to her, pulling on the gloves from his pocket as he eyed Savannah in the mirror. She attempted to hide how rattled she was as he pulled his hoodie off and shucked it to the side, showcasing his sweat-soaked, muscle-shirt covered torso.

Austin grabbed up a set of 45's, and couldn't help but smirk at her surprised expression. He sat down, rested the weights on his thighs, laid back, and did chest-flys with the heavy weights. He made it look easy, but his arms were on fire as he did twelve reps before sitting back up and resting the dumbbells on his thighs once more.

Her eyes were wide as she looked at him then glanced back to her brother who was entranced by the television.

She huffed as she sat her weights to the side and turned to him. "Why are you here?"

He gave her the slow grin of his that he knew drove her nuts. "I'm pumpin' iron. What's it look like?" He even curled his bicep, a little icing on the cake.

"Dammit, Austin, you know what I mean? Daddy would…You— you have your own gym."

"Well, Jax said y'all had all the equipment I needed for a work-out…I have to admit, Savvy, I couldn't agree more." His brow went up as he watched her cross her arms over her chest, like his presence was the epitome of annoyance to her.

His statement had taken her off guard, and she narrowed her eyes at him before standing and huffing off.

Austin couldn't help but laugh; she was so damn hot when she was pissed and he really loved the challenge she gave him.

"Damn, man. I swear, you can piss her off so easily. What'd you say *this* time?" Jax shook his head in amusement.

"All I said was that this gym had all the equipment I need, nothin' more." Austin shrugged.

Jax gave a hearty laugh and focused back to the television.

Austin did two more sets before taking a water break.

"So," he began as he filled his water bottle up then chugged half of it. He turned to Jax, who came to take the bench Savannah had occupied just ten minutes prior. "Who was that hot little blonde you were carousing with yesterday?"

"Oh, that's Stella Jenkins. Buck's daughter."

Austin eyed Jax suspiciously. "You gonna ask her out?"

"C'mon, Aus, I dunno. She's like family…" But the blush on Jackson's face said otherwise.

"Well, she was eye-fucking the shit out of you, bro."

"It's too soon."

"Is it though?" Austin asked and lay back down on the bench, all too aware that Jackson looked like he was thinking about that question a bit too hard.

CHAPTER 12

*D*allie grumbled as she headed into the waxing mare's freshly cleaned and hayed stall, Austin close on her heels. She wasn't really feeling it today. She was tired, irritated to hell and back, and didn't want to see or look at Austin Montgomery at all, but here he was, the only ranch hand available to help her bring the Friesian foal into the world. Her father had a meeting, her brother was in Bremond, and Wyatt was in the middle an interview.

Dallie had checked the mare last night and knew it was only a matter of a day before Sadie would be ready to give birth, so she'd watched as her appetite waned then got her cleaned up good this morning. Now, here in a matter of minutes to be exact, the baby was coming sure as the world, as Dallie eyed the water sac that had appeared within the last ten minutes and went to go grab an assistant.

"Easy girl," Dallie said as she stepped back to give the horse the privacy she needed to begin foaling, feeling her anxiety as she brushed her hand down the mare's snout. "Back up, Austin. She doesn't like that you're in here."

Austin's sigh sounded annoyed, but Dallie didn't try to overanalyze it; he was going to be her hands in this process as she was almost six months pregnant herself and didn't need to be stooping and pulling a hundred-fifty to two-hundred-pound horse out of its mother.

Dallie waited for the mare to go from standing to laying then approached, placing the mare's head in her lap, careful of her big belly. Cole had been upset that she was even considering being in the stall at all, but she wasn't sure this would be a smooth birth and had felt it only necessary. After all, Dallie's touch would help soothe the mare as it always did when she touched the horses. She immediately felt an easiness sweep over the horse and felt herself relax in turn.

"Ok, stand ready but relaxed, ease your shoulders," Dallie coached softly to Austin as he awaited with gloved hands at her instruction. "She should start the process very shortly."

The mare gave a low whinny, and Dallie stroked her forehead and cheek. She hummed softly as the horse's breath grew ragged and watched her belly as the contractions began. "That a girl," she said.

Within minutes, fluid began exiting from the water sac as Dallie spotted one foot then another. Good, she was birthing normally and Dallie wouldn't need to come down and dig the baby out of the mare's womb. Dallie sighed in content.

"Oh wow, I see hooves," Austin said barely above a whisper, looking over her in awe, and Dallie couldn't help but smile back at him. Despite her mood towards him, a birth was an incredible sight to witness, albeit graphic and gory at times, and Dallie had delivered many a foal in her day.

"Watch for the nose to come next and assist if you see the baby struggling. You might need to break the amniotic sac if he can't do it on his own."

"Oh, good, it's a boy?" Austin asked.

"Well, I don't know for sure but that's what we say until we know."

"Ah, gotcha," Austin answered.

276

They waited and watched as the mare pushed, her breathing and body movements frenzied.

"Tell me what you see, Austin," Dallie insisted as she couldn't see from this far away over the mare's big belly—or her own.

"Uh, I still just see hooves," he said as he came a little closer, lifted his hat, swiped his forehead and replaced it.

Dallie nodded and continued to stroke and hum to the mare. Another couple pushes of her belly and Austin stated that he could see the nose.

"Good, ok, just keep a close eye." She rubbed the mare's neck. "Good girl, you can do this. Push some more. Let's get that baby out."

The mare seemed to hear her and did as instructed. "I see the head, oh my God," came Austin's surprised voice.

"Ok, step in a little closer, just be ready if he needs you," Dallie instructed. They both watched as the mare pushed again and the head of the baby was fully out, now for the hard part, the shoulders. The mare gave a grunt as she pushed again, her big body straining to expel the foal in her womb. "Good girl, good girl."

They watched as the shoulders appeared then his belly. He was so little compared to his momma and black as night, he was gorgeous. Tears came to Dallie's eyes as she watched him, exhausted from birth and trying to pull himself the rest of the way out.

"Ok, you can tear the sac now, I just want to make sure he can breathe."

She watched as Austin stepped forward and tore open the amniotic sac. "Should I pull him?" Austin asked, looking over to Dallie, his amber eyes flashing at her.

"Gently, very slowly, let the process happen as it was intended."

Austin did as he was told and grabbed the little foal by his thorax and eased his hips gently up and out of his mother's pushing body. Austin gave a little chuckle as the pony was free. "It is indeed a boy, I can see that now."

"Are you sure you aren't just looking at the umbilical cord?" Dallie gave a giggle.

"Oh, that's what it is," Austin stated, sarcastically. "No, the term 'hung like a horse' is one I'm all too familiar with, I'll have you know." He gave her a wink; she rolled her eyes.

She didn't need to know that and furthermore, didn't care as the strain on her back reminded her *exactly* how she'd gotten pregnant in the first place.

"Do I need to cut the cord?" he asked, looking over at the forceps of her opened bag.

"No, it should separate by itself. Let's give it a minute. Let them rest."

Dallie continued to observe and stroke the mare, who'd turned her head to look at her baby, sniffing him as the colt inched toward her.

"Look at him, he's so cute," Austin said, thinking the same thing Dallie was, and their eyes connected in astonishment at the miracle of the birthing.

But then Dallie sensed fear in the mare as her hands stilled on the horse's throat. She looked down to see the mare nuzzling her colt, he wasn't moving.

"Austin," her voice trembled. "Check his nose, is the amnion gone?"

Austin's hands moved to the freed snout of the foal, nothing was obstructing it, and he nodded, watching in horror as the baby grew limp.

"Shit, check his airway," Dallie hissed as she tried to move off the ground, using the mare's mane to hoist herself up. She stepped up to the colt just as the mare jumped up and snorted, the placenta still attached to them both, jerking the baby in the process. "Dammit, grab her. I've got to check his airway," Dallie stated and switched places with Austin, who grabbed the horse's head and cooed to her. The mare's uneasy whinny jolted Dallie into action as she opened the foal's mouth and swept for debris, grabbing for her bag and applying a breathing mask to his nose as she got him into position for CPR. She gave the respirator bag a set of squeezes and checked for a pulse, tears coming to her eyes when she didn't feel one. "No, this isn't happening."

"Dallie," Wyatt's voice called to her from outside the stall and she looked up at him.

"He's not breathing," she cried and placed her interlocked hands on the baby's thorax, just beneath his triceps. She began chest compressions.

"Shit," Wyatt stated and opened the stall door to assist.

The mare began to grow restless in Austin's hands, watching her baby with angst.

"Talk to her, Austin. Sing to her," Dallie grated out, her back straining in protest as she pumped the baby's chest with all her might.

"Dallie, let me take over, you don't need to—"

"Get the bag ready for breaths," she interrupted, her mind on the sole task of bringing this horse back to life.

Wyatt did as she'd asked, and she was vaguely aware of Austin's smooth voice serenading the mare as she worked on the foal. Time stood still, an invisible clock ticking in the back of her head, counting down how long the baby had been down. She tried to focus solely on performing high quality CPR and counting the compressions and breaths as she and Wyatt worked seamlessly together.

Just when Dallie's back, hamstrings, and knees began to ache and her heart was breaking in defeat, tears streaming down her face, the foal finally began to breathe and move. Dallie huffed out the breath she'd been holding and sat back on her heels, exhausted and elated at the same time. She watched as the little colt moved around, seeking his mother, feeling Wyatt's arms pulling her to her feet. He held her waist for a moment as she reeled and he steadied her, his brown eyes seeking hers as she blinked and tried to center herself.

"You ok?" he asked and looked down at her round belly.

She grabbed it and rubbed, gulping, aware that she'd outdone herself. But she was indeed alright, just tired as all get out now after the CPR and stress of the situation. She nodded.

"Let me go grab you a chair and a pillow," Wyatt insisted and propped her against the stall door as he exited.

"You alright?" Austin asked and moved to her side, watching her face in concern. "You did great, by the way." His bright, straight smile lit up his entire face, and Dallie could immediately see why her sister would be so taken with him. That smile was downright sexy. Dallie couldn't help but smile back as she looked down at the colt interacting with his mother.

"You did too," she stated truthfully and patted his shoulder, recalling that he'd sang "Free Bird" to the horse. "You sing really well."

"Hey, thanks. I was just doing as my boss told me to do." He gave her a wink. "I'm glad he's alright."

"That makes two of us."

Suddenly, Dallie's head reeled and she felt her feet give out. Strong arms encircled her, pulling her into a hard chest, and her eyelids fluttered closed.

"Dallie," a deep voice called and her eyes opened into Austin's burning amber gaze. "Hey!" He cupped her cheek and looked her over. "You don't look so hot. I think you might need a doctor."

"I *am* a doctor, ya know?" Dallas giggled and tried to right her feet, only to slip again. Austin held her tighter to him and began to scoop her up. She felt strong arms beneath her knees and on her back. Dallie sighed, feeling dizzy, but his strong cologne filled her nostrils and seemed to awaken her some. Immediately, she felt embarrassed by being so feeble in front of this man, the man who'd put her father in the ER three days prior, who'd slighted her sister, but she didn't have the energy to demand he put her down. Dallie let Austin carry her to her father's office and sit her down onto the couch as her head continued to rotate on a foreign axis.

Austin moved to the soda machine and pulled out a Sprite, popping the top and handing it to Dallie. "Drink this," he stated and made sure her hands were around the can firmly before coming to sit beside her.

"I have to go check on the colt and the mother. I have to—"

"Right now, you have to take care of yourself and your *own* little one." His hand moved unconsciously to her belly, and she looked up at him, surprised at his boldness. "This is baby number two, right?" he asked. She nodded, sipping the drink, feeling her senses starting to slowly return.

"Do you want children?" she asked, her statement as bold as his hand on her was.

He looked down and gave a slight grin, his eyes sparkling when he looked back up at her. "I do actually." The statement shouldn't surprise her, but it did somehow; Austin didn't seem to be the fatherly type. He was too rugged, too wild, too unconventional. He was tattooed, rode a motorcycle, brought random women to random places to sleep with. He was unstable and unruly, but he oozed sex appeal, and Dallie understood why Savannah would want a man like him, especially under the circumstances of her breakup with Sidd. Austin was as different from Sidd as night was to day.

Dallie and Savannah had different tastes in careers, hobbies, interests, and obviously men. She'd not discussed this man with her sister much this week, there'd not been much time for girl talk with all that had happened in the last few days, but she'd known Savannah had stayed two nights in a row with him. Savannah wasn't one for one-night stands or sex with random strangers, Vanna was far too smart for that, and Dallie secretly wondered what had happened and why her father had been out for his blood.

Suddenly, the baby kicked in her belly, poking at the hand still atop Dallie's skin and Dallie grinned. "See that, she likes me," Austin chuckled and winked. "She might be the only one in the family right about now." He moved his hand off Dallie's belly, his gaze staring out into the quiet room.

"You care for Savannah." It wasn't a question, Dallie realized suddenly, although how she knew this was beyond her.

Austin's amber-colored eyes returned to hers and he gave her a crooked grin. "She's amazing."

Dallie felt the stirring in her stomach; she knew what that statement meant, and her heart jumped in her chest. Surprise, admiration, and awe filled her.

Suddenly, Wyatt sprang through the door out of breath, "There you guys are."

"Sorry, Dallie wasn't feeling well," Austin answered and motioned over to Dallie who continued to drink her Sprite.

"Well, our colt is already on his feet. I disinfected the cord. It separated, and Sadie delivered the placenta. All is right as rain." Wyatt's smile was big and bright and brought forth one from Dallie.

Wyatt and Austin didn't look exactly alike but favored a great deal. They were both golden tanned, tattooed, and sandy blonde— save the black hair Wyatt still dyed and his piercings. They weren't built the same; Wyatt was taller and more lanky, while Austin was broader and stronger. Austin's beard was fuller and his eyes lighter than Wyatt's, but one could tell they were brothers. A sudden thought occurred to her, like an epiphany, and she laughed to herself. Come to think of it, Wyatt didn't look like the fatherly type either, but he had three beautiful sweet girls of his own. *Anything is possible*, Dallie thought and looked back over at Austin.

"Looks like we make a good team after all, Montgomery." She elbowed him, and he laughed.

Dallie made sure the little foal was nursing and had his first bowel movement, passing meconium, before leaving the barn to head home for the day. She hadn't seen her father or her brother, much to her disappointment, but she was too tired to stay any longer. She needed rest. A nice, relaxing bath and a good meal.

Lily was in rare form that night, and Dallie was glad Cole got home early because she needed to crash after she made dinner. She thanked her lucky stars that she wasn't on call tonight as she drew up a bath.

Cole bathed their daughter and put her to bed while Dallie let her sore muscles absorb the Epsom salt of her lavender bath and when she was all pruny, she got out and rubbed her skin with her new sweetpea and magnolia lotion that was handmade locally before throwing a low-cut gown over her head. When she stepped out, the room was lit in dozens of candles and her husband lay naked atop their bed, stroking his hard shaft in his right hand.

Dallie's brows went up and she couldn't contain the giggle in her throat or the sudden arousal that pulsed through her like high voltage.

"Mmm, well this is a surprise," she murmured as she stepped closer to the bed.

"I was afraid I was going to have to finish without you, Dr. Kinsen-Callahan," Cole's deep voice made her insides shiver.

"You wouldn't dare," she hissed teasingly and narrowed her eyes at him.

"No, I wouldn't. Your hands feel so much better than mine do."

"Oh, I was thinking of a place even better than my hands—and mouth." Her grin was devilish, if his gaping mouth was any indication.

"Why don't you show me what you had in mind, angel?" His hands moved to her hips as her knees hit the bed and she straddled him. "Mmm," he groaned as her hands peeled her gown off her head and tossed it aside. "Aren't *you* a sight for sore eyes, sexy mama?"

"Ugh, Cole, you know I *hate* that nickname," she protested even as she moaned from the feel of his hands on her bare breasts.

"Yes, I do, I'm sorry. You can punish me all you want for it." He teased even as he pulled her hips down to his erection and began rocking them into it, his mouth covering her taut nipple. She moaned aloud as her need for him pulsed deep within her.

"Oh, God, Cole. They're so sensitive. Oh, that feels good."

He chuckled as his opposite hand began to knead her other breast, then he switched out. He leaned up to kiss her mouth after her nipples were thoroughly tortured, and she unleashed the passion dwelling within her at the touch of his hands and body on her own.

"Oh, Dallie. Come to me, my love." His hands trembled as he guided his hard sex into her and they both gasped and shuddered. It had only been days, but it felt far longer as her body acclimated to the stretch of his thickness inside her.

"Mmm, Cole," she whimpered as he settled her atop him, her legs shaking in protest as she began to move over his steely member.

"Oh, yes, baby, ride me."

And she did, letting her desire drive her even as her muscles ached. Nothing existed but the pleasure that arced between the two of them, the exquisite torment of his hard manhood sliding in and out of her, hitting all those sensual sweet spots. She whimpered and climbed and soon came apart to his touch as his hands squeezed her breasts and his mouth nibbled at her nipples, sucking and nipping just how he knew she liked it.

"Cole, I—I can't," she cried as her legs protested and she stopped moving, splaying her hands across his hard chest.

"I got you, baby." He grinned and flipped them over, coming to his haunches as he pulled her hips towards his. He slid his sex back inside her dripping, wet center and angled her hips up towards him as he plunged and withdrew, over and over again, hitting more places inside her and drawing moans from them both.

"Oh, God, Cole. I'm gonna—"

"Yes, angel, come for me." His gorgeous green eyes held hers as his deft fingers caressed at the ridiculously sensitive folds of skin between her legs and she cried out as she climaxed once more. He chuckled, watching as a tear slid down her cheek, her eyes never leaving his as her sex contracted around him in beautiful release. "That's my girl," he groaned as he continued to drive into her. He gripped her hips tighter and arched his back, pushing his length even deeper and getting another moan from Dallie's throat.

"Cole," she gasped, loving the look on his ruggedly handsome face as he hammered into her, so serious, so sexy, as he chased his own release. He pumped faster, harder as her hands moved over his muscular abs and up his chest, coaxing him on, gripping his biceps as he leaned into her and spread her legs wider.

"You want it, baby?"

"Oh, yes, give it to me, Mr. Callahan. Give me all of you. I want it all." She dug her heels into his ass and held on for dear life.

His smirk was sinister as he gripped her bottom in his hands and pistoned into her with all his might. Dallie ignored her protesting legs, her screaming quads, all she focused on was the feel of his sex tickling yet another spot deep within her. She felt the stirrings begin again somewhere unreachable, yet he was there, hitting it, a spot she didn't know existed. She whimpered and gasped as wave after wave, hit after hit, began to make her mind go numb and her body throb in the most delicious ways possible.

"Cole, Cole, oh, God, oh—", she had no clue what she was about to say as her brain exploded in a sea of sparks and her sex clenched hard around him. She literally screamed out in sheer pleasure as his cock hit that incredible spot over and over again. His roar was loud and deep and rumbled them both as he gave a hard thrust, climaxing even as her orgasm still seized her in violent spasms, milking him into a series of gasps and groans.

When she returned from her own sexual high, her husband was still trembling and shaking as he held her tightly to him, his muscles rippling so beautifully it took her breath.

She gave him a knowing grin and raised a brow as his breathing returned and he lowered her hips. He slid out of her and laid beside her, pulling her into his big, strong arms.

"Mmm, Dallas, that was amazing." He kissed her cheek and neck and licked at her sweaty flesh there before moving her hair behind her ear and smiling down at her. She just gave a satisfied sigh and kissed his lips. He returned it as his hands moved over her, coming to a rest on her big belly. "How's my baby tonight?"

The statement never failed to stop her heart and make her melt. "She's as perfect as her father is."

"Ha." He always balked at that statement, telling her he was far from perfect, but in Dallas's eyes, Cole was as close as she ever wanted a man to be to it.

"I have to admit, your pregnancy has made for interesting and rather exciting positions, wifey." He grinned that sexy grin of his that had her mind reeling.

"I can't agree more, husband." She kissed his nose and giggled.

"Have I told you how very much I love you, Dallas Kinsen-Callahan?"

"Hmm, not today you haven't, my sexy man."

"Sexy?" He gave her a silly look. He knew he was sexy; he'd given her three intense orgasms in the span of minutes, some of which were brought on by the mere feel of his muscles beneath her palms, not surprisingly. *"You're* the sexy one." His hands kneaded the back of her thigh and she moaned aloud, the muscles tight from being on her knees over the dying foal. "You okay, angel?" He squeezed and massaged even as she whimpered and groaned. "Rough day?" he asked, concern in his eyes.

She only nodded, she wouldn't tell him how rough because he'd be upset at her for overexerting herself and beg her to cut her hours in half, of which she couldn't do.

"Let me massage you then, sweetheart." The twinkle in his eyes had her giggling again and she let his slow, sensual massage turn into more mind-blowing sex.

Later, as they both lay in sexual bliss, her husband's rough breath in her ear and his chest pressing into her back, she let her mind wander. His hands absent-mindedly stroked their kicking baby as her eyelids fell, exhausted from the day.

She let her memory go back to Savannah and Austin, the unlikely couple, and she couldn't help but smile. As different as they were, they seemed good for one another. Not that Dallie knew Austin very well, but she'd seen how unfit Sidd was for Savannah, it had been evident in the few holidays and get-togethers they'd had with him. Austin was spunky, full of life and mysterious like Vanna was. And Vanna could be sassy—like their mother—on occasion. From what Dallie had ascertained from their conversations, Savannah had been sassy to Austin many times and he'd come back for more, which meant he could handle her moodiness too.

Dallie recalled the look in Austin's eyes as he told her that Savannah was "amazing". She recognized that look. It was infatuation, which was good. He was infatuated with her little sister and that made Dallie happy. Dallie'd once been infatuated with Cole. Now, she was married to this beautiful man whom she had one equally as beautiful daughter and would soon have another.

As if reading her mind, Cole kissed her shoulder languidly then the curve of her neck.

"What are you thinkin' about, angel?" he asked as he slid the covers up to her chin, tucking her into his arms.

"Vanna," she answered.

"Is she ok?"

"I think Austin might be fallin' for her." Dallie smiled as she tilted her head to look back at her husband.

"Is that a good thing?" he asked, thoughtfully.

"I dunno yet."

"Only one way to find out, right?" he chuckled, knowingly.

Dallie closed her eyes. "Right."

But even as she surrendered to sleep, Dallas Kinsen-Callahan suddenly knew Savannah and Austin were gonna be perfect together; she simply felt it.

"an we just address the elephant in the room, real quick?"
"Uncle Jack—"
"Daddy—"

"Jackson Edward," Natalie's shrill voice called over the rest of the murmuring, and Vanna huffed over at her father.

"Well, everyone's thinkin' it, I'm just the one sayin' it," he scoffed and lifted his gaze to Austin, who stood propped against the wall of Morgan's sage green kitchen wall.

"You want me to leave?" he asked, shrugging and pushing himself upright.

"No!" Morgan stepped forward and put a hand on Austin's shoulder, signaling him to stay put, as he looked over at Jack. "Uncle Jack, Austin is handling security and it's important that he's here."

"Can we just focus on the problem, Dad?" Jackson bellowed, frustrated as he crossed his arms over his chest.

"Well, California Dreamin' here *is* part of the problem," Jack grumbled under his breath. "And last I checked he was workin' for *me!*" he yelled over at Morgan.

"Daddy, stop your belly-achin'." It was Dallas who elbowed him and gave him a scowl. He clamped down immediately and waved at Morgan to continue.

"As I was sayin', we need to continue to be vigilant. Keep our eyes peeled for anything suspicious."

The *entire* Butler/Kinsen clan sat in the kitchen of Morgan's house in a family meeting that had been called that Monday night—one week and three days since the break-in. The week had been fairly uneventful, everyone had gone to work like normal, save for Vanna, who'd continued her hiatus, painting and composing—and trying hard to keep her distance from Austin as her dad had asked. She'd helped her mom with housework and dinners, she and Dallie had gone to lunch and shopping one day, and everything had seemed to be fine until one of the sensors had gone off that Sunday night and alerted her dad of someone on their side of the property. He'd chased them off with his rifle in tow, the blast of which had woken everyone else up, thus prompting this meeting.

"He's tryin' to break us down. Get us riled up," Austin stated. "He's thriving on taking away our sense of peace."

"Well, he's succeeded," her grandmother, Corrine, stated, lifting a brow.

"The harassment isn't gonna stop," Austin stated, confidently.

"So, what's the solution then?" Vanna's mom asked.

"We shut this guy down," Morgan said.

"And how do we do that?" Dallie asked, looking over at Austin, and for the first time, Vanna saw what looked like respect in her sister's eyes as he held her gaze. It gave Vanna pause.

"Morgan and I are trying to find some way to tie him to his crimes. A chink in his armor so to speak. I have a confidant who's been doing some digging, and the dirt on this man continues to pile up. It's just a matter of time before he's caught red-handed."

"But at what cost?" her uncle Nathan asked.

"What do you suggest I do, Dad? Sell him the land?" Morgan smarted. "We'll all be worse off than we are now."

"So, how do we catch him?" her Aunt Jordan asked.

"We fight back," Morgan suggested.

"This isn't *Roadhouse* for God's sake," Jackson smirked.

"Wait! We're just as powerful as he is. This is our damn town. We have more money than he does. Why are we putting up with this shit?" her father asked, slamming his fist on the table.

All was quiet for a moment as they digested his words. He was right. Vanna chanced a glance over at Austin then, his bearded face surprised by her father's words.

"We threaten him back," Kelsey suggested and leaned into Morgan, whose arm tightened around her waist.

"With what? Bodily harm?" Jackson scoffed again.

"We run him out of here," Nate answered. "What does he have that we don't? Lawyers? Money? Security? We have all of that and more."

"We could bribe him," Dallie proposed.

Her father mulled that over then shrugged.

"Or we just let him continue to bully us," Morgan stated angrily.

"No," Savannah offered. "We've all suffered enough. Morgan had a suggestion, and—"

"Absolutely not," Austin countered, and she held his gaze for the first time in almost a week.

She'd come over an hour earlier than everyone else at Morgan's prompting, and he'd proposed that Vanna do something that she'd thought was completely ludicrous. He'd told her to run against

McClintock for mayor. First of all, she lived in Houston, second, she planned to return to Houston, and third, why did he possibly think she would want to be mayor of Abundance?

"It's only a hoax, Vanna," he'd offered. "But if you run, no one will vote for him, and he'll be forced to leave. He'll have no power. If it's you who runs against him, you'll win, hands down."

It was brilliant but insane at the same time. Their current mayor, Victor Leach, was retiring and no one had stepped forward to take his place. Enter McClintock who technically wasn't approved to even run yet, since he was not a resident of Abundance. But Morgan planned to hold a council meeting and announce Vanna's intent to run. It was something McClintock wouldn't be expecting. Nor would her family, which was why they had to believe it too.

"What am I missin' here?" Her father looked over at Vanna then, breaking the gaze she had on Austin's handsome face.

"I proposed that Savannah run for mayor, against McClintock," Morgan admitted.

"Are you *out* of your mind?" her Uncle Nathan yelled over at Morgan then. "She'll be a walking target, more so than you are. You're a fuckin' coward if you—"

"It could work," Vanna offered. "Just listen," she screamed, attempting to outspeak her family, her voice growing higher than any other in the room.

She remembered Austin's reaction then as it was now. "You're gonna lie to your family?" he'd asked, his eyebrows raised, plump lips pursed.

"If that's what I have to do to protect them, then so be it," she'd smarted back.

Her gaze flew to Morgan's now, and he gave her a subtle nod. She looked to Austin, whose eyes challenged her, then her gaze settled to her mom and dad, who sat across from her.

"If you run for mayor—?" Jax began.

"That means you're staying home?" Dallie's excited voice chimed in.

"Vanna, is that true? You're home to *stay?*" Her mother's hand went to her chest.

"I'm more than qualified for the position," she stated, not directly answering the question, but holding their eyes just the same.

"Why don't *you* run for mayor, Morgan?" It was Austin who asked.

"Because it won't look legit," her father answered. "The entire town knows Morgan's had run-ins with McClintock. He'll expect that. Plus, Morgan already holds a seat on the town council. It'll look like a shoo-in. Savannah is completely unexpected. It'll be a slap in the face." Her dad eyed her. He could see right through her malarkey, but he didn't give her away.

"It could work," Vanna's Paw-Paw said and grinned over at her.

"It'll put Vanna in danger," her mother said.

"More danger than we're in now?" Savannah retorted. "We're all walking on eggshells around here, waiting for this man to actually harm us."

"Isn't this what the police are supposed to do?" Jax asked, frustrated.

"Other than zoning, the police can't do much," Austin stated.

"So much for a restraining order," Kels murmured.

"So, are we in agreement then?" Morgan asked.

They all sat quietly, looking around. Vanna taking in their solemn faces for a moment, the concern, stress, and anxiety of the last couple weeks coming to a head, and she nodded. "It must be done."

Her eyes returned to Morgan's and he nodded again. She saw Austin shake his head, out of the corner of her eye, and storm out the back door.

~

*A*ustin took a deep breath in as he tried to calm his anger. Damn Morgan and his 'brilliant' ideas. This was too risky. Savannah would have a direct target on her back and the shooter was a man with a reputation as shady as the man they were all already hiding from. Austin was furious. With Morgan. With the situation. With Vanna for just agreeing to this without considering the consequences. Trevor was doing all he could but without concrete evidence, the FBI couldn't move in yet. They were all sitting ducks for Sim's antics.

Austin heard the door open and tried to calm down, but his hands were shaking. He took another deep breath in and was shocked when he heard Vanna's soft voice behind him.

"Hey." He felt her palm go to his shoulder and he spun around quickly, wrapping his arms around her.

"You're the dumbest genius I know, Savvy. What the hell are you doing?" His eyes burned into those gorgeous Caribbean blue-green spheres of hers and his heart did a flip flop.

"I'm trying to prevent a war?"

"You mean *start* one?" He couldn't contain the growl in his throat at the thoughts of her being in danger. It scared the hell out of him.

"You know that's not what I want." She angled her face up, and he looked down at her gorgeous mouth, the most gorgeous mouth he'd ever seen.

"Savannah, this man is very dangerous."

"He started a war with the wrong family. It's time to show him who he's messing with."

"Dammit, you're so much like your fuckin' father sometimes, I swear to God!" Austin sighed heavily and unhanded her, his fists clenching involuntarily at his sides. "I've been to war, remember? I know what happens. There are casualties. Casualties that you can't anticipate. People are gonna get hurt. Are you prepared for that?"

Her palm reached up to cup his cheek, stilling him, stilling his anger. "Are you afraid?"

"How are you *not?*"

"Because you'll keep me safe."

"Oh, Savvy," he ground out and pulled her back into his arms as his forehead leaned against hers. "And what happens if I can't?" He closed his eyes, remembering Jerome's body as it practically disappeared right in front of him.

"You will. I know you will," her voice was barely above a whisper as she tilted her face up to his and his head fell. His lips captured hers and savored their softness against his own.

He moaned aloud and cupped her face, deepening the kiss as she leaned into him, her breasts and belly hitting his chest and torso, scorching his flesh like a branding iron. He reveled in the feel of her against him as his hand moved into her wavy curls. It had been so long. He needed to be inside her, needed to have his cock buried within her delicious heat. His tongue brushed hers and her mouth opened to its coaxing. Her tongue stroked back and her hands moved up his shoulders to wrap around his neck. He shifted them then and his hips pinned hers to the railing of the back porch. His mouth continued to torture hers until they were both breathless then he lowered his head to her throat.

He smirked. "If I'm gonna keep you safe, Miss Kinsen, I'll have to get even closer to you than I already am, spend more time with you…" His teeth grazed her pulse point and she shivered, sending a jolt straight to his groin.

"What'd you have in mind, cowboy?" she asked as she pulled back to look at him. Her dark, perfectly-shaped brow arched and he instantly fell in love. Just like that. Head over freakin' heels. Dammit! She had him, every single damn inch of him in her grasp.

He smirked. "Oh, I think you know *exactly* what I have in mind."

She giggled, and his heart soared at the thought of having her once again.

"Well, isn't this cozy!" came a deep growl, and Austin and Vanna shot apart as if a cannon had gone off. Vanna straightened her shirt, and Austin moved to her side, staring out at the clearing as his erection painfully waned.

"Daddy! We were just—"

"I know what you were doing. Save it. Vanna, go inside. I need to talk to Austin."

"No," she huffed and crossed her arms over her chest. "Whatever you have to say, you can say in front of me."

Damn, she was so fuckin' hot when she was being feisty. It made Austin want her all the more.

Her dad seemed more amused than angry that she'd defied him, and he smirked, "Fine." He took a seat in one of the rocking chairs and looked out the screen into the darkness of the night. "He could be watchin' us right now, ya know?"

Austin watched Vanna shiver and hated her obvious discomfort.

"You two care for one another, I see. And I'm gonna use that to protect my daughter," Jack stated and looked up at them.

Vanna gulped, and Austin frowned. "What do you mean, Jack?"

"I mean, you're gonna protect her. You were in the Army, you know your way around a gun, and you know how this shit works... better than any of us, apparently. So, who better to protect her than you? Plus, you care about her well-being. And I'm gonna use that to my advantage."

"But Daddy, you wanted us to keep our distance—"

"I know, I know. But y'all are gonna find some way to be together, if that's what y'all want to do, am I wrong?" Jack looked up at Austin with a scowl.

It was true. And now Austin's suspicions about exactly *why* they needed to "keep their distance" were confirmed. Damn Jack Kinsen!

"Jack, I'm a horse trainer, not secret service."

"Now, you'll be Savannah's body guard...unless you want me to hire someone else." Again, the man smirked. Sonovabitch, how could he read Austin's thoughts like that? He knew Austin would be nuts with worry no matter who Jack assigned to protect Savannah. It had to be Austin—Austin and no one else.

"No, sir. I'll do it."

"Good. It's done then. You'll start immediately." His smile was diabolical and he stood and extended his hand to Austin. "Now's your chance to redeem yourself, Montgomery." His green eyes, darker than his daughter's, held Austin's in a challenge. He shook Austin's hand and leaned in to the ear opposite Savannah. "Consider this your one and only reprieve, Montgomery. If you let anything happen to my daughter, my idle threats of the past will turn into promises."

With that, Jack turned and walked back inside.

CHAPTER 13

"*I*s this really a good idea?" Jax asked, even as a slow grin spread over his face.

"Looking at naked chicks is *always* a good idea, cuz," Morgan scoffed.

"Damn straight," Austin agreed and opened the doors of the Prickly Cactus, Abundance's one and only strip club.

His eyes adjusted to the darkness inside after several minutes, and they greeted a large bouncer who ushered them to a table in front of the center stage. Austin wasn't quite sure what to expect when Morgan had made the suggestion; he couldn't imagine the small town would even *have* a strip club, much less one with half-way attractive ladies in it. But as he looked around at the topless dancers, he was rather surprised to say the least.

Hell, it was Abundance after all. There was something different about this town, he'd seen fairly quickly after meeting Dallie, Savannah, and Kelsey, besides wasn't there some country song talking about how God had blessed Texas and brought angels down from Heaven? He would have to agree because the ladies were drinking some mighty good water or milk or something...or perhaps the beer was just more potent.

A brunette shooter girl came by, scantily clad in a low-cut white top that was tied up beneath her big breasts, black bralette showing beneath it, and short denim shorts, displaying long tan legs. Austin couldn't help but laugh at Jackson's surprised expression as his gaze fell over her.

"Well howdy there, cowboys, what y'all want to drink?" Her heavily made-up eyes zeroed in on Austin and she gave him a wink.

"Oh, I—uh," Jax began, only to be cut off by Morgan.

"We'll take a couple pitchers of beer, please? Bud, if you got it on draft."

"Sounds good, handsome," she said and winked over at Morgan.

When she walked away, Morgan hissed at Jax. "Don't give yourself away, jerk off."

Austin shook his head in amusement. If they were carded, Jackson had a legitimate-looking fake ID. But wouldn't it be some shit if they got thrown out on those grounds? At least they weren't here to get shit-faced; it wouldn't be a repeat of what happened to Jax at the Rusty Spur, Austin had already told him that in the truck on the way here. They were just out to have a few beers and hang out.

Austin's gaze moved over the lit dance floor to the half-naked dancer on the pole in front of them. She was blonde, pretty, and had breasts as fake as the color of her platinum hair.

He looked over at Jax, whose eyes were riveted on the dancer now crawling on all fours towards them on the jetty of the stage.

"Hey y'all," she cooed and licked her lips as she sat back on her haunches, bringing a hand from her thigh to her breast. "We have a newbie?" she asked and eyed Jackson knowingly.

"Yes, ma'am, got a rookie here," Morgan patted Jackson's back and laughed.

"Not new to—uh—certain things, just never been to a strip club," Jax asserted and cleared his throat.

"Well, how about I welcome you good and proper then," she stated seductively and began an enticing dance. She rocked her hips and rolled her body to the thumping beat of the overhead music. She turned, removed her undergarments and bent over, showcasing a plump backside before heading back to her pole to swing, prop, and move over it with notable skills.

It was a good dance, it was impressive, but it didn't do a thing for Austin. At any other time, he'd be relishing this opportunity for a good tease, a bare show of beautiful smooth bodies, women whom he couldn't seem to get enough of. He'd been to many a strip club in the past. He'd flirt with the shooter girls, watch the strippers, get a lap dance or two and thoroughly enjoy every second of it. He'd not known when or if he'd ever see another set of tits when he went off to war. He'd control himself, he wasn't one for taking strippers home like some of his buddies were known to do. No, he'd never been quite *that* desperate for a woman. He'd usually call up an old friend to help set him up or meet a girl at a club or bar and take her out on a couple dates before seeing where it ended up. Despite his recent behavior, there had been maybe five women total he'd taken home after just meeting them. It wasn't something he was proud of, but hell, he was a testosterone-filled man. He'd always been a smooth-talker and it didn't take long for it to pay off and he cashed in on the rewards. But tonight was different; the desire he felt wasn't aimless. It had a face. It had a name. And it claimed not just his dick but his heart too.

That desire was Savannah Grace Kinsen, and she sent his mind into orbit. He'd slept with her one night and now, he was ruined to any other female, it would seem. She was smart and sexy and funny and sassy, and he wanted to drive back to Kinsen Ranch that instant, grab her up, and claim her once more with the mind-blowing abandon he had just a month prior.

Had it only been a month? Was that even possible? Could a man really only have one sexual experience—ok, more like 3 or 4—with one woman and actually be in love with her? A month ago, he would have said, "No fucking way," but now he wasn't so sure. For he yearned for his sweet Savvy unlike he'd ever yearned for any other woman before. She'd been all he'd thought about since burying himself inside her and waking the next morning with her tight little body curved into his.

Right now, she was safe, at home with her father, mother, niece, sister, Cole and Kelsey. They were having movie night with Lily, so Morgan had suggested the boys go out. They'd been taking patrolling shifts the last few days until they found security guards they trusted. Wyatt had perimeter duty tonight, along with Jack and Cole, who would have declined the invite anyway, Morgan had told Austin—gentlemen that they were.

When Jax, Morgan, and Austin had gotten into the truck twenty minutes earlier, it had been Morgan who'd smirked over at Jax, stating just the place they should go to soothe his "heartbreak and sullenness".

"What's your name, cowboy?" A set of tits asked Austin, and he looked up into big, blue, doe eyes and a head full of blonde ringlets.

He gave her his signature smile. "Austin." He tipped his hat.

"Mmm, you're one sexy cowboy." She looked him over in unbridled interest. "Want me to take you to the V.I.P. room and show you how *I* ride?" She winked and moved her hand over her right breast, stroking it leisurely.

At any other time, Austin would have given her a "Fuck yeah, baby," taken her outstretched hand and let her work him into a sexual frenzy with her tight, little body, but the only thing she did for him was make him want Savannah all the more. He grinned and motioned over to Jax. "Actually, darlin', I brought my boy, Jackson, out tonight. See, he's all kinds 'a tore up from his recent break up and needs a woman like you to make him forget all about ol' what's her face." Austin dug into his back pocket, fished out a hundred-dollar bill from his wallet, and tucked it into her garter belt. He gave her a wink and whispered under his breath, "His first time to a strip club."

At that, the blonde's smile dripped venom as she eyed Jackson, who gulped audibly at her. "Oh my goodness, you poor darlin'. I've got just what you need to feel *so* much better. Come with me, baby boy." She took his hand, and he looked uncertainly over at Austin who gave him a terse nod, and off they went, leaving a laughing Morgan and Austin to watch them walk away.

"Good for him, he needs to have a little fun for a change."

"Only been with the one chick, huh?" Austin asked.

"Yeah, been together since they were babies, well pretty much anyway."

"I mean, hell, if that's all it takes then it's kinda impressive, I have to say."

"That's all it took for me. Just one woman." Morgan smirked and looked off, not at the dancer in front of them but beyond. "I fell hard at fourteen and never recovered."

"Fourteen, huh? Damn. That's young."

"It was like an electric jolt went through us when we met and shook hands for the first time. No other woman has ever affected me like Kels did. I tried to move on, but I always came up short without her. So, I caved. That Friday night at The Spur."

"Turned out to be a pretty damned interesting night, I'd say." Austin laughed.

"For you too, huh?" Morgan eyed Austin suspiciously, noting that he wasn't entranced by the dancers either as they attempted to put on a good show for the two men before them. They might as well have been invisible for all the good their moves did them. "Savannah."

Just her name got Austin's heart palpitating. He gave Morgan a big grin. "I'm sure Kels told you everything about that night, huh?"

Morgan nodded. "I also see the way y'all have been lookin' at one another. I'm really not that surprised to be honest. You two aren't that different, ya know?"

Austin took a sip of the beer that was brought to them at that moment, looking away even as he knew Morgan was onto something. "She's on the rebound though," he stated as much to himself as to Morgan, knowing it was true and that knowledge cut into him like a knife wound.

Morgan smirked. "You can't really be on the rebound when your relationship's been in the shitter the whole time." Austin glanced back over at him, letting him go on without a response. "Savannah's always marched to the beat of her own drum and not many people can keep up with her. You keep her on her toes and she doesn't really know how to take that." Morgan laughed. "Y'all are good for one another." He gave Austin's elbow a nudge. "She really likes you, ya know?"

Just then, Austin's phone started buzzing from his back pocket; the notification for the app he'd set up for the security system was going off and he felt anticipation seize him.

He grabbed his phone and unlocked it, bringing up the app and touching the notification badge. He could see one of the cameras; the motion sensor had been triggered, and the video was live. He couldn't make out much aside from flames.

"Shit," Austin grumbled and clicked on the live feed.

"What's wrong?" Morgan asked and moved closer to try and see what Austin was looking at.

"Looks like McClintock has finally shed first blood."

"What do you mean?"

"I mean, go grab your cousin. We gotta go! Right fuckin' now. He's set something on fire."

~

Savannah paced out on the porch, waiting for the men to return as Kelsey sat crying on the front porch swing. Her dad had just gone inside to man the cameras, stating that the other guys would be there in a minute. The dog was out here with them, so Vanna wasn't worried. Caesar laid on the rug at the door, practically dozing, all the world, a pup at peace.

Dallie, Cole and Lily had gone on home for the night as Cole didn't want his pregnant wife or daughter to be any more upset than everyone already was.

Savannah's dad had cussed up a storm and Kelsey had gotten upset when his and Cole's phones had started alarming simultaneously during the movie notifying them of activity on the building site of Morgan's.

The trailer had been set ablaze by McClintock's minion, assumedly. Her dad had immediately called Morgan, who said he was on his way and told them all to stay put and be on lockdown. Only after her father had checked all the security cameras around their immediate perimeter did he feel it was safe enough for Cole and Dallie to leave. They'd already called and said everything was fine on their end. Savannah's mom had made the rest of them coffee and they sat solemnly, awaiting a reply.

Now, Savannah took in a deep breath as Morgan's big black Ford F-150 pulled into the driveway. She felt relief shoot through her, sharp and calming, as Morgan, Austin and her brother stepped out.

Morgan was the first to reach the porch and Kels ran to him. They embraced tightly and kissed fiercely, tugging on Savannah's heartstrings.

"It's destroyed, nothing's left," Morgan asserted.

"The lots?" Vanna asked.

"Fine. It was just the trailer. It was contained by the gravel, thank God. But my blueprints are gone." He huffed and stroked Kelsey's back as he frowned down into her face.

"I'm so sorry, my love. I'm so glad you're ok, though," she whimpered, kissing his cheek. "Let's go home now, Morgan. Please?"

Morgan nodded over at Vanna and moved away, Kels in tow, as Jax and Austin came onto the porch.

"Hell of a way to end my first night at a strip club," Jax grumbled and huffed as he opened the front door, stepping over Caesar's pert head on his way inside.

"Strip club?" Vanna asked, surprised. "So *that's* where you boys decided to go?" She felt anger lick at her veins. Just the thought of a naked woman being anywhere near Austin made her blood burn.

"It was Morgan's idea for the record." Austin shrugged and came to stand next to her at the porch railing.

"Why am I *not* surprised," she continued, feeling both irritation and jealousy. "So now you're contributing to my brother's juvenile delinquency?" Austin snorted and began laughing heartily. "What the hell is so funny?"

He bent double, gripping his stomach, trying to catch his breath as Vanna fumed and tapped her foot on the porch.

"Sorry, I didn't even know people still used that word," he answered her after tears came to his eyes and he'd gotten his laughter out. Savannah seethed in anger. "And last time I checked, your little brother is much older than a 'juvenile'."

Her eyes narrowed and she shoved a finger into his chest. "Perhaps this wouldn't even have happened if—"

"Whoa, easy there, darlin'." Austin put his hands up in defense. "I *told* you we needed to keep our guard up. It's why we installed cameras in the first place. Don't worry. I'll be scanning them over first thing in the morning and looking for evidence. We handed copies over to the cops tonight too and we're getting 24-hour zoning and surveillance here on the ranch. I just told your dad all of this on the phone."

Savannah sighed. Yeah, so the fire started on a night when they hadn't been expecting anything—it could have happened at any time —but it really stuck in her craw that it had to be tonight while they were getting their rocks off in some skanky strip joint. Her anger flared once more.

"Well, did you enjoy yourself?"

Austin, whose handsome face had been looking out at the clear night they'd been blessed with once more, glanced over at her and turned his body toward her. He gave her a lopsided grin. It infuriated her. "Not as much as I'm enjoying myself right now, believe me."

Vanna scoffed, but before she could cross her arms, Austin was pulling her hard into his tight chest. She almost moaned at how solid his muscular frame felt against her. He looked down into her eyes, his tan cowboy hat covering his forehead, his amber eyes burned into hers.

"Savvy, there's no place I'd rather be than right here with you."

"I know better than that load of bullshit."

"Oh, you do, huh? You seem to have this idea in your head that I'm some heartbreaking, wild-ass playboy. Well, guess what? I'm sorry to disappoint ya, baby, but I ain't."

"And you seem to have it in your head that I'm some weak and desperate female who needs protection, but I'm not."

Austin laughed big. "Baby girl, there isn't a *thing* about you weak or desperate. That's what I love about you, Savannah Grace." He grabbed her around the waist then and lowered his head, seeking her lips and finding them as a moan vibrated from her throat. She let herself be lost to his words and lips as his big palms settled at her lower back. He didn't deepen the kiss but held it to just their lips, and Savannah was surprised by the tenderness of it. Her hands came up and rested on his broad shoulders, and he pulled back slightly to look at her. She gulped. "If I could have you just like this for the rest of my life, I would never step foot in another strip club."

She wasn't really sure how to respond as she just stared back into his amber eyes; eyes that seemed to assess every aspect of her in that moment. There was no hint of sarcasm, no phoniness, all kidding aside—just raw, real, genuinely clear resolve.

She could lose herself in his eyes, the curve of his bearded jaw, the furrow of his blonde brows. He was beautiful and all she wanted right then was to be his. Fully and truly.

His mouth widened into a slow smile that took up his face then. "I wanna take you out, Savvy. On a date. Soon."

Savannah was too stunned to respond; she could only nod. That sounded amazing. A date. When was the last time she'd even been on a date?

Austin leaned in to kiss her again, the briefest of touches. His lips explored hers, as if doing so for the first time, with a slight brush and coax. He sipped at her plump lips as if he were drinking from them then his strong tongue slid in and she felt herself melting into his strong arms. She wanted him again. To feel his big frame on top of her, feel his big shaft filling her, feel herself be lost to him all over again. She wanted to beg him to carry her back to the hayloft at that very moment and spank her bare bottom like he had that night a month ago, to rock her world and make her forget all her prior lovers again. But he was pulling back, and her mouth felt ravished and unsatisfied, her womanhood humming to be overtaken by him.

"Go inside now, darlin'. Lock up and I'll see you in the morning. Bodyguard's orders." Austin winked, and Vanna nearly whimpered and begged him not to go just yet, for she longed to spend the night with him once again. "Caesar, let's go home, buddy."

Savannah did as he'd instructed, allowing his strong, capable hand to assist her to the door. When he pulled her knuckles to his lips, her panties grew damp and her mouth went dry even as her heart soared. She licked her lips as his eyes fell over her once more. She felt unabashedly sexy in that instance. He smiled again, tipped his cowboy hat, and waited for her to close the door and lock it behind her.

What the hell had just happened? Was she actually *falling* for Austin Montgomery? Damn. Hell might have just frozen over.

~

The entire trip back to Morgan's log home was in silence. Kelsey had volunteered to drive but he'd given her a curt shake of the head and she'd simply gotten into the passenger seat of his truck and taken his outstretched hand in her own as he drove the mere two miles to the house.

Once inside, after turning on the lights and locking the door. He threw his keys on the coffee table and pulled her into his arms. He buried his face into her hair, inhaling her, and for a moment she thought he was crying then he pulled back slightly and took her face in his palms.

His sapphire eyes unraveled every cell of her being as she drowned in their blue depths.

"I was so scared, Kels," he began. "When Austin said the word 'fire', all I could think about was you, that you were in danger, and I wanted to die. I wanted to kill the man who'd threatened you and make him suffer. I can't tell you how relieved I was that it was only the office trailer."

"But Morgan your blueprints, your designs, your—"

"Can all be replaced," he countered and kissed her lips softly. "You, my sweet honey locks, you *can't* be."

He stepped forward, closing the remaining distance between them, and slanted his mouth across hers, his hands fell to her back and he pulled her roughly into him. She moaned and ran her hands down his chest and around to his back, kneading the hard muscles there.

"Oh, Morgan," she cooed as a hand moved to cup her breast and his mouth moved to her throat.

"I can't live without you, Kelsey Jean. I can't and I won't."

With that, he picked her up in his arms and cradled her to his chest as he took the stairs quickly, in a rush to get to the bedroom. She couldn't help but blush as he practically threw her down on the bed and covered her body with his, his deft hands making quick work of her clothes. He swiftly unbuttoned his jeans and unzipped himself as she pulled his face back to hers for more scorching hot kisses and his tongue plunged in, claiming her mouth. He moaned this time and she felt his knee part her thighs as he moved his torso between them. Suddenly, the head of his thick sex pierced her wet opening and she whimpered, not believing how much she'd missed having him inside her; it had been mere hours since their last sexual union.

"Mmm, yes, baby."

"Kelsey, you're my everything. You always have been. How could

I have ever thought I could just fuckin' walk away from you? Oh, God." He grunted and reached for her breasts.

"Shh," she soothed him even as her thighs wrapped around his middle and her sex milked him into mindless abandon. He thrust deeper, his hips angling, pushing himself even further inside her as his mouth covered hers again.

"Fuck, Kelsey, this feels so right, honey locks. *You* feel so right." His hand moved to caress her tingling bud.

"Oh God, Morgan, I'm gonna—" she didn't finish before her world was splitting apart and she was losing herself to him. He rode her orgasm and lowered his mouth to her nipples, suckling and kissing as she cried her climax.

"Forgive me, Kelsey. Forgive my stupidity. Oh, how wrong I was." He pleaded even as his hips relentlessly began hammering into hers, his body a missile set to pleasure her.

"I forgive you, Morgan. How could I not?" she gasped as her body began unraveling all over again.

"Take what you need, baby, what I kept from you for so long. God, I was such a fool."

She gripped his hard ass and held on as he came down lower on top of her, his chest covering hers. Her hands moved to his shoulders then as his fell to her hips and he tilted them up at an angle to his, bringing her bottom off the bed. "Morgan," she whimpered, feeling her womanhood clench.

"I love you, Kels, I love you so much."

"Mmm, Morgan, oh, God, I love you," she cried as her womanhood contracted and her mind split open again in a starburst of ecstasy.

When her orgasm subsided, Morgan pulled out and turned her over on all fours, coming to his knees. She felt his fingers part her before his rock-hard member claimed her again. She gasped and moaned as he began thrusting into her from behind. She leaned down and angled her bottom up, hitting his thighs with each thrust of his hips.

His palm gave her a sharp smack on the bottom before gripping her hip to steady his rhythm, his other hand moving into her hair and tugging gently. "Do you know how much I love fucking you, Kelsey Jean? How much I missed it? Missed this sweet body of yours?"

"Mmm, yes, fuck me, baby. Harder," she moaned, her body responding to her lover's sex as Morgan did as she coaxed. "Oh, oh, Morgan."

"Fuck yeah, I'm gonna come, baby."

"Oh, me too... Oh, God." His grip on her hip and in her hair tightened as her world split and they cried out together in perfect sync as their bodies caved to the sexual energy spiking between them.

Morgan's hips continued to gently pump into hers as his climax abated. Kels felt her center clench him until slowly she came back to earth, her breathing normalizing. Gently, he pulled away and she flipped over and into his arms; into the arms of the man who'd had her heart long before she'd realized she'd even given it away.

He grinned lazily down at her, the moonlight bathing his russet skin in bars of silver and blue. His hair was unkempt and he was sweaty from their lovemaking. His lips were sparkling along with his beautiful blue eyes.

"I never hated you, Morgan. It's important that you know that. You hated yourself enough for the both of us, it would seem." He said nothing, just gulped audibly in response. "Please, can we stop dwelling on our past and move forward? I don't want to rehash it each time we get upset. The baby died and a part of us died along with him, but we're here now, alive and well, and it's vital to our relationship that we don't focus on the things we can't change. We were kids. We ain't kids any more." Her eyebrows went up even as his hand cupped her cheek.

He kissed her lips softly, gently, as if he'd never done so before and was testing their softness. When he pulled back, he smiled at her.

"Marry me, Kelsey." It wasn't a question, she noted. It was a command. She smiled slowly in response. "I should have made you mine years and years ago. It would appear that fate won't have it any other way."

"Morgan, I would *love* to be Kelsey Jean Butler."

Morgan gave a deep, sexy laugh and moved his hands down her back to pull her into him. "Honey locks, more beautiful words have never been spoken."

~

"*W*ell, well, if it isn't 'Sharp-Shooter' Montgomery," the deep voice of Brody Sims grated out as he approached Austin. "What are you doin' in Abundance, Texas, old friend?"

Friend. Now there was a word that Sims wouldn't know if his life depended on it.

"I think we both know the answer to that, Sims." Austin's arms remained crossed over his chest and his brows drew lower over his eyes. He was propped against his Jeep, outside the Rusty Spur, of all damn places. He'd tracked Sims here to discuss what he'd seen on the video footage of Morgan's building site—what he'd hoped the idiot had been dumb enough to miss…and luckily, he had. "You appear to enjoy the criminal lifestyle, it would seem."

"Criminal?" Sims scoffed and shrugged.

"Let's cut the bullshit, Brody. I got a tape here to link you to a fire that happened on private property the other night. Got a witness testimony to you breaking and entering the Butler residence too."

"You ain't got shit," Sims' voice deepened and he reached toward a holster on his hip.

"Not so fast there, slow poke. You know I'm quicker'n you. If you pull it, you better aim true, otherwise you'll be a dead man faster than you can blink." Austin had moved his hand to unclasp his own holster, his palm itching to arm himself. His jaw ticked as he watched and waited for the bigger man to draw first.

Sims hesitated, as Austin knew he would. He frowned. "What do you want, Montgomery?"

Austin gave a smart-assed grin in return. *Indeed.* "I want McClintock the hell out of this town and you're gonna do the hard work for me."

"The hell you say—"

"I can link you to him. I have bank account information. Phone calls. Records going back a long time. I can shut your ass down. Right now, in fact. Trust me, I'd love nothing more than to arrest you and haul you to Leavenworth right this minute."

"Leavenworth?" he smirked. "Who the hell are you, Montgomery?" his gaze roved over Austin, concern showing in his eyes. "Military police?"

"This is bigger than that and you damn well know it, asshole. You think we don't know about you, 'Castor'? Don't know about the past you thought we weren't smart enough to dig up? You didn't think there were witnesses to your corruption? You can't keep people quiet forever, Sims. Little birdies will always tweet when threatened. You, of all people, should be *well* aware of how that works." Sims' big jaw dropped, and he gaped at Austin then. "Yeah, dumb fucks like you rarely go under the radar as long as you have. But your time's up. So, you can either choose to do as I ask or I take you in. The choice is yours! I suggest you choose wisely."

Sims practically growled and a litany of vulgarities flew from his mouth. He spat and crossed his hulking biceps across his chest. "What do I have to do?"

Ha ha! Victory. This had been as easy as taking candy from a baby, like Austin knew it would be. Like he'd told Trevor it would be.

"I'll bring a wire and trick him into believing me. Sims was all brawn and no brain after all. This can work," Austin had insisted when he'd sent the tape to Trevor to verify that they were indeed looking at Sims as the perp. Trevor had been pulling closed files and, essentially, red flags on Sims. He was certainly going to end up in a maximum-security facility before all was said and done as Trev's persistent digging had led to the unearthing of unsolved federal crimes from money laundering to murder, all involving Sims—and ultimately McClintock. Now, they just had to link the two, and wiring Sims in order to get a confession out of Max was the way it was going to happen.

"You're going to take *these*," Austin stated and handed him a wiretap and some bugs. "And you're going to follow my instructions to the T." Austin decided to hit a nerve; he knew how homophobic Brody had been during boot camp, getting grossed out when he had to shower with a bunch of other dudes. "If at any point you don't cooperate in this investigation, consider the fact that somebody much bigger and dumber'n you will be butt-fuckin' you for the remainder of your life and consider—"

"Jeez, Montgomery, you don't have to give me gritty details. Fuck!" Sim's grimaced and shuddered. "Just tell me what the hell to do and I'll do it."

CHAPTER 14

"So, do I get to find out now why I'm dressed like I'm going to a ball? You're not taking me dancing, I hope. I'm super clumsy. I—"

"Nope. I ain't tellin' you where we're going, but I can tell you that it doesn't involve dancing, not for you and I anyway." Austin winked over at her and the sheer sexuality of it nearly caused Vanna to shiver.

He looked so good tonight and he smelled as sexy and 'dangerous' as always. Her heart hammered as her eyes descended his hard-muscled body. How was it he could pull off a white collared button-down and black blazer in a pair of tight dark denim jeans? And even a pair of black snakeskin cowboy boots at that? Lord help. Every pore in his golden-tanned skin oozed sex appeal, and Vanna's female parts hadn't stopped vibrating since she'd gotten into the small cab of his Jeep...and it wasn't the motor that was causing it. She'd been amped up since two nights ago on her parent's front porch where he'd tortured her with a sultry kiss.

She hadn't left the family property since then. They'd all been shell-shocked over the fire and aside from those who worked, everyone had stayed home—and under the watchful eyes of the handful of parked police cars that surveyed the perimeter of their five-hundred acres of land.

Vanna had taken to composing to get her mind off the reality of the situation. It was easier than facing the fact that a madman was threatening them and torching their property, threatening their lives, their legacy, and their future. Vanna had been playing the piano, entranced in her work last night when she'd looked up into the doorframe to see the handsome blond man staring into her soul, his gorgeous golden-brown eyes taking her breath away.

"Tomorrow night," he'd said after a few moments of silence had passed between them.

"Huh?" she'd been confused at first, her senses overwhelmed by his overpowering presence.

"I'm taking you out. On that date I'd promised."

"Oh," she'd gulped and felt liquid heat flood her lower belly.

He'd approached, moving off the door frame so lithely and gracefully that she'd practically swooned. He'd come to sit down beside her on the booth, giving her that panty-dropping grin of his.

"I can play too, ya know?" Vanna had just gulped unable to form words in her muddled brain. "This one is one of my faves."

He began playing "Angel of Music," from Phantom of the Opera and she'd gasped and looked up at him in surprise. His grin had deepened, hitting his eyes, and her heart melted in her chest as she watched his long, straight fingers dance across the keys of her baby grand piano. He'd stroked them with such grace and elegance, bringing forth a beautiful sound from the metallic cords.

God, she was such a sucker for piano fingers! She'd hopped up then and grabbed her violin from its case on the settee, quickly bringing the lower bout to her chin. She'd skillfully pulled the bow across the strings, synchronizing with him in perfect harmony as they drowned the room in one of her favorite melodies of all time from the beloved musical of Andrew Lloyd Webber's. She'd closed her eyes and lost herself to the gorgeous congruence of string instruments being struck simultaneously. They'd played through the chorus, Vanna passionately taking the lead as the song intended then relinquishing it back, a lover's dance, in the key of C major.

When they'd finished, she'd looked to Austin, whose gaze had burned even hotter into hers, his eyes flashing something she couldn't quite place. It had held her captive, suspended in space and time for a moment. But then a slight movement in the doorway had drawn her from her entrapment as she saw her father smiling over at her, beaming from ear to ear.

He'd given them applause, and Austin had tipped his hat to Vanna as she'd bowed gracefully with a giggle. "You should bow too, maestro," she'd stated.

"And take *your* spotlight? I think not, Ms. Prodigy." Austin's grin had been playful and his eyes admiring as he'd moved off the bench and taken her hand, kissing her knuckles. "You blow me away, Savannah Grace. Every. Damn. Day." He'd ducked his head so that only she could hear him, moving closer to her, his voice a deep whisper. "You make my heart beat faster and slower at the same time. How's that even possible?"

She'd held his eyes as her belly did somersaults and her voice disappeared. After a moment, her father had cleared his throat. "You two performers want dinner? It's ready."

They'd seemed to come out of their trance then and Austin had given a soft chuckle and turned. The hateful glare her father usually wore for Austin had been absent, for his green eyes—just a shade darker than her own—were soft and warm, such a stark contrast from the anger she was used to seeing whenever Austin was around that she'd practically balked.

They'd had a pleasant dinner of roast beef, green beans and potatoes, talking about work, the weather and her cousin, Elias, who was coming to visit soon from Corpus Christi. Afterward, Savannah and Austin had sat out on the porch, taking in the rainy night, cuddled up on the swing. Austin had seemed to be relaxed in her presence, while her brain fired off jittery neurons, attempting to rein in her arousal at his smell and touch. Just when his silence had begun to completely unnerve her, she looked up at him and her heart had down a flip-flop as his eyes filled her entire soul with wonder. She'd gulped as his face lowered to hers. Oh, how she'd wanted to beg him to love her like he did in the hayloft. She needed to lose herself, to fall into mindless gratification, to fill her senses with him and him alone. His lips had hovered, inches from hers, and she'd thought she'd die from anticipation before he'd ultimately kissed her. But finally, his lips found hers and she'd arched her back off the wood of the swing to press her mouth harder to his, getting a low chuckle out of him—only fueling her sexual stimulation.

"You're the damnedest woman. You know that, Savvy?" he'd asked, a man far too content for his own good.

"Well, you're the biggest jerk who ever lived," she'd pouted, not really understanding where her frustrations came from.

He'd seemed to understand her predicament even as he gave her a crooked grin, amused at her torment. "If only we had the house to ourselves right now. I'd carry you upstairs to your bed, strip you naked, and have you begging my name as I made you mine all over again. Believe me when I say, I want it as much—er, probably *more* than you do, darlin'. But your folks are inside. I really don't wanna push my luck tonight."

He'd licked the pouty lips in front of him, patted her bottom, stood and adjusted himself before heading off into the rain.

Now, they were entering the city of Dallas, the nighttime skyline making her smile as the big glass and metal buildings towered over them. "Ah, Dallas. Well, aren't you fancy, Mr. Montgomery?" She looked back over at him.

He pulled her knuckles to his lips, getting a shiver from her. "Hey, I'm just doing what I can to sway the multi-faceted Doc over here. I doubt that much impresses you, am I wrong?"

"To the contrary, actually. I enjoy life's simple things."

"Dually noted, mon chéri."

"Mmm, I love a man with an accent," Vanna teased, getting a big laugh out of him.

They passed multiple landmarks she knew and recognized; the Perot Museum of Nature and Science, Reunion Tower, Pioneer Plaza, and the Giant Eyeball before parking in a lot adjacent to the Majestic Theatre. Savannah eyed Austin suspiciously, but he gave nothing away as he paid to park, stuck the receipt in the window, and took her hand as he helped her up and onto the curb in her strappy gold heels. She'd donned a taupe, form-fitted, sequin-top cocktail dress. It was V-neck and sleeveless with flowy thin material beneath the waistline. It flattered her figure and the color complemented her skin tone. She'd bought it just that afternoon with her mom and sister when Austin told her to dress in business casual, formal but not formally. Whatever the hell that meant. As soon as he saw her, she could've wiped the drool from his chin. She figured, she'd nailed it.

The sights, sounds and smells here in the city were different than on the ranch. It was louder, more crowded, more...*polluted* than home. Suddenly, Vanna recalled Houston, and for a moment, she was taken aback. It was like a punch to the gut because it reminded her of Sidd and his betrayal.

How easy it was to forget where she had to go back to—and in the not too distant future—what she had to look forward to. And a city, Houston, was the *last* place she could imagine being.

Austin seemed to sense her hesitancy and stopped mid-walk, looking down at her. "You okay, angel?" He brought her chin up with his index finger and looked into her eyes.

She swallowed hard, trying to thwart her misgivings of the future and just enjoy the moment with him, the date, his wonderful surprise at driving her over an hour out of town. She forced a smile on her face—for how could she not smile at the sexy wrangler before her? He was gorgeous, every flawless inch of his skin, the dimple in his cheek, the sparkle in his eyes, quite unlike any color she'd ever seen—or painted—before. She wanted him in a bed, a shower, a tub, on a beach—wherever—just next to her. She wanted his hard member buried deep inside her, calming the hunger that coursed through her system when she was near him. "I—I just, I thought I forgot my purse," she recovered and pulled her wristlet up.

He shook his head, as if she were silly. "Good. I was starting to wonder if you'd regretted coming out with me."

Was he kidding? He simply *had* to be kidding. Who on earth would regret allowing this man to take them on a date? She scoffed. "As if!"

"You're gonna wish you'd brought a shawl, I'm afraid," he regretfully said as he ushered her through the doors of the chilly theatre. "But tonight's your lucky night. If you get cold, I'll drape my jacket over you and mark you…just in case that sexy little dress of yours entices any single guys around here." He looked around dramatically, his brows furrowing, and Vanna laughed and swatted at him, rolling her eyes. "I'm serious. I should've brought some duct tape for my boner."

Savannah tried to hold in her cackle as they approached the ticket booth, and Austin pulled two tickets from his jeans pocket.

The valet took the tickets, tore them and handed the stubs back as Vanna took Austin's extended elbow, looping her arm through his big, muscular one. She stopped in her tracks as she looked up at the big banner.

"Phantom of the Opera? Wait…you—"

"I bought the tickets before I even knew. I mean, I had an inkling…well, a gut feeling, really. But when I played the song and got the reaction I did outta you, I knew I'd hit the jackpot."

Tears came to her eyes then. "Oh, Austin. I—I don't know what to say. I've never actually seen it live."

"What?" he balked. "Even *I've* seen it live, like more than once to be exact." He looked around, as if he should be worried he'd divulged this information. She laughed again.

"I mean, I've wanted to. I begged Si—" Dammit! There it was once again, the ache shooting through her heart so fast, a knife wound that bled harder now the longer she'd had time to think about how long Siddharth had been deceiving her. She'd been such a fool.

"Well, my 'angel of music'. You'll be seeing it live here very soon. And I'll bring you to see it as many times as you want me to. You just say the words, darlin'."

Savannah felt her lips quiver as she held in a sob. God, he was being such a perfect gentleman. If she hadn't really wanted to see the show, she'd just say, "Fuck it," and tell him to take her to one of the fancy, high-rise hotels nearby where she could show him just how grateful she was for his thoughtfulness. The realization of how perfect his timing was after their stunning musical union last night wasn't lost on her; it had been a perfect fusion that had jarred her very soul. Vanna felt her heart overfill with sheer joy; it both terrified and thrilled her all at once.

Austin smiled then and his finger chased the unbidden tear that ran down the length of her cheek. "Sidd won't ever have a chance to break your heart again, Savvy. I intend to mend every single piece back together that he tore apart, no matter how long it takes."

His words stunned her into silence and her waterworks stopped as quickly as they'd started. What was he saying?

She didn't have time to consider before they were being ushered into the theatre and were taking their seats. She looked around the beautifully decorated playhouse, the history evident in every piece of its gold embellishments, curtains, and architecture. She looked onto the dimly lit stage and up to the covered and tethered chandelier and got goosebumps. She'd waited to see this musical since she was a girl. Her parents, of course, would have taken her but between all her own activities and Dallie's and the ranch...and her baby brother, it just got pushed off each time she'd meant to ask them to go. She'd romantically assumed that eventually the man she loved would bring her one day, but it simply hadn't happened...until now.

She looked over at Austin and when she did, a tingling began in her heart and worked its way out to the rest of her. She gasped softly at the realization, for she knew what it was, although she'd never felt it before until that moment. But the more she tried to push it away, argue with it and dampen it down—it couldn't be, it wasn't—the more it fought towards the surface, like a swimmer in the water coming up for a much-needed gulp of air.

Savannah simply *couldn't* be in love with Austin Montgomery. There was no way! It was too soon. She was on the 'rebound', she was still reeling from a break-up, her heart was in pieces as Austin had said minutes prior...but her thrumming pulse and reeling head stated otherwise. Her soul vibrated with fulfillment and her womanhood tingled in yearning, but her stomach wasn't ready for this new knowledge and it fought the notion, repelling it back into her throat.

"Darlin', you look as if you've just seen a ghost." The concern on his face, made her gulp. "I mean this place is rumored to be haunted, but—"

Vanna attempted to coax her rational brain to help her out of this situation, but it was firing in so many different directions, it couldn't help her if it tried. "I—I need something to drink," she blurted out and scorching heat filled her core as Austin's big palm splayed across her uncovered knee. She whimpered internally, loving the feel and look of his golden-tanned hand on her olive skin.

"We're not allowed to have drinks in here. Can you wait until intermission?" His eyes did her in, and she lost all train of thought.

The lights dimmed then, signaling the start of the show and the doors began to close. What had he asked her? *Think, Savannah, think dammit!*

Oh, yes—drinks! Her mind recovered and she gave a quick nod, smoothing her dress and attempting to quiet her pounding heart, even as Austin's unnervingly delicious hand stayed put on her knee.

He grinned over at her as the performance commenced and leaned into her a little more, her body all too aware of his shoulder touching hers, burning a hole through her epidermis.

She tried to focus on the actors and the music, but it was so hard with Austin's hot, hard body so close to her—close enough to touch, close enough to tease—but it wasn't until the chandelier was uncloaked that she became finally immersed in the musical.

She found herself humming along, closing her eyes as she remembered playing the music and dancing along to the movie she'd watched with her mother, father, sister, and baby brother one Christmas. Oh, how she'd always loved beautiful music, tragic romance, and mysterious endings. Intermission came with the thundering of the chandelier "falling" and Savannah nearly leapt out of her skin as she cried out in surprise—the power of the moment as intense as her emotions at that point in time.

Austin laughed even as Savannah held a hand to her breast in shock. "Oh my goodness. Did you know that was gonna happen?"

"You honestly didn't?" he asked, surprised at her dramatic reaction. "C'mon, Doc. Let's go grab you a drink or two to calm your jangled nerves." He winked. She didn't know if there were enough drinks *in* the place to calm her ridiculously jangled nerves.

What kind of self-loathing idiot *falls in love with an irresponsible, rogue womanizer after getting her heart broken barely a month prior?* It was all the heat of the moment, mere wishful thinking, poor timing, and high emotions. *Nothing more,* her genius brain clarified. She wasn't in love. She was in lust—pure unadulterated lust. She was simply trying to bury her heartbreak in a fantasy. After all, that's what it had been, hadn't it? A mere fantasy she'd fulfilled one night in a bar—on a whim—and her body just hadn't gotten enough of this delectably rugged cowboy. That was it. She just needed another round in the sack to satisfy her womanly cravings, then this silliness would end.

At the bar, Austin ordered Savannah a cosmo, and himself a beer, and they sipped their drinks easily. Austin propped himself at the bar laconically, giving Savannah the remaining bar stool, and they looked around at the patrons, dressed in wear that ranged from incredibly formal to extremely casual.

Austin seemed to pick up on her thoughts as she watched, with raised brows, a lady in a feather shawl walk by in a sequined ball gown. "I guess we fit somewhere in the middle, huh? I feel a bit underdressed in my Wranglers now." His amber eyes sparkled in amusement.

Savannah pursed her lips as her eyes fell to appraise him in his jeans. The man could fill out a pair of pants, she had to give him that. The dark denim was loose on his hips but hugged tight to his muscular thighs and his crotch, making her antsy to see beneath the zipper. She knew how good his firm ass looked in them, she didn't need for him to turn around to confirm it. She had a mental image of its enticing form burned forever into her memory; she'd only watched him work in tight jeans at least a dozen times since she'd come home to Kinsen Ranch.

He looked pleased as her eyes came back to his—she suddenly realized she was gawking—and gave her a cocky brow that told her he knew his powerful physique was impressive. Damn him! "Speaking of Wranglers, Savvy, it appears you're attempting to visualize what's *inside* mine." *Oh, yes, I am...because I know what it looks and feels and* tastes *like... and I want to again,* she wanted to scream. His eyes told her that he, too, wanted the same thing she did. They warned her. And by God, she didn't heed it.

She simply stared back, not speaking, not breaking eye contact as his fingers moved to hers then up her bare arm. Her flesh broke out in goosebumps, but she dared not budge. She held her breath as his frame came ever closer, his hip bumping her knee. She gave a breathy gasp as he ever so subtly turned his stance into her, brushing his zippered crotch across her knee.

"Dammit Savannah, if you keep looking at me like that, I'm gonna have to take you to the bathroom, slam you against a wall, and devour you like the hungry tiger you seem to have turned me into."

His words made her insides clench in anticipation even as his tone startled her. She'd never been taken against a wall and the thought thrilled her.

Just then, the lights began dimming again, and he gave her a knowing grin.

As he downed his beer and she threw her drink back with equal fervor, she set her mind. She was going to sleep with Austin again. One more time. Then she'd be able to move on with her life. She just needed to get him out of her system. It was going to be as simple as that.

～

*T*he ride home was quiet, quieter than Austin could've anticipated. It did a number on his nerves, wondering if it was because Savannah was unhappy with their date or if she was simply as rattled as he was by what happened at the bar just three hours earlier. He'd been so tempted to take her hand, lead her into the bathroom, and make good on his statement of taking her against the wall as the blinking lights called the audience back into the auditorium. But he'd hesitated. She'd given him a look and he hadn't been real sure what it'd meant. Now, he was still trying to decipher it as they rode back down the highway towards Abundance.

Savannah had appeared more restrained during the second act of the show, withdrawn even, and later at the romantic candlelit terrace-top dinner they'd gone to afterward, as if something had changed in her. He'd been unable to figure out exactly what, but now he was taken off guard and he didn't like it—not one bit.

Austin had always been confident, self-assured, to the point of arrogance. It was simply his nature. But now with the overwhelming feelings he was having regarding Savannah Kinsen, that confidence was waning. He seemed to be aware of the stifling heat within the cab of his Jeep, despite that the A/C was going full blast; it had nothing to do with the temperature.

"Thank you for taking me out tonight, Austin. It was amazing," Vanna said as he pulled the Jeep to a stop in front of his bungalow. Perhaps she was uneasy, but he'd be damned if they went one more night without slaking the ever-growing lust between them; the wait had been absolute torture.

"It was my outright pleasure, sweetheart," he cleared his throat and puffed out his chest, summoning his inner proud peacock. He turned his body slightly toward her and grabbed her hand from her thigh, rubbing his thumb across the back of it, loving the contrast of her softness to his callouses. "Wanna come in for a bit and have a drink?"

She nodded, biting her lip nervously and it was all he could do not to pull her onto his lap and satisfy the undeniable urge to have her, right then and there.

He came around to assist her out of his Jeep, looking around cautiously before unlocking his front door and motioning for Savannah to go first. She did, and he shut the door and locked it behind himself, grateful Wyatt had Caesar for the night, for more reasons than one.

"I have wine. Want another glass of Malbec?" Austin asked, noting Vanna's blue-green eyes burning sizzling holes into him as he shucked his blazer off and tossed it onto the chair in the corner. Savannah just nodded, looking unsure of herself as she rubbed her arms. "Sit for a spell. Get comfy." Austin gave a weak chuckle, his stomach tying in knots even as he moved to make their drinks.

Had it really been that long since he'd had a date that he was actually nervous bringing a girl to his room? What the fuck? He was a grown-ass man of thirty-two years old. Was he *that* rusty? No. He was in love and Savannah Grace Kinsen wasn't just any girl; she was *his* girl and he really didn't wanna screw this up.

When the wine was uncorked and he filled the glasses mid-way up, Austin handed Savannah her glass and clinked his own against it before sitting down on his bed next to her, his elbow bumping hers.

He heard her intake of breath as she shifted, and his skin burned with the heat coming off her. Damn, if he wasn't throwing the glasses down and tackling her in that moment. But, he didn't. Her nervousness was rubbing off on him and he cleared his throat, trying to think of something to talk about even as his brain searched dumbly, his body tingling from the closeness of her. He took a sip of the wine and mulled his options over.

Austin saw his guitar out of the corner of his eye and moved to grab it as he set his wine glass down on the night stand, realizing he could serenade Savannah into his bed as easily as he could talk her in. He grinned as he pulled his Fender CF-60 from its case and set it on his thigh, turning his body toward Savannah as he began to strum the chords of Bon Jovi's "Bed of Roses." Austin saw immediately as he broke out into song that he'd pulled her right in as her eyes grew dark with desire and she gnawed her lips. He belted out passionately, her eyes never leaving his as he threw the words seductively out at her.

When he finished, he lost all control of his senses as she licked her plump lips in anticipation. He shoved the guitar off into the floor —very gently—and leaned in, capturing her lips with his own, one hand cupping her cheek as he deepened the kiss. The dark-headed beauty pulled his other hand to her breast, and he felt as if he were being bathed in sizzling flames.

"Mmm, Austin," Savannah murmured and moved her hand to his chest, gripping his shirt in her fist as she set her wine glass next to his on the night stand.

"Fuck, Savvy." She was making him lose his mind as she kissed him like a woman finally unleashed, her tongue fighting with his for control. He squeezed her breast and flicked his thumb across her pebbled nipple. When she whimpered, his hands moved to her hips and he grabbed her and pulled her onto his lap. Another sexy moan from her had his hard cock leaping in his jeans as his mouth moved to her throat. "Oh, God, baby girl. I want you so *fuckin'* much," he groaned as he licked the sweetness from her skin and kneaded the full breasts through the sequins, which suddenly irritated the hell out of him. They were so cold and rough and the skin beneath was so hot and soft, he knew. He needed to touch Savannah's bare flesh, love every inch of it, and he suddenly despised the dress that fit her curves so well. He longed to eradicate the barrier between them and moved his hands to her thighs even as hers began unbuttoning his belt and jeans. The feel of her hands on the part of him that wanted her most had him reeling and when the heel of her palm hit the head of his erection, he arched up into it. She moaned again and he swore he was climaxing in that instant.

"Austin," came another breathy rasp against his lips.

"Yes, my sweet, sexy Savvy?" His thumb grazed her inner thighs, and she shivered.

"Mmm, I want…" she trailed off as his fingers rubbed the apex of her thighs and he gasped as he realized there was nothing separating her center from him. She gave a deep blush and it turned him on even more.

"Oh baby, you're not wearing any—"

"They—they're crotch-less."

Sonovabitch! His cock strained desperately against his tight denim, seeking her silken heat like a missile. "Fuck *me*," he groaned as she unzipped him and he dipped a finger into her wet folds.

Her back arched up in response and she grabbed for his bulging erection, unable to free him from the jeans due to their angle. He chuckled in bittersweet agony.

"Mmm," Vanna moaned as he began pumping his finger inside her. "I want you to do what you said you were going to do to me at the bar. Please?" She looked back into his eyes, and he couldn't help but grin at the eagerness there.

"Anything my lady desires." Austin kissed her again, reluctantly pulled his finger from between her legs, and stood up. She wrapped her legs around him as he waddled to the wall, their mouths ravenous for one another.

"God, I've waited so long to be inside you again, Savvy. You have no idea," he breathed out as he pressed her to the wall and steadied her legs around him. He shucked his jeans and ran his hands up her slender thighs, kissing her lips gently before gripping his cock and guiding it to her sex. He pierced her opening gently, slowly, letting her tight little core stretch around his thick length. He practically whimpered as he eased inside her silky heat—it felt unbelievably good—his thighs shaking with restrained need. When she threw her head back and ardently moaned, it was all he could do not to fuck the living hell out of her. She was so sexy and delicious—and all his —as his steely member filled her inch by delectable inch. He was bare he suddenly realized, but try as he might, he wasn't gonna be able to pull out. He only slid further in and groaned out animalistically as his shaft became fully engulfed in her nectar-drenched sweetness. "Oh God, sweet angel. I've just found Heaven and I don't ever wanna leave."

Her arms went around his neck and he watched her gorgeous face as he plunged in and out of her over and over again, intense pleasure seizing every fiber of his being. "Mmm, darlin', you're so tight. Am I hurting you?" he asked, making sure, even as she moaned again. A sexy, hungry kiss was his answer, and he pressed his chest into hers, continuing to arch his hips up, thrusting into the hot, silken core of hers he couldn't seem to get enough of.

"Please, don't stop, Austin. Oh, oh, yes." Her breathy sighs nearly did him in as her climax approached rapidly, but he held his own back, waiting for her. This was all about her and pleasing her; he was in love with her—he realized once more—and her pleasure was all he strove for in those moments.

He grabbed her hands and pulled her arms up over her head, pinning her wrists with his. His other hand moved to grip her bottom as he lunged hard. "Come for me, Savvy. Let me hear you scream my name, like our first night."

Austin drove deep, gaining speed, angling her up so that he could hit her G-spot and have her shuddering beneath him. As he did so, she cried out, calling his name as her orgasm took her. He gave a deep chuckle—happy he could satisfy this little sex kitten he'd created. He kissed her forehead, moving from the wall as her insides continued to grip him in deep contractions. He laid them down on the bed, staying inside her as he removed his shirt then flipped them over to where she was on top. He began pulling at the dress, anxious to free her and see her naked in all her glory.

Savannah smiled bashfully as the dress came over her head and she threw it aside, her eyes darkening. His hands immediately went to her beautiful breasts, cupping and kneading, teasing her light brown nipples with his thumbs and index fingers. She moaned and moved her hands over his chest. He began to pump into her again, his cock aching for release, but her look stopped him. "I want to uh —" she began, "I want to do something."

"Anything, sweetheart. You name it. I'm all yours." Austin propped his arms behind his head and studied her. "You miss the cowboy hat, don't ya, darlin'?" He winked and groaned in sweet agony at seeing her impaled on his dick, her trim body with curves in all the right places.

"Well, yes, but—"

"Sav, what is it?" he asked and leaned up, propping his arms behind him, incidentally thrusting his member even further into her. His eyes rolled back in his head and he grunted. "Just tell me, your sweet body is about to drive me over the edge." His hands moved up her arms and down her back. His lips kissed her cheek, her shoulder, her collarbone. She shivered.

"I wanna go down on you and—"

When she didn't continue, he asked, "You wanna suck my cock?" He grinned big at her shyness—and at the anticipation of having her mouth on him. She looked down, biting her bottom lip and nodding. "You know that little shy card of yours turns me on like nobody's business, right? You keep playin' it and you're bound to not be able to walk tomorrow."

Savannah gulped, and he took her lips, savoring the feel and taste and texture of them as his tongue plunged in. He could only take the torment so long though as her hips began to grind into his. "Damn baby, if you're gonna do it, you better do it. I'm about to blow my load and hear me when I say, it's gonna be a mouthful." She gaped at him as she pulled back, and he couldn't help but laugh. "I'm not kiddin', Savvy. I've been savin' up for this one." Badgering her was too damn easy; he couldn't resist. "Don't worry, angel." She frowned slightly even as she began to pull herself from his lap. "I'll pull out and shoot it on your tits if you'd rather me do that." He winked again, and the hunger in her eyes made him growl in longing.

"I—I've never—" But she didn't finish as she took his outstretched hand. She pulled him to the edge of the bed, kneeling down in front of him, and his heart stilled as her sultry green eyes looked up at him. She took in his long, erect cock, jutting out at her and worried her bottom lip.

"Think you can take it?" he challenged, knowing full well she got over half of it down her throat last time. Why did she seem so hesitant?

Her eyes moved to his left knee and she gasped at the huge, ugly scar there that covered the entire area, running up his thigh and down his shin.

"Oh, Austin," she murmured, and he gritted his teeth at the memory of that day. Her fingertips lightly traced the raised and disfigured tissue there, but the skin was numb and had been for years now, if only he could numb the pain so easily. She seemed to sense his unease. It wasn't like anyone had ever seen this part of him, aside from his family. Even at the gym he wore a knee sleeve that covered the worst of it. She kissed his prosthetic kneecap tenderly and gave him the sweetest smile; his heart literally melted.

Then as if the moment hadn't happened, she gingerly took his hard length in her hand and began to squeeze and pump it before her lips warily enclosed the tip of him.

"Mmm, do you taste yourself there, darlin'? You taste so sweet, don't you?" he asked and watched her lips take his glistening shaft, glistening from her wetness. She moaned as she took him further into her mouth.

Austin gasped on a groan and licked his lips as he watched her silky, hot mouth move over him with beautiful purpose and her fist shifted to the base of his cock, squeezing and stroking him. "Oh, baby girl, you have the most beautiful mouth I've ever seen." It was completely true. Savannah had a mouth made for this, for his cock—for *him*—and she was loving it like she'd done it a thousand times before. She took his sex all the way down her throat so easily for someone who wanted to "try something" like she'd not done it before; it blew his mind. She seemed to be really good at it. Had she really only done this with him? No way. She simply had to have given head before. Whatever the case, Austin wasn't complaining as she continued to suck and stroke him into oblivion and he felt his climax building. His jaw clenched and his hand moved into her dark hair, gripping her scalp and gently guiding her to his member, in and out, fighting the urge to thrust into her mouth. His head flew back and he groaned as her other hand moved between his legs to cup his scrotum. "Oh, God, Savvy. That feels amazing."

Savannah's fervor seemed to increase as her speed picked up, and Austin knew it would be any second before he ejaculated into her mouth, but he didn't want to shock her or gross her out—in case this *was* her first time performing a blow job—so he pulled her shoulders back before it was too late. She seemed completely put off, and he couldn't help but laugh as she gaped.

"Austin!" she protested.

"I'm *sorry*, I was trying to spare you."

"I don't *wanna* be spared," Savannah countered even as he pulled her up and moved them back onto the bed. Austin chuckled again at her expression and reversed his position, pulling her atop him as his head fell between her legs. He felt her mouth and fist take his sex again as his tongue licked at her swollen bud and he thrust two fingers into her center. She moaned around his cock, and he felt so close to expelling his pent-up desire into the mouth that was working him—once more—with incredible dexterity. Soon, he heard her fall apart again as he tormented her flesh and felt her sex clenching his fingers. Only then did he let go, feeling the wave of pleasure overtake him as his seed spewed into her throat. He groaned and pumped as he continued to feast on her wet folds, her cries of pleasure egging him on.

As their breathing normalized, he kissed her peach fuzz-covered lips and slowly removed his fingers from within her. He laid his head on her thigh and looked up at her, her hand still gripping his semi-erect shaft, her eyes seeking his.

"Oh, Savvy. How I've missed you, darlin'." Austin kissed her thigh and stroked his hand down it to grip her ass cheek. "You're really good at giving head, you know?"

Savannah blushed. "I—that was the first time I've ever—"

"Swallowed?"

She nodded. "I only did it long enough to get it up. Never got to finish what I started."

"Well, feel free to go down on me anytime you like." He winked with a laugh.

Austin moved back up to the head of the bed where Savannah's maple hair spilled out across his pillow in shimmering ribbons. He looked over her exquisite, womanly form, his sex hardening again as his eyes stopped at her round breasts and their erect nipples. He propped his elbow up and rested his head in his hand.

Savannah blushed and looked down, bashfully biting into her lip. "You're not having post-coital regrets, are you, Savvy?" Austin asked. She scowled, but before she could respond, he added, "You're worried about your dad. Don't. You're a grown woman."

She shook her head. "No, Austin. I'm not worried about my dad." The look she gave him was so tender as she moved into his arms, aligning her beautiful body with his. She stared into his eyes and cupped his cheek, running her hand over his beard. Her dazzling green orbs fell to his lips and she worried her own again. His hand went to her shoulder and he took a strand of her hair, twirling it around in his fingers. The love he felt for her swelled in his heart, but as much as he wanted to confess it, he felt that now wasn't the right time. Her hand moved down to his chest and she traced the cross tattoo there. She looked back into his eyes as his hand settled on her curvy hip. "No regrets," she whispered. "Tonight is ours."

With that, she leaned in and kissed him. He took her face in his hands and moved his body to cover hers. That was correct. Tonight was theirs, and he planned to rock her world for the remainder of it.

CHAPTER 15

Savannah awoke to muffled grunting and deep cries. For a moment, she forgot where she was, but slowly, it all came back to her and she realized she was in Austin's bed, feeling her arm and leg thrown across his muscular frame. Sweat had pooled on his chest where her hand rested and across his forehead, she noted, as the first hint of sunrise peeked in through the windows.

"No, no," came a raspy whimper from Austin's lips. He was dreaming...better yet having a nightmare as his body trembled and his hands gripped the sheets on either side of him.

At first, she wasn't sure whether to wake him or not. Then as his body began practically convulsing beneath her, she knew she couldn't just let him come out of it on his own; he might hurt himself...or her.

She gripped his shoulder with one hand and touched his face with the other, her thigh wrapping around the back of his. "Austin," she cooed and shook him gently.

"I'm sorry Laquanna, I'm so sorry," he began to sob and tears hit Savannah's eyes, her throat tightening at the sorrow so evident in his voice.

"Austin, wake up." She shook him again, a little harder this time. His muscles tensed beneath her arm and leg, and he groaned as if in pain. "Austin!" she screamed aloud, and the violent jerk of his body coming upright made her gasp as she went with him. He gripped her like a lifeline, his sandy blonde brows drawn in confusion.

His breathing was ragged as one hand smoothed over her back, the other cupped her cheek. "Savannah." Her name on his lips was like a prayer, and it made her insides turn to Jell-O. His eyes bore holes into her soul and he kissed her forehead before pulling back to look her over. "Did I hurt you?" he asked, his face softening.

"No, I was afraid you might hurt yourself though. You were having a nightmare."

He didn't respond but turned his head from her, embarrassed.

"Hey," she murmured and took his face in her hands, "it's alright. I have nightmares too." He gave her a weak grin, his jaw clenching. "Who's Laquanna?"

Austin gulped and looked down, his hand covering the one on his cheek. "Jerome's wife. She came to see me in the hospital. She wanted to know what happened. It was the first and only time I'd told the story...well to anyone outside the military, until I met you." His eyes came back to Savannah's and her heart literally swelled. He'd opened up to her that night on her parent's back porch; unlike he'd ever opened up to anyone. Now, to her surprise, he continued, "People who haven't faced death on a daily basis don't understand what it's like, what it does to you, to your mind." He looked down. "It changes you. And there's nothing that can prepare you for the devastation. Jerome was different. He handled it all so well. He was one of the most positive people I've ever known. He had faith so unshakeable. We all fed off of him. He was really good for us." Tears streamed down his face, and he wiped his nose with the back of his hand.

Savannah couldn't help but feel Austin's raw emotions, tears stinging her eyes, her chest tightening. "I'm so sorry you lost him, Austin. Truly, I am."

"I didn't just lose him. The bomb—it—there was nothing left of him, Savvy. Nothing to bury. We had a casket with no body in it. No closure. For his wife...or child...or me." Austin covered his face with his hands, his body racked in intense sobs. Savannah pulled him into her bosom then and his arms went around her as he cried. She stroked his curly, mid-length hair and his back, absorbing his anguish. She rocked him and murmured sweet nothings to him, letting him expel his grief, feeling he'd held this inside for far too long. "He was the best friend I've ever had, and I blame myself for his death. I was the team leader. The captain is supposed to go down with his ship."

"I'm sure if Jerome was the man you say he was, he wouldn't feel that way about it. He wouldn't trade your life for his."

"No, he wouldn't. He would've died for me...and he did. But now, his wife has to live without a husband, his child will grow up and not know how amazing his father was."

"His memory lives on though. You honor him by living."

"You have a poet's heart." Austin pulled back slightly, sniffling and giving her a soft grin.

"*There's* that sexy smile I've come to know and love." Savannah's eyes held his and the warmth in them had her soaring. He licked his lips and looked at her mouth for the longest time. She felt desire pool between her legs as he moved his body closer, his grip on her shifting from comfort to possession.

"Savvy." The tenderness in his gruff voice touched a nerve deep within and her insides clenched in anticipation. "I'm gonna make love to you now."

The way he said the word 'love' took her breath away, and Savannah gulped even as Austin's mouth descended to hers and he kissed her with a passion unlike anything she'd ever felt before—different than last night or their first night together. It was hungrier, more desperate, as if he were kissing her like it was the last time he'd ever get to; his lips and tongue stroking hers like kissing was an art form that he'd mastered and was showing her his proficient talents.

"Mmm." The moan from her throat excited even her, and when his body covered hers and he began to caress her naked breasts and belly and thighs with lazy, slow, unhurried hands, she whimpered, frantic for him to be inside her. "Please?" she begged even as he centered himself between her thighs and his velvet-tipped shaft penetrated her wetness. "Oh God, Austin," she gasped and gripped his big, muscular shoulders, her head hitting the pillow as he thrust deep inside her in one smooth motion.

When he said he was going to make love to her, he wasn't kidding, for his body became one with hers as his thrusts turned into deep caresses. How it was even possible to have a caress from steel Savannah didn't know, but Austin made it possible as his hips moved in a rhythm so adoring that her body greedily devoured every stroke he gave her. The whimpering from her lips was foreign to her ears as they climbed together, looking into each other's eyes, the pleasure building within like a volcano ready to erupt in an explosion so powerful that nothing would survive in its wake. It was about to happen and nothing could've prepared her. For the force of her orgasm was so profound, it literally sent her into earth's orbit where she collided with supernova after supernova, touching Heaven and returning with such clarity that it shook her to the core. Her fingernails dug into Austin's back as her entire frame quaked in deep, violent spasms. He'd come with her, spilling himself inside her, crying her name in ecstasy with deep groans and gripping her body in a way that told her what she already knew. He held her bottom and back with such possession—but such tenderness—she knew he was never letting go.

Just like that she'd fallen in love, hard and true. There was no going back, she saw as she looked into his gorgeous amber eyes, and he smiled at her, knowingly. He'd felt it too—the pinnacle, the tipping point. His body had told her what his lips hadn't, and Savannah couldn't deny her heart—or his.

Austin held her for the longest time, stroking her face and watching her, before withdrawing, leaving her center feeling bereft.

But he laconically pulled her with him to the shower and began all over again, taking her pleasure to new heights as he did things to her she'd never had done before. It was exquisite and unbelievable, not just the sex but the love she felt oozing from every pore of his skin, coming from his lips, his hands, his manhood. It was the most amazingly beautiful feeling Savannah had ever felt in her life and she never wanted it to stop.

Later, they were putting their clothes on, Austin donning a pair of jeans and a rust-colored polo shirt that made his eyes pop, and Vanna put back on her dress from last night. It, thankfully, had no wrinkles, she noted as she adjusted it over her breasts and looked in the full-length mirror on the bathroom wall. She caught his eyes on her as she looked at her reflection and grinned at him. If they didn't have to be at city hall in an hour, she would jump his sexy ass all over again. Then again, her sex was so tender after all the action she'd experienced in the last eight hours.

"Have I told you that you're the most stunning female I've ever laid my eyes on?" Austin asked as he approached and embraced her from behind, resting his bearded chin in the crook of her neck.

Vanna giggled. "You can tell me that as much as you want to, Mr. Montgomery."

She realized she had only a touch of mascara and a hint of lip gloss on—thanks to her wristlet—and he was still calling her stunning. She hoped the dress and her curly tendrils made up for that fact, but considering his reaction and the semi-hard erection suddenly digging into her bottom, she knew it did…although, he was probably biased.

"You ready?" he asked and kissed her neck as his hands descended to her thighs. "Or do we need a few more minutes?" he teased, his tongue licking at her neck.

How was it possible that she was aching for him all over again? What was he doing to her?

Savannah moaned even as she said, "We should go."

He hummed an, "Umm, hmm," in her ear as he cupped her

breasts and squeezed, getting a gasp from her. "I love that your panties have a huge hole in them. I'm gonna be thinking about that this *entire* meeting and how much I can't wait to stick my dick through it." He arched his hard-on into her bottom, driving his point home.

Had her body not been quivering in desire, she would have laughed—not to mention that she was completely embarrassed by that fact now, and sitting with her legs crossed the whole time as a draft moved up her skirt wasn't going to be ideal.

Austin seemed to sense her sudden distress and turned her around. "You don't have to do this, you know? We're gonna get McClintock. One way or another, he's going down. He'll never see that seat, let alone sit in it. I can promise you that."

Austin had something up his sleeve, Vanna could feel it, but he hadn't told her what it was and she wasn't going to ask. But she felt a duty to her town, it was strong and relentless, and had kept her up at night thinking about it. She wasn't kidding herself, but the thoughts of staying here in Abundance had been dancing around in her head. She might not have to go back to Houston, and the more the time continued to sneak up on her, the more she dreaded going back to the city that had failed her. She couldn't explain it; she'd rehashed the options over and over again, but she felt compelled to take a part in keeping her town safe and its best interests in mind.

She thought about all this as they drove to Morgan's office that rainy Monday, he'd called her while she was on her way and asked her to meet with him first, he had something he wanted to talk with her about.

They entered his complex, and Austin caught Vanna's eye again while they rode up the elevator to Morgan's suite. She could only imagine what was going through his head as an eyebrow rose and his eyes descended to her thighs; he made her feel unabashedly sexy. Her cheeks were red as they stepped off the elevator and approached Morgan's secretary's desk.

"Dr. Kinsen? It's a pleasure. I'm Sally. Please go on in. Mr. Butler is waiting for you."

It had been a while since she'd been greeted with her title, but she smiled at the lovely brunette dressed in a white button dress suit and headed back to her cousin's office.

"Vanna," Morgan greeted her with a smile, his eyes warm as he took her hands in his. His dark beard was neat and trim and his hair was spiked. He looked dashing in a slate-colored three-piece suit with a royal blue shirt and matching tie. "Austin." He shook Austin's hand and motioned for them to approach a table with a blueprint atop it. "Thanks for coming."

"Of course. Wow. This—is this Terra?"

"Yes, what of the original design I could recall from memory," he smirked. "I've been racking my brain and suddenly, I remembered... you're an engineer. Why hadn't I asked you prior to now? I've been struggling with a way to incorporate an irrigation system. I was wondering if you could help me with it."

Vanna grinned. "I'm honored." She looked down, seeing where the lots would be, the gardens, the farm, and her mind began analyzing and assessing the placement, like a computer. "Where's the closest water source?"

Morgan pointed to the river, and Savannah's brain began computing her thoughts.

"Got a blank piece of paper?" she asked, and Morgan pulled a piece of draft paper from a stack on a nearby shelf.

Soon, Savannah had a sketch in place and was drawing it into the blueprint with ease, erasing, and reworking it efficiently. "Now, don't worry about the mechanics of it all at this point in time. I'll get a schematic going of that, but in the meantime, show this blueprint to your team and I'll do some research on the best materials to use." She finished drawing and stepped back, looking over to her cousin. The two men seemed stunned by her speed and intelligence, but instead of being intimidated, like she always was, Vanna felt proud.

"Oh...kay. Wow. Thank you. That was—"

"Un-freaking-believable," Austin finished and his sexy eyes raked over her with admiration; Savannah's heart soared.

Morgan checked his watch. "Ah, crap. We need to go." He gathered a briefcase and led them out.

Sally waved to them, and they took the elevator back down to the ground floor, walking the short distance to city hall. The clicking of Vanna's heels echoed in the big marble foyer as she looked nostalgically around at the paintings of her town on the mosaics that ran the length of the wide hallways.

"This should be fairly easy. Just sound convincing. You're one of the most genuine people I know, cuz, so this shouldn't be difficult for you." Morgan escorted her and Austin into the chambers and kissed her cheek before taking his seat behind the podium.

Ed Johnson was the head of the council and he couldn't be more pleased as he gave her a big smile and shook her hand with equal fervor. "Dr. Savannah Kinsen, I'm utterly thrilled that you're considering this position. I know I speak for all of us when I say, we would be tickled pink to have you for our mayor."

Savannah nodded and smiled back in return, thanking him for his kindness. She didn't miss the look Austin gave her as they sat behind a table off to the side of the lectern. Butterflies filled her stomach as the members began to file in, one by one, some greeting her eagerly, others eyeing her suspiciously. Austin gave her thigh a squeeze under the table, reassuring her even as her womanhood sang at the closeness of his enticing frame next to hers. She just looked over at him and nodded, pulling confidence from his presence.

Soon, Ed was greeting the council members, calling the meeting to order, and introducing Morgan to speak as he'd been the one to call this emergency meeting. Morgan thanked him and began. "First of all, thank you for coming on such short notice. As you know, our town—and my family—is being targeted and I, for one, am gravely concerned for our future. A parasite has seen its way into our midst and our legacy and all we've worked for is at stake. Which leads me to why we're all here." He smiled over at Savannah then, his blue eyes sparkling. "My cousin, Dr. Savannah Kinsen, has recently moved home, and she's interested in running for mayor."

Gasps, mumbles, and excitement filled the space as the voices of the ten council members all spoke at once.

"She's not a resident," came the voice of an old man Savannah didn't immediately recognize, one who'd also given her snake eyes when she'd entered.

"Nonsense," Peggy Freeman countered. "Savannah was born and raised here. She's as much a resident of Abundance as any of us." She gave Vanna a nod and a smile.

"Let's hear what she has to say, shall we," Ed stated and motioned for Savannah to rise.

Her heart leapt into her throat then and she felt her legs wobble as she stood. She smiled and adjusted the mic in front of her. "Thank you. Thank you all for meeting with me and agreeing to give me this opportunity. I know that my announcement is sudden, but contrary to what you may believe, I've been considering this for some time now. Houston hasn't been home to me in a long time." Savannah looked down, knowing that she spoke the truth. "Abundance means so much to me...my family and the families of this town are my top priority and keeping them safe is what I want. I would make a good mayor. I'm fair, I'm considerate of our values and interests, and if given the chance, I will keep the order that was set forth almost two hundred years ago. A man has come to our town, a man who longs to change it into something that would alter our principles that were founded on small town living." She paused and took a sip of water from the glass before her. She looked to Morgan and smiled. "Abundance is a town that thrives on its name. It's a place of community, of love and friendship, cooperation and dedication, and Morgan Butler has a vision that will bring that idea to life in his newest project. It will benefit the entirety of the town and bring homes, jobs, and local economy back into the fold. He and I are going to work together to make our town better and not for our own interests but the betterment of Abundance." She watched as the council digested her words.

"And just where does commerce fit into that vision?" came a gruff voice, and Savannah almost gasped as a white-headed man in a white cowboy hat and grey suit stood in the opened doorframe.

"This is a closed meeting, Mr. McClintock," Ed hissed and stood.

"And as the future mayor of the town, I deserve to be a part of it," he smirked.

"Future mayor!" Morgan scoffed and stood too, "You have some nerve."

"Answer the question, Ms. Kinsen," McClintock demanded, and Vanna felt Austin's strong shoulder pressed to hers in an instant as he, too, came to stand, his growl soft in her ear. "What the hell does an astrophysicist know about business—or politics for that matter?" He laughed. "Not a damn thing! Don't y'all see that this is a bunch of bullshit? These two are playing you, folks. She's a shoo-in. Morgan Butler is grasping at straws because he doesn't have a leg to stand on." McClintock moved into the room and pointed to Morgan.

"You'd better watch who you're talking to, McClintock," Morgan smarted back.

"And you'd better up your game, son. What kind of fool doesn't see right through this charade?" His hands waved dramatically before his eyes locked on Savannah, and she felt fear as dark pupils started back at her. "Why in hell would a woman of her caliber give up NASA to come here to this measly place?"

"If you think our town is so *measly* then why are you running for mayor of it?" Peggy asked, heatedly.

"Because no one else is."

"*I* am. And I *will* win. You can bet on that," Savannah spoke up, her anger flaring at that moment.

"We'll see about that, sweetheart. But it's good to see what I'm up against," McClintock retorted, his eyes descending her body, making her feel violated. "Let the games begin, Kinsen." He laughed even as he began to walk out of the room, bringing a wave of nausea to

Vanna's throat. The door closed sharply behind McClintock, and Savannah felt an arm come around her shoulder, protectively.

Her heart hammered as she looked into Austin's angry, red face.

What had she done? She'd squared off with the enemy. Was she really ready for this?

~

"So, uh, you doin' anything tonight?" Jax asked Stella as he led her around the back pasture, getting her used to Calliope, their newest quarter horse, a seven-year-old buckskin filly.

Stella gave a cute little giggle and looked down at him, her hazel brown eyes sparkling. Man, she was beautiful. And she turned him into a bumbling idiot when she was around, making his palms all sweaty and setting his heart to fluttering. He felt as if he were hovering somewhere between weakness and nausea, but at the same time with uncontainable excitement.

"What'd ya have in mind, handsome?" she asked.

"Well, it's Friday night. We could go grab some dinner, a movie, whatever ya like." He pulled the horse to a stop and the look Stella gave him had him tripping.

"As long as I get to go with *you*, I don't care where it is."

His heart lurched and he gulped. She'd been saying things like this all week, dropping hints and standing so close that his blood felt like it had turned into a river of scorching desire. Being so near to someone with the sheer sexual magnetism of Stella Rose Jenkins was like standing in awe of the Grand Canyon or Niagara Falls, one wasn't simply immune to her beauty for she shone like the sun.

And Jackson had fought it until he just couldn't do it anymore. After all, Cassidy hadn't called, she hadn't come to see him; he'd not seen hide nor hair of her since she'd broken up with him a month ago and she did, *indeed*, break up with *him*...and practically told him not to waste time waiting for her. So, Jax was simply doing what his father and Wyatt had encouraged him to do, enjoying his youth, seeing what else was out there, and asking the smokin' hot girl that seemed to be into him out for a date.

And she'd just said yes. Jackson was ecstatic, but at the same time it felt like a premature celebration; his heart ached with bittersweet contentment. Stella seemed to sense the change in him for she reached down the horse's neck to the halter he held and took his hand. He tilted his head back and looked at her. The sincere understanding smile shining back at him gave him pause and he couldn't stop the warmth that spread through his chest. He gave her a smile back.

"What time ya wanna go?" he asked.

"As soon as I get off this horse."

Her eagerness made him chuckle. Was she always so delightful? Or was it just with him?

"Aren't you hungry?" she asked.

Now that she mentioned it, he was a little hungry. He shrugged. "We should probably clean up first."

She blushed then and it was so unlike her that it took his breath. How could she get even more beautiful than she already was?

He hadn't seen Stella since Christmas before last and man, she had literally blossomed overnight. Not that she hadn't always been a looker; her mother was a gorgeous movie star who Stella took a lot after. And it wasn't that he hadn't noticed before now, but he assumed that being single made her more attractive to him now. Or he'd been so absorbed in Cassidy that no other girl had caught his eye. Either way, now his eyes were fully opened and he was enjoying what he was seeing. He just hoped he wasn't jumping the gun.

"Of course you're right." She huffed and recovered. "How about six?"

Jackson looked down at his watch. It was 4:30 PM now. "Ok. I'll come to your house and pick you up."

"Jax, you're so old school. I love it." She gave him another sexy giggle. He was a bit taken aback. How was coming to pick her up for a date considered old school? Was he *that* out of the game?

He led the filly back into the barn and helped Stella down off the horse. She gave him a kiss on the cheek and patted his chest. "I'll see you in an hour." Her eyes fell down his body and back up and she winked, the promise there undeniable.

Once again, Jax wondered if this was premature. He knew he wasn't over Cassidy, not by a long shot. Had he just made a big mistake in asking Stella out?

He turned to see Austin standing there, propped against the stall wall, giving him a knowing grin. "Well, well, looks like you're in for a fun night, stud." Austin laughed.

Jax scowled. "I just—"

"Don't tell me you're *already* having doubts, dude."

"I dunno, A.J. Stella's great, really, but—"

"But?" Austin's blond brows shot to his hat.

Jax hadn't been oblivious to the way Austin and Savannah had been acting the past week. Things had changed between them. His sister and Austin were an item now, it would seem. They'd gone out a couple times and she'd even had him back at the house for dinner the other night. Not to mention, they'd all noticed Savannah hadn't been home at night much this past week. She'd been staying with him. And she seemed happy. Really happy. And so did Austin.

So, Austin should understand Jax's misgivings about talking Stella out on a date. If Austin really cared for Vanna, how could he even *think* about another woman, let alone go on a date with that person? So why was Jax doing this? And how could he even dream of getting Stella's hopes up? He was on the rebound after all; what if he broke her heart, without intending to do so? She was like family. He'd not only have to deal with his Uncle Buck, he'd have to deal with his father too...and his mom.

Austin stepped forward then and patted Jackson on the shoulder. "Ah, hell, J.D. Stop worrying so much and just go out and have fun. Don't put any expectations on it and you won't have this pressure you've put on yourself, huh?"

He had a point, but pressure was all Jax felt, well that and nervousness, anxiety…betrayal. But Cassidy had broken up with *him* dammit, not the other way around, and for all he knew, she was going out with someone tonight herself.

Jax puffed his chest out and nodded to Austin, led the filly in, brushed her down and ran to the house to shower and change.

He was ready in no time and headed out after dressing in a pair of relaxed fit jeans and a stripped sage green polo shirt. He threw his tan Stetson back on because he knew Stella loved it—she seemed to have a thing for cowboys and he was going to use that to his advantage.

He exited the basement door, as he didn't want his family to know what he was up to. Good or bad, he didn't wanna hear it.

He cranked the old turquoise blue '57 Chevy that had once belonged to his great-grandfather and had been handed down to him by his sister when he'd turned sixteen after Cole had put a new engine in it once again and touched the paint up. It was looking spiffy and Jax knew Stella was gonna love it. If she was into the country boy swag, she would be putty when she rode in his antique truck, for sure. He turned on the radio as he pulled out onto the highway and set it to classic country, feeling his cowboy roots take hold.

It wasn't long before he pulled into the gated drive of the Jenkins' property and punched the code in that Stella had texted him. It opened slowly and Jackson drove up the driveway, stopping out front of the mansion he'd seen many times over the last twenty years. His anxiousness returned as he came to the door and hit the doorbell, praying his Uncle Buck didn't answer.

He was relieved to see Stella there, donning a white mini-skirt and a fitted red t-shirt with the words "Don't flatter yourself cowboy, I was looking at your horse" across it in white letters. She was complete in a straw cowboy hat and red leather cowboy boots. Her hair was curled, she wore more makeup than usual, and had a long white pearl necklace and leather wrap bracelet with silver rings on her fingers.

Jax laughed at her shirt and pointed to it. "That's hilarious."

"Thanks." She gave him a grin and his heart did a flip flop. "Bye Daddy, I love you." She moved out of the door quickly and began pulling it closed, but not before Jax heard Buck say, "Be home by eleven." She huffed, rolled her eyes and pulled the door to. "God, he's annoying."

Eleven seemed like a fair curfew to Jackson, but he just shrugged and motioned for her to go in front of him. They descended the stairs of the white-pillared home, and Stella stopped as she saw the Chevy.

"O-M-G, you brought the Chevy. I freakin' love this truck, Jax." She giggled and kissed his cheek. He opened the passenger side door for her and assisted her in. "You're adorable." Jackson gulped, stopping in his tracks at her batting eyelashes before finally moving off to get into the driver's side, his hands shaking as he shoved the key into the ignition.

The engine started with a deep rumble, and Stella squealed in delight. He couldn't help but smile over at her infectious radiance. She was stunning.

They rode in silence as the twang of Alan Jackson's voice crooned to them and the wind from the opened windows softly whipped their hair as the city limit signs came into view. "So...you like Tex-Mex?" Jax asked.

"Are you kidding? Did you seriously just read my mind?" She swatted at his bicep and gave him another cute little giggle.

When they pulled up to the best Tex-Mex restaurant in Abundance—it had been there for over thirty years—right on Main Street, Jax cut the engine and got out. He came around to Stella's side and opened the door for her, taking her hand. "Are you trying to score brownie points?" she asked, seeming impressed. He just gave her a grin and looped her arm through his, taking the side nearest the road before opening the door for her to go in ahead of him. "Wow, you're *trying* to make me swoon tonight, huh, Jax Kinsen? You must be shooting for first base." Stella gave him a wink, and Jax literally balked, his eyes going wide.

The thoughts of rounding *any* base with her at that point seemed both mind-blowing and incomprehensible. She seemed to realize how off guard she'd taken him, for she laughed and swatted at his chest. "Relax, cowboy, I'm only kidding." But the sudden disappointment in her face had him wondering.

They came to the hostess stand and she led them back to a brown leather booth. The sounds of Spanish mariachi music filled the air and the smell of chargrilled meat on a cast iron skillet hit his nose. Jackson smiled over at Stella as the hostess gave them their menus and walked off. He removed his hat and set it in the seat beside him; Stella followed suit.

"You really *are* the last true gentleman, you know that Jackson?"

Jax only blushed in return. He knew he was an old soul and hoped that wasn't throwing her off. Perhaps that had been the problem with Cassidy, maybe he'd been *too* old-fashioned, not quite modern enough for her tastes? The thoughts of Cass had his stomach roiling. He felt a soft hand cover his and looked up to see Stella all out gazing at him.

"Did I upset you?" The concern on her face made him smile.

"No, not at all, darlin'. Why would you think such a thing?" He peeled his eyes off hers and pretended to peruse the menu, the thought of food at that moment making him sick.

Stella pulled her hand back and began reading over her menu, looking as unsure of herself as Jackson had ever seen her. He recalled Austin telling him to simply have fun and not to put any pressure on the "date" so he made a joke about the refried beans, getting a laugh out of Stella and his unease began to settle.

They ended up ordering sodas, guacamole, and overstuffed steak burritos, of which they didn't finish, but all in all their conversation was light and easy, much to Jackson's relief. They discussed the ranch, Stella's modeling, their families, movies and coffee. Jax started to relax midway through the meal, until Stella brought up an upcoming modeling gig.

"I'm gonna be modeling some western wear in San Antonio in a couple weeks; Momma got me the gig just yesterday. You should come with me. You'd be perfect!"

Jax immediately shook his head, the thoughts of being photographed over and over again completely unappealing to him. "That's alright. I'd rather not," he stated honestly.

Again, the disappointment on her face made his chest hurt. She looked down, and he felt his heart rip as she cleared her throat. "I'm sorry. I was being completely presumptuous, how stupid of me."

"Stella, you aren't stupid. Not at all."

"Do you like me, Jackson?" she huffed out then gasped softly as if she hadn't really meant to ask him that aloud.

How could he answer that question honestly? He was still recovering from his breakup and she was one of the most gorgeous females he'd ever laid eyes on. He gulped and tried to figure out how to answer her.

Stella looked away and Jax swore there were tears in her eyes as she pulled her lips in. He couldn't stand to see her agony, it made the already gaping hole inside his chest even bigger. He reached his hands out to take hers, the ones she was pushing her hair behind her ears with.

"Hey, look at me." She did as he asked, looking so unsure of herself that it made him wince. "You're utterly gorgeous, Stella. And yes, I do like you," he admitted. How could he not? "I like you a lot, in fact. You're funny and full of life and you make me laugh." That got a grin out of her. "I just, I can't stand the thought of having my picture taken from a million different angles. I'm—well, to be honest, I'm camera-shy." He blushed.

Stella laughed then and squeezed his hands in her own. "Why on *earth* would you be camera-shy? You're sexy as hell." Again, her cheeks went bright red and her beautiful green-brown eyes went wide. "Shit!" she swore and looked down. "When I'm around you, Jackson, I have a hard time controlling myself. I'm sorry."

He laughed; she was so good for his bruised ego. He squeezed her hands. "Don't be sorry. I love your honesty." It was true. At least she wasn't walking on eggshells around him, afraid to be herself, like Cassidy had been the last several months.

Stella gave him a big smile then and he pulled his hands from hers when the waiter came with the check. As he was paying it, he caught Stella's eyes on him and felt hot beneath his collar.

He became as nervous as a turkey in November as they headed back out to the truck. *Now what?* Jax thought. As much as he wanted to pretend that he wasn't going to kiss her before night's end, he knew that the odds weren't in his favor for her being let down easily. And as sweet and carefree as she was, he might just end up bedding her; he was simply too vulnerable right now and his heart—and body—enjoyed her luminous spirit far more than he wanted to admit. Her parent's had picked the perfect name to fit her personality; Stella was a "star" in every sense of the word.

As Jackson contemplated the dilemma he was in, he suddenly remembered the rodeo was in town, for his cousin Elias had texted him earlier and he'd forgotten to respond—*Whoops!*

"So, uh, the rodeo's tonight if you—"

"OMG, yes! Take me! Please?" she begged and sidled up next to him in the seat.

He chuckled and threw his arm around her as she pressed into his side. "Alright, cowgirl. We've missed the first hour of it." He checked his watch. "But we'll be right on time for the exciting stuff."

∼

*J*ackson had been correct. The excitement had begun the minute they'd walked into the Abundance Fairgrounds to find a seat on the metal bleachers that had been set up in the large field. The arena was standard sized with stadium lights illuminating the enclosure of dirt in front of them. He'd scanned the railing and pens, looking for the guys he knew would be there to rodeo, for most were friends of his, as well as his cousin, Elias Kinsen. He'd waved when he saw Elias and ambled over, glad to see him.

"Howdy, cuz, how are ya?" Jax asked as he patted Elias's back and laughed, pulling him in for a half-hug.

"I'm good. I texted you earlier, asking where you were, brohoof." Elias lifted his cowboy hat and gave him a beaming smile.

Elias was twenty-four years old, as tall as Jackson and just as broad. They could almost pass for twins, virtually, only Elias had dimples, darker hair and his eyes were a lighter green than Jackson's. His mother, Veronica, had blue eyes and dark hair, just like Jackson's mom. She and his Uncle Gavin had been married five years before Jackson was born, Elias came that next year. His sister, Avery, had followed four years later; she was Jax's age.

Elias, much to his father's surprise, had followed in his Uncle Carson and Uncle Jack's footsteps. He was a cowboy through and through—and a championship calf roper at that. He was fast as lightning and had hung out with Jax many summers during their childhood, learning all things equestrian with him.

"*Now* I see why I didn't get a text back," Eli scoffed and looked behind Jax to a surprised Stella. "Who's the babe, cuz?" he asked with a whisper in the ear opposite Stella.

Jax blushed ten shades of red before turning to Stella, who looked back and forth between the two of them like she'd just developed double vision. "Have I entered the *Twilight Zone?*" she asked with a giggle.

Jax's voice finally took hold. "Stella, you remember Elias, right? Eli, this is Stella Jenkins."

"Stella? My my, darlin'. I sincerely apologize. I didn't recognize you!" Eli's eyes looked her over in unreserved appraisal that Jax couldn't fault him for. It had probably been a good four years since he'd last seen her. Back then she'd been a lanky kid with chicken legs and knobby knees. Now, she was all woman, and if Eli's gaze was any indication, he was memorizing every curve.

"Eli's in town for the rodeo," Jax told Stella, who nodded at him.

"Yes, ma'am." He tipped his hat at her. "Gonna be around for a little while. I'll be crashing with my lil' cuz here...if he's cool with that, o'course," Elias stated, elbowing Jax.

Not only did Jax and Elias look alike, they also got along well. Their four-year age gap hadn't been a problem—not with Jax being as mature as he'd always been—especially in these last few years. They were both easy-going, easy to please, and liked a lot of the same things. Elias was so different from his father, Gavin, who was a business man with no trace of a rugged side. Jax's dad and uncle had often teased that Gavin had been adopted.

"Of course! The girls'll love seeing you. Vanna's in town, ya know?"

"Nice, it'll be a regular ol' family reunion." Elias chuckled and looked back over at Stella. "Well, I got to get back to Ringo. Put him up for the night. I placed third. Sorry that you guys missed seeing it; it was *mighty* impressive, I might add." He tipped his hat to Stella once more, who grinned back in reply, before saying, "I'll call you later, Jax."

After Eli left, Jackson and Stella found a seat in the stands and she shivered from the night air as she moved closer to him. "I'd forgotten that your cousin was a calf-roper," she noted as she watched the first barrel racer galloping into the arena. "God, it's uncanny how much you two look alike."

Jax gave a laugh. He'd always known it was true, but hadn't really thought much about it until she'd said it earlier. "He favors me more than Alex or Ethan do."

"I don't recall meeting either of them. Did I?"

Jax shook his head. "They're around Dallie's age. I don't think you've ever met them. It's been a few years since they were down here last. They live in Cheyenne. Both are married with kids and help run CK Ranch."

Stella nodded then groaned softly as she watched the racing cowgirl knock over a barrel before heading out of the arena at full speed. "So, there's four boys and three girls, huh? Big family, the Kinsens." Jax hadn't really thought about it, but yeah, they were a rather big family, especially when they all got together now with Alex and Ethan's broods at three kids a piece. "I would love to have a big family. I mean I have my cousins Chandler and Heather, but being an only child kinda sucks, I'll be honest."

"Your parents adore you, Stella."

"I know, but I'm spoiled and sometimes it shows." She gave him a knowing grin and he shrugged, getting a gasp and laugh out of her as she shoved him. "Seriously though, I don't like being an only child. I would've loved to have a brother or sister. Someone to fight with and be close to like you and your sisters are."

"It has its ups and downs," Jax admonished, but despite that his sisters tended to be overprotective of him since he was the baby, he adored his family and wouldn't change a thing. He couldn't imagine how lonely and uneventful his life would be without his sisters and cousins. Stella and Heather were seven years apart, her and Chandler were eight, and Stella had always stood out. "You know, my grandfather taught my grandmother how to barrel-race in her teens?"

"Really?" Stella smiled over at the blonde girl on horseback as she rounded the pink canvas tented barrel closest to them.

"Yeah, my mom was a state championship barrel-racer too. She went to the US finals several times."

"Your mom is one of the most graceful riders I've ever seen on horseback." Stella looked back at him in awe, and he grinned; it warmed his heart that she admired his mother so.

They stayed for the bull riding, watching as each rider lasted just mere seconds before getting violently bucked off. After one particular cowboy was badly injured and carted off to an ambulance, Stella appeared to be rattled; Jax knew it was time to make their leave.

She held one hand to her chest, the other interlocked with his.

Jax enjoyed the feel of her soft palm on his calloused one and the cool breeze that blew as they walked back to the full parking lot. Stella shivered once more on this windy May evening.

"You cold?" She nodded in response as he opened the truck door for her and helped her into the seat. Once he got in and cranked the truck, he turned the heat on. "I'll get it warm for you. Slide over here."

Stella gave him a soft smile and came over to sit beside him as he looped his arm over her shoulder. She smelled so good, like fresh sweet lilies and peonies and a spice he couldn't put his finger on. He felt content next to her, to his surprise, and a tender jolt hit his heart as she lay her head on his shoulder, her blonde hair falling across it. He longed to touch the soft curls, lift them to his nose and inhale, for she was putting him under a spell.

"Do we *have* to go home? It's barely ten," she moped, and he had a sudden overpowering desire to kiss her pouty lips.

"We'll go sit out in the pasture for a little while. I'll start a fire. Would you like that?" She simply nodded, sending her curls bouncing, and Jackson laughed.

Things had been quiet since the fire at Morgan's building site, but they hadn't taken any chances. Kelsey had a body guard even while she was teaching and they'd hired someone to watch the cameras 24/7. Austin hadn't let Savannah out of his sights, and Dallie, his mother, grandmother, and Aunt Jordan didn't leave home without one of the guys escorting them wherever they went. Every single one of them were packing, not that they hadn't been all along, but they were loaded and ready. Tonight was no exception; Jax had his forty-five strapped to his hip.

When he pulled up to the gate of the back pasture, he got out, looked around and unlatched it with his key. He did the same once he got back in the truck and drove through it.

Stella sensed his caution and asked him about it, of which he relayed all the details. She grimaced as they came to stop in front of the fire pit, and he cut the engine. "Can we just stay in the truck?" she almost whimpered.

"I didn't mean to scare you, darlin'," Jax admitted, regretting that he'd even told her. He hadn't wanted to upset her. "There's no need to worry. I'll protect you." He put a hand on his gun.

He looked down into her face, lit by the bright glow of the moon, grateful for this clear night as he could see her every feature.

"I know you will. You're big and strong." Her hand moved down his right shoulder, gripping his bicep, and he felt desire flood his senses, stopping the laugh that came to his throat. He was about to say that he wasn't big and strong, but she made him feel like Superman at how her eyes appraised his body.

She was so utterly beautiful. Young. Innocent. Unaware. And he was still recovering from the damage Cassidy Boyd had done to his heart. He had to speak up and stop this before it started. He felt weak and vulnerable, his body's demands outweighing his mind's protests as he felt her soft palm settle on his chest.

Stella seemed to sense the change in him for she immediately pulled her hand away and eased back some. "I have to tell you something, Jackson." She looked anxious, pursing her lips. "I—I've had a crush on you for a long time."

He should be surprised by this knowledge, but he truly wasn't, despite that he knew Stella was just flirty by nature—like his Aunt Vivian had always been. After all, she'd been hitting on him for weeks now. Jax took in a deep breath and continued to watch her.

"I know you're still heartbroken and I don't want to push you into something that you're not ready for but—"

"I know." He looked down at his hands to tear his eyes from hers. They were so deep, he was going to drown in them if he wasn't careful. "You're amazing, Stell. I want you to know that. Truly and completely. But I *can't* rush into this. I'll only end up hurting you and I won't be able to live with myself if I do. I still love Cassidy. Please understand. It's gonna take time for me to— I don't know if I'll even be able to—"

"You *will* move on, Jax. I'll help you. If you'll let me."

He felt her soft hand cup his cheek and he tried his damnedest to resist her, but the pull was too strong. When her soft lips brushed his, the deep, satisfied grumble in his chest surprised him. How could it feel so good to have another woman's lips on his when he was still in love with his ex? It wasn't possible, was it?

Nothing could be further from the truth as his hands moved to Stella's face then into her hair as he deepened the kiss and thrust his tongue into her hot, hungry mouth. The eager tongue that stroked his back caused a spark to ignite inside him and he was suddenly fully engulfed in licking hot flames that shot straight to his groin. He felt his shaft began to stiffen and moaned into her mouth. That was all the response she needed, for her hands moved to his shoulders and his fell to her waist as she moved onto his lap, straddling him. He felt a hot center press against his bulging zipper and gasped as desire overtook him.

"Oh, God, Stella," he grunted as she rocked her hips against his growing erection, her mouth assaulting his, their tongues tangling together in a delicious frenzy.

"Mmm, Jax." Her head flew back and she arched up, her breasts hitting his chest. His hands fell to grip her bottom and he thrust his pelvis against hers involuntarily.

Alarm bells began going off in his head, warning him to slow down, to stop this, to dampen this hunger that was born from lust and nothing more. But she smelled too good, so feminine and sexual, and he was weak and starving for it.

Jackson felt sudden wetness cover his crotch and looked down, his hand moving to her inner thigh. He rubbed his fingers together realizing the viscous liquid wasn't what he originally thought it was.

The metallic scent hit his nose just as Stella gasped and groaned, covering herself. She moved off him quickly and whimpered, "Oh, my *God*!"

When she pulled her hands back, they were covered in blood.

~

*S*tella cried all the way home. She was completely mortified beyond belief. How could she have started her period, tonight of all nights? It wasn't due for days. She pulled her knees in and looked out the window to keep them off Jackson; she might not ever be able to look him in the eyes again.

He'd quickly went into action, reaching into the dashboard and pulling out paper towels, but the damage was already done. They both had blood all over them and Stella had never wanted to hide under a rock more in her life than the moment she realized she'd bled through her white panties and skirt and onto his jeans.

When he pulled up to the house, she was fumbling for the door lock.

"Stella," Jax began. "It's really okay, I promise. It happens."

"Thank you for tonight, Jackson," she interrupted. "I'm so sorry I ruined your clothes." She let out a sob and grabbed for the door handle.

"Hey." He grabbed her hand to stop her, scooting closer, his voice in her ear tearing her heart a little. "I'm not mad. Or upset...or grossed out. I swear."

"You may not be, but I'm all those things right now, so, please, let me go?" she was begging she realized as she pulled away and practically threw herself out of his truck. She slammed the door shut and walked the suddenly long distance to her front door. She opened it gingerly, praying her father wasn't anywhere near it.

She couldn't be that lucky; he rounded the corner just as she closed it behind her.

He gulped as his eyes took in her white skirt, soaked with deep red blood. He dropped the whiskey glass in his hand, inhaling sharply, as his eyes came up to hers. The sound of shattering glass echoed in the foyer and Stella gasped.

"I'll *fuckin'* kill him!" Her father roared and stalked over to her.

Her hands went up even as humiliation filled every corner of her being. "No! Daddy, it's not—I—I started my period!" Her fists grabbed for his shirt just as he started to move to the front door, his face alight with anger.

The sigh of intense relief that huffed out of his big chest steadied her and tears hit her eyes again. "Oh, baby, I'm sorry," he stated as he moved to embrace her. She held her hands out.

"No, I need to change. I don't want to ruin your clothes too," she whimpered and the pitiful look that she received from him made her angry. "I'll be upstairs wishing I was dead." She threw back over her shoulders as she ascended the stairs.

When Stella got to the bathroom, she began filling her bathtub with hot water and body wash and threw her soiled clothes on the ground, letting her tears fall as they may. She crawled in and bawled like a baby, feeling naïve, ashamed, and in the poorest of spirits. Her body had betrayed her to the man she'd been crushing on since she was sixteen and on their first date, of all times, she'd soaked him in menstrual blood. She felt like an amateur and an idiot.

A knock came at the bathroom door and she sniffled. "I'm ok, Daddy," she assured him.

The door opened, and he stepped inside, coming to sit at her vanity, facing the chair away from her even though her nakedness was completely covered in bubbles.

"I know you're embarrassed, but it's not the worst thing that could've happened, you know?"

"You're a guy, how can you *even* understand?" she grumbled and sniffled again.

"Baby, you can't be mad about something that's a natural process."

Oh, yes I can, now go away! she wanted to scream but didn't. "I really care about him," she whined instead.

"I know. That's why I'm telling you that it's okay. If a little blood is all that's gonna scare him off, then you don't need him anyway. A real man knows how a woman's body works."

She looked down, sighing. She knew he was telling the truth, but it didn't take the sting away from her cheeks when she thought of how awful it was, what horrible timing her uterus had.

"Your momma's water broke all over my brand-new shoes, you know?"

"It did?"

"Oh yeah! But it didn't matter because I was so excited to meet you I couldn't have cared less about my shoes. We were walking down the street when I pulled her to me for a kiss and it happened. She was so embarrassed, I remember. I didn't realize that it could splash like that, but it did." His deep laugh made her smile.

But that was different, her father'd had a baby to look forward to meeting. All Jax had gotten was blue balls—thanks to her. Her lips quivered as another surge of mortification hit her.

"I know it's not the same, but still…"

Stella smiled. That her father cared enough to try and comfort her meant the world to her. She was a Daddy's girl and she adored him, even if his protective nature annoyed the teenager in her sometimes. "Thanks, Daddy. For trying to cheer me up. I appreciate it. It was just really bad timing." When his curious eyes looked over at her, she blushed, hoping he didn't understand what she'd meant. "On the first date, of all times!" she admonished.

He looked away, then leaned onto his thighs, sighing deeply. "I thought he'd hurt you, Stella. I've never been that angry in my entire life."

"Dad! You know Jackson's not like that. He would never force himself on me. He was a perfect gentleman tonight."

Buck shook his head, grinning. "I figured. He's a lot like his dad. Jack put the G in gentleman. As lucky as you'd be to have a man like that in your life, he'd be twice as lucky to have you, my little star."

She giggled. "You're just biased, Daddy."

"And you're getting pruney." He gave her another handsome grin. "Finish up and come downstairs. I'll make us some popcorn and we'll watch the classic movie of your namesake." He gave her a wink and blew her a kiss, leaving her to her thoughts.

He'd had a point, she thought and smiled to herself as she soaped up. But most of all, she was lucky that Buck Jenkins was her father; he treated her like a princess. She only prayed the man she ended up with would be half the man he was.

~

*A*ustin looked up into the clear night sky and smiled over at the dark-headed beauty looking through the telescope.

"Found it!" Savannah called out and laughed.

"Sweet," he murmured and wrapped his arms around her from behind. "Star Savvy in the Libra constellation."

"Good choice on the constellation by the way. If you'd have picked Pisces, we wouldn't have been able to see it this time of year...we would've had to wait until fall time."

"I knew this...which was why I chose good ol' Libra." He knew no such thing and the smirk she turned around and gave him told him that. She laughed again and the richness of it warmed his heart. God, he was so in love with her.

"I didn't even know one could buy a star. I mean, I should've I guess, but—"

"Well, I planned to buy you Jupiter, but you wouldn't *believe* how much they wanted for that freaking planet!"

Her head flew back as she chortled, the echo reverberating into the open land surrounding them. It was the most beautiful sight and sound Austin had ever heard and he smothered her in a searing kiss as he pulled her into his chest and down onto the blanket on the grass.

Savannah grunted in surprise as her back gently hit the fleece and Austin's body covered hers. A soft moan passed her lips as his mouth moved to her collarbone and shoulder as he pulled her cardigan down. "Don't you wanna see it?" she asked, and he pulled back just enough so he could look into her face.

"All I see is you, my sweet Savvy. Nothing can compare to your beauty. Not a star, not a planet, not even a nebula."

"Oh," she giggled. "That you even know what a nebula *is* is such a turn-on."

Score a thousand points for me, Austin thought. He'd been googling planetary jargon just so he could come up with new things to talk to her about. It had been enlightening and also induced mind-blowing sex as it *indeed* seemed to turn her on, as she'd said.

She moaned as his mouth returned to hers and his hands cupped her breasts, relishing the heat coming off her as if he were freezing to death and she was the warmth he needed to live.

Austin heard a rustling in the trees behind them and Caesar gave a low growl next to him. He immediately jumped up, unholstering his gun, and pointing it ahead of him into the deep brush as quick as a flash. He stood there, braced over the woman he loved, eyes focused, breathing steady, waiting for the bastard to show himself. Just then a doe stepped out and froze as she looked at him. He sighed heavily and moved to Savannah's side, dropping his gun and placing his forty-five back in its holster on his hip.

Savannah moved forward into his arms then and he reassured her. "I'm a little jumpy— apparently. Sorry, darlin'."

"Damn, you're fast on the draw." Her brow went up.

He laughed, feeling his nerves began to calm. "I was called 'Sharp-Shooter' in training camp."

"I've got a few nicknames I could call you," she murmured and kissed his neck.

"Mmm, do tell, angel." She giggled, her hand falling to the front of his jeans. When she squeezed at the bulge growing there, he moaned. "Mmm, Savvy. You gotta stop doing things like that out here. I gotta be on my A game."

She pulled back, and he frowned at the worry etching her face. "I'll be glad when I can walk out here without having to look over my shoulder." She pulled her knees to her chest as she looked around, shivering all the sudden.

"I'm sorry." He placed his arm around her shoulder and pulled her into his chest. "You did well today though."

He was referencing the squabble that had taken place during the chaotic meeting of the town council, regarding McClintock's seat. Max was pissed, saying the council was setting him up for failure since they'd deemed Savannah eligible as a candidate for mayor despite her lack of permanent residence in Abundance. Peggy Freeman had been the one to remind Max that he wasn't a resident any more than Savannah was, since he'd wanted to play that card. It was when he'd demanded a public debate that all hell had broken loose.

"The town council has always voted in the candidates for mayor. That will not change. We do not need an open debate," Ed had said.

"She's not a politician," Max snapped.

"Neither are *you*," Savannah had retorted. "But if you want a debate then you shall have one."

All eyes had gone to her and she'd blushed but held her ground, defiantly raising her chin. Austin had fallen even more in love with her then as he was now, watching her gaze up into the stars she was so passionate about.

"What do I even know about a debate? I'm in over my head here. He's gonna chew me up and spit me out."

"You're smarter than him. Don't even worry about it. I'm hoping to have him in the can before he even has a chance to embarrass you. If I had my way, he'd already have disappeared before now."

The look she gave him was weary. He hadn't told her about his and Trevor's secret operation, and he didn't intend to. The less she knew about it, the better off she'd be. She seemed to understand this without him having to divulge.

She looked around again, better settling herself against him. "I'm sorry it's come to this."

"Don't be. You aren't at fault here. Max and his greed are to blame," Austin remarked.

They sat in silence for a while and Austin pondered the future. The open-endedness of Savannah's stay here and that she'd not mentioned when she would be returning to Houston. He knew it was inevitable. Space was all she talked about; that and her paintings and music. He knew it was only a matter of time before she had to go back to NASA and the thought hit him harder than he ever expected it would. She was swiftly approaching the two-month mark of being on hiatus and it was going to come faster than either of them were ready for.

He couldn't stop the words that came to his lips. "When are you going to tell your family that you don't plan to stay?"

Her blue-green eyes tore into him, and he immediately regretted asking the question. She looked away, her lips twitching, then she stood and planted her hands on her hips. "This is my decision, not yours!" She huffed. He stood too and put his hands out. "They're *my* family."

"You're gonna get their hopes up." *And mine!*

"You should mind your own damn business."

"Savannah, you can't be mayor of a town if you're not going to be *in* town."

"You don't think I know that!" her shrill voice echoed out in the pasture. "I know exactly the dilemma I've caused, okay? I don't need you to remind me."

"Then pull out of this election before it's too late?" There he'd said how he really felt.

"No! McClintock needs to know he can't win."

"And at what cost?" Austin retorted. "Someone's gonna get hurt. He's not gonna stop until he's made his point. Is your family's safety worth this?"

"What the *hell* do you think I'm doing this for?" she hissed and shoved at him. "That man makes me cringe. I know what he is."

"Then renounce the seat."

"And let him have it? Without a fight? Why?"

"For your own safety."

Savannah shook her head. "You don't understand me at all, do you?"

They stood silent for a moment before Austin felt the hair on his arms raise in awareness. But he was too late as he called her name and watched Caesar's hackles raise as the dog shot up, growling furiously. She'd started walking away and the sharp sound of the gun blast assaulted Austin's ears as he watched the bullet enter her flesh.

"No, no, no," he cried as he caught her in his arms and heard the gunfire hail around him. He could do nothing but run.

CHAPTER 16

*A*ustin rocked back and forth in his chair, in the surgical waiting area of the hospital. Savannah was in surgery, he was covered in her blood, and all he could do was pray now as he waited for his brother to join him.

All he'd focused on after Savannah was shot was getting her away from the spraying bullets as he'd run for cover to his jeep. He'd seen the vast amount of blood covering her and tore his shirt off, wrapping it tightly around her thigh in a makeshift tourniquet to staunch the flow of blood. Then he'd cranked his jeep and raced to save her life, for he'd known there was a chance that the bullet had hit her femoral artery. He prayed all the way here, just as he was praying now.

Please, God. Don't take her away from me. Please? Hot, salty tears ran down his cheeks. He ignored the chill of the air venting on his bare arms, ignored the blood staining his hands, thin tank top, and jeans, and simply let his mind settle only on praying for the woman he loved to survive.

He looked up into the doorway to see his brother standing there.

"Dammit, I'm sorry, I got here as fast as I could. Have you

checked your fuckin' phone?" Wyatt grumbled even as he moved forward.

Austin jumped up and pulled his older brother to him, grateful for his presence, glad he'd been the first to arrive. No, he'd not checked his phone. He'd not even been aware of his phone until they'd rushed Vanna off to surgery. Then he'd called Wyatt and began to pray.

"I was too late. I was too fuckin' late. Jesus, I'll never forgive myself." Austin cried into Wyatt's shoulder as Wyatt patted his back.

"It's not your fault, brother. Don't blame yourself."

"*Where* is she?" a deep voice asked from the doorframe, and Austin looked up to see Jack Kinsen standing there. Austin's heart plummeted as rage took over his boss's face, and Jack marched forward, grabbing Austin up by his shirt. Austin's back was slammed against the nearest wall with such force his teeth rattled. "You son of a bitch. You were supposed to be *protecting* her!" Jack spit out in a growl.

"Jack, I—"

A big hand gripped Austin's neck tightly, forcing his head up to look into Jack's blood-shot and intent eyes. "If my daughter dies, I'm gonna kill you. Do you hear me?" Jack's murderous gaze only made Austin feel like an even bigger piece of shit. If Savannah died, Jack wouldn't need to kill him, Austin would do it himself.

"Daddy, stop it!" Dallie's voice rang out loudly and hurt his ears.

"Jack, let him go," Wyatt begged. "This isn't his fault." Wyatt's hand came to Jack's big shoulder and Jack practically roared in fury.

Jack's ragged breath fell over Austin's face even as his hands shook and his grip tightened. Austin's lungs burned for air, but he also felt relief in death's cold embrace, for without Savannah he didn't want life.

"Jack!" A shrill female voice called.

Jack's hand fell from Austin as he took a step back. Grief over-took the older man and he fell to his knees, his hands covering his face. Austin coughed, trying to pull air into his oxygen-starved lungs.

After he was able to breathe again, he looked around at the Kinsens—Jack, Natalie, Dallie, Jax—at their worried faces, their disappointment, their anguish. In that moment, he truly hated himself. He felt worthless and undeserving to be amongst them.

Suddenly, a man in scrubs with booties and a surgical cap came into the room. "Are you the husband?" The surgeon immediately looked at Austin, the one who'd brought Savannah in. He didn't deny or confirm the doctor's question, he simply stepped forward, ready to hear the news, good or bad and embrace his destiny, whatever that might be. If Savannah had been called home to Jesus then Austin was going to follow her. "The surgery was a success. She's gonna pull through. She's lost a lot of blood though. We're gonna need donations."

"I'm type O negative, take all you need," Austin stated and put his arm out.

The doctor smiled. "Thank you, son. I'll send the nurse in."

"So, she's ok?" Natalie asked and approached, placing a hand on Austin's shoulder as Jax assisted his father to stand.

"Yes ma'am. The bullet went straight through the muscle. It missed her major arteries, miraculously. Your quick actions helped too, young man."

Sims had always been a shitty shot. Austin thanked God for that now, even as his blood boiled in rage at the thought of Sims. He was going to destroy him. There wasn't going to be anything left when Austin was done with the bastard.

Austin looked down, sighing in a myriad of emotions, then he felt a soft frame embrace him and a lavender and vanilla scent hit his nose.

"Thank you, Austin," Natalie stated as she hugged him. "Thank God for you. You saved her life." A beaming smile lit Savannah's mother's face, and Austin couldn't help but smile back at her, even as his heart felt like it might explode. "Can we see her?" Natalie asked as she turned back to the doctor.

"For now, she's sleeping in recovery and will be for some time. I'll have the nurse fetch you when she awakens, but it's important that she rests and gets blood transfusions. She's lucky." He looked back at Austin, and nodded before turning to leave.

Thank you, God! Austin literally fell into the nearest chair, his adrenaline rush finally waning. His hands shook as he buried his face in them, grateful and upset all at once.

The nurse came to get him to draw blood not long after. They asked him a million questions, especially regarding his last inking, and took a pint of the life-giving fluid. He begged the nurse to take more but she looked at him as if he were nuts. Hell, the process took long enough as it was, and Austin was antsy to get out of that seat, check in on his sweet Savvy, and call Trevor back. He was given a large bottle of water and escorted to the waiting room, where everyone save for Wyatt still sat, awaiting news on Savannah.

Jack looked up at him, the rage on his face now gone and a look of gratitude replacing it. Man, the guy's moods were unpredictable. Although Austin understood all too well, he felt them too. Anger. Pain. Fury. Fear. Appreciation. Loathing. If Jack was feeling a quarter of those things, then it would explain his need to expel his emotions in any way possible.

"Baby, why don't you and Jax go on home and me and your father will stay? You look exhausted," Natalie cooed to Dallie and patted her cheek as Dallie's head rested on her shoulder.

"No! I have to see my sister. Make sure she's ok," Dallie insisted. Jax pulled her into his arms for a hug as tears hit her eyes.

Her soft sobs tore into Austin's heart as he sighed and waited with them. He checked his phone and as much as he wanted to call Trev back, he couldn't leave, knowing Savannah might wake up and he not be there.

Just then a nurse came forward and gave them a weak smile.

"She's awake." She looked around and Natalie closed her eyes in relief, grinning softly. "She's asking for Austin."

Austin's heart hammered in his chest as he stood. He moved forward only to be blocked by Jack's big frame in front of him. "Give her our love, Montgomery. And thank you for your quick thinking." He patted Austin's bare shoulder and nodded.

"Of course, sir. I'm her bodyguard after all." He gave Jack a weak smile.

"You did well, son." Jack's head fell. "I'm sorry. That man's gonna pay for what he did though. If it's the last thing I ever do." The determination in Jack's eyes matched Austin's and he gave the older man a nod before Jack stepped aside.

Austin moved to follow the nurse and as soon as he crossed the threshold of her room and saw his sweet angel laying covered in blankets, looking like death warmed over, he began to sob.

"Oh, Savvy," he moved to embrace her gently, his head falling to her neck.

She cooed to him, her voice weak, "Austin, I'm sorry. I'm so sorry."

"No, baby. I'm sorry. I should never—"

"Shh...no apologies. Promise?"

He laughed even as tears fell down his cheeks. "I promise. Damn, you're a sight for sore eyes. You look gorgeous even so close to death's door, love."

"You're *so* full of crap," she joked.

"You're the most beautiful thing I've ever seen, Savannah Grace." He kissed her cheek before pulling back and kissing her hand.

He was just about to tell her how in love with her he was, but he was interrupted as Natalie and Jack came in and he stepped back letting them gush over her. He simply watched and waited, making sure Savannah could see him as her anxious eyes searched for him when he was out of view.

Dallie and Jax came next and Austin propped himself against the wall, planning the course of action he was going to take regarding Brody, his anger and hate melding into a stew of bloody fury.

A little while later, when Savannah's eyes succumbed to sleep, Jack took watch while Austin called Trevor back.

The first message he'd left had been a warning. "The falcon is about to strike. On my way, but the bird may land before my arrival. Be on the ready." Trevor had left it as both a voicemail and a text message, but Austin had been too busy wooing his woman. If he'd been more prepared, Savannah never would have been shot.

The next message Trevor had left not long after the first had been brief; "Operation blue falcon has commenced." Austin was glad, but it didn't take the anger away. He wanted to be the one beating the living fuck out of Brody.

Trevor answered with a simple, "I'll have to call you back Mustang, our falcon is squawking as we speak."

"So long as I get to pluck a few feathers, T-man."

"No need, brother. It's done."

Fuck! He was simply gonna have to take his anger out in another way. And if they already had Brody then McClintock would soon follow.

It gave Austin great relief, but he wasn't taking any chances, not with this family's lives still at stake.

"I want to see him in the burn bag, Trev."

"It will be done, my friend. Don't worry. The skies are clear."

It was over. And Austin should be pleased. But he felt guilty and nothing in the world was going to change that. Once again, he was responsible for a casualty of war. Thank God that casualty hadn't resulted in death, but the sting of Austin's negligence was still poignant.

He sighed and pinched his nose, closing his eyes briefly before heading back into Vanna's room. He propped himself back against the wall and watched Jack, who sat beside his daughter, stroking her hand that was interlocked in his.

Neither man said anything as silence filled the room. Dallie and

Jax had left already and Natalie sat sleeping in the chair next to Savannah's bed, her head resting back.

"There's nothing I wouldn't do for my family," Jack began, his voice soft and calm. "My children and my wife are everything to me. I would die for them and I would *kill* for them."

"He's been apprehended," Austin answered, and Jack's head came up to look at him.

"He's gonna go to prison, I assume?"

"The worst," Austin assured him. "He'll pray he was dead." Austin crossed his arms over his chest.

"I shouldn't have blamed you. That was wrong of me, Austin."

"I understand. I blame myself; it shouldn't have happened. Period."

"Accidents happen."

"That was no accident, Jack. That bastard planned to take her down. I had a feeling McClintock would retaliate. Savannah was a threat. He doesn't like threats." Austin closed his eyes again, anger filling his veins. He should've been better prepared.

"You did all you could, son. You've spent every waking minute with her. He was waiting for that perfect moment. It just so happened that he didn't succeed when he took it."

Austin couldn't stop the tears that fell down his cheeks, thinking of Jerome and how ill-prepared he'd been for that attack too. "Sims always had poor aim, thank *God*."

When he opened his eyes, Jack was assessing him, his mouth curved in a crooked smile. "You're in love with her, aren't you?"

Austin's gaze fell to Savannah's beautiful face, her long, dark eyelashes resting on her high cheekbones, her perfect lips relaxed. She was blissfully unaware of her surroundings, unaware of how much Austin adored every cell of her being.

"I should've known," Jack scoffed, and Austin looked back at him. "These girls just creep their way into your heart and once they got their hooks in you, it's all over."

Austin gave a soft chuckle. It was true. That's exactly what had happened. He'd been blindsided by the power Savannah had over him, the spell she'd put on him...and he'd been helpless to stop it.

"I got one question for you," Jack said and brought Austin back to reality.

"What's that, sir?"

"When you plannin' on letting *her* know?"

~

*J*ax knocked on the Jenkins' door and waited, tucking his arms behind his back. When his Uncle Buck answered, he tipped his hat to him and smiled.

"Howdy," he stated.

"Good evenin', son," Buck stated and stepped back. "C'mon in. Stella's in the living room."

"Great, thank you."

"Can I grab you a beer?"

Jax gave his uncle a smirk. "Now, if I say, 'Yes,' and take your daughter out then I'll be drinkin' and drivin', and if I say, 'No', now that's just plain rude...way to trap me, Uncle Buck."

The older, broader man gave him a hearty laugh and smacked him on the back. "You always were smart, Jackson. Now I admire you, kid."

Buck showed Jax into the living room and he looked around for Stella, but she wasn't there.

"I swear I left her here. You know how girls are, she's probably run upstairs to put makeup on or change her clothes or somethin'." Buck shrugged and shook his head. He motioned for Jax to take a seat and he took the couch opposite his uncle.

The man wasn't even related to him by blood, but that had never mattered. Their families were as close as two families who weren't kin could be, same as with the Boyds. His Uncle Buck and his mom had gone to school together and been best friends decades before Jackson was born. When his mother had moved back to Abundance, she and Vivian had bonded when she'd trained Viv for a movie on his grandfather's ranch years and years ago. Buck and Vivian had met at a charity ball in Dallas some nineteen years ago and had gotten married before Stella came just four months later. The dual friendship and connection his parents had with the Jenkins had lasted over the years.

As if reading his mind, Buck asked. "Do you remember the trip we took with your folks to Cancun all those years ago?"

Jax shook his head. He was too young to remember that, but he'd been told about it periodically over the years—what a great time they'd had.

"Stella was still in the womb, but she was there with all of us." He chuckled and took a swig from the bottle in his hand. "Man, it doesn't seem like that long ago. You were just a little tyke, enjoying the water and sand, and covering me up in it." Buck sighed. "Damn, time flies."

"I thought I heard that Kinsen voice," came a female voice Jax recognized well.

He looked up to see his gorgeous Aunt Vivian coming towards him, clad in a black romper, her blonde locks pinned up on her head and her lightly tanned face free of makeup. She was just as stunning as always, her brown eyes sparkling up at him.

"Aunt Viv," he exclaimed and stood to embrace her. "When did you get back?"

"Oh, just yesterday. Let me look at you!" She smiled as her eyes roved him. "My, you're so handsome. I can't believe how tall you are and broad." She shook her head and sighed. "God, I remember when you were just a baby, Jackson. When did you get so big?"

"I literally just said the same exact thing, darlin," Buck replied. "You remember our trip to Mexico with him and Jack and Nat and how he buried me in sand?"

Vivian laughed at the memory and moved over to sit next to her husband, who threw an arm around her shoulder. "I remember." Jax sat back down, his eyes searching for the missing Stella. "Oh, hon, she's gonna be a while. As soon as she heard your voice, she ran upstairs to primp."

Jax blushed. "She didn't have to get all dolled up for me."

Vivian rolled her eyes. "Like that's even an option."

"Ah, she's a teenager, it's what they do." Buck shrugged.

"How is your sweet sister doing?" Vivian asked, her hand going to her chest. "When your mother told me she'd been shot, I almost died. I couldn't *believe* it!"

"She's doing okay, the pain was worse yesterday on day three than today. They'd told us it would be. The swelling was down some and they gave her several rounds of antibiotics. She should be discharged today or tomorrow. She's already sick of the food." He laughed so as to try to ease some of the tension he felt talking about Savannah being shot. It still made his blood scream in his veins that someone had tried to kill her, a man Austin had known from his training camp days—a man who'd been hired by Max McClintock to take her out.

"It's gonna take some time to recover from that, but I'm glad it missed the bones and arteries."

It had. She might be looking at some future nerve damage, but little victories were to be celebrated, Jax guessed. "She'll be on crutches for a time and out of work for a while still. But the doctor is confident she'll have a full recovery." Well, *almost* full, anyway, the surgeon had told them.

"Nat said that the shooter's been apprehended and the damn fraud behind it all," Buck added, and Jax nodded in response.

"Well, if you talk to your mom before I do, you tell her, I'll be coming to see them very soon. As soon as the jet lag is gone." She gave another dazzling smile and again, Jax nodded. "Stella was so embarrassed about what happened, Jackson. I didn't even know what to say to comfort her."

Jax frowned. "She had absolutely nothing to be embarrassed about, Aunt Viv."

"Well, but that's just her, Jax. She always wants everything to be

374

perfect."

"Well, life ain't perfect and sometimes we just got to take the good with the bad."

Buck raised his bottle in a "cheers." "Amen to that, son."

Jax heard the sound of flip-flops on the stairs and turned to see Stella. She was clad in yellow shorts and a flowy, white peasant top, her hair framing her lovely face, her eyelids were shaded in smoky hues and her lips were painted a lovely coral color. He stood as she came forth and removed his hat, nodding his head to her. "Stella."

"Hi, Jackson," she said softly, blushing as she looked down. "What a pleasant surprise."

He gave her a crooked grin as his eyes fell down her slender legs. She looked beautiful, as always. "You look lovely." He reached his hand out to take hers, and she looked wearily at her parents before taking it and moving toward him.

"Bye, Mom and Dad. See ya later." She pulled him with her as she turned and walked into the foyer.

"Wait a minute!" Vivian called to her. "You're leaving?"

"We'll be back. We need to talk. Sheesh."

"I was gonna invite Jackson to dinner. I didn't know you were going out."

Stella huffed as she turned and looked up at Jax, impatient and annoyed. He just gave her a smile; he'd let her be the deciding factor on that. "You wanna have dinner with them?" she asked.

"I'm down for whatever you wanna do, darlin'."

Stella rolled her eyes and turned back around, stating to her mother, "Fine. We'll stay for dinner. Let us know when it's ready. We'll be outside."

With that, she pulled him the opposite direction and he followed, giving his uncle and aunt a chuckle as he let Stella lead him outside to the deck where the pool was.

"We shoulda taken a swim," Jax admitted. The water looked inviting on this warm May day.

"Maybe next time." She grinned and looked him over, making

him even hotter beneath his collar as they sat beneath the covered porch in swiveling, cushioned rocking chairs. "Assuming my menstrual cycle stays in check," she smarted off.

"Stella," he protested.

"I'm really sorry, Jax."

"Please, don't apologize. I know you were embarrassed—"

"I was *horrified*. That would be a better word to describe it."

"I know, but it really wasn't that bad."

She gaped at him as if he'd just lost his mind. "I looked like I came from an animal sacrifice, are you kidding me?"

Jax couldn't help the chuckle at the back of his throat. It came full force as her mouth opened wide and he couldn't hold it in. He belted out, and she jumped on him, punching at him playfully.

"Jackson, you stop laughing right *now!*" she scolded.

He grabbed her and began tickling her in the ribs, pulling her into his arms even as she laughed uncontrollably. She fell into him, and he cradled her to his chest, brushing her hair away from her face. Her head settled on his shoulder as one hand cupped her cheek, the other falling to her hip. He took in her beauty, her youth, her softness, letting it invade his system.

The stress of the last few days had taken its toll on him and he'd needed the laughter to put things into perspective. Stella seemed to sense his line of thinking for she said, "I guess my issues are trivial when compared to your sister's, huh?"

Jackson immediately frowned, thinking of the bullet wound in Vanna's leg, and almost growled in anger.

Stella's hand came to his cheek then and he calmed. He smiled down into her face and leaned in to kiss her lips. The movement was slow, unhurried, and sensual as his mouth moved over hers. He closed his eyes and let himself be swept away by her; her smell, her sweetness and the sexy little moan that answered his tongue as it stroked across hers. He teased her with it, exploring her mouth with slow caresses then deep plunges as he made her melt against him.

When he pulled back, his member was hard against her hip and his heart was pounding.

"Maybe we should have gone out," she admitted, her eyes darkening in desire.

"Maybe it's better we stayed." Jax frowned. Stella's brows drew down in question. "Here, with your parents, I'm less likely to get in trouble with you."

~

"*H*e's in custody?" Jack asked as Austin drove his Jeep down the road.

"Yup."

Trevor had brought McClintock to the compound just an hour ago. Between the wires Brody had successfully set up and the confession, Max was going down—*Finally!* And not even a great lawyer was going to be able to save his ass.

"Now's your opportunity, Shooter, if you want it," Trev had told him.

"I can be there at eighteen hundred. I'm bringing a friend."

"Ten-four. We'll be here."

Trev had then sent Austin an encrypted message with the exact location—latitude and longitude—and he'd walked over and told Jack, "Judgement Day has come."

Jack didn't need for him to elaborate, he'd simply nodded and followed Austin. Jax had come to take watch for the night, Austin's sweet Savvy sleeping blissfully unaware of the violent rage brewing in her father and lover's veins, their yearning for blood as strong as their love for her.

"So, why did Sims even shoot if he knew they were both going down?" Jack asked.

That had been the question that had kept Austin awake the last several nights. If Brody had listened to Austin and done what he'd asked for fear that he would end up in Leavenworth, then why the hell had he upped his ante by attempting to kill Savannah in the first place? Why had he followed McClintock's instructions? Austin could only come to one conclusion and it made him want to kill the bastard even more than he already did. Brody had done it out of retribution. Sim's had known there was no way McClintock would go down without going down himself and as a slap in Austin's face, he'd shot his girlfriend. Or he'd missed on purpose, sabotaging his boss's instructions, saving Savannah's life essentially but also getting in the "last word". Either way, Austin was gonna beat the absolute fuck out of him and enjoy every single hit.

Austin scowled in reply and shook his head, unable to answer his boss's question.

As if reading his thoughts, Jack said, "I want McClintock," and rubbed his clenched knuckles. Austin knew Max would be hurting something fierce come tomorrow; he remembered all too well what it felt like to be on the wrong side of that big fist.

"I'd expect it no other way, sir."

Jack nodded, and Austin stepped on the gas.

A little over an hour later, they were heading back to the Jeep—appetites satiated, knuckles bleeding and bruised despite the gloves they'd worn—when Austin said, "I got dibs on the nest of another bird whose feathers need to be plucked." Jack's brows drew in question. "Think Luther would be up for it?"

Jack hung his head as he climbed in the passenger side of Austin's Jeep. "I dunno if that's such a good idea."

"It's now or never, boss."

"If it's up to Luth, Austin, he'll kill the man... I don't know if he needs that on his conscience."

"He deserves to get a chance to face him though, don't he?" Austin could tell Jack had a hard time with that.

After a long silence, Austin cranked his Jeep and waited for an answer. Jack pulled the phone from his back pocket, scrolled through his contacts, pressed a button, and put it to his ear.

Austin heard a, "Hey, buddy. Guess what day it is? *Judgement* Day. Yup. We'll be there in twenty."

Jack hung the phone up, and Austin headed down the blacktop, following Jack's instructions to Luther Boyd's house. Austin thought about how much Dan Wilson had this coming to him; how the man had almost destroyed Annabella Smith, how much he'd had taken from her as a young woman. No, Luther didn't need this on his conscience, but it would never be clear if he didn't have some way to appease his growing rage. Austin and Jack had gotten theirs, now it was Luther's turn.

Luther came out of his house as Austin's headlights lit up the front porch and driveway and hopped into the back. All was silent as Austin drove to the address Trev had given him; the one where Dan Wilson—rapist, attempted murderer, and sexual assailant—was staying. Before anyone had a chance to budge upon parking in the long, gravel driveway, Austin turned and addressed the man whose eyes held a wrath he was all too familiar with.

"Now listen, you can't make too big of a mess in here, Luther."

"But—Then why the hell did you even bring me here?" he asked angrily.

"Look, I have my connections...but I can only do so much," Austin warned. "Otherwise, you'll go to prison and there's not a thing I can do about it."

Luth huffed, scowled then cursed. "Fine!"

They all moved to get out, but Austin stepped in front of the two older men as they stopped at the door of a ratty, old, dingy trailer. "Let me go first." He could tell Luth was getting irate, but this had to be handled delicately or they were all gonna be in serious trouble. Trevor had pulled some strings but he'd said to "keep it in check." And what kind of soldier would Austin be if he didn't obey direct orders?

Austin gave three hard knocks, and they all waited patiently for long moments—sure that no one was gonna answer—before a very old-looking man gently pulled the door open. Austin felt his lungs blow out a hard exhale as his eyes fell over the callous bastard that had hurt Luther's wife so badly. This man was feeble—*all hunched over and everything*—skinny, white-headed, and had a nasal cannula in his nose attached to an oxygen tank. Austin didn't know what he was expecting…but it sure as hell wasn't this!

"Can I help you, son?" he asked, and Austin's stomach plummeted to the floor. He couldn't let Luther assault this old man; it would be outright cruelty in its grossed form.

Austin sighed heavily and turned to Luther then, seeing his eyes fixated on the decrepit Dan, but it was Dan who spoke first. "Luther Boyd?" his eyes squinted and he coughed even as he moved to push the screen door open for them. "Is that you?" he asked.

Luth was speechless at first, taking in the scene before him. Then he finally found his voice, "Jesus, I guess you didn't get off scot-free after all, huh, Dan?"

Dan coughed again and held his small chest, the sound akin to the death rattle. "Lung cancer. I only got a month at most." He moved towards an arm chair and beckoned them in with his hand. "I would offer you a beer, but I don't have any, Luth."

He sat down and looked all the world like he'd just run a marathon, his chest heaving with every breath he took. "I reckon you and Jack came to right my wrongs, I reckon?"

The white-haired man looked to Jack then, who stood behind Luther. They'd all been drawn slowly inside, the shock pulling them forward like magnets.

"Jack, I never thought I'd see the day when I'd say, 'It's good to see you', but it's true."

Jack laughed humorlessly. "I can't say the same for you, Dan."

"No, I suppose not."

"Well, I guess we won't be needing to pluck any feathers," Austin mumbled under his breath. "Looks like the parrot's already molting."

"Ha," Dan laughed. "Sorry, I couldn't let you boys go out with a bang."

"One punch might just break him in *two*, Luth," Jack grumbled and patted Luther's shoulder. "Let's go!"

"Wait," Luth said and stepped forward.

Jack's big arm shot out and his palm gripped Luther's bicep. Luth turned and reassured his friend with a nod and Jack let him go.

"For the last thirty years, all I've thought about is how much I would enjoy beating the life out of you, Dan. For what you did to my Bella, what pain you put her through, how horrible it must have been for her to endure the Hell you four wrought upon her. I've wanted to see you suffer…more than almost anything."

"Well, you got your wish," Dan stated and showcased his thin, withering frame.

"Yes, I did. But guess what? You didn't achieve what you set out to accomplish. Bella gave birth. To four of my children in fact. I'll be a grandfather one day. And Jack. Yeah, Jack here already is. But you…you pissed your life away. Over a stupid *lie*. I'm glad to see you suffering… and I hope you rot in Hell."

With that, Luther turned and walked out Dan's door. Austin and Jack followed.

❧

"*A*unt Nat?"

"Cassidy, sweetheart, are you alright?"

"No. I need for you to come get me." Cassidy paused and sighed heavily into the phone receiver. "I'm sick. I'm at work and I can't get Momma, Daddy, Kelsey *or* my worthless brothers to answer the phone. I knew you always stay up late so I—I would've called Jackson, but…" Cass trailed off. Her Aunt Natalie would understand why she didn't call Jax, *couldn't* call him.

"I'll be there as soon as I can, Cass."

Cassidy apologized, thanked her Aunt Natalie and hung the phone up. She wrapped her arms back around her belly and rocked back and forth in the break room chair. Her stomach started cramping again and she moaned in pain. She'd held on as long as she could but knew it was inevitable that she call someone to come get her on her night shift as her Crohn's had been flaring up the last day and a half and was now thoroughly inflamed. She hadn't embellished to her co-workers or the ER doc as to how sick she really was. She didn't want to end up in a bay all night long or admitted for the weekend. She just needed her bed. She needed sleep and she needed her heating pad. A week of bland eating and de-stressing would have her back to herself in no time, but even as she tried to convince herself of that, as bad as she'd felt since breaking it off with Jackson, she wasn't sure she wouldn't end up hospitalized before all was said and done.

Cassidy moved from the chair she'd been perched on for the last half hour and headed to the locker room to grab her belongings. She then told her supervisor she was leaving and headed out the ER entrance to wait. The night was cool but felt good to her hot skin as she threw her bag down on the bench and sat down. She sighed again and thought of how this breakup had taken a toll on her body and spirit.

Jax was amazing...and she'd left him to seek a life apart from him. She'd begun to wonder if she'd made a grave mistake. For if she was so free now that they weren't together, why did she feel so trapped? More "trapped" than she had when they were a couple.

The last several weeks had been uneventful, boring even, and she'd missed him with an ache that pierced her soul. And just when she'd thought she would go to him and confess her blunder, she'd heard today that Jax was dating Stella Jenkins. The 'outflux' of her bottled up stress had started not long after.

Natalie pulled in sooner than Cass had expected and she eased up off the bench and threw her bag over her shoulder as she walked towards the blue Nissan Murano.

"Hop in, sweetie," Nat said as she rolled the window down.

Cass opened the back door, threw her bag in, shut it back and opened the passenger door. Natalie Kinsen's beautiful smile greeted her and she lowered her head, reminded of Jackson.

She grumbled an apology as she got in and closed the door behind her. When Nat grabbed her hand, she looked up into the sapphire eyes that were the same shape as the man's she loved. She could've burst into tears then but tried to hold herself together.

"Don't you dare apologize, Cassidy," Natalie soothed. "I'd just left Vanna's hospital room to head home and work on my novel and no, it wasn't an inconvenience...I wasn't home yet, plus I needed the night air to give me time to think, and I'm glad for the opportunity to talk to you."

Cassidy didn't really understand why she was saying that, but nodded all the same.

"How's Vanna doing?" Cass couldn't hide her grimace, thinking about sweet Savannah being shot.

"She's doing well. She's set to be discharged tomorrow actually. Your sister is with her by the way. I think they were watching *The Longest Ride*; she may have silenced her phone." Natalie pulled out of the well-lit hospital lot and turned back onto the road, the darkness surrounding them like a cloak. "So, you're in a flare?" Nat asked. "Are you taking meds again, Cass?"

Her meds had been weaned down, but that was before she'd ripped her own heart out of her chest, before the stress was all-consuming, when her disease was stable.

When Cass shook her head, Natalie sighed. "Do I need to turn this car around and take you back to the ER?"

Cass shook her head. "No, I'm ok. I just ate something that didn't agree with me."

For the most part, Cass had been lucky when she'd been diagnosed with Crohn's at sixteen. She'd gone on biologics and had done well. She didn't drink much alcohol and had to avoid certain foods, but unless she was extra stressed or didn't sleep enough, she was like any normal eighteen-year-old.

"I know this has a lot to do with my son."

Cass dared a glance back at the mother of the man she loved. Natalie had a hard look on her face.

"I hurt him. I don't deserve him."

"That's not true. You both deserve each other and you both love each other."

Well, he was dating Stella so that wasn't entirely true.

"He doesn't love Stella," Nat said as if reading her mind. "He loves *you*. He knows it, I know it, and you know it. Let's not kid ourselves. So, why aren't y'all together?"

Had Jax really not told his family about why Cass broke up with him? "I—"

"Shoot straight, Cass. I was young once too, remember?" Natalie's tone was soft as she smiled over at Cassidy.

"I thought I wanted freedom. I don't want him to wait on me when I go off to college. I mean, what if I don't come back?"

"That's fair. But you've realized that it's not entirely what you want, huh?"

She shook her head, feeling tears sting her eyes.

"Oh, sweetie. You know I moved off to Chicago at your age, right?"

Cass looked at her confused.

"I was pregnant though and the man I loved only ever loved himself. You and Jax are so good for one another, Cass. I know you're young and my husband doesn't get that you two can have true love at this age. See, Jack and I were older when we got together. I was twenty-eight and he was thirty. He felt like he had to learn from his mistakes in order to appreciate true love, but I don't think that just because your love is young and new it means it can't be as genuine as a love born from tragedy." She squeezed Cass's hand and continued. "I went away to college and I pursued my writing career. I deeply regretted leaving. And coming home was sweeter—but harder—than I ever thought it would be. You're seeking your career, your life goals, and trying to find out more about yourself. I bid you good fortune, but always remember where you started. It's not wrong to seek knowledge, Cass. Be true to yourself. And if you and Jackson are meant to be then it will find you. Just don't run from home thinking you'll fix yourself. The problems aren't always where you think they are."

They'd gone a great distance, Natalie's hand holding tightly to hers. Cass just tried to absorb her words and digest them as best she could. She really wasn't sure what the hell she was doing or if she was even running from home as much as running to something new. She felt so drained and frustrated. She laid her head back on the headrest and closed her eyes, letting the steady sound of the tires hitting the asphalt and the soft sounds of easy-listening tunes on the radio lull her into stillness.

"Did you know that your father and I were once sweethearts? Did he ever tell you that?"

Cass smiled to herself, keeping her eyes closed. "Yes, I remember, he always greeted you as his 'first love'." She giggled.

"We were sweet together, but not like you and Jax. Luther and I weren't in love, despite what he says. Troy was all I thought about by fifteen years old, but I look back now and realize I was seeking his approval more than anything else. He had a hold on me, a death grip, and until I was free of him, I didn't realize how much he'd possessed me or how free I truly was outside of his grasp. I gather that you don't feel that way about Jackson?"

Cassidy opened her eyes and looked over at Natalie. She shook her head, frowning. "He's the most thoughtful, wonderful, self-less person I know." Cass looked down. "But I crushed him. And now he's with Stella. How can I ever tell him I was wrong? And how can I ever make it right again? I still don't know what my future holds."

"Sweetheart, none of us really know what our future holds."

"But it's not fair to ask him to put his life on hold while I—"

"Life isn't fair."

Cass huffed; what the hell was Natalie Kinsen trying to say?

"Cassidy, you should talk to Jackson. Love is stronger than anything else in this world. Stronger than hate or evil or fear. If you two love each other then no matter what, you'll be together. Trust me."

CHAPTER 17

Savannah struggled to get out of the car, pain ricocheting up her leg. She groaned and took her father's outstretched hand.

"I got you, baby. Lean against me."

She did and rested her shaking hip against his as she wrapped her arm around his shoulder, his arm going around her waist. The effort of merely pulling herself from the car seat had drained all her energy. She took in a deep breath and looked up at Austin who held the door, a whining Caesar at his side.

"You ok, angel?" he asked, his look one of deep concern.

She almost swooned but simply gave him a small nod as the effort—and ability—to speak in that moment had been taken from her.

"Alright, let's take it slow, Vanna. Take a step forward," her father suggested.

Savannah hopped forward, her left leg raised slightly off the ground. When she was clear of the door, Austin closed it and came to her left side, pulling her arm around his neck and wrapping his arm around her waist. Together he and her father lifted her as they ascended the stairs. Austin moved aside as her father lifted her into his arms to carry her into the house, turning to go in through the door sideways. He didn't set her down until he got to the couch and did so easily, being careful of her injured leg. Austin came to her side as her father moved away, placing pillows under her left leg to elevate it.

"Want some hot tea, sweetie?" her mom asked and made a move towards the kitchen as Vanna nodded.

"Here, let's get you comfy, darlin'." Austin grabbed another pillow and stuck it behind her back before pulling a blanket from the back of the couch to cover her t-shirt and sweat pant clad frame. He'd been so sweet and adoring, not that he hadn't been before she'd gotten shot, but Vanna knew he was blaming himself for what happened, although she didn't blame him, not in the least.

The last five days had been tough as she'd recovered from the bullet wound and surgery to put the ligaments and vessels back together. She was very lucky in that the gunshot had missed her femoral artery and her bones. She thanked God she hadn't been as bad off as she could've been and that she wouldn't need any more surgeries—and possibly no physical therapy. It had been a clean shot with no embedded bullet fragments and had gone in and out of her flesh. She would be well enough to put weight on it a couple weeks and healed up within a month to a month and a half.

She'd dreaded the conversation she'd had with her boss, Royce, but he was just glad she was alright and told her to focus on herself, that her work could wait. It had been an easy discussion and left her feeling confident, despite that she wasn't eager to return to Houston any time soon anyway. Right now, she was grateful to her supportive family and glad to have them taking care of her.

"Need anything, baby?" her dad asked and squeezed her hand. She shook her head and gave him a sweet smile. He returned it and leaned down to kiss her head. "Alright, I'm gonna go down to the barn then."

"I got 'er, boss," Austin stated and sat down at the end of the couch, looking over at her.

Austin hadn't left Savannah's side for more than a few minutes at a time. It was humbling to see him doting on her, but also infuriating in that she was weaker than she'd ever been in her life. He'd assisted her to the bathroom and back, into bed and out—she'd refused burdening her mother or pregnant sister. Even after she'd gotten crutches, Austin was still there to help, refusing to let her go it alone.

He looked handsome today despite the ruggedness of his unshaved face and overgrown beard. His amber eyes looked tired and were slightly blood shot, his clothes were rumpled, and he had dark circles beneath his eyes. He hadn't slept well, no better than she had, since the night she'd been shot.

Savannah didn't remember much and what she did came in pieces; she presumed her mind had blocked some of it out due to shock and she was *definitely* experiencing post-traumatic stress disorder. Any loud noise had her heart racing and the nightmares hadn't stopped since that first night.

She recalled the sound of the gun blast, feeling the bullet come out of her thigh, and falling into Austin's arms as he'd run with her to his Jeep, the sound of gunfire surrounding them. She could still hear the sound of the tires peeling out of the gravel, and looking down to see her leg covered in dark red blood. She must have passed out after that because the next thing she remembered was calling for Austin—after she'd awoken from surgery.

The apprehension on his beautiful face had scared and touched her, seeing her family had relieved her, and when Kelsey had come the next day, the sobs of gratitude and fear made Vanna realize just how lucky she'd been to be alive. She'd been shot—by a rifle…and by a man who'd been trained in the Army—and she'd lived to tell the tale.

Now, she gave Austin a grateful smile even as he frowned at her and pulled her hand to his lips, closing his eyes and blowing out. "Get some sleep now, my angel of music. I'll be here when you wake up, ok?" He pulled the blanket to her chin and tucked it around her sides.

She only nodded as exhaustion took her.

It didn't seem long before she was awakened by the sounds of clinking in the kitchen and the soft droning of the TV.

"Oh good, you're awake," Austin smiled down at her as he set a steaming bowl down on the coffee table. "It's dinner time, gorgeous."

She didn't reply as she pulled her weary body up to a sitting position and peeled the blanket from her frame.

"Bathroom?" he asked knowingly, and she nodded.

When they were back, she settled onto the couch, taking the hearty bowl of vegetable-beef soup Austin handed to her, her tummy growling. Austin gave a low chuckle and moved a pillow onto her lap to set the bowl on. She thanked him and smiled. He smoothed her hair down as he motioned to a small plate with a piece of corn-bread on it.

"It's good, by the way. Like, *really*, really good." He grinned and her heart soared. "Your dad and I are gonna watch *The Mandalorian*, he hasn't seen it yet."

Savannah just nodded with a smile, too groggy to speak, and ate contently as they began streaming the show Vanna had come to love.

When she awoke again, presumably hours later, the house was dark and her screams ripped through the stillness.

Savannah felt a broad chest against her own and strong hands rubbing her back. "Shh, you're ok, baby girl. I've got you. You're ok. I'll never let anything happen to you. Never again." Austin's rough, soothing voice called to her in the darkness.

She looked around and tried to calm her pounding heart and ragged breath, her eyes adjusting. She realized she was still on the couch as the light from the hallway upstairs turned on and her father's big frame stopped on the landing. He gazed worriedly down at her as her mother approached his side.

"Oh, sweetheart, another nightmare?" her mother asked, her sad eyes ripping a hole into Vanna's chest.

Vanna just looked up at them, suddenly noting her death grip on Austin's back, realizing her legs were wrapped just as tightly around his waist. She pulled back some and looked into his apprehensive face.

"I'm sorry," she croaked out, feeling both embarrassment and agitation at the situation.

"You have *nothing* to be sorry for, baby girl," he crooned and kissed her lightly on the lips.

Her parents must have gone back to bed, for within a few minutes the light was off. Savannah's eyes adjusted, thankful for the light on in the kitchen.

"PTSD," Austin murmured, and Vanna suddenly remembered the nightmare. It was the same as always—fear, blood and gunfire; feeling the pain and being overcome with dread.

It was something he'd experienced too, after being bombed in Afghanistan and watching his friend vanish in the blink of an eye. Her situation was far less intense but that didn't diminish the trauma of it. Austin must have sensed this.

"It's one of the worst things you've ever experienced, right?" he asked. She nodded, unsure what to say, feeling a bit theatrical at the moment. "Don't feel bad, Savvy. It was a horrific experience. For me too."

She felt even guiltier then, knowing the shooting had made his own PTSD even worse. She lowered her head as tears stung her eyes.

"You saved my life, Austin," she blurted out.

His eyes looked over her face as he gulped. His palm cupped her cheek. "If something had of happened to you, Savannah... I wouldn't have been able to live with myself." The sound of his hard swallow took her breath away. He sighed. His amber eyes looked into hers.

"Now, I understand all you went through. Not entirely, but—" she trailed off, feeling stupid for saying that.

"Sympathy pains, I get it. Your attempt at twinning?" He pointed to her left leg and smirked, trying to lighten the mood.

She gave him a weak smile and her leg started to protest its position around his waist. She grimaced as she tried to ease it down to the couch.

"Here, let me help you," he insisted and gripped her knee gently as he moved from between her legs. She felt bereft and reached for him, not wanting him to leave her side just yet. "Don't worry. I'm not going anywhere, darlin'." He kissed her cheek as he sat down on the floor and took her hand.

It was then she saw the blanket laying in front of the couch.

~

"Jax! You made it." Tanner patted Jackson's back with one hand and handed him a beer with another. "I wasn't sure you were comin'."

"I told ya we'd stop by, man," Jax stated with a chuckle as he moved his arm tighter around Stella's waist. "Y'all remember Stella, right?"

"Are you kiddin'?" Jared smirked as his eyes roved over Stella's curvy frame. "Who the hell could forget a set of tits and an ass like that?"

Jax felt his blood boil and he practically growled as he stepped forward. But his cousin, Elias, was quicker as he moved to Jared's side and swatted him hard on the back of the head.

"Hey, ass-clown watch your filthy mouth before I bust it for ya," Eli scolded.

"Ow, dude," Jared grumbled and rubbed the back of his head with the hand that he wasn't holding his beer with. "I'm just statin' a fact."

"You don't get to be disrespectful just because you're drinkin'," Eli continued. "Now apologize to Ms. Jenkins here or else I'll call up her daddy and you can take it up with him."

"You're a fuckin' buzzkill, Kinsen."

"Yeah, well, it beats being a douchebag like you, Campbell."

"Fuck you, Eli," Jared retorted back, but just as he started to shove him, Eli knocked him off the hay he was seated atop of and to the ground.

"Like I said, *watch* your mouth." By that point, Elias had his fists drawn and was standing over Jared.

Jax just shook his head and rolled his eyes. Defending a woman's honor was simply in the Kinsen's bloodline. It came as natural to them as breathing did...and apparently so did fighting.

He and Stella had gone parking after they'd caught a movie earlier that evening. They'd made out for a time, rounding second base, before Jax had finally stopped Stella's roving hands. They'd been dating over a week now, and he knew it was only a matter of time before they went all the way, but his heart still wasn't healed from his split up with Cassidy. He would dream of her, think of her, and couldn't whole-heartedly move on just yet. He still loved her, and even though hanging out with Stella had been a fun distraction, he was hesitant to take it further than simply making out; it wasn't fair to her. His heart just wasn't in it. He'd used the fact that they needed to stop in at Tanner's to hang out as an excuse for why he'd suddenly stopped kissing her just ten minutes ago. He'd moved her hand off his erection, pulled his lips from hers, and cranked the truck. The disappointment on her face hadn't been lost to him as he'd peeled out and headed east.

Tanner had a small plot of land and a one-story log home, close to a lake. It was out in the 'boonies' and Jax had gone hunting and fishing with him on the property in the past. Tonight, Tanner had invited them over in celebration of his birthday. He had a big fire going and as Jax looked around, he saw some old high school friends of his among the crowd.

He waved to a few of them and walked over, tipping his hat as Elias joined him.

"You're showing me up, cuz," Jax mumbled as he punched at Eli's shoulder.

"Didn't mean to. I just hate that piss-ant, even if he *is* your friend.

Wasn't trying to steal your thunder, Thor." Elias laughed and tipped his hat at Stella. "Miss Jenkins, you look lovely this evening."

His eyes were much more appreciative of the beautiful blonde next to Jax than Jared's lustful ones had been and Jax couldn't help but smirk. Elias had a thing for Stella. It hadn't been completely oblivious to Jackson the day he'd reintroduced them, although Jax presumed Stella was none the wiser.

"Thanks, Elias," Stella cooed and grinned back at him.

She *was* indeed lovely tonight, not like any other night, in her denim jeans and skin-tight black halter top that left her slender, muscled torso bare. She'd worn a black felt Stetson and boots to accessorize. She was a cowboy's wet dream come to life; too bad Jax simply wasn't her cowboy.

"Want a beer, Jax?" she asked and kissed his jaw, looking up into his face as her dazzling eyes sparkled back into his.

What he wanted wasn't a beer, but he nodded anyway and gave her a smile. She ambled off toward the cooler, waving to a girl Jax recognized as a friend of hers, and stopped to talk.

"Man, she's something else, Jackson. You got your work cut out for ya." Elias laughed, even as his eyes appraised Stella's plump backside.

"I just wish I..." Jax trailed off, not sure how to explain to his cousin what he was feeling.

"If you're not into 'er, you need to tell 'er. Don't string her along, Jax. That ain't fair."

"I know." Jax sighed heavily and looked into Elias's no-nonsense eyes. "I like her. She's one of my dearest friends. She's amazing, honestly. I just—"

"You love Cassidy."

"Yes! I do. I can't stop loving her. I want to move on, but..."

"You've always loved Cassidy, Jax." Eli patted his shoulder. "I get it."

"I mean, Stella's completely refreshing."

"But...she's not Cass."

Jax watched Stella talking with her friend Jamie. She laughed and the sound of it was musical and radiant. It made his chest tight to think of hurting her, of letting her down. But this was all a façade. On the inside, Jax was aching. He wanted to love Stella, wanted to make her his, but she could never be, not the way she deserved, not when another woman would always shine brighter than her in Jackson's eyes. Elias was right, Jax had to tell her the truth. That as much as he wanted to, he couldn't do this anymore.

Stella sauntered over and her smile made his insides clench. She handed him a beer and clinked the neck of her own bottle with his then she leaned in to kiss him. It was a sweet, soft kiss that promised more and as much as he wanted to fight her tongue as it plunged into his hungry mouth, he couldn't. The moan that came to his throat deepened as her mouth slanted and her chest hit his as her arms went around his neck. When she pulled back, Jax gulped and heard a big gasp. His eyes flew from Stella's to Cassidy Boyd's and just like that, he stepped back as if struck by lightning.

Where had she come from? The pain in her gorgeous hazel eyes reverberated in every part of him as her gaze went to Stella, where Stella's body touched his, where it seemed to sizzle as if lit by a torch.

"Ca—Cassidy," Stella stuttered and pulled her arms from Jax's neck. "W-what are you doing here?"

"Me!" Cass grated out angrily, her fists clenching at her sides. "What are *you* doing here, you bimbo?" Cass took a step forward. "You enjoying my leftovers…bitch."

Whoa! That escalated quickly, Jax thought.

"Now, Cass, just—"

"You're *supposed* to be my friend. But I can see that doesn't count for shit in your eyes, Stella Rose Jenkins."

"Cass," Jax stated and stepped forward, the tears that fell down her cheeks physically hurting him.

"No! You! You said you loved me. I take it that doesn't mean *exactly* what I thought it did. I can't believe you two. I—I never wanna see you again." Her pointing finger seemed to include them both as she stalked off in a fit of rage.

Jax was immediately following her, all thought of anything else left behind, as he couldn't stand to have her walk out on him again. She would never get another chance to do so. He wasn't gonna have it. Not now. Not ever. She was his. She was always gonna be his and it was time he let her know that.

"Cassidy," he called to her, but she was gaining speed. He ran, following her jean clad legs and pulling on her pink tank top. He pulled her sobbing frame into his arms even as she pushed and fought at him, her protesting squeaking in his ears. He finally got her to calm down as he pulled her stark against his chest, rubbing her back and letting her cry for a time.

"I hate you, Jackson. I hate you," she whimpered against his chest, the sweet smell of her wavy strawberry-blonde locks filling his nostrils and soul with renewed energy.

"Hate me all you want to, my sweet hummingbird. I ain't letting go. Never. I love you, Cass. I love you with all my heart."

"Then why were you kissing *her*?" Cassidy grated out as she shoved hard against his chest, but he wouldn't be swayed so easily.

"Baby, she was kissing *me*."

"You kissed her back!"

"I know. I'm sorry. I was weak without you."

"Please, tell me you didn't fuck her?" Cass pouted as she looked up at him, her beautiful green-brown eyes burning a hole into him.

"No, baby, I've only ever been with you."

"Why are you dating her, Jackson?" Her sobbing had stopped but her voice was unsteady.

"I—" Jax's mind went blank. "I needed a break from my pain. She distracted me." He shrugged, and Cass pulled away from his embrace, crossing her arms over her ample chest. Before she could say anything, he felt anger hit his face. "You were the one who left me, Cassidy, remember? You're the one who told me not to wait for you, if I recall."

She looked down, knowing she had no right to make him feel bad for seeking a reprieve from his heartbreak. She stared at her shoe, the one she was scuffling in the gravel road they stood in, away from all the prying eyes of the crowd beyond.

"I was wrong, Jax. So wrong." Her ragged sob tore deep into his soul, but he let her say her peace. "I love you. I never stopped. I know I'm going to Georgia and I don't know when or if I'll be back, but the thoughts of being without you are killing me. I can't just turn my heart and my feelings off. I mean, I didn't, but this has been hard. I thought I was— I'm sorry. God, I don't want it to be like this." She was rambling, but he understood her emotions, he'd felt them all too.

"Cass, I want us to be together. Even if that means we have to have a long-distance relationship for the next four years. I don't care."

"And if I decide to stay in Georgia?"

He shook his head. He couldn't say what she wanted him to say. He wasn't moving. He wasn't leaving home.

"We'll cross that bridge when we get to it, huh?" he asked and stepped forward to take her hands, enjoying the comfort he felt from her touch.

"You're okay with all this uncertainty?" she asked.

"Life is one big uncertainty, darlin'. We don't know what's gonna happen from one day to the next. All I know is that I love you, Cassidy Jane, and I don't want to be without you. And after your reaction to seeing me with another woman, I take it you want me back." He gave her a big smile even as tears continued to flow down her cheeks. She nodded. "Then what are we doing, hummingbird? You're the one I want. You're my woman, not Stella. You, baby. Let's just enjoy what time we have left until you leave for school. We'll figure out the rest as it comes."

She smiled and the joy of it warmed his heart. He pulled her back into his arms, loving the feel of her soft, petite frame against his. It felt good. It felt right. And he knew he'd never find its equal in another ever again. He felt at peace in her embrace. She was home. She was his, and he was gonna fight like hell if she ever decided that's not where she belonged again.

When her soft, full lips touched his, he was in Heaven, soaring high above the clouds and he cupped her cheeks as his mouth moved familiarly over hers in both dominance and submission equally. His tongue eased in, and she melted against him as she kissed him back with matching fervor. His hands moved to her waist and hers went up his arms to rest at the back of his neck as he picked her up and pinned her to his truck door, kissing her as if there was no time left in the world. When one of his hands came up into her hair, she moaned hungrily and his body was alight with the flames only she could entice. He was fully alive once more and his body and soul were starving to quench the raging desire mounting within him. He found himself thrusting against her pelvis even as her legs wrapped around his waist and she cried his name as his mouth moved to her neck, his hand squeezing her big breast, loving the desperation in her voice for him.

"Oh, Jax, let's get out of here, please?" she begged even as he fumbled for the car keys in his pocket.

When he opened the door and got in, her mouth and hands were all over him as he cranked the truck and he shoved the transmission into reverse.

She unbuttoned his jeans and stroked at his erection as he drove, in a frenzy that made him mindless.

He was going to pull off the road, he was going to take her right there on the seat, and he was going to show her the love that spilled from every pore of his skin, every cell of his body, every shred of his soul. He was going to love her like there was no tomorrow and he was going to prove to her that she was his, fully and completely.

～

*S*tella felt her heart plunge as Jackson ran off down the dark, gravel driveway after a sobbing Cassidy. She gulped even as her chest throbbed and tears stung her eyes. He'd chosen Cassidy. As unsurprised as she should be by that revelation, all she could do was drown in a sea of misery as she gulped and tried to appear unrattled as she shattered into a million pieces on the inside.

All eyes moved to her as she bashfully looked around. Jamie's fist covered her mouth, and Tanner frowned over at her.

Jared broke the silence first as he laughed. "Well, Stells, I guess it doesn't matter *how* fine your ass is now, huh?" His drunken gaze roved over her once again and she shivered, rubbing her suddenly chilled arms. She gulped again and looked away, his eyes unnerving her. "Looks like you'll be needin' a ride home, huh, lil' cowgirl?" he asked and moved forward as they all heard Jax's truck crank and peel out. Her hammering heart jumped into her throat as he came ever closer. "I can give you the ride of your life, sweetheart. What do ya say?"

"*I* say, keep your fuckin' mouth closed and your hands to yourself." Elias stepped in front of her just in time to block Jared from coming any closer. "The last thing she needs right now is to be ambushed by *you.*"

"Let's allow her to decide that, shall we?" Jared grumbled.

Elias turned and his handsome face stared into hers. His bright green eyes were piercing yet soft as they looked into hers. "Stella?" his deep voice made her shiver.

All she could do was shake her head and step closer to him, resting her cheek on his bicep, forcing her tears down. "Please, take me home, Eli?" she whispered and dropped her hand into his.

"Ohhh," Tanner scoffed, "burn, J-rod." Tanner shoved at Jared, laughing hysterically and everyone else followed, but Stella was too mortified to respond as Elias led her to his truck. It was a burgundy Chevy, and Stella robotically moved into the passenger seat once he'd opened the door for her. The cab was flooded in light before Eli climbed into the driver's seat and started the engine.

Once they were on the road, he spoke up.

"I, uh, I don't actually know where you live, you'll have to tell me."

She nodded and motioned for him to turn left onto the highway.

"I'm really sorry about what happened, Stella."

Tears once again burned her eyes as she thought of how heart-breaking it had been. First, she'd hurt Cassidy, second, she'd been jilted by Jackson and third, she'd been humiliated. "I should have known it would come to this." She'd known Jax wasn't over Cass, but that hadn't stopped her from pursuing him, hadn't stopped her from falling even harder for him, hadn't stopped her from throwing herself at him like some sex-crazed harlot. God, she was a fool. "He's loved her as long as I've known him. Why did I ever think I had a chance with him?" The tears streamed down her cheeks no matter how much she tried to stop them.

"Don't beat yourself up. You're great, Stella Rose. You deserve to have a man who will worship you. Jax just isn't that man. You'll find the right one though, if you haven't already." He gave her a wink as they came to a traffic light, and she couldn't help the smile that came to her lips.

Elias was charming, she'd give him that. And he'd defended her against Jared tonight, twice. And now he was taking her home. She was grateful for him and told him so.

"No need to thank me, m'lady. I was only taking care of a damsel in distress. What kinda knight would I be if I didn't rescue you?" Another sexy wink and she could feel her tears starting to wane.

Elias was handsome. Tall. Muscular. Rugged. Dashing. All the qualities she loved in a cowboy. Why in God's name was he single? Perhaps he just hadn't found the right one yet, himself. She wanted to ask him but refrained as he looked over at her for directions.

"Oh, sorry, turn left here." She pointed and guided him from there.

He was silent, giving her time to gather her thoughts. He finally spoke as he pulled into the long, paved driveway of her home. She gave him the numbers to punch in on the keypad and he did so, waiting as the heavy, wrought-iron gates opened before pulling through them.

He stopped in front of the garage, the motion sensors kicking on as he cut the engine. He turned to her then and sighed heavily. "Look, I know Jax needs to apologize to you, but tonight, I'm gonna do it for him."

"You're a good man, Elias Kinsen, and a good cousin." She smiled into his dimpled face, noticing them for the first time as he returned it.

"Well, love makes men do stupid things…or so I'm told anyway." He laughed, the sound comforting to Stella's ears.

"Thank you, Eli. For not making me feel like an idiot or a floozy."

"You aren't either of those things, and I'm sorry you were made to feel that way."

"You have nothing to apologize for, but all the same, thank you for your kindness."

He gave her a nod and said, "I'll walk you to the door and see you inside."

"You honestly don't—" she was interrupted as he opened his door and stepped out. He came around to her side and opened the passenger door, extending his hand to her. She took it, blushing, and let his hand interlock with hers as he shut the door with his other hand. He looped her arm through his and walked them laconically to the house.

"It's a beautiful night. Such a shame it had to end like it did." He looked up.

"Agreed," Stella stated and, too, looked up into the cool, starry night.

"Oh, look." Elias stopped and pointed. "A shooting star. Quick, make a wish."

She giggled even as she watched the sudden flash of a meteor's entry into the atmosphere. She closed her eyes and wished for true love, as silly and cliché as that was. When she opened her eyes, Elias was grinning down at her. "What?" she asked.

"That's good luck, ya know?"

The beauty of his beaming pearly whites made her giggle again. "I need some good luck after tonight."

"Well, I'd say your wish might be coming true then, don't you?"

His gaze left her breathless. She was all too aware of his powerful sex appeal, his clean, fresh scent mixed with leather and beer, and the ease she felt in his presence. She felt the strength of his hand in hers and smiled, glad he'd been so good to her when she was so vulnerable.

"I best get you inside before Bobby 'Buck' Jenkins has my head. He might've given me this here cowboy hat, but he'd take it right off me if I didn't deliver you home properly."

Stella looked at him funny; when had her dad given him that cowboy hat? "Oh," she suddenly remembered, "Mom and Dad are out tonight. They won't be home til late. You wanna come in?"

His eyes roved her face and stopped at her lips. Tension seized her, sexual, hot, and licking as it coursed through her veins. What was happening? "I probably shouldn't, Stella," he answered with a frown. When she pulled her lips in and looked down, his big palm cupped her cheek and his index finger brought her chin up. "I want to, believe me. But you're not the only one unguarded right now."

She suddenly wanted to know why he was "unguarded". Had his heart been recently ripped out too? Was he in love with someone who didn't love him back? And why on earth did she desperately care so much? She gulped, feeling ashamed at her wanton brazenness.

"Hey." He stepped closer, his masculine command overwhelming her senses. She felt his chest bump hers and fought the urge to press her palms into the broad expanse of it, feel the muscles that poked through his tight t-shirt. "Don't look at me like that," he scolded with a crooked grin and a chuckle, his sweet breath on her face causing her to gasp. "I made a wish on that star, too, and I named it Stella."

She would have laughed had his eyes not been burning so deeply into hers; she was awestruck. Was he crushing on her? Was he *serious*? And how had she not noticed how beautiful his facial features were until now, how well-built he was beneath his clothes? "You're beautiful, Elias," was all she could say as her eyes fell over his muscular, trim frame.

He laughed big even as his thumb stroked her cheekbone. "I thought that was supposed to be *my* line."

She cupped the hand holding her face, and he pulled a deep breath in. "You could be a model. In fact, Jax was supposed to go with me to a shoot Friday. Dammit." She huffed and looked down, suddenly remembering that she was now partner-less.

"I'll go with you," Eli stated much too quickly, and Stella's eyes shot up to his, evaluating him.

"You will?"

"Yes ma'am." He winked again and his eyes fell to her lips. "Should I seal it with a kiss?" His brow went up, and before she could decide how to respond, his lips were lowering to hers and he was kissing her.

His lips were soft yet firm as they pressed ever so lightly to hers. He slanted his mouth and tugged gently on her lips as her body eased into his, his arms wrapping gingerly around her. He didn't deepen the kiss, he just lightly caressed her lips with his own plump, full ones until she was aching for more. She moaned even as he began to pull back and she felt the smile tug on his lips as she leaned into him for one more smooch.

"I've been wanting to do that since I saw you at the rodeo."

Her head was reeling and her heart was pounding, unsure of her reaction to him. Was this ache between her legs misplaced? Was she simply pining for Jax and Eli was a good stand-in? What was she doing? This was too soon, right? She simply licked her lips, hungry for more as Elias's index finger touched her nose and his hand cupped her bicep, stroking her with the tenderness of a lover.

"Give me your phone, Stella," Eli commanded, and Stella pulled it from her jeans pocket and handed it over, after entering the code.

He smiled even as he began putting his number into her contacts. He handed it back to her and took her arm again, leading her up the steps as she continued to float away on cloud nine.

He waited for her to take the key out and unlock the door. He saw her in and stood in the foyer, arms across his chest. "I would stay for a bit, but I know myself and I don't wanna rush you into something you're not ready for." His tone and eyes were serious and had her gulping once more. "But I want you to know that I'm just a phone call away. I texted myself from your number, so I got yours now too." He pulled his phone out and shook it at her, giving her a crooked grin. "I'll call you later, if you'd like."

How could she say no to that? She nodded.

"Well, m'lady. I bid you goodnight." He winked and leaned in to kiss her cheek, her heart hopping up into her throat as his soft lips lingered there for a moment before he turned to leave. She shut the door behind him and locked it, turning and falling against it in over-whelming shock and elation.

She pulled out her phone suddenly and searched for his name in her contact list, scowling when she couldn't find it. She then checked her last text message and laughed aloud as she read, "Beautiful Elias."

Wow! He *was* beautiful. And that beautiful cowboy had just turned her night from horrific into heavenly.

CHAPTER 18

"Ok, ok, my eyes are closed," Savannah admonished with a giggle, covering her eyes as she'd been instructed by Austin. She was excited, for it was the first time she'd been out of the house all week and she was starting to get antsy. He must have sensed it somehow because he'd told her to get dressed, they were having lunch in town then he had a surprise for her.

The week had gone by painstakingly slowly as she'd simply rested and tried to let her gunshot wound heal up. Austin and her mother had taken turns changing out her dressing; the wound had finally stopped oozing yesterday. She'd stayed the night with Austin last night, but much to her dismay he'd not tried to have sex with her since before she'd been shot. Not that he owed her sex—it wasn't like he was her "official" boyfriend or anything—but being so close to him in his bed and them finally having some privacy had her whole body tingling. She tried not to let her disappointment show when morning came and he'd jumped right out of bed to make them coffee, but she was down-right irritated.

"What's wrong, darlin'? Are you in pain?" he'd asked and moved back to her side, seeing her grimace as she sat up in bed, dragging her bum leg with her.

Vanna couldn't tell him she was horny as fuck and needed him to remedy it—she was too modest to say that—so she'd just lowered her head and sulked, letting him draw his own conclusions. His index finger had come to her chin then and he'd given her that sexy as sin crooked ass grin that made her melt.

"Hey, the pain will subside, your leg will heal up, and you'll be back to being yourself in no time, alright?"

How could he not see how erect her nipples were beneath her thin tank top? That she was practically melting beneath his touch? She whimpered as his hand moved up her uninjured thigh. She drew her lips in and her eyes burned into his. He finally got the hint, his blonde brow shooting up, and he rubbed his beard.

"Once you're all healed up, angel, I'm gonna worship this sweet little body like I've been without it for years instead of weeks."

That statement had made her gulp as he'd looked her over from head to toe, his index finger stroking down her naked bicep, making her feel unabashedly sexy and incredibly exposed all at once.

When had she become so damn sexual? And how was it that she couldn't get enough of this man? It frightened and thrilled her.

Austin had leaned in then, his ruggedly handsome face coming ever closer, those sexy amber eyes of his doing unimaginable things to her already flustered sex. When his lips touched hers, she wrapped her arms around his neck and plastered herself to his chest. He chuckled even as her tongue plunged into his mouth and he took it, stroking ever so gently at it with his own. When he pulled back, she was gasping for air and licking the taste of him from her lips, her body ablaze in consuming flames of lust.

Austin had chuckled again and Vanna had huffed, her sexual frustration at an all-time high. She crossed her arms over her chest as he said, "My sexy little Savvy, you ain't the only one being tortured here." He'd suddenly moved her hand to his crotch and she'd gasped at how hard he was beneath his pajama pants. "Trust me when I tell you, I've had this same raging boner for days now." She frowned again, not understanding why he'd not just taken care of it. Wasn't that what guys did? "I want you so much right now, darlin', but I would hate myself if I were to open those stitches back up or hurt you in any way, so as much as I abhor not being able to have my way with you, I'm gonna wait until you're at least walking before I plant myself between your legs. Because believe me, when I do, I intend to stay there for a *very* long time."

She'd gaped at him and gotten another searing kiss before he'd moved off again and began making their coffees, all the while she was all too aware of every ripple of his back muscles, the plumpness of his sexy ass, the deepness of his golden tanned skin and the allure of those big, inked arms she couldn't wait to have wrapped around her again. Her whole body throbbed in need and she knew she was probably going to have to masturbate at some point in the day in order to have some peace if she had to wait another week to have him inside her. She'd bit into her lip and tried to calm her aching womanhood even as he ambled off to the shower, but the thoughts of his enticing, muscular naked body beneath the spray had done nothing to ease her desire.

When he'd come out all too soon, she'd been touching herself and just as she'd pulled her hand from her shorts, he caught her. The contrast of the white towel wrapped around his tanned hips and the beads of water covering his broad chest and arms had made her moan aloud. His face turned diabolic in nature as his eyes had fallen over her. She'd whimpered, and he moved, shucking the towel and gripping his manhood in his fist.

"Were you thinking about me, baby girl?" he asked as he moaned and stroked his cock, pumping it easily as he walked forward. "By all means, don't let me interrupt you, darlin'. Carry on."

The blood that had shot into her cheeks was a combination of arousal and embarrassment, but she couldn't stop her hand from moving back down into her shorts to quiet the burning ache inside, the situation too enticing to resist.

Austin groaned as his own hand fell to touch hers. "As much as this turns me on, *I* want to be the one giving you pleasure, lover," he'd trailed off and before she could respond, his knees were on the bed and he was easing her shorts down her hips. He'd gripped her bottom in one palm, the butt cheek of the uninjured leg, and opened it slightly. His head fell and he began loving her with his mouth and fingers, lying flat on his belly. She'd been unbelievably wet and his stroking did her in in a matter of minutes. Her climax came violently upon her and she'd cried out in both relief and pleasure, watching as he licked her clean even as she shuddered and came down from her high. His eyes were devilish as they moved between her womanhood and her eyes and she waited to see what he would do next. He'd smiled and moved, popping back up on his knees, his angry erection jutting out at her.

His fist returned to his hard shaft and he'd pumped it slowly, watching her eye it with both arousal and agony. Suddenly, he slid the steely member between the delta of her thighs, bumping the tip of it against her swollen bud.

"Mmm," she'd grated out and slid down an inch closer to him, craving that massive girth filling her up to the hilt.

But Austin wasn't pushing himself inside her, only stroking her back and forth with the head of his manhood, ever so slowly and erotically. It'd felt amazing and yet she wanted so much more. She'd arched her hips up to his and whined but that crooked smile returned to his face.

"Patience, love," he'd moaned as one hand gripped her waist, the other fist pumping his length a bit faster. She closed her eyes as he bumped her bud again and again with the velvety soft tip and she felt herself sliding over the edge once more.

"Oh, God, oh, Austin," she'd called out as she tumbled once more, her head falling back to the pillow as she reached for him in mindless liberation.

He'd moved closer to her as her fingers skirted the V of his lower abdomen and hips and traced up to his taut belly, fingering the muscles there. His fist stroked harder and faster, so hard and fast it almost looked painful, before he was groaning and pressing his member to her belly, shooting his seed onto her bare flesh there, as her shirt had ridden up to her breasts.

"Oh, fuck, Savvy, my sweet angel." He'd groaned out and expelled his breath in ragged gasps and huffs. "Damn, that was sexy, baby." He'd squeezed her waist and his hand moved to her injured thigh. "I didn't hurt you, did I?" The concern on his face nearly had her tearing up, for the emotions filling her in that moment couldn't be tapped down.

She'd just shaken her head and let him clean her up. He'd assisted her into the shower and not long after, she was dressed and ready to go.

Now, they were stopping and she was giddy, a combination of how much she'd enjoyed herself earlier and simply being in Austin's company. He made her happy. He filled her heart and soul with joy and excitement and hope. She heard his Jeep door open then felt the rush of air as he opened hers a moment later.

"Alright, no peeking, Savvy. If you do, I'll spank that sexy, little ass of yours," he growled playfully and she tingled at the word 'spank', her mind going back to that sweet memory in the hayloft.

He helped her out and she felt him lift her up onto the curb as she covered her eyes with her hands. He told her to keep her eyes closed and positioned the crutches at her side, she took them and settled herself on them. Finally, he told her to open her eyes.

When she did, she was staring at an empty store front on Main Street and she looked back at him in both amusement and confusion.

He chuckled, adjusting his Stetson and fumbling with his keys. "I rented it."

"Why?" she gave a little laugh, herself.

"Come on in," he stated as he unlocked it and held the door open for her.

She entered a large, open space with white walls, tile floors, and a coffered ceiling. It was about 1,500 square feet that could have be used for anything really. It was a blank canvas with big windows in the front and a counter to the right where a cash register or desk could go. But why was he showing her this and what on earth was he renting it for?

Savannah gave a nervous giggle again as he assessed her, waiting for her brilliant brain to pick up on what he was aiming for. She had no clue. "Are you opening an antique toy store? Or trying to take me back to the day we met or—"

"It's your art gallery," he interrupted, and she literally gulped.

Had she heard him correctly? She looked around the room again and balked. It would make a *perfect* place to display her work. Obviously it needed some work, but it had great potential and the windows were placed perfectly. The lighting would need to be redone and they would need to—

"W—Why would you do that?" Why had he assumed she wanted to display her work? Hadn't she already told him that she wasn't going to do that?

"Because your paintings are amazing and need to be seen. I was walking by here last week and saw it was vacant and I couldn't resist."

As much as his thoughtfulness touched a place in her heart, the audacity of him assuming he knew what she wanted angered her all the more.

"You made a mistake," she barked. "You need to break the lease."

"What?" he asked incredulously.

"You heard me! I already told you that I'm not ready for the world to see my work. Why do you think I haven't signed my paintings? I don't—I'm not gonna stay here in Abundance!"

The surprise and disappointment on Austin's face was tangible and it hurt every nerve-ending in Savannah's body. He looked down then back up, anger darkening his face.

"But you became interim mayor. You—"

"It's only temporary, Austin."

She'd been elected just two days ago, gratefully accepting the title and making an inspirational and powerful speech about how short life was, how one shouldn't give up on their dreams, and how she and Morgan were going to make their community proud by working together to make Abundance even brighter, stronger and more self-sufficient. Her words suddenly felt like ash in her mouth as Austin frowned and crossed his arms over his chest.

Why the hell did he care? Was *he* here to stay permanently? The thought of him leaving hurt her more than she wanted to admit.

"That's not how you made it sound in your speech," he threw back as he turned to look out the window, the cowboy hat shading his face from her. He was quiet for a few minutes before he said, "I guess that was all a bunch of horsepucky, huh?"

He turned back to her, the accusation in his eyes piercing her heart. She gulped and looked down.

"Little Ms. Astronomer is too good to come back home. Too good for this town. Too good for—" he trailed off, letting the statement hang in the air, but if Savannah could've read his mind, she knew he would've said, "Too good for this cowboy."

He huffed out a hard breath and lowered his head again, shaking it. "Fine. I'll break the lease, if that's what you want. I'm sorry. I shouldn't have assumed I knew you so well."

That statement hurt more than being shot in the thigh had and she felt unsteady on her feet for the first time since she'd been on crutches. The pain in his face made her wince. He stepped forward, seeing her teeter.

He was to her side in two strides, but his eyes were hollow as he looked at her and she wanted to cry and tell him she was wrong and stupid and being a total and unfeeling bitch, to ignore her and kiss her, but too soon, they were leaving the empty room, the room that was as empty as her soul suddenly felt in that moment.

411

*S*tella was more nervous today than she'd ever been on a photo-shoot before. She couldn't tell if it was because of the way Elias was looking at her or the fact that his bare chest was far more impressive than she'd ever anticipated. What was it with these Kinsen men and their big, broad frames and hulking biceps? He was the picture of fit with his olive-toned chest and arms, row upon row of defined muscles, six-pack abs, and the sexy V that disappeared into the denim jeans that hugged his thick thighs and firm ass far too tight for comfort.

She was literally salivating as the oil beneath her palms made her hands slide over his rock-hard torso. It didn't help that her bikini top was thin as her nipples brushed his pec muscles and his hands were propped on her hips as she looked up into his eyes.

The photographer and director had eaten Eli up the minute he'd stepped onto the set, just as she'd suspected they would. They took in his ruggedness, hat, and sexy eyes, and when he'd taken his shirt off, they'd literally cheered in glee.

"He's perfect, Stell Bell." Her assistant Tony immediately began drooling over Elias's big, muscular frame.

She'd made the introductions as Elias smiled big and greeted everyone, as if he had any hope of remembering their names once this was all over.

Now, they were posing provocatively on the set of a ranch in San Antonio for a new jeans company as his hands moved from her hips, to her thighs, to her face. Their chests kept bumping as they stood still and let the cameras flash, the instruction of the director guide them, and their looks to each other as sincere as they intended to be.

"It's a long time to stay so still," Eli whispered beneath his breath as his head lowered at the director's order.

"I know, I'm sorry. I'll take you out for a steak dinner later to make it up to you," Stella replied and arched her breasts into his chest as the director, Nero Mosley, asked.

"Beautiful. The chemistry between you two is making my dick twitch," Nero said.

"Gross!" Eli scoffed, "Is this guy for real?" Elias scowled, and Stella couldn't help but giggle at his furrowed brow. He was such a gentleman after all. She should've warned him of Nero's filthy mouth. Her father didn't even know how bad he could be at times.

"He's a bit dramatic."

"Ya think?"

"Move this thigh in between hers," Nero grabbed Eli's thigh and pulled it into Stella's crotch.

"Jeez, I'm sorry," he mumbled as his knee hit her pubic bone.

Stella tingled all over and not because it hurt.

"Alright, move your hand here." Nero pushed Elias's hand up Stella's ribcage to rest beneath her breast and her flesh tingled at how close his palm was to that part of her. The director then took their faces, pushing them close together. "Angle your face down, I want your lips closer to hers."

Again, Stella's skin felt electrified and she gulped as the cameras flashed, instructed to kiss Elias's jawline as he arched his head back.

"Gorgeous. I love it. So fucking hot, Stells. Now, kiss his shoulder. Elias, lower your head and look like you are about to do the same."

Stella's flesh tingled as Eli's soft lips hovered at her bare shoulder, her lips pressing softly into the bulkiest part of his bicep.

"I'm so glad you're doing all this to me and not with someone else," Elias said as they were told to bring their faces back to look at one another, her hand resting up on his shoulder. "I have to admit, I'd be real jealous if it was Jax."

At Jax's name, Stella swallowed and her eyes fell.

"Sorry, I—"

"Don't be. I'm not." Stella recovered quickly and smiled up into his face.

"Fucking gorgeous, Stells. Give me another big smile, hon. Just like that. Elias, where's your smile? Are you gonna let a gorgeous fox like that beam up at you without cracking one yourself? C'mon kid, work me up. I wanna be swollen and ready to fuck by the time this shoot is over."

"Jesus," Eli swore. "This guy is disgusting. And he needs to watch his mouth talking to you like that before I bust his lip."

Stella stifled a laugh. She wouldn't correct him and tell him Nero was actually talking to Elias and not her, for she loved that he was coming to her defense...once more.

"And on that note, I'm gonna do something to spice this shit up a little. Stells, let's take that top off, sweetheart. I want to see skin to skin, babe."

"Is he for *real?*" Eli's tone was hard—a combination of anger, surprise, and arousal all wrapped into one.

"It's ok." She put her hands up when Elias's body stood at attention.

"Don't take your top off, Stella! That's ridiculous. This isn't porn." He tried to stop her even as her hands moved to untie her bikini top.

"It's alright, Eli." She smiled before turning her back to him.

"Stella," he protested and grabbed for her hands, but she shooed him off.

Her assistant, Tony, came forward then with a shawl and her pasties. They'd done this dozens of times before and in a matter of minutes, she was ready and handing her top off to Tony, who smiled playfully up at Elias.

When she turned, Eli avoided looking down at her chest, his red cheeks, making her feel sexy.

"I have pasties on, Elias," Stella stated with confidence, but knew Eli was a gentleman and wouldn't stare at her no matter what.

"Alright, Eli, lean against the fence. Hands on her hips. Stella, lean into him. Chest to chest."

She felt Eli grunt as her breasts settled against his bare chest and he looked away, uncomfortably.

"Look at her, Eli. She doesn't bite. Well, not hard anyway." Nero chuckled, diabolically.

Eli practically growled as he looked down into her face. "You don't have to do this, you know? You *do* get a say."

She smiled at him, dismissing his anxiety. "It's really ok, Elias. I'm not offended."

Too bad *he* was because the feel of his hard body against hers had her sex aching in bittersweet agony.

"Alright, let's sex this up, shall we?" Nero stated. Again, Eli huffed, obviously not liking where this was going. "Stella, kiss him, slowly." Stella arched her head up and leaned in, letting her lips brush over his as Eli's face lowered to hers. Her hand came to his jaw and she angled her head. "Hold it right there," Nero instructed once more. "Pull back just a tad, you two. Eli, hands down to her bottom, just hover there. Stell, hands on his chest. Pull back. Look at his lips. Perfect! Alright, lay your head down on his chest. Eli, hands on her back, hold her like you'll never let go. Love it. You guys are fuckin' naturals. Ok, Stella, give me that pouty look I love. Beautiful. Now, pull back. Eli kiss her. Softly." Eli's kiss had her moaning, his lips barely touching hers. "Perfect. Now, Eli, look into her eyes. Eli, open your eyes."

Stella looked up at Eli, and he was frowning. "Sorry, Stella," he grumbled, and she felt the solid ridge of his hard erection pressing into her thigh.

She just smiled. "It's ok, Eli. It happens," she admonished. He gulped. He didn't like that answer.

"Look at her lips, Eli. Stella, tilt your head. Eli, hand up to her face. Head back, Stella. Head down, Eli." The instructions went on and on, until Stella and Eli were fully aroused and moaning, his bulky erection solid against her as his hands and mouth moved over her bare flesh. At one point, Eli grunted as she rubbed his manhood unconsciously back with her pelvis as it moved against her.

"Damn, Stella," he breathed out on a groan. His hand fell into her hair and he kissed her hard.

"Yes, fuck yes. I love it," Nero exclaimed.

By that time, Eli was throwing his hands up in frustration. "Are we done here?" he asked and pulled Stella against him, defensively.

"Yup. I need to go rub one out. We're good. Thanks, guys." Nero came over and high-fived Stella. Eli's grip was firm as Nero shook his hand and he scowled as the older, pudgy man walked away. He looked down into her face, anger darkening his green eyes.

When Tony came over, he draped the shawl over Stella's shoulders, and Eli pulled her to him as they walked to his truck and got in. His hands were shaking as he pulled his shirt on and cranked the truck. By then, Stella had pulled her own shirt back on.

She looked up, surprised, as the truck shuddered to a stop in a gravel lot still inside of the property, Eli turning his body towards her.

He took deep breaths in as he tried to regain his composure. "Please tell me your dad doesn't know about this guy?" Before she could respond, he continued. "I don't want you working with him ever again. He's a sick fuck and I didn't like that at all."

"Eli, I—" Stella's brows drew in protest.

"Stella, I felt like he was watching us hump each other. It was revolting."

"Then why were you so turned on by it?" she smarted back.

"I was turned on by *you*. I was touching you, kissing you. You were half naked pressed against me. It was only a natural response."

She crossed her arms over her chest and harrumphed back at him.

"Let me finish," Eli scoffed and looked out the front window, his hands shaking on the wheel. "Your father would have killed that man. There's no way he would have let him talk to you like that. You won't work with him again!"

The finality of his statement couldn't be argued with; he was right. Buck Jenkins would have Nero's head on a spike and come to think of it, the last two shoots had been even weirder than this one had been. Stella didn't need this gig. She was a model and star all her own, despite her parents' fame. This had only been set up because she was in the area.

When Eli stopped at a traffic light, she reached out and took his hand. "Thank you, Eli," she stated truthfully. "For taking up for me and being a good sport. I'm sorry."

"You have nothing to be sorry for, my shooting star. I'm sorry if I seem to be overreacting. It's just—I couldn't stand the way he spoke to you, the way he looked at your body like he did. Like he wished he was touching you like I was. It made my skin crawl." Eli huffed out. "I hope I haven't messed anything up with your career. I just couldn't take it anymore."

She just smiled over at him. "I believe I owe you dinner, Elias."

"You don't owe me a single thing. Being in your presence is more than enough." When she frowned, he pulled her hand to his lips and kissed it. "But I *have* worked up an appetite. I'm all sweaty and sticky though. I'd like a shower first, to wash off more than the oil."

"Yes." Stella laughed. "I need one too." She showed him her sticky hands.

They rode in easy silence before they pulled into the luxury hotel Stella had booked for them. It was a beautiful high-rise right in downtown.

"Man, this is nice. I don't know if I've ever stayed anywhere this fancy before, Ms. Jenkins." He tipped his cowboy hat at her, and she practically swooned.

He pulled their luggage from the back and Eli scoffed as she tried to take hers from him. "I'm stronger than I look, Stella. If I can wrangle calves, I can manage two bags." He winked.

She smiled and led them through the lobby as a piano tinkled in the background. The foyer was large with dark marble tiles underfoot and cascading chandeliers hanging from high mirrored ceilings.

After they checked in, Stella taking both their separate room keycards, she waited at the elevator door as Eli pulled their bags in and the valet pushed the button for the eighteenth floor.

Eli smiled over at her and she couldn't help but blush. "I'm still glad I came with you, you know?"

She gave him a grin. "What time do you have to be to the stockyards tomorrow?" She was referring to the rodeo Elias had to perform in starting tomorrow night. They'd worked it out so that the photo-shoot didn't interfere with his calf-roping events which lasted two nights.

"I'll probably go in by four so I can do some practicing."

When the elevator stopped on their floor, they got off. Elias thanked the valet and declined his offer to take their bags. Eli was such a stud, and as she stopped at her room and he saw her in, carrying her luggage and setting it down, she couldn't help but gape at his rippling muscles once again. He turned to her and tipped his hat again. "Well, I reckon I'll meet you outside your door, say in an hour?" he asked, and Stella grinned and nodded. "I guess I should dress up for this dinner?" His smirk had her reeling. She couldn't wait to see how dashing he'd look in a suit. Again, she nodded. He winked and turned to leave.

She called to him and he stopped and turned back around.

"M'lady?" If he tipped that damn cowboy hat one more time, she was jumping his bones, she didn't care how desperate it made her look. She couldn't stop her audible gulp and bit on her lip. His eyes fell to her lips then and they darkened with what looked like desire. He stepped forward, closing the distance between them. He took her chin between his thumb and index finger. "You're much too good of a person to allow anyone to treat you any such 'a way as that man did, Stella Rose. He doesn't deserve to breathe the air you do."

With that, Elias Kinsen leaned down and kissed her. He kissed her breathlessly, allowing his tongue to slide in and do incredible things to her insides, unraveling the very fabric of her being, until she was panting and yearning for more. Then he pulled back and grinned devilishly before he left her room.

And just like that, Stella was over his cousin, Jax.

~

*A*ll the Kinsens, Butlers, and Boyds got together two Saturdays later to celebrate both Jack's birthday and Morgan's "reunion", as they called it, save for Savannah's uncle Carson and his brood, and her grandparents who were under the weather.

Gavin, Veronica, Avery, Elias, Stella, Buck, Vivian, Jack, Natalie, Dallie, Cole, Lily, Jax, Cassidy, Kelsey, Morgan, Luther, Bella, LJ, LJ's girlfriend-Amber, Levi, Nate, Jordan, Wyatt, Angela, and Austin's three nieces were all in attendance, along with Austin and Savannah. The house was packed and loud as hell with thirty people in it, but Austin was on cloud nine as he watched Vanna moving easily along on her left leg.

It had been a relief to say the least to see her up and mobile and not hobbling—and so far without nerve damage—as she walked without a noticeable limp as Austin did. It was bad enough that he had to live like that, she shouldn't have to.

Things hadn't been so great between them after he'd shown her the gallery he'd rented for her. He'd felt defeated that day, although he somewhat understood, he was annoyed with her for not even trying and telling him she wasn't staying in Abundance. If she didn't plan to stay then how come she didn't seem so eager to leave? It was bullshit and she damn well knew it too. She was procrastinating going back to Houston. He wasn't stupid. It was written all over her face. Well, now, he just had to find a reason to make her stay. Even if it meant throwing her family's happiness in her face, he was gonna do whatever it took to keep his dark-headed dream girl there with him. He loved her. He worshipped the ground she walked on and the thoughts of her being so far away from him were unfathomable. Didn't she see that she belonged here? On the ranch. With him. With her family. Couldn't she see how happy they were?

He smiled over at his boss as he handed him a beer. "Big crowd," Jack said with a laugh.

"Ah, crowds don't bother me too much. Vanna, eh, she could leave them, but I can see she's glad to see everyone." Austin looked over at Vanna, laughing with Cassidy and his niece, Katie, and smiled. It was good to see everyone reconnecting, despite that Stella kept glancing over at Cassidy with guilt, as if she'd stabbed her in the back. They still needed to reconcile, but who was he to say? Jax had told him nonchalantly what had happened the weekend before and he'd actually laughed.

"It must be nice to have two hot chicks fighting over you, stud," Austin had stated and howled with laughter, getting a scowl out of Jackson. But he could understand not wanting bad blood between Cassidy and Stella, their families had been too close for far too long to have something as simple as a misunderstood love triangle between them.

Well, if Elias's hand on Stella's hip and Cassidy's hand interlaced with Jackson's were any indication, there was no misunderstanding...at least, not anymore.

"So, you still haven't told her how you feel, huh?" Jack asked, bringing Austin back to reality. It hit him hard in the chest, and he recoiled, feeling his guts tighten as Vanna's gorgeous sea-green eyes held him captive. Her mere glance had him stumbling all over himself.

He looked back to his boss, who glanced at him as if to say, "You gonna answer me sometime today?"

Austin shrugged. The timing hadn't been right, or so that's what he told Vanna's father.

After all, she'd shut him down, popped his bubble, and deflated his confidence all in one shot that day she'd "rejected" his gift. Yeah, it might not be what she wanted at the time. But it was what she loved to do. It was what she was good at! It was who she was. A painter. An artist. A musician. A lover of beauty and fine things. And he was head over freakin' heels in love with her.

So why the hell couldn't he *tell* her that?

Because the last two weeks he'd thrown himself into work, into playing guitar, into giving her time to heal and see him for who he was. He was hoping she'd change her mind, humble her heart to him, accept his gift. He'd not done as she'd asked. He'd not broken the lease and he'd made his second payment on an empty building with a heavy heart.

He'd picked up a couple gigs in local bars in hopes to inspire her to break out of her shell a little, and Savannah, her mother, and sister had actually come to see him play, much to his surprise, and he'd played his heart out for her, singing to her as if no one else existed but her. Because in all truth, she was the only person he could see from those stages. The aura that surrounded Savannah blotted everyone else out and his heart rejoiced in her presence, basked in the love he felt for her.

But even now as he held her gaze without breaking it, she was the first to look away. She'd done that very thing too many times lately and it left him swamped with doubt. What was she waiting for? What was she wanting from him? What was he failing to provide for her? Was his original assessment correct? Was he unworthy of her? Was she even in love with him? And if not, where would that leave him?

If she decided to go back to Houston, he would follow her. Although he was happy here in Abundance and didn't want to leave, he *would* if it meant he could be with Savannah. But the fear that had plagued him was the answer to the question he was too frightened to ask—Did she *want* him to go with her?

He tried convincing himself that she loved him. That he was being silly. Their lovemaking had been down right earth-shattering... But her continued avoidance of him had him overwhelmed, his confidence shaken to the core. He was a former military man haunted by his own flaws and short-comings. After all, what did he have to offer a woman like Savannah Grace Kinsen? She was a doctor, a brainiac, an engineer, an artist, a violinist...and he was just a simple country boy with a raspy voice and a bum leg.

It was Wyatt who picked up on Austin's sullenness after they'd all made their rounds around the kitchen, filling their plates with various grilled meats and side items, most of which Austin knew he'd pay for the next day, and they were all seated. Jack thanked everyone for coming, said grace, and they dug in.

"For someone who didn't leave her side two weeks ago, you sure are pretty far away from her now," Wyatt said under his breath, as he looked over at Vanna who sat across the table from them, next to Kelsey.

Leave it to his brother to notice the obvious. Austin just shrugged, not wanting a lecture or advice on women and relationships. What the hell did Wyatt know anyway? He'd had the same woman since high school.

"Wanna know what I think?" Wyatt continued, like Austin's death stare wasn't enough to shut him up. "I think it's *her* who's running from her feelings."

Austin gave his older brother his undivided attention, setting his fork down in annoyance after taking a bite of potato salad.

"You've thrown the resident genius for a loop and she doesn't know what to do."

"Alright, Dr. Phil, so what is it that I'm supposed to do now?"

"You always were the charmer, lil' bro. I'm sure you'll figure it out." Wyatt winked.

"Alright, that's it!" Stella jumped up then from the end of the table. "I can't take it anymore."

"Stella, what on earth?" her father balked and tugged at her shirt.

"No, I have to say my peace. It's been weeks and I can't live with myself anymore. I have to say something."

"Good, I'm glad the guilt is eating at you, you tramp," Cassidy Boyd shot up and pointed across the table to Stella's chest. Half the table gasped.

"Whoa now, ladies. This ain't the time nor place," Jordan Butler pulled on Cassidy's arm.

Cass jerked her arm away and sneered at Stella then. "You're a home wrecker! You have some nerve to even show up here today."

"You two were broken up, Cassidy. Quit being such a drama queen." Stella crossed her arms over her chest.

"Like that makes it any better. Don't excuse yourself for what you did."

"At least I didn't sleep with him," Stella smarted back, and Jax stood, huffing and holding his palms out in truce.

"He's one of the *few* in town," Cass retorted, pursing her lips.

Vivian gasped and scowled up at Cassidy. "Now, wait just a—"

"Alright, where's the boxing gloves? Let's take these two outside and hose 'em down, shall we?" Luther tried to laugh to break some of the tension, but it didn't work.

"Now, Cassidy." It was Natalie Kinsen's calm voice that took the spotlight then. "As you can see, Stella has moved on. No harm was done, and we do things when we're young that we aren't proud of." Natalie's brows went up as if she and Cassidy were in on something that no one else knew.

"That's right, young lady. Dammit! Natalie and I were sweethearts once, long before Jack and I were best friends. You don't see any bad blood between me and Jack or her and your mother, now do ya? C'mon, you two were raised as friends. Don't let your feelings for the same person cloud your love for one another. Friends and family. That's what matters. It's over now. Let Stella apologize and move the hell on." Luther huffed as he sat back down, his eyes boring holes into his youngest child.

Cassidy seemed to calm some and looked back at Stella, whose face was streaming tears. It took her a minute to regain her composure. Elias took her hand then and kissed it and she gulped before saying. "I *am* sorry, Cass. I never meant to hurt you. I was wrong. I don't want this to destroy our friendship. I love you. And I love Jax... not like that. Y'all are my family. Please. Forgive me for—" Stella hiccuped, unable to finish, but Austin caught Jax as his eyes went from Stella to Cassidy and clearly, Cass was rattled.

Cass nodded and her head lowered. Bella got up from the table then and motioned for Cass to follow her into the living room.

Vivian did the same with Stella and everyone was quiet for a moment before Luther shrugged and started eating again. Everyone else followed suit.

Soon, the table was laughing again, and Stella and Cass's red faces were rejoining the table. Austin was surprised at the sudden drama and mending that had taken place at such an unexpected moment. Perhaps he should confront Vanna like that but he knew she wouldn't be reacting the same way. Vanna was too private to have her dirty laundry aired for all the world to see. He remembered how unhinged she'd been when her father and uncle had caught them red-handed in the hayloft that day. He recalled how amazing his first night with her had been. Being threatened by her father and uncle had been worth every second he'd spent with her.

Vanna laughed at something Nathan said, and Austin's heart stopped in his chest. God, she was so beautiful and her laughter was music to his ears. He wanted to hear it again and again and he wanted to be the one making her laugh.

It wasn't long before people were done eating and the banter was so loud it was practically deafening.

Morgan then stood and clanked his beer stein with his fork, bringing the attention to himself. "Everyone, if I could have your attention please?" He could be so damn suave when he wanted to be. "I have a few announcements to make. First, as you know, my cousin Savannah here is our interim mayor. I want to congratulate her on the fine job she's done as of late. We have a plan in place for Terra, ground has broken on the community farm, and thanks to her, our irrigation system is not only top of the line, it's revolutionary, and will sustain the gardens for decades to come." Applause surrounded the table, and Austin couldn't help but smile at the flush on his lover's cheeks. She was so oblivious to how amazing she really was. "We've picked out her plot of land here on the property and I've personalized some blueprints, now, if only she'll just let me get started on it." Austin balked at that and Savannah shook her head, frowning, as if to say, "Drop it, Morgan."

The fact that she'd refused Morgan's offer to build her a home, made Austin feel even more hopeless. She didn't have a place in Houston, so why would she be so opposed to having one built here, where her family was? He couldn't stop the pain that rippled through his heart. If she didn't want a house on her family's land, how could she possibly want *him*? "And last but certainly not least... Last month—as some of you already know—I asked Kelsey Jean Boyd here to marry me."

The women at the table all squealed in unison. How was it that they could harmonize like that—and so shrilly too?

"And as you can see by that big rock on her finger, she agreed," Morgan chuckled as he looked down at the lovely Kelsey, clad in a yellow cotton dress that complimented her hair and skin tone.

She shot up into Morgan's arms, and they embraced in sweet familiarity. Morgan kissed her with a possessiveness and passion that Austin envied. God, he wanted Savannah to look at him like that again. Or had she ever? He wasn't sure at that moment as he chanced a look at her. Tears streamed down her cheeks and she smiled up at her cousin and best friend, even though she and Austin had known about the engagement for some time now, the impressive solitaire on Kel's finger was new.

Austin's head lowered. Perhaps he'd imagined Savvy's feelings for him, maybe he was the only one who'd felt something that very first night they'd spent together. After all, Austin had been a means to an end for Vanna; she'd been at the bar searching for a one-night stand, and he'd been the perfect target. Her words stuck in his craw then as he remembered her begging him to 'pound her'. It had been almost humorous then. It wasn't quite so funny now though.

He stood to leave but as he did so, Morgan glanced over at him. The smile that came to Austin's lips wasn't as genuine or as big as his friend deserved, but he tried anyway. Morgan raised his glass to Austin and Austin nodded, turning to seek the exit, and shield his heart from any more pain.

But Natalie Kinsen was quicker and her match-making ways once more took Austin off guard.

"Austin, Savannah, Cole, you all could play our lovely bride and groom-to-be a nice, romantic tune, couldn't you?" *Damn that dark-headed beauty and her conniving ways,* Austin thought even as he nodded to her and glanced over at Vanna, who looked like she was about to pass out.

"I'll just grab my guitar, Mrs. K," he winked and headed toward the front door.

He wasn't aware that Morgan had followed him until he cleared his throat as Austin turned with his guitar case, pulling it from his bike.

"Got a sec, Aus?"

"What's up, buddy?" Austin's eyes drew questioningly at the smirk on Morgan's face.

"So, I've been thinking, A.J. You know my dad plans to retire at the end of this year?" Morgan asked. Austin just nodded in response. "Well, as you know, I don't know the first thing about runnin' a horse ranch, plus I'm busy with my own business and my seat on the council." Again, Austin just nodded. "You wouldn't be interested in being my foreman at Starlight Valley, would you?"

Austin was taken aback. Blown away that Morgan had asked him; both honored and surprised.

"You're good with horses, you were in the Army, and people listen to you... It was actually Uncle Jack's idea. He thinks you'd make a good leader." Morgan's brow went up and a slow smile took his face.

Jack? *Really?* Wow! Had his boss actually changed his mind on how he felt about Austin? No. That couldn't be right. Jack just wanted Austin to quit so that he would be rid of him and Austin would be further away from Savannah—albeit it only a few miles away. It still flattered Austin though that his boss, whom he'd not been the best employee to, would recommend him for foreman of his sister ranch.

Before Austin could respond, Morgan patted him on the back. "You don't have to decide now. Take some time and mull it over."

With that, Morgan winked and they headed back inside.

~

*D*allas watched as her sister nervously removed her violin from its cover, Austin's eyes never leaving hers.

God, it was so obvious how they felt for one another. Why were they both being so darn stubborn? Vanna belonged here—at home—and with *him*, and Dallie didn't understand why she didn't see it.

They'd literally had the awkward conversation about it days ago, and Dallie told Vanna to pull her head out of the clouds. Vanna feigned indifference, thinking Dallie couldn't see right through her, but Dallie did and called her out.

"Stop denying who you are, Vanna. You've always been too hard on yourself. But it's time to make a decision and take the dang hook out of his mouth. Sheesh!" Dallie had stormed off, a bit angry at herself for sounding so harsh, but Vanna had always been so wishy-washy with her feelings. Dallie didn't get it. She, herself, had gone away for a little while, but she'd come back home and was happier for it. Why was it that Vanna didn't see how much she belonged here?

Dallie smiled up at her husband then, who kissed her cheek and sat their adorable little blonde daughter on her lap, before he moved over to the piano. Lilian clapped for the trio as Vanna sat down in a chair adjacent to Austin's. He grinned over at her and adjusted the mic in front of him.

"This one here's a classic. One of my faves from the king of rock n' roll himself." Austin's smooth voice echoed in the piano room as everyone quieted down and moved in closer. Vanna's eyes growing big as she gulped and looked back at Austin to begin.

He did, with a chord Dallie and probably most of the people in the room were familiar with. His deep voice began singing "Can't

427

Help Falling In Love" and Dallie couldn't stop thinking it was as much for Vanna as for Morgan and Kelsey. She stifled a giggle.

Vanna's violin chimed in at the right time and the harmony of guitar and violin filled the space as the audience was awed by their undeniable talents. Music flowed through their blood, it connected them unlike anything else could; it was yet one more thing these two unlikely lovers had in common than not. Cole entered in at the chorus, his fingers stroking the piano with ease.

Dallie grinned as she looked over at Morgan and Kelsey. Both their eyes glistened in unshed tears and when the song was over, everyone clapped in delight and Morgan pulled Kelsey to him for a smoldering kiss.

It was good to see the two of them back together as fate had intended when it had intervened on a day much like this one some seventeen years prior. Dallie would never forget the electricity that had sparked from one to the other when they'd touched hands. Everyone had seen and felt it, like heat lightning on a clear summer night.

Austin, Vanna, and Cole played another several songs at their audience's requests—a Kid Rock and Sheryl Crow classic, one from Metallica, another from Journey, and finally "Oh Come, oh come, Emmanuel," with Austin at the piano, Cole strumming guitar, before they stopped and people started to slowly head out.

Dallie hugged her friends and family members, glad to see them —even if it was only for a short period of time. Vanna mentioned getting all the girls together for a bachelorette party for Kelsey, and Kels nodded in agreement. Stella and Cass hugged, and Dallie smiled over at them, so glad her little brother hadn't destroyed an eighteen-year friendship over his immaturity.

Speaking of which, Dallie suddenly had an unbelievable urge to go check on the colt that she and Austin had birthed merely a month ago. She noted the darkening of the skies as she looked out the window nearest her. Most everyone was gone now save for her, Cole, Lily, Eli, Jax, Austin, Savannah, Stella and Cassidy, her mother and father. She looked over at her father then. He seemed to sense her trepidation as he stepped towards her.

"I need to check the horses," she said as he took her arm.

"Jax, you and Eli grab the gator, round the horses up, it's about to storm."

Just then everyone's phones went off in unison, a deafening of alarms that pierced the stillness.

Dallie's hair stuck out on her arms and she felt it before Austin ever said, "It's a severe thunderstorm warning."

"Alright," her father said. "Girls, head down to the basement. Austin, you and Cole come with me and Dallie."

Cole started to protest, but Dallie wouldn't have it. He knew where her heart lie as he'd known since the day he'd married her. "Vanna take Lily. Dallie and I'll be back shortly."

Vanna looked at Dallie in apprehension before she grabbed Lily and she, their mom, Stella and Cassidy ran down to the basement.

Jax and Eli were out the door, on the gator, and gone by the time Dallie, Cole, Austin, and Jack got into his truck. The skies were gray with an impending blackness heading in from the west. Dallie's heart hammered in her chest and she held onto her father's headrest as he peeled out and headed down to the barn. Horses were rearing and whinnying as lightning flashed in the distance and Dallie's apprehension grew as their fears became her own.

She got out of the truck as soon as her dad parked it and ran to the little colt's stall, looking him and his mother over.

"Close all the hatches and make sure the barn doors are shut once all the horses are in," her dad commanded. Dallie, we need a head-count," he commanded.

Dallie could already tell him how many weren't there and feel their trembling as she stroked Cobalt's and Sheba's muzzles, cooing to a whining Caesar.

"Something's not right, Dad. This isn't their normal behavior... even for a storm," she admonished and watched as Cole and Austin began closing and locking the Dutch doors that were open around the perimeter of the barn. They worked quickly and in unison as the skies grew more ominous by the minute.

"Where are Jax and Eli?" her father asked as he checked the latches on the stalls, throwing open the doors that had missing horses. "They're taking too long."

Dallie checked another horse, feeling an impending doom from the buckskin mare as she tried in vain to calm her. "They're so anxious, Daddy." Dallie grimaced even as she tried to relinquish her anguish. "It's not working."

"What are you saying, honey?" His big palm gripped her bicep and he looked into her eyes with worry.

"This isn't just *any* storm, Daddy."

She didn't want to say it aloud, but he knew where her thoughts were heading. Their home and barn had been spared in the past. All she could do now was pray they would be once more.

He scowled at her before grabbing his phone up from his back pocket. He began checking it, she figured the radar, as she walked towards the front of the barn, feeling the wind picking up as she did so.

She tried to hone in on the ten horses out in the back pasture, letting her mind drift to where they were and subconsciously call them in. It was crazy. Her gift didn't work that way, but it was worth a try. After all, her brother and cousin were out there trying to round them up and this storm would be on them within minutes. Their lives were at stake. She calmed her mind, calmed her heart, and stilled her fears even as thunder roared loudly in the distance.

She summoned the horses in her head, and when she opened her eyes, she looked up at Cole and Austin, who were breathless as they came inside, four horses in tow as they ushered them forward. The stallions took to their stalls, grateful to be indoors as Austin and Cole closed the stall doors behind them.

"We gotta hurry, it's going green out there," Austin replied and looked beyond her to her father.

He scowled at her and brought his phone to his ear, calling Jax she assumed.

"Baby, I know how important these horses are to you, but we're running out of time," Cole begged and looked down at her rounded belly.

"Just a couple more minutes, please?" she gripped his shirt, and he huffed in frustration.

"Jax?" her dad called into the receiver of his phone and she could hear screaming on the other end of it as Jax answered him back. She couldn't make it out but knew it only echoed what she already knew was coming.

It was then that the sound of two dozen hooves overpowered their ears, and Dallie laughed as she ran towards the back of the barn to the back gate where the six horses stood. "It worked," she stated in relief as Cole and Austin moved ahead of her to lead them in.

"Jax, just get out of there and head to the house. We got 'em." Her dad grabbed her arm then, steering her to the truck. "Close the barn doors and let's go. There's a twister comin.'"

CHAPTER 19

*V*anna's heart leapt into her throat as she held her niece to her chest and prayed for the safety of her family as the wind whistled past the window. Damn it, why were they out there in this? Didn't they know how dangerous a tornado could be?

Once the girls were downstairs, their phones had gone off once again, upgrading the storm from a severe thunderstorm warning to a tornado warning, just as quick as that, and panic had begun to rise in her throat. Vanna had been used to this most of her life. Living in Texas, they were in tornado alley. They had always been lucky though, never having to deal with more than roof damage and broken windows, some downed trees and power outages. Savannah suddenly prayed with everything inside that this time would be no worse than the others.

She texted Kelsey, and Aunt Jordan to get to their basements as quick as possible. She knew Cass and Stella had done the same as their phones had all been chirping notifications as thunder boomed around them.

Her mother sighed and moved closer to her on the couch, taking her hand as Vanna started to tremble. Even as a child she'd hated thunderstorms, despite how beautiful the sky became during them.

"It's gonna be alright, baby," her mother cooed as Vanna felt hot tears stream down her cheeks.

She tried to nod but fear seized her as a flash of lightning made the power surge. She jumped. Lily pulled back from her bosom and looked up into Savannah's eyes then, taking her face in her tiny little palms. Her little blue eyes sparkled as her lips pursed. "Aunt Vanna, are you scared?" she asked.

"Aunt Vanna doesn't like storms, Lil," Vanna's mom stated.

"It's gonna be ok, Aunt Vanna. Mommy and Daddy, they're comin' right back and Paw-paw Jack too. Uncle Jax and Uncle Eli, and that bearded cowboy that sings real good."

Vanna couldn't help but laugh at her niece's sweet precociousness. Oh, to be so oblivious to her surroundings. Deep envy filled her then.

"That's right, sweet baby. They're on their way back now." Her mother's conviction did nothing to quench Savannah's fears as her voice wavered at the end.

Vanna gulped back her fear and said another prayer of well-being just as the lights went out and rain began to pelt the roof. The wind whistled again and she couldn't help the way her body shuddered as a loud boom of thunder vibrated the house and darkness surrounded her.

Lily began to sing "Jesus Loves Me" as her little hands stroked her aunt's arm, and Vanna felt out of sorts being comforted by a four-year-old instead of vice versa.

Her mother's head fell to her shoulder and she could hear Stella and Cass whispering as their faces lit up with the light from their phones.

"They're here," Cass stated and jumped up suddenly as they heard the front door open and footsteps sounded on the hardwoods above them.

"Oh, thank God," Savannah's mom stated and sighed.

Dallie was the first down the stairs and Lily bounded out of Savannah's arms and into her mother's. "Mommy! Daddy!" Lily greeted her parents as Cole's head popped out from behind Dallie.

"It's ok, baby, we're here," Cole soothed her and kissed her plump cheek as Dallie cradled Lily's little frame to her chest, coming to sit on the couch across from Savannah and Natalie.

Vanna smiled at her sister, glad to see her, although she and Cole were now soaking wet from the rain.

Eli and Jax came next, much to Vanna's relief. Cass and Stella ran to them, embracing them as another bolt of lightning lit up the window.

Vanna shivered, eagerly awaiting the arrival of her father and Austin—not wanting to be a drama queen but felt her heart hammering uncontrollably in her chest. She looked up to her brother, who caught her eye first.

"You ok, sis?" he asked as he took Cassidy's hand and led her to the love seat near the couch Savannah sat on.

She tried to nod but couldn't.

"Daddy and Austin are okay," he confessed and gave her a smile. "They were right behind us. They'll be down in a minute."

But as the sound of the roaring wind and storm grew louder and another rumble shook the house, her fear suddenly overcame her logic.

She ran for the stairs and took them two at a time, her need to verify her father and her lover's safety superseding anything else in that moment.

"Vanna," Eli called but she ignored him, ascended the stairs, and came through the door frame just as another lightning bolt lit the room up like it was daylight.

"Daddy," Vanna cried, her voice cracking. "Austin?"

Neither man answered her and her stomach soured with horror when she noticed the door was shut and locked. Where the fuck were they? She heard Caesar bark and patted his head in relief as he came to her, knowing the dog wouldn't be far from his master. "Hey buddy, where's your daddy?"

"Vanna?" Austin's voice called to her from the kitchen and she ran forward just as the sound of something cracking behind her caused her to cry out. The crash of broken glass and the feel of wind and rain on her skin caused her to fall and cover herself as the stigma of her PTSD took control of her.

She was overcome with panic as a set of strong arms gripped her biceps and forced her up and into a hard chest. "Savvy? Are you hurt?" Austin asked as he looked her over, but she could see nothing beyond the terror and whimpered.

"Is she ok?" Vanna heard her father's voice in the background.

"Yeah, I don't think she's cut, but she may be in shock."

"Go on, I'm right behind you. Let me clean up my mess."

"Aus—Austin?" Savannah murmured as he lifted her and cradled her in his arms. He headed down the basement stairs slowly, carrying her as if she were lighter than a feather.

"Savannah?" Jax called as he came into view. "What the hell happened? We heard glass breaking."

"I broke a vase in the kitchen, trying to get back into the living room," she heard her father say behind them.

"No, it—it was a tr—tree," Vanna's head swam as she tried to remember.

"Here. Lay her down," her mom said.

"Dallie, would you grab me that pillow? Jax, you got an ice pack down here?" Austin asked.

Jax ran to go retrieve it as Austin laid Vanna down on the couch, his beautiful face coming into view.

"You're okay." She sighed and cupped his cheek, her fear thwarted by his presence.

"Only the *good* die young, sweetheart." He winked.

She felt her feet go up as he cradled her head and soothed her. "Now, I want you to look at me, alright, angel? Focus on my face. Listen to my voice." That wouldn't be hard to do. He had like the sexiest voice ever and he'd always been easy to look at. She gave him a smile. "There's my beautiful girl and that smile I can't get enough of. It's ok, now. It's all gonna be okay."

Vanna was only aware of him and his overpoweringly amazing smell and aura; it didn't matter that he was wet and getting her wet in turn, or that the storm was raging outside now in full force, the wind and rain hammering the house. All that mattered was that her family, her loved ones, were safe.

~

"I'll take Park Place, thank you very much," Austin smarted with a laugh and paid Dallie, the banker.

"Now, wait just a minute," Savannah protested.

"Nope, this is the name of the game, darlin', Monopoly, and I am an entrepreneur—not unlike your cousin, Morgan Butler."

Vanna planted her hands on her hips and scoffed. "You already have houses on St. James Place and Baltic Avenue."

"I know and guess what?" He dramatically threw his money down next to Dallie, getting a giggle out of Lilian. "I'm about to buy *more* houses."

"No fair! I had to take a mortgage out the last time I landed on your space."

"Well, then start hooking, baby, because Daddy don't play fair." He winked.

Dallie burst into laughter even as Vanna gaped at him, and Austin laughed maniacally.

They'd been without power now for two days and had resorted to playing board games in candlelight. All their homes were fine—Dallie's, their parent's, their grandparent's, Uncle Nate's, and Morgan's, save for downed trees and power-lines all over. Dallie and Cole had some broken windows and needed to have the roof replaced due to water damage but all in all, nothing major, thank God, had occurred from the storms...not on their

SHANNA SWENSON

land anyway. Luth and Bella's and Buck and Vivian's homes were unscathed.

It was as if the EF-4 tornado had bounced around; some homes were demolished—reduced to nothing—while some appeared as if nothing had ever occurred. Town had been spared, but there were homes on the east end of the county that were gone. It had been guesstimated that only five lives had been lost. They would know more in the coming days and weeks that followed.

Certain roads were still impassable and the power was still down all over the place.

Savannah had addressed the public yesterday, urging those that didn't need to be out to stay home and those that had resources and money to donate them. Projects were underway for reconstruction. Vanna, Morgan, and Austin had spent the better part of the last two days helping others with shelter, food and water, medical care, clean-up and safety measures. But until the power-lines were safely restored, the power would remain off. She'd been told it should be up by next week, until then the Red Cross had come in and a state of emergency had been declared for Greyson county—their county—and two other surrounding counties who'd suffered similar damage.

"I'm sorry, Savvy, but I like to win," Austin countered as Vanna pouted up at him, standing to refill her glass. He pulled her into his lap then and kissed her pout away. "As soon as Dallie and Cole leave, I'm taking you home," he whispered in her ear. The promise in his voice was undeniable and her sex clenched.

Things had been different since the night of the storm. Her heart felt content even as her mind wasn't certain of what it wanted. Although they hadn't been intimate, what with being so busy with storm cleanup and all, she and Austin had gotten even closer than they'd ever been. She'd seen his strength and determination these last two days, his humble soul and his giving heart, and she'd fallen in love with him all over again. It was as if fate had answered her questions in the most subtle ways possible.

"Well, if you two are done messin' around, I'll take my turn now,"

438

her father grumbled and rolled the dice. He scoffed when he drew a card and ended up in jail. "Damn. How's that for luck? Allow me, Miss Kinsen." He winked at her and took her glass from her hand as he stood. Austin's arm went tighter around her waist and he chuckled over at Lily and Cole plotting their next move. Vanna couldn't help but grin and place her forehead on his, loving the feel of his strong, inked arm around her.

Just then the doorbell rang and her father walked over to answer it on his way to the kitchen.

Her mom was just moving her game-piece, the thimble, as they heard a voice from the front door. Vanna looked up to see her father step back and she gasped as she looked up to see who was coming in.

It was Siddharth Bhushan.

"Sidd?" Vanna asked as she stood from Austin's lap. "Wh—what are you doing here?"

He approached, looking apprehensively at her father, who crossed his arms over his chest, growled, and looked over at Vanna then, a reproachful look on his face. It was as if he asked, "Want me to make him leave? 'Cause I would *love* to."

Savannah just gave him a curt nod, telling him it was alright without having to say the words. He backed up but didn't move off as she'd expected.

"Savannah, uh, can we talk outside?" Sidd asked and motioned towards the front porch.

She looked up at her father again then back to Sidd and nodded. He turned and was out the door in a matter of seconds. She followed and pulled the door closed behind her, noting the cool May breeze and the sounds of tree frogs, cicadas, and crickets singing into the night.

He turned from the porch railing to look at her, and she took in his weary green eyes, olive skin, and plump lips. His dark hair had recently been cut and he was clad in his usual linen button down and grey slacks, his grey blazer was missing.

She crossed her arms over her chest and waited, waited to hear why he'd come here.

"Did you fare well during the storm? I heard it was really bad."

"It was! A lot of roads are still impassable. I'm surprised you were even able to get here."

"I needed to get out of the city for a little while."

She almost scoffed but didn't. "People died, Sidd, we still don't know how many."

He looked off again and came forward. "Well, you look great, Savannah." His eyes roved over her and he gave her a faint smile. He wasn't a big smiler by nature, at least, not that she'd ever seen.

"I was shot." She bet he'd missed *that* fact too while his eyes burned through her thin V-neck blue cotton dress. They didn't have power, therefore no one had A/C, and it was hot during the day and at best seventy degrees Fahrenheit at night.

He just looked back at her blankly, like she'd lost her mind. He obviously didn't take her seriously though as he said, "I made a mistake, Savannah. I fucked up. And I'm sorry."

This wasn't happening. He wasn't coming here to try and get her back. There had to be another reason. He wasn't the groveling type. But then again, he wasn't one to make spur of the moment decisions either.

"I want you back. I miss you." Did he really just say that? What a douche-bag.

Savannah smirked. "What happened to your *girlfriend*?"

He lowered his head for a moment then moved closer to her, within arms reach. He didn't answer her question, but said, "Savannah, you and I belong together. We're so much alike, we—"

She was vigorously shaking her head. She'd not realized how different they really were until they were apart.

Just then the front door opened, and Austin came out of it, looking back and forth between them. "Hope I'm not interruptin' anything, Savvy," he crooned and his sexy voice renewed her.

She smiled over at him as he sauntered up next to her, throwing his arm possessively around her waist and pulling her into his side.

"I'm sorry. We haven't met." Austin extended his hand to Sidd.

Siddharth looked frazzled as his eyes moved from Savannah to the intruder. "Uh, Savannah and I are in the middle of something. Do you mind?" His hand shooed at Austin as if he were an annoying fly. He apparently didn't know the Austin she did or he wouldn't be so crass with him.

"Name's Austin Montgomery. You must be Sidd." He leaned into Vanna then and loudly whispered, "You're right, darlin', he *is* a total fuckhead."

Uh oh! Austin finally had Sidd's attention as Sidd's eyes hovered on him, evaluating him. "Savannah, who the fuck is this? A cousin?"

"Well, damn, Sidd. That hurt! Ya see, contrary to popular belief, us Alabama folk don't go around fuckin' our cousins. Not only is that shit illegal, it's also rather disgustin' if you ask me. Don't be rude! You know Savvy's got a hell of a lot more class than that," Austin antagonized, his deep accent picking up more twang. Savannah put her hand to Austin's chest, and stifled a giggle, stopping him from moving forward as he practically growled at Siddharth.

Sidd looked as if he'd been slapped. He gaped up at Vanna, looking as if she'd just confessed to something horrific.

"Don't look so damned shocked. You ain't the *only* one around here with a healthy sexual appetite."

Savannah could feel Austin's eyes burning into her skin as they moved down over her body.

"I mean, I'd be a damned idiot to let this sexy angel fly by without takin' notice."

"Wait! You two are—"

"Ding, ding, ding," Austin chuckled cynically. "He figured it out, darlin'. You're right. He *is* pretty smart, after all." His handsome face looked down into hers.

Again, Savannah had a hard time keeping her laugh at bay. After all, the look on Sidd's face was worth it. He'd humiliated the hell out of her that morning in Houston.

Sidd took a step back and shut his mouth, paling even as he looked down. "I guess I didn't realize you'd move on so quickly." The accusatory glare he shot Savannah then finally got Austin angry. She'd never seen his face so intense before and it frightened her.

He shifted her back behind him and took a protective step forward.

"You *demanded* she give the ring back to you, you sonovabitch, so don't be slinging shit around here unless you wanna get covered in it. Savannah owes you nothing! She's not tied to you anymore. Now, she may not be a violent person, but I can turn into one fairly quickly when the occasion calls for it. So, I suggest you get the hell out of here before I turn into your worst nightmare."

With that, Sidd looked them both over as his face flushed and he scoffed before turning on his heel and leaving.

"Happy trails, motherfucker," Austin mumbled under his breath, and Savannah let her breath out. "God, what a prick. The nerve of that guy. Sorry, baby girl, I didn't let him finish what he was sayin'." Austin turned then and looked down into her face. "I'm sure it was so very important too."

She laughed at his sarcasm for a moment before his mouth was on hers. She moaned into his lips and he deepened the kiss, pulling her tightly into his hard chest.

As his tongue moved over hers, she felt herself fall into him and her hands fell to his waist, holding him as if she were afraid she would fall.

Suddenly, he was lifting her into his arms and she was swooning as he moved off the porch and into the driveway.

"Where are we going, Corporal?" she cooed seductively.

"To do what I've been wantin' to for weeks now."

∾

*A*ustin silently thanked the good Lord for the fact that Jax's Chevy was unlocked as he opened the door and sat Savannah down into the driver's seat. She quickly slid over as he, himself, slid in and pulled the door closed.

She giggled as her hands went at him and his erection went from semi to raging in an instant. "We're gonna do it in my brother's truck? Gross. I'm sure he and Cass have done it in here."

"Don't care," he admitted as he grabbed her up and pulled her atop his lap. He gripped her bottom and squeezed hard. "I haven't spanked this sweet little ass of yours in too long, darlin'. You're overdue."

The whimper that escaped her lips had him tripping as he leaned her against the steering wheel and kissed her lips with all the pent-up passion he'd held back. Within seconds, she was putty in his hands and he was crazy with lust.

"God, I need to be inside you, my sexy Savvy. Claim you. Own you." He was rambling but didn't care, he'd never felt so possessive of a woman in all his life.

Seeing Sidd at his boss's front door and watching Savannah walk out with him had made Austin crazed. He'd gone on the defense, like he'd been when his team was in jeopardy. Obviously that man hadn't come to hurt Savannah and the situation wasn't anywhere near as dire as the one his team had been in while in Afghanistan, but he'd felt compelled to safeguard what was his.

Austin cupped Savannah's breasts, kneading the firm mounds in his palms, loving the noises that escaped from her throat as he did so. He grabbed for the hem of her dress, needing to touch her bare flesh, feel it in his hands. His hunger for her had his hands shaking in a frenzy.

Once her dress was off, he tackled her bra and threw it aside before his lips found her nipple and pulled the hard peak into his mouth, loving it as his hands moved back to her plump bottom. Her arched back and cry of pleasure nearly unraveled him. His hands moved to his jeans and he freed his erection with a quick zip and jerk of his hips. Before he knew it, his cock was piercing her opening, filling her, and he was pulling her hips down onto his, getting her as close to him as humanly possible.

"Oh, my baby girl," he moaned even as she gasped. His hands moved up her waist and back to her breasts as she began to ride him, rising and falling over his hard shaft. The sight of her curvy body fucking him was the most beautiful thing he'd ever seen. He looked up into her sparkling eyes as his hands moved to steady her, assisting her as they loved one another's bodies. "You're mine Savannah Grace Kinsen. This body," he stopped only long enough to kiss her full breasts with soft, sweet pecks of his lips as his hands stroked up and down her waistline, "this body is mine. It'll *never* belong to anyone else." His eyes fell over her round breasts, her slender belly, the delta of her thighs that worked him into mind-numbing abandon before coming back to her gorgeous face. She bit into her bottom lip and moaned as she chased her release, her grip on his shoulders tightening as he thrust up with her lunges.

"Oh God, Austin," she whimpered.

"Too much, angel? I'm sorry. I'm crazy fuckin' possessive right now." He grunted even as her sex clenched around him.

"No, it's so hot. So. Fucking. Hot." She cried out as her body was racked in spasms, her orgasm coming upon her.

He grinned in triumph even as he held himself back from his own climax. He flipped them over, moving her to the seat, before she could fully come down off her high and thrust hard and true as he settled between her legs, gripped her bottom in his palms as he pistoned into her, over and over again.

"Oh God, oh God," she cried out again in climax, and he moaned as his own sex screamed for release.

"Tell me, Savvy. Say it. Tell me you're mine, sweet baby."

"Mmm, Austin. Oh, God. I'm yours. I'm so completely yours."

And with that, he fell, into a void of exquisite bliss and exploding stars as he cried her name into the tight cab of the truck.

~

*A*ustin awoke alone in his bed, immediately realizing that Savannah wasn't there. They'd made love all night. After they'd finished in Jax's truck, they'd, regretfully, had to go back into the house to grab Austin's keys. Jack and Nat hadn't said a word, but the avoidance in their eyes told Austin all he'd needed to know. They knew what he and Savvy had just done. They *had* to know.

Once they'd gotten into Austin's bungalow, they'd done it again... and again...and again. He'd not been able to fully quench his thirst for her—he wasn't sure he would ever be able to do so—and she'd finally fallen to sleep out of sheer exhaustion in his arms.

Austin had followed not long after, looking down at her gorgeous face in the moonlight, dark ribbons splayed out around her head. He'd smiled before kissing her forehead and pulled her into his chest, loving her soft, warm frame pressed so intimately against his.

Now, he started, panic seizing him as he realized she wasn't in the bungalow. He was completely alone. Had something happened? And why wasn't she there?

He jerked the covers from his bare hips and jumped up, his knee protesting as he did so.

He winced. "Savannah?" he called even though he knew there would be no answer.

Austin patted Caesar's head as the dog whined next to the bed. He grabbed his shorts from the arm chair, threw them on and zipped them up. He then moved to his closet, choosing an old Dallas Cowboys shirt. He threw it on over his head as he shoved his feet into a pair of sneakers and fumbled for his keys on the table next to the door. He pulled it open and looked around briefly, seeing nothing amiss, before he started to jog, Caesar on his heels.

Where would she go and why hadn't he woken up when she'd left? He wasn't usually a heavy sleeper.

He checked the barn first, as it was on the way to the house, even though he'd known he wouldn't find her there. Wyatt gave him a confused look when Austin breathlessly asked if he'd seen Savannah as he'd entered the front barn door.

"Lose your girlfriend already, brother?" Wyatt asked and laughed.

But Austin didn't think it was funny. Savannah wasn't actually his girlfriend. He wanted her to be. But he'd never asked her to be. Hell, he'd not told her he loved her either, worshipped the earth beneath her feet, and wanted her to be his for all eternity. And he silently prayed that wasn't why she'd disappeared on him so suddenly. He seemed to keep fucking things up with her and he didn't really understand why.

He jogged faster, heading through the back yard. He stumbled on a rock and felt his left ankle jerk sharply. He winced but didn't stop even though the pain shot from his ankle up to his knee and it began to throb in protest. He ignored it, for nothing mattered but getting to the woman he loved and finally telling her how he felt as dread began to cloud his thoughts.

He climbed the gate with ease and gingerly jumped down onto his right leg—his left knee pounding like a toothache. He hauled ass up the back-porch stairs and heard voices coming from the open window.

"Vanna, honey, we understand." Austin heard Jack say.

Oh, thank God. She *was* here.

He stormed up the landing and hammered the door violently, hearing gasps as he did so.

"Sorry! It's me...Austin. I—I just wanted to talk to Savannah."

All was silent for but a moment then the door was jerked open, and Natalie Kinsen greeted him with weary eyes. He looked at her momentarily before his eyes settled on Savannah.

She was standing, beautiful as ever in a grey dress suit and lilac silk shirt, hand to her chest, lips quivering as she stared back at him.

"Savvy, baby, what's going on?" Austin looked around briefly. Jack gave him a frown, but that wasn't unusual, so he looked back at Savannah.

She looked down and shook her head. "I have to go to Houston."

"No! Why?" Austin huffed and came forward, his knee screaming in pain. He would have collapsed had her sad eyes not held him still in time.

She was leaving him. She was returning to NASA. Houston. Where she belonged.

Had he said something wrong? Done something wrong? Was she choosing Sidd instead of him? Why was this happening? No. He couldn't let this happen. He had to stop her, had to tell her how he felt about her. "I'll go with you," he stated truthfully. He would follow her to the ends of the earth if that's what it took.

She was shaking her head again, and Austin felt his heart break into a million pieces. He'd been right. She didn't want him. He wasn't good enough for her. He didn't deserve her. "Don't make this harder than it has to be. Please, Austin?" she begged and another piece of his soul ripped away as a tear slid down her cheek.

Her pleading was heart-wrenching. The void inside his chest widened. This was a bad dream. He had to wake up. *Oh God, no, please?*

"Vanna, we *have* to go, honey." Her dad checked the watch on his wrist, and Austin noticed for the first time that Jack wasn't wearing a cowboy hat. So, her father was going to Houston with her. As happy as Austin should be that Vanna wouldn't be going alone, he couldn't hide his disappointment that it wasn't him who would be accompanying her. He gulped even as Jack moved forward and took Vanna's elbow, steering her around.

Do something, you pussy! his mind screamed at him. "Savannah, wait!" Austin called and ran to stop her. The anguish in her beautiful green eyes prevented him from touching her, but his insides shrieked for him to confess their secret. "I love you, my angel of music. Please, don't go."

He was aware of Natalie's gasp in the background and Jack's smirk, but he was focused solely on the woman he loved and her reaction to what he'd told her. Her eyes closed and another tear escaped. He wanted to grab her, pull her to him, and kiss her until she succumbed to his resolve, but his time was running out.

Jack moved his arm around Savannah's waist and nudged her. "Baby, that man just told you that he loved you."

"I—I know," Vanna whimpered.

"You've reached for the stars all your life, Savannah Grace. Planet earth isn't such a bad place to be grounded, you know?"

Savannah simply gazed up at her father. She'd made her mind up and no matter what, she wasn't changing it. It didn't matter that Austin had told her he loved her. He was too late, and as her reproachful gaze moved to him, he felt his guts tear in two. Half his soul was walking away, out the door, escorted by her father who just gave him a hard smile over his broad shoulder. Austin felt his left knee give out and fell to his knees as agony encompassed every part of him. He'd only thought he knew what pain was in Afghanistan; true pain was losing the woman he loved more than he'd ever loved himself and observing her walk out of his life, knowing there wasn't a damn thing he could do to stop her.

CHAPTER 20

*N*atalie Kinsen smiled as happy tears hit her eyes. Austin Montgomery was in love with her daughter and he'd confessed it. Only he wasn't aware that Vanna reciprocated his feelings.

She'd called Nat an hour ago to come and get her so that Savannah could go meet with her boss in Houston and give him her notice of resignation. She and Savannah had been talking about it for weeks now and Vanna was on the fence about what she should do, torn about leaving her dream job but wanting to come home. Natalie knew what she would do long before her daughter did and it seemed now that Vanna had made the right decision—as Nat knew deep down she would.

"Would you like some coffee?" Natalie cleared her throat and looked down at Austin, whose shoulders shook in distress and exhaustion.

"Is it a remedy for heartbreak?" he asked, running his hands through his unruly blonde curls.

"It helps," Nat answered.

"That pain that feels like your soul has just been torn open with vise grips… that's not a heart attack, right? I mean, it's just a normal response when the person you love takes your heart with them as they walk out on you, am I wrong?" he asked, and Nat shook her head. "Ok, good, just making sure I don't need to go to the ER." He groaned and gripped his left knee, and Nat gaped at the huge scar there.

"Oh, dear, Austin. Let me get you an ice pack. That looks swollen."

"How can you tell?" he scoffed, humorlessly. "Looks as bad as it always has to me." He drew himself up onto his haunches then stood and flexed his knee before limping forward. "Sorry I barged in, Mrs. K. I should probably go."

"Go where?" she asked and motioned for him to take a seat at the breakfast table.

"Ah, you know, go nurse my broken heart. In a bottle of Jack would probably be a good start, don't 'cha think?"

Natalie giggled. "I can see why my daughter is so taken with you." When Austin looked up at her in confusion, she continued. "Vanna hasn't always been the best with knowing what she wants. She's a bit indecisive at times, despite that she's determined and when she sets her mind to do something she goes all in. She's headed to Houston to quit, Austin. She's not leaving to go back there."

"What?" He looked up at her in equal parts surprise and shock. "No. She can't. We have to stop her." He started to stand, but Natalie shook her head and rested her hand on his forearm, stopping him.

"She's already made her decision. Besides, she's not the same woman she was before Sidd broke her heart and crushed her dreams. NASA isn't where she wants to be anymore. For a time, it was all she wanted, but with age, what makes our hearts content seems to change as we do. Like that old saying about when one door closes, another opens. When our hearts are unlocked, our desires are transformed and our priorities change."

"Yup, you're a writer, alright," Austin smirked. "I'm not surprised Savvy is so talented. It's in her blood."

"Well, so is being stubborn. It's a Butler trait, I'm afraid."

"Ha, tell me about it! Morgan is a real pain in my ass sometimes." Austin looked down at his hands.

"Nate told me that Morgan offered you the position of foreman at Starlight Valley." Austin looked up, surprised by her boldness, but she wasn't holding anything back now. "You should take it."

"What about my job here?"

"Jack will understand. You'd make a fine foreman, Austin. After seeing how protective you are of my daughter, I know you'll far surpass Morgan's expectations. Besides, I heard you were a great leader." She winked.

Austin sighed and lowered his head again in heavy thought. "I don't know about *great*... I got a man killed."

"We don't measure success by the times we've failed. Only by the times we failed to get back up and try again."

He looked up at her then, his amber eyes burning into hers. "Vanna had two great role models raising her. I understand now why she's so amazing."

Natalie gave him a beaming smile. "Speaking of... it's time we showed *her*, don't you think?" Austin's brows drew and Nat laughed. "You and I have an art gallery to put together." She looked over at the clock above the French doors. "And we have a little more than twenty-four hours to do it."

~

"You ok, baby?" Savannah's father asked and took her hand in his as they rode back to Abundance.

They'd left Houston by nine that morning after breakfast at a little bistro in downtown, not far from the hotel they'd stayed at last night. She'd been at NASA most the afternoon prior and met her father before dinner in the hotel bar.

Her meeting had gone well. Her resolve hadn't faltered and her boss had been both happy for her and discontented by her resignation. Savannah had gone into the meeting with the intent to give up her full-time position but Royce Staton had talked her into staying on with NASA on an as-needed basis—for future projects, collaboration and council as her expertise was "highly regarded". It pleased her that he thought so much of her and her work and she'd felt that the situation was a win/win; she could leave Houston behind but still be called upon when the time came that she wanted to contribute. She could teach, assist, guide and work remotely and, on occasion, come to quarterly meetings but she could now focus on her art, her music, the town she loved, and herself for a change.

She smiled over at her father then. "I am. Better than I'd hoped for."

"You made the right decision." He made it sound like a question.

"Yes, I did."

"You're happy?" Jack brought her hand to his lips and kissed her knuckles, his handsome face and jade green eyes evaluating her. She nodded. "That's all a father ever wants for his children. That and to see them loved."

Savannah smiled again. Now all three of his children were happy, but she needed to get something off her chest. "You were wrong about Austin."

"Was I?" he smirked. "Or was I *right* about Austin?"

Vanna's brow furrowed. "You hated him."

"Hate is such a strong word."

"Daddy," Vanna scoffed.

"I hated Sidd… Austin I just disliked immensely."

"He must have grown on you."

"Or he proved himself worthy of my daughter, which was what I figured would happen."

"No, you told me he was, and I quote, 'going nowhere'. Your words."

Her father shrugged. He didn't want to be in the wrong. "But I didn't say he was beyond saving or that it wouldn't take one very special woman to bring him back to life."

Vanna smiled, contented knowing she'd been that woman for her amazing Austin.

"But he *is* a Longhorns fan," Jack grimaced, playfully.

"Dad." Savannah giggled.

Her father was quiet for a moment then looked back over at her solemnly. "I'm *glad* I was wrong about Austin, Savannah. So very glad." He gave her a slow smile, and she tried not to cry.

She was glad he was wrong about Austin too. Although, going back to the day she'd met him she would never have imagined things would've gone like they had or that he would be confessing his love for her just two months after their first night together. Life was funny and love was completely unpredictable.

Savannah was so absorbed in her thoughts that she didn't realize the truck had stopped and they were parked out front of a shop in downtown.

"Why've we stopped?" she asked, wanting to be back home as soon as possible so she could see Austin.

"Oh, your mom said she needed—"

Savannah gasped, realizing as she looked out the window that the shop Austin had shown her just weeks ago was now lit and occupied. A twinge of guilt and sadness filled her. He'd had such conviction for her to take this place and turn it into an art gallery, now she wouldn't get the chance.

She found herself opening the passenger door, stepping out and being drawn toward the shop. It had white curvy lettering on the front glass door and as she closed in on it she read "Savvy's Sanctuary."

"Oh my God!" she exclaimed and turned to see her father behind her with a beaming smile on his face.

"After you, my dear," he said and opened the door for her as she realized the window displays had her paintings propped on easels being showcased.

She entered the now filled store. The walls were cream, the floors hardwood, the ceilings white and her paintings were everywhere, on podiums, pedestals and with spotlights shining down on them. This gallery was set up and ready. And she'd had no idea.

She felt tears come to her eyes then as her palm covered her mouth and she stepped forward, taking it all in.

Just then she heard boots on the floor and saw Austin's big frame enter from a curtain in the back. He froze when he saw her, looking both anxious and eager. The tears fell then and she couldn't have stopped them if she'd tried.

He took a step forward. He looked good, so handsome, and fresh. He wore jeans, a fitted gray Army t-shirt and his cowboy hat, although this one looked brand new and it was black. He gulped and rubbed at the back of his neck, before dropping his hand to his side. "I—I wasn't sure what to think the other morning when you left. I thought," he paused and closed his eyes before quickly opening them again, "I thought you were leaving me. Going back to Houston for good. It was your mom who told me you were going back to quit. Please tell me that you didn't give up NASA?"

Savannah quickly shook her head. "No, I went to resign, but we worked something out."

Austin audibly sighed. "I'm so glad." He gave her a sexy grin and she could have melted into a puddle on the floor. He looked around. "Do you like what we did to the place?"

Savannah's eyes followed his and she smiled as she looked around at the windows, the perfect lighting, the creative ways they'd displayed her art. It was stunning. The décor was earthy tones and they'd used minimal backgrounds and props so that the colors from her work were the brightest things in the room.

"I think we about caused Google and Pinterest to crash researching how to display artwork."

Savannah laughed and looked back at her blond, beautiful cowboy. God, she loved him so much. He was everything she could have ever wanted and so much more.

"Thank you. This...this is amazing."

"I know you didn't want it, but don't worry, your mom found

someone who knows their stuff to run it so you won't be troubled with any of the business side of it. Oh, and the first round of paintings, all the proceeds are going back into this town you're running to help aid the storm victims. Again, your amazing mother set all that up."

Savannah laughed softly. How thoughtful and perfect!

"Your mom and Kelsey did the displays, I did the heavy lifting, and I've learned Jax and I aren't shabby painters either?" He pointed to the walls and ceilings. "It was a team effort, I have to admit."

"Y'all did a wonderful job. It looks incredible."

"You, you my darling, you look incredible. You're a sight for damn sore eyes." His eyes grew wistful and he closed the distance between them, taking her hands. "I've never wanted so much to go to Houston in all my life, but your mother swore to me you'd be back. Do you hate this?" he grimaced as he tried to read her mind.

She shook her head and sniffled. "I love it. It's perfect."

"We can change the sign on the door if you want more anonymity. It was Dallie's idea to personalize it and well, obviously, *I* chose the name." He blushed and her heart swelled.

She shook her head and gave a little giggle. "You might as well capitalize on that coining," she teased.

"Right? I think I might just patent it."

Savannah all out laughed and didn't miss the way Austin gazed at her. He leaned his forehead down to hers. "God, I missed you so much, my sweet Savvy. Please tell me I'm not the only one? You're home to stay, right? If you say no, I'm going with you, wherever you go. Timbuktu, Antarctica, Africa, it doesn't matter...I can't be without you."

Savannah couldn't help but grin again. How was it he could always say the most freaking perfect things at the perfect times? "I missed you too, Austin. So much." She looked at his lips and suddenly, she was pulled into his chiseled arms and her breasts crashed against his chest. She moaned as his lips fell to hers. His tongue possessed her mouth and she let herself be taken away by him.

When he finally pulled back for a breath, they were both panting. She cupped his beard-covered cheek and smiled up into his ruggedly handsome face. "And, if I *were* to leave Abundance, what would you do for work?" she teased.

He scoffed. "I'll find something. I'll have you know, darlin', I'm a very talented man. I was told this by a soon-to-be-famous prodigy. She's a genius—doctor, astrophysicist and engineer. I greatly value her opinion." His nose touched hers and she swooned as his hands came to rest around her waist. "Now, I reckon she'll have to start signing her work so as people know it's hers."

She grinned knowingly. "I actually *do* sign my work. I always have."

His brows drew, confused. She pointed over to her closest painting, one of a bright pastural landscape with an array of horses grazing in the background and smiled as he moved from her side to inspect it. His hand pulled her with him and she waited for him to find her little scrawl. She finally pointed to the bottom corner, where the initials SGK sat catty-cornered and blended subtly into the painting.

He grinned at her seductively. "You sassy little *minx*." She laughed and he pulled her back into his arms. "I should've known, you're always so clever. It's such a turn-on." He looked her dress suit clad self over appreciatively.

His hand cupped her cheek then and he stared into her eyes, his amber orbs pulling her in and she was hopelessly lost. "I love you, Austin James Montgomery," she admitted.

"Finally!" he exclaimed before leaning down and taking her lips in a scorching kiss.

EPILOGUE

ONE YEAR LATER

"*V*anna, just breathe. Gosh," Kelsey cooed to Savannah even as the bride-to-be sat down and let her niece fan her. "You got me nervous too, dang it, and I don't get nervous."

"Oh, honey, you look utterly gorgeous," her mother came to her side and took her hand, patting it.

"You do, sister. Absolutely," Dallie assured and brought the infant back to her breast to nurse.

They were all in the bridal suite: Savannah, Dallas, their mother, Lily, Kelsey, Gracie, and Cassidy, awaiting their cue to enter for the ceremony. Savannah *did* look gorgeous. After all, her makeup was perfect, her maple-colored hair looked like something out of a magazine half-up half-down, cascading in ringlets down her back, and her wedding dress was the perfect blend of lace and silk, simple yet elegant as she looked herself over in the mirror. What they failed to remember was how much Savannah hated the spotlight and she knew as the bride that all eyes were gonna be on her, the thought made her want to hurl the little bit of food she'd eaten all day up.

"It's gonna be alright, Aunt Vanna," Lily surmised. "They're all gonna be looking at *me*." The lovable light brown-haired doll smiled over at Savannah and her heart practically melted. Lily Rose was missing her two front teeth now and her lisp was almost as adorable as she was. Her blue eyes glistened into Vanna's as Savannah looked her over, her rose pink flower girl's dress shimmering back at her.

"You're right about that, sweet girl. They'll be too busy adoring you to even take a second glance at me." Oh, how she wished those words were true.

A light knock came on the door, and Vanna's heart leapt into her throat as her father came through it after her mom told him to enter.

"My God, baby. Look at you." Jack Kinsen beamed as he looked his youngest daughter over, trying hard to hold back his tears as his jaw clenched. "You're simply stunning."

Her father was as handsome as ever adorned in a dark-grey suit with a light silver vest and tie and his ever-present Stetson, only tonight it was silver instead of tan.

"Thanks, Daddy." She blushed.

"Momma," Jax stepped forward in his own grey suit, navy-blue vest and tie, a black hat on his own head. "You're up. I just walked Grandma down. Vanna, wow!" He smiled and kissed her cheek. "You're gonna knock your groom for a loop." Jax laughed and puckered his lips over at Cass before taking their mother's arm.

"Breathe, my daughter. Focus only on the man you love. No one else will exist. I promise," Natalie admonished, kissed her husband and looked up at him, eyes shining, before turning to exit with Jackson.

Her father just grinned back at his wife's departing back before looking back at Savannah. "It's—uh—it's true actually. As adorable as this one here was." He pointed over to Dallas, who'd now pulled the baby to her shoulder and was burping her. "Once your mother came down that aisle, I didn't see anyone else."

Savannah smiled big. That should make her feel better but it didn't and her stomach plummeted as the wedding coordinator stepped in, clipboard in hand, to get them all lined up and ready.

Oh, God! This was it! She was about to be showcased—not unlike her work in the art gallery that was now a huge landmark in their town—in front of over a hundred people.

The last year had gone by fast. Sims and McClintock's trials and sentencing had taken place just recently, both had been found guilty on multiple counts of charges including fraud, extortion, embezzlement, arson and first-degree murder to name a few. Savannah felt vindicated, her leg was fully healed, and she'd never been happier to be home and thriving amongst her family and peers.

Kelsey and Morgan had gone to Vegas the weekend following Vanna's gallery opening, spontaneously pulling along Savannah, Austin, Cass, Jax, and both sets of parents with them, and gotten hitched in a quaint little chapel on the strip. It had been impromptu and casual and they'd had a blast. Kelsey was now six months pregnant and happier than Vanna had ever seen her.

Jax and Cass were happy too, sustaining a long-distance relationship with surprising ease. Cass was enjoying her classes and doing well in college, as Vanna knew she would. Jax would visit her once a month when she couldn't get away to come home, stating that he enjoyed traveling but maintained that he wasn't moving away permanently. Only time would tell where their relationship went, but Savannah felt they were gonna make it, for that sparkle had never left either of their eyes.

Savannah's cousin Elias and Stella were adorable together. Elias was modeling alongside Stella now when it wasn't rodeo season and Stella had broken into some new movie roles as of late.

Dallie had given birth to Gracie Marie Callahan on July 21st. She was a Cancer, and Vanna loved having yet another water sign in the family. Gracie was a beautiful baby with green eyes and brown hair like her daddy. She was sweet and easy-going and at a little over eight months old had all their hearts wrapped around that tiny little finger of hers.

Savannah had been sworn in as mayor of Abundance last June and she and Morgan had recently finished a large portion of Terra Viridis. It was beautiful, revolutionary, and the pride of their small town. Austin had taken the job as foreman of Starlight Valley when her uncle Nathan had retired in December and the job fit him to a T. He was a great supervisor and enjoyed his work and position immensely.

Morgan had built the house Vanna and Austin would be living in —following their honeymoon to Paris. It was a beautiful gothic Victorian style two-story home with peaked roofs, flying buttresses, turrets, a huge deeply arched entry way with French doors, bay and circular windows, a huge front porch, and grey cedar shake siding and river stones. It was stunning—and eccentric like the two of them.

Savannah was almost more excited to spend two weeks with her soon to be husband in one of the most romantic cities ever than to actually be getting married to him. She knew it was only because she hated the spotlight and she was utterly exhausted. Plus, she'd been his since their first night together—a ring and a piece of paper was just technicalities to her. Love didn't need anything more than two hearts committed solely to one another, as far as she was concerned.

She remembered the night he'd asked her to marry him. It had only been a few days prior to Gracie's birth on a starry night, not unlike the current one, on a blanket gazing out into the night that Austin had turned to her and said, "You know this night is almost perfect."

"Almost?" She'd giggled even as her hand reached for the buckle of his jeans. She'd kissed him in longing and snuggled into his embrace as his arms went around her. He kissed her back in equal passion then pulled back and looked into her face.

"Yup. It would be utterly perfect if you were on your way to becoming my wife. I mean, you *are* building a house. It would only be fitting if you had a big, strong husband and a family to go along with it."

"Oh? Did you have something in mind?" she asked as his hand reached into his back pocket.

He pulled out a ring box and her heart literally stopped. "Well, *I* myself am big and strong, among many things, plus you know, Dr. Savannah Grace *Montgomery* sounds pretty damn good."

She started to say, "It absolutely does," but her voice caught as he opened the blue velvet box and a dazzling, starburst diamond ring glinted back at her. She gasped.

"I love you with everything in me and have since the night I made you mine in that hayloft of your father's. So I say we make it official. Marry me, Savvy," he'd commanded and she'd laughed and cried in sheer happiness as she'd vigorously nodded.

Now, that day was here and her father's bulky arm steadied her on the heels she wasn't used to as she fell in line behind Lily.

"You okay, baby doll?" Her father asked and pulled her arm through his. She only nodded, for the flood of blood to her ears took her concentration away. "You're gonna have Austin absolutely speechless when he sees you." The faint smirk on her father's face faded as he looked her over from head to toe. "God, you look so much like your mother, Savannah Grace." His green eyes grew wistful and she smiled up at him.

"You're not getting all sappy on me, are ya, Daddy?"

He scoffed but again his rugged face grew serious. "I love you so much, my daughter." He leaned in and kissed her forehead. "And I'm thankful you and Austin are so happy together."

"I love you too, Daddy. And I've never been happier to be caught in our hayloft by you that morning."

Her father gave a big laugh even as she leaned up and kissed his clean-shaven cheek.

The sounds of the organ pulled her away and soon, her father was guiding her forward into the dimly, candlelit room decorated in navy, pink and silver accents. But as she took in the faces looking at her, once she saw Austin, that was it.

He was gorgeous as ever, his tall, muscular frame clad in a dark grey suit and vest almost identical to her father's. His head was bare though, sans cowboy hat, his thick, unruly blond locks tucked behind his ears. His sandy-blond beard was trim and his amber eyes

461

sparkled like stars. When his eyes caught her coming down the aisle, his stance wavered and his mouth fell open. He covered it with his hand and she saw him trying to rein his emotions in before he quickly removed it and gave her that sexy grin of his that had led them to this moment.

She felt the world stop as she was guided towards him, walking along the white runner, amid the white roses, through the open French doors and onto the veranda overlooking their town. Her father led her beneath the altar that her uncle had built for him and her mom over thirty years ago. The air was crisp and the night was clear and perfect as the stars and moon blessed them with splendid light.

As the formalities were said and her father tearfully lifted her veil and handed her over to Austin, she watched a tear fall down Austin's cheek too and he smiled blissfully over at her as he wiped it nonchalantly away.

"Savvy, you—Wow! Just—wow!"

"I see I won the bet, Montgomery," Jack joked under his breath and playfully punched at Austin's bicep.

"Yeah, you did," he grumbled and moved to pull out his wallet.

Her father belted out in laughter and patted Austin on the shoulder, leaned in to kiss his daughter, and moved away to his seat.

"You bet against my dad you wouldn't cry?" Savannah's voice finally took hold as her groom stepped forward and interlaced their hands, facing her.

"Truth is, darlin', I knew I probably would, but you know how dumb us guys are. We gotta badger each other about being 'real' men." He shrugged, and she couldn't help but swoon for him, so grateful that the relationship he had with her father was an amicable and lovable one now.

Austin's eyes burned into hers as the preacher began to speak. He was focused solely on her, and she on him, and when the time for Austin's vows came, he surprised her and pulled out a little notebook. It touched her as he quoted more Shakespeare, spoke of the heavens bringing them together, and thanked her entire family for giving him a second, third and fourth chance. He had everyone laughing—typical Austin—until he looked up at her again, his face growing serious and another tear ran down his golden-tanned cheek.

"Savannah Grace Kinsen," he said on a sigh and shook his head, "I never knew how dead I was inside. How much I truly lost that day in Afghanistan. Until I met you. Your bright soul sparked some invisible wick inside me and brought me to life again. My angel of music...and art, and beauty, and stars." He looked up into the night sky, gave a soft laugh then gazed back down at her. "I love you so very much, Savvy. And I promise to show that to you every single day I live. From this moment until the day I die."

Savannah couldn't stop the tears that poured down her face if she tried. When the preacher announced them as man and wife, Austin pulled her into his strong arms as if he were starving and she was the feast of a lifetime. His lips seared hers in a passionate kiss that had her melting into him. Nothing existed but them. They were soaring through space and time and they were one, Mr. and Mrs. Austin James Montgomery.

When he pulled back, he leaned his forehead against her own. Then he took her hand, turned, and beamed out at their audience as he showcased his wife for the first time.

The piano and violin music began as they headed back down the runner and Savannah's nervousness eased some. He pulled her into the bridal suite and back into his arms, mindless of the wedding party behind them.

"Austin," she protested even as his lips descended to hers once again. "Save some of it for our honeymoon," she teased as he growled against her throat and inhaled her new perfume.

"I don't know if I can, darlin', you look and smell like absolute freakin' sex on a stick and now you're my wife. Do you know how hard that makes me? God, what the hell *is* that?" He inhaled her again and the feel of his nose on her neck made her break out in goosebumps.

"It's called 'Irresistible'." Her brows went up as his head came up and he gave her that sexy smirk that melted her panties right off.

"Well, angel, I gotta tell ya. It's *workin'*."

She would have laughed if he wasn't kissing her again and pulling her against him like he needed to eliminate all barriers. She was hot, throbbing, and panting before the door opened and Morgan came in.

"Guys, *seriously?* Can we at least get through the reception before you tear each other's clothes off?" Her handsome, dark-headed cousin scoffed and shook his head at the two of them.

Savannah looked down and noticed the disarray they were in and pulled away from her husband, blushing. She had to wipe the lip stick that was smeared across her chin—and his—straighten her veil and readjust Austin's tie.

Austin smirked as he took her hand and kissed it before letting Morgan lead them back to the altar for pictures, where her Aunt Jordan was.

After many funny, sexy, and breath-taking pictures taken by her talented and beautiful red-haired aunt, they entered the reception hall. Applause erupted around them before Savannah was pulled into Austin's big arms once more and was twirled around the dance floor as a spotlight focused on them.

"Have I told you how utterly stunning and gorgeous you are tonight, Mrs. Montgomery? God, that sounds *hot*, don't 'cha think?"

Savannah giggled and nodded. "You look mighty sexy tonight, yourself, husband."

"Behave, wife, you're gonna give me a raging boner in front of all these people." He looked around in feigned apprehension, and Savannah giggled again. "Thanks for being a good sport." He knew she hated crowds, being the center of attention and all these formalities. She only nodded. "I just wanted to share this moment with those we love."

He motioned over to her family then his own—Wyatt, Angela, his nieces, his sister- Sierra, brother-in law-Thomas, two boys and parents sat.

His sister, Sierra was as attractive as her brothers with a great personality. She had quickly taken to Savannah and the rest of her family and Savannah was so happy to have more nieces and now nephews to love. Austin's parents, James and Patty, weren't anything like she was expecting, but in a good way. Her father-in-law was a retired Army sergeant with a tall and broad build—similar to Austin's—with white hair and a bright smile. He was a big teddy bear, she'd seen right away. Austin's mother was a petite little blonde with a cute giggle and a no-nonsense attitude. Savannah had loved them immediately.

"I know. Me too," she admitted. She laid her head on her husband's shoulder and took in the moment, his voice singing along with the song, his big palm across her bare back and his lips on her temple. He smelled amazing and she couldn't wait to be his wife in every sense of the word.

"You tired, darlin'?" he asked. She only nodded. "I can't wait to consummate our marriage," he murmured with a moan. "But if I need to wait—"

Savannah pulled her head off his shoulder then and looked up at him, cupping his cheek. "I'm *not* waiting. The minute we get to that room—"

"Shh, it's coming back." He looked down between them and she laughed again and shoved him lightly. He didn't budge—not an inch. "How's our baby?"

Savannah grinned. She was just six weeks along, not even showing and she'd only found out day before yesterday. Austin had been utterly ecstatic. So far, she hadn't suffered from morning sickness and prayed that she wouldn't...at least until after the honeymoon.

Before she could answer, he said, "Speaking of, I have a gift for you. And I got this before I even knew. I think you're gonna get a kick out of it."

At that time, their first dance ended and they were applauded once again. Austin thanked everyone and reached for the mic the DJ handed over to him. "Thanks, Al. And thank you to our friends and family who joined us tonight on this very special occasion. I want to give my wife— wow, that feels so good to say." Austin's eyes raked over Vanna and she felt heat spike through her center then. "I want to give my wife here a gift. Morgan, bring it on out, buddy."

Savannah watched as Jackson and Morgan brought forth a big wrapped box. She grinned up at him as they began to tear the paper off and open it. She stepped forward to see what it was as they lifted a beautiful wooden rocking horse and placed it atop the closed box lid.

She stifled a giggle and looked over at her husband in surprise and awe. God, he was so adorable.

The crowd seemed to be awaiting her response for they didn't understand the symbolism of the gift and unease started to rip into her. They were gonna know she was pregnant and she wasn't ready to tell anyone—not that Kelsey, Dallie and her mother didn't already know.

She looked apprehensively up at her husband, who, like always, knew exactly what to say and when to say it. "I don't reckon all of you know the story of how Savvy and I met, huh? Well, laughably, it was in an antique toy store fighting over a rocking horse that looked much like the one you see here."

With that, the crowd laughed audibly and Savannah relaxed some, feeling the tension ease. She moved towards Austin, into his outstretched arm and grinned up into his handsome face.

"Unsurprisingly, Savannah took it away from me," another laugh came from the crowd and Austin shrugged, "I fell head over heels for that feisty little fox that morning. She, on the other hand—well, Savvy didn't think I was too funny then. She would later change her mind." His eyebrows bobbed and he handed the mic back to Al as the song changed and he pulled her into his arms. "Do you like it?"

"I love it. It's perfect." She looked back at the gorgeous replica of the horse she'd purchased for Lilian that cold March morning. "Morgan made it?"

"Yup! I thought it would look great in the nursery." His eyes were so sincere that she teared up.

"Oh, Austin. I love you." She kissed him with passion then her brain intervened and she looked up into his face in amusement.

"What?" He laughed at her expression.

"I never asked you...why on earth were you buying an antique rocking horse in the first place?" After all, his nieces were much too old for them and, well, his nephews too as a matter of fact.

"Darlin', some things are just worth fightin' for." He smirked then kissed her again as he pulled her back into his solid embrace.

~

*J*ack Kinsen chuckled, walking alongside his granddaughter to the barn. Lily Rose was in rare form as she sang "Deep in the Heart of Texas" aloud and giggled. Jack's heart swelled to bursting in her sweet, precocious presence and his mind and heart overflowed with memories of his wife all those years ago, in a pasture singing that very song, not too far from where they were now. His life had only gotten sweeter and better since that day, despite the horrors, tragedies and downs of it. Falling in love with Natalie Butler Cameron had been the best day of his entire life.

He looked down at his adorable five-year-old granddaughter, looking like her mother once did, wearing jeans, a pink button-down, a brown cowboy hat and matching boots. Her light brown ringlets fell from the hat, resting on her tiny shoulders and she beamed up at him, resembling a jack-o-lantern with her missing teeth. Jack couldn't help but return it, for his heart was wrapped all around that little finger he held within his own.

"Paw-paw Jack, what are we gonna do today?"

"Anything your little heart desires, darlin'."

"I wanna ride."

"I figured as much." Jack chuckled deeply. "Which one will it be today?"

He picked her up and swung her around as Victoria, a palomino broodmare stuck her head out of her stall to greet them. Jack stepped forward and let Lily's hands cup the mare's cheek. She giggled and leaned her head against the horse's forehead. He smiled again. God, she was so much like her momma.

"Well, I don't think you should ride *her*, Paw-paw."

"And why not?" he scoffed.

"She's gonna have a baby. She doesn't need the extra weight."

Jack's head came up quick as lightning and he looked over at Wyatt and Jax as they stopped, hearing her remark too as they'd been ambling towards them. They'd literally just gotten this mare yesterday and the owner had told Jack she was in heat and ready for breeding. Could he have just been wrong? Dallie had yet to examine her, but would be doing so shortly.

"How do you know that, kiddo?" Jack asked and propped Lilian on his hip.

She gave him a heart-stopping smile and shrugged. Jack shook his head. No freakin' way!

"You just know, don't cha, baby?" he asked. She nodded. *Unbelievable. She has the gift too.* "You can feel it, can't you?" he asked again, mesmerized. She nodded once more.

"You've *got* to be kidding me!" Wyatt exclaimed with a laugh.

"What?" Lily asked and looked at the men like they'd lost their minds.

"You're more like your momma than we originally thought, Lily Rose," Jack answered her, and she turned in his arms to hug him. He held her tightly against him and closed his eyes as happiness oozed from his pores.

Another horse whisperer. Here. On their ranch. In their family. Dallie wasn't the first and she wouldn't be the last. Dallas's legacy. The Butler/Kinsen legacy would *indeed* live on.

THE END

ACKNOWLEDGMENTS

I want to give a sincere, heart-felt thank you to all my betas and ARC readers. To Jamie, Britney, Jennifer, Nicole, Brittany, Claire, Jacob—I couldn't have done this without all your support and love for these characters.

To all my writer and blogger friends, of **all** genres, who took the chance on Abundance, fell in love and have continued to support me in this journey—Jen, Veronica, Danielle, Trisha, Cat, Cassie, Jess, Emina and Katie to name a few.

To all my fans worldwide—my readers, my family and friends, my husband and his never-wavering encouragement. Thanks for being one of my most trusted soundboards, honey, even though you're not a reader—LOL :-*

That y'all took the time to trust in and "spur" on this indie author means **everything** to me!
Thank you so much for reading my works!

I love each and every one of you.

AFTERWORD

Well, as Porky Pig always said, "That's All, Folks!" (From Abundance, Texas, anyway)

Thank you so very much for reading this book! If you enjoyed it, please be sure to leave a review on Amazon, BookBub or Goodreads; it makes it possible for other readers worldwide to be able to see and read it too.

If you've enjoyed the Abundance series, tell a friend about it, loan them a copy, or give the books as gifts. Be sure to follow me on social media, and of course, stay *tuned* because this author is only just getting started.

I've got an anthology coming this summer (it's a paranormal romance), a dark, twisty, steaming hot collaboration you won't wanna miss and a football romance series—both coming in the Fall —(the prequel of which is in my anthology *The Fire Within: Conquered by Love*)

I've also started writing many other works (sci-fi and fantasy) that I look forward to sharing with you in the future, so stay tuned readers.

Until next time!

Sincerely,

Shanna Swenson

ABOUT THE AUTHOR

Shanna Swenson is a cardiac sonographer by day and a weaver of various tales by night.

She's been an avid reader all her life and began writing at the age of fourteen. She finally published her first novel, *Abundance*—after it sat patiently on her laptop for well over fifteen years—and hasn't stopped writing since.

Shanna fits her zodiac sign of Cancer to a capital C and enjoys life's simple things—sunsets, rain, and coffee to name a few.

When Shanna's not reading or writing, she enjoys action and horror movies, pro football, hiking, Yoga, and traveling with her own "knight in shining armor".

You can find her on the following social media platforms.

Her website is www.shannaswenson.com

facebook.com/shannaswen

twitter.com/shanna_swenson

instagram.com/shannaswen_author

goodreads.com/Shannaswen

amazon.com/author/shannaswenson

pinterest.com/shannaswen

bookbub.com/profile/shanna-swenson